FLASH POINT

A Selection of Titles by Colby Marshall

The Dr Jenna Ramey series

COLOR BLIND
DOUBLE VISION
PLAIN SIGHT
FLASH POINT *

The McKenzie McClendon series

CHAIN OF COMMAND
THE TRADE

* *available from Severn House*

FLASH POINT

A Dr Jenna Ramey mystery

Colby Marshall

This first world edition published 2016
in Great Britain and the USA by
SEVERN HOUSE PUBLISHERS LTD of
19 Cedar Road, Sutton, Surrey, England, SM2 5DA.
Trade paperback edition first published
in Great Britain and the USA 2016 by
SEVERN HOUSE PUBLISHERS LTD

British Library Cataloguing in Publication Data
A CIP catalogue record for this title is available from the British Library.

ISBN-13: 978-0-7278-8632-3 (cased)
ISBN-13: 978-1-84751-737-1 (trade paper)
ISBN-13: 978-1-78010-801-8 (e-book)

All Severn House titles are printed on acid-free paper.

Severn House Publishers support the Forest Stewardship Council™ [FSC™],
the leading international forest certification organisation.
All our titles that are printed on FSC certified paper carry the FSC logo.

Typeset by Palimpsest Book Production Ltd.,
Falkirk, Stirlingshire, Scotland.
Printed and bound in Great Britain by
TJ International, Padstow, Cornwall.

For Courtney, whom I'll always want to share a closet with during a thunderstorm.

Acknowledgments

Though I wrote *Flash Point* alone, many exceptional people helped bring it into the world.

First and foremost, to the incomparable Faith Black Ross: when we started this series together, I had no idea I'd just met an editor I would trust implicitly with my writing and feel so at ease with. For being a phenomenal editor, for inspiring me, for being one of my heroes, and for being my friend: thank you. To the sensational team at Severn House Publishers: I can't thank you all enough. It's an honor to be a part of the Severn family.

To my biggest cheerleader, advocate, and my own personal superhero – my agent, Rachel Ekstrom. Your steady guidance keeps me on track, and your enthusiasm for my career energizes me. I'm thrilled to call you my ally, partner, and friend. To the whole team at IGLA, thank you for your hard work and dedication. And to the dynamic team of Danny Baror, Heather Baror-Shapiro, and everyone at Baror International: thank you for giving me the chance to have my book seen all over the world.

As always, thank you to those who have helped me find my place in this industry. To Pat Shaw, Amanda Ng, Ken Coffman and the Stairway Press family, and the charming and terribly witty Loren Jaggers: thank you for your tireless hours and full-throttle attitude. Thanks to Matt Stine & 27Sound Entertainment for my the rockin' internet digs. And to Bob Stine, who I'm pleased to call not just a mentor, but a friend: for introducing me to ITW, lending a hand when I needed one, and steering me in the right direction to get my books off the ground, words will never be enough. You are – and always will be – one of my favorite people.

Researching elements that end up in my stories is important to me; a special thank you to everyone who pitched in to keep my details as accurate as possible (except where I specifically took license to use a little artistic freedom). To Dr Richard "Dick" Elliot for his invaluable consults on forensic psychiatry and profiling. To Kelly Hines, Rick Campbell, Dr Tyler Darnell, Courtney Hatlee, R.N., Lynne McElheney Squarez, Sarah Kitchens Chancellor, and Margeaux & Doug Copeland, for providing your expertise for various scenes/settings. Thank you to Kimberly Thompson and Abby DeLuca, for your assistance in language pathology, and to D.P. Lyle M.D. for putting me in touch with a terrific linguistics contact. To Tiffinie Helmer, for her knowledge on hunting knives. And thank you to Randy Olson, for taking time out of his busy day to make sure I still knew how to do math.

Thank you to the many other writers, for their advice and encouragement: Y-Nots, Purgs, Pitizens, and ITW Debut Class. A special thanks to Jenny Milchman for sharing her know, and to Kay Kendall and Rick Campbell: thank you for your support in all facets of life.

Thanks to everyone who makes my day to day life a place where creativity can survive *and* thrive. To my theatre families at Theatre Macon & Macon Little Theatre – especially my YAC kids for many laughs and even more inspiration, and to Ellen Wilson & Spencer Maddox, friends I can count on. To Emily, Paige, Sasha, and the Millers for time to type without "help" from those not tall enough to ride rollercoasters.

To Danielle, James, Will, Nikki, & Falkor, for everything you do for me and are to me. To JP, for keeping my "wife" happy, and for going all the way into the pages of a book to marry her. To Herbie and Riley, who add zany zest to the otherwise mundane. To Meg, because I couldn't make it without you. And to Courtney, for believing in this series – and me. The dedication says it all.

To Ashlee, for reading every word I've written for almost a decade. Thank you for being what I need at any given time. Thank you for allowing me to name a character in this book for you. Now, any time I'm wishing you were right here in my living room, all I have to do is open up my laptop and you are.

To Mom and Dad: thank you for cheering me on, spurring me forward, and loving me. Thank you for valuing my happiness, sharing my triumphs – I owe so many of them to you. And to the littlest members of my family, for their hugs and laughter, energy and spirit. I love you.

Finally, to David, for not just understanding my dream, but for taking it on as your own. After all we've been through the past few years, you've amazed me, kept me sane, stayed steady, been a force of nature. David, you truly are my champion.

Last but certainly not least, to my readers: be this your first or fifth book of mine, thank you for reading. I wish you a pulse-pounding ride, full of twists, and excitement. And as always, I hope this story will keep you reading late into the night!

One

Chaos.

Cold sweat dripped down Beo's sides under his black cable-knit sweater as he rushed through the crowded room, frenetic energy driving him. Fear pulsed through him like it had a blood supply of its own as all around him screams and frantic movement hit him like he was running a giant, terrifying gauntlet. In the planning stages, he'd known it would be like this, but the real moment was different. Faster. Blurrier.

Scarier.

He nearly slipped as his foot hit something slick. He looked down briefly to see the puddle of crimson he'd skidded through. His breathing caught in his throat, panic gripping his chest. *Don't think about it.*

But even if he'd been wearing blinders and hadn't seen the body thud to the floor in his peripheral vision, the air inside the room wouldn't have let his mind drift. Body odor, urine, feces . . . metallic blood. All were present in the muggy heat of the building where everywhere black-clad figures moved swiftly amongst patrons, killing each and every one in his path.

Had Beo not consciously known he was on their side, it might have overwhelmed him.

Out of the corner of his eye, Scarlett spun and whirled like a ninja through the crowd. He knew it was her simply by the way she moved. Precise. Deliberate.

The blade of her dagger caught the chandelier lights just before she plunged it between the ribs of the man in the white-collared shirt before her. The guy grunted as Scarlett slipped the knife back out as seamlessly as she'd thrust it in. In one more swift, solid movement, she pivoted around the clean-cut, thirty-something man, grabbed a handful of his dark hair in her left hand to pull his chin back, and swiped her dagger left to right across his throat.

Scarlett's hand grasping the man's hair let go, and without another look, she rushed in another direction.

Beo's gaze didn't follow her, though. He stood, vision fixed on her victim.

The man sputtered while he choked for breath. Eyes wide with panic, he sank to his knees. Beo's stomach clenched. Scarlett had the skill to have spared this guy a lot of agony if she'd gone for a quick jab into the side of the neck, but slicing across the trachea and making him suffocate was more her style. Dramatic. Showy. *Poor bastard.*

Beo ripped his stare away and urged his feet forward. In front of him, a tall and slender black-clad figure held a knife in a blonde young woman's back, rooting her to the spot like she was partly skewered. *Damn. Scarlett's kill was bad enough, and I had to turn away from* that *and see* this.

The girl cried soft, breathless tears, her eyes on her assailant's second knife – the filet knife lingering over her forearm. Just like Scarlett's reaming from moments ago, Mr Darcy could end this girl's suffering with a few quick stabs. Only, Mr Darcy's reasons for whatever it was he was about to do to the girl weren't like Scarlett's. Not a display but rather something much sicker.

Dear God. She could be Sabine's age.

From the left, a machete came wildly out of nowhere and dropped the girl.

'We don't have time for this shit. Keep up your hobbies in your own spare time,' Atticus growled at Mr Darcy.

Beo trudged on, looking for any business left to finish, but the black masked figures outnumbered the others. And yet, the choppy, desperate gasps of Scarlett's victim seemed to seek out his ears through the din of whines, sobs, and groans. The image of Mr Darcy holding the girl skewered in front of him burst forth in his mind. Hard to fathom how all these sick motherfuckers had ended up together in this one room.

Beo whirled around, his own knife grasped tightly at his side. His feet urged him forward across the floor until his boots splashed into the fresh stream dripping from Scarlett's victim's throat.

He stared into the man's eyes as he raised his knife, not sure whether the eyes of the man looking back at him were begging for help or mercy. Not that it mattered. Beo, for one, wasn't here because he enjoyed suffering.

'Clear it out!' a yell from the other end of the room rang out.

Beo glanced at his digital watch. They'd been in for just under two minutes. *Right on schedule.*

All the black figures bolted for the doors, leaping over bodies and dodging pools of blood.

Quite the opposite, actually.

Beo plunged the knife into the side of the man's neck, ending it. He watched him fall face first on to the wood grain. Shame it had come to this, but it had. For all of them.

Scarlett had her reasons. He had his.

Now, all that was left was for them to get the fuck out.

For now, anyway.

Two

'And you promise to be a good girl for the teacher.'

Jenna Ramey tucked a stray blonde strand behind her three-year-old daughter's ear as she knelt in front of her. How had she let her dad and brother talk her into this? She was about to leave Ayana in the wide-open, in public, for the first time since she could remember. Sure, her elaborate system of locks and passwords for the house had been a pain in the ass for everyone, but she'd proven time and time again that it was also *necessary*. Anything could happen in a place like this . . .

Ayana, however, didn't seem nervous at all. Her chubby hands grasped the straps of her purple Hello Kitty backpack as she nodded in earnest.

'And if you need *anything*, you tell the teacher to call me, OK?'

'If you take much longer, she won't have to tell the teacher, because she'll be old enough to drive off, buy her own phone, and call you herself,' Charley said, rolling his eyes.

Jenna shot a glare at her brother. 'Look, Charley, I know you don't *agree* with everything I've done to protect Ayana over the years, but I think you'd at least *understand* it and cut me some slack.'

He looked down at Ayana. 'The teacher laid out coloring sheets over there. You know, ever since you drew me that picture of the Cowardly Lion, I've *really* wanted one of the Scarecrow, too. What do you think?'

Jenna bit her tongue as Ayana nodded and rushed toward one of the low tables, where she slung her backpack to the floor and grabbed an orange crayon.

'You let her watch *The Wizard of Oz*? Seriously?' she snapped.

'Oh, come on. She's seen the barracuda eat the main character's wife in *Finding Nemo*. No one even dies in *The Wizard of Oz*,' Charley answered. 'And maybe I'd cut you more slack if all these crazy shenanigans you've put us through to protect Ayana had actually *worked*. Claudia found us anyway, so obviously there's no need to keep racking up costs on the child's future therapy bill by continuing to deprive her of socialization with kids her own age.'

Jenna didn't look at her brother. She couldn't, because as much as she hated it, he was right.

As Jenna watched Ayana scribble on the white construction paper, she sighed. So few things were normal about A's childhood, thanks to Claudia. Her dad was gone. She had hardly been let out of the house the past year. It wasn't fair to A, but then again, Claudia's effects on their lives weren't exactly fair to any of them.

The ring of Jenna's phone echoed through the preschool classroom so loudly that everyone – including the toddlers – turned to stare at her. She grabbed the phone from the back pocket of her khakis.

'Sorry,' she muttered, wandering toward the door even though she wasn't *quite* ready to walk out of it and leave Ayana here. She pressed the button to take the call. 'Jenna Ramey.'

'Jenna, it's Saleda,' came the voice of her superior, Saleda Ovarez. 'Drop everything and meet me at headquarters ASAP. We've got a situation.'

Jenna's gaze darted back toward Ayana, who was still coloring at the table, not paying any attention to the fact that her mom was still in the room. Jenna's heart picked up as her imagination ran wild with scenarios where she came back to pick Ayana up only to find her daughter was missing. After Claudia had left that note about Yancy, they'd gone months on tenterhooks waiting for her to do something awful, but Jenna could just imagine how the one time she dropped her guard would be the one time when Claudia would swoop in and take advantage. Just like always.

She shook the thought away. *She'll be fine.*

'With the Northeast Strangler case?' Jenna asked, surprised. They'd been working on the serial killer's case for a few months now, unfortunately. The guy had a very distinct pattern of a new victim every two weeks, and it had only been three days. She was planning to go in to the office and pick up where they'd left off yesterday when she finished here, but the only reason Saleda would call an ASAP on that case would be to fly out because there was a new crime scene to investigate.

'Negative,' the Special Agent in Charge of the FBI's Behavioral Analysis Unit said. 'We're handing the Northeast Strangler case off to another team. We've been called in about another crime scene. A bank here in DC.'

A bank?

'Local police aren't handling their own bank robberies anymore?' Jenna asked, confused.

'I said it was *at* a bank. I didn't say it was a robbery,' Saleda replied.

Jenna shook her head, trying to clear it. Maybe it was her daughter's first day of preschool. Maybe it was that she hadn't had her coffee yet. But somehow, this didn't make sense.

'I don't get it.'

A long pause.

'Look,' Saleda said, 'I probably shouldn't tell you this over the phone, since the locals want to get your objective opinion walking in, but you should probably be ready for what you're going into. A group of masked people stormed a bank in town this morning. They didn't take a thing, but they killed everyone inside. *Everyone.* And it was apparently brutal, Jenna.'

Jenna tore her eyes from Ayana. Even after all the years she'd gone after monsters – serial killers, rapists, and mobsters – as a forensic psychiatrist with the FBI, she still couldn't stand to talk or hear about the gruesome crimes she investigated with her daughter's innocent face in front of her.

'That still doesn't explain why they're calling us in,' Jenna said. They were based in DC, sure, but the FBI didn't have jurisdiction here unless there were crimes across state lines or there'd been a kidnapping.

'Locals invited us to consult,' Saleda said.

Or that.

Mass murder at a bank where nothing was taken. Surely someone was missing something. Unusual, though, the locals thinking they needed the FBI.

'They'd usually rather have a serial who kills their own family before they bring us in,' Jenna muttered.

'Yeah, but maybe they're afraid this time, it *could* be their families,' Saleda replied. 'Jenna, twenty-one deaths, not a robbery, and no sign of motive except . . .'

'Except what?' Jenna blurted, impatient.

'I know this is your little one's first day at school and everything, and I don't want to make any of this worse for you or make you more nervous than you are . . .'

Jenna's chest tightened. 'Unless you tell me Claudia is responsible for this, I doubt I'll be more worried than I already am,' she lied.

Even though she'd arranged with the school for her brother, her father, *and* Ayana's dad's cop brother Victor to stay with Ayana all day at preschool with explicit instructions that A was to remain in their line of vision at all times, she still would never be confident her mother couldn't weasel her way in if she wanted to.

'All right,' Saleda said, her voice grave. 'They left a message at the crime scene. It says no one in the city is safe. Whoever they are, they promise they're going to attack again.'

Three

Jenna Ramey pulled her beat-up Blazer into a church parking lot across the street from the bank. The police had setup a command center from the spot, and she'd need to check in. After putting the SUV into park, Jenna shot off a quick text to Charley, asking if Ayana was OK.

She sent the same one to both Vern and Victor – someone bad could intercept one phone easily, but three phones would make it harder to contaminate the message. If Claudia did get in, Jenna would find out from one of the three. Not to mention they had a list of safe words to respond to her check-ins, and none possessed a written version of the passwords that would change depending on what time she texted. Claudia had no way to possibly know, so if something went wrong, the wrong word back to Jenna from any of the three would tip her off fast.

Jenna looked out at the crowd of cops swarming the parking lot as she waited for replies, and her gaze met Saleda's. Her superior waved for her to come on over, the raised eyebrows and bugged out eyes telling Jenna that Saleda's patience was thin. She glanced back down at her phone. The red light blinked.

A text from Victor: *Plankton*.

She backed out of it and opened another from her father.

Disarray, Vern's text read.

Nothing from Charley yet, but Jenna smiled. Both of those were the right responses. Everything was fine.

She turned off her ignition, climbed out of the Blazer, and strode toward Saleda.

'Glad you could make it *and* finish your favorite song at the same time,' Saleda griped.

Jenna ignored the snipe. 'The rest on the way, or is Dodd getting the jump on us as usual?'

Saleda glanced toward the bank. 'Porter and Teva are on their way from Quantico together. I assumed Dodd was on his way, too, but now that you mention it, we should probably check and make sure he's not already inside. He does like to do that.'

'So, close to a dozen UNSUBs stormed this area this morning with weapons and slaughtered everyone inside,' Jenna reviewed, a convenient change of the subject. 'They didn't take anything, but all the perps made a clean getaway before first responders arrived, correct?'

Saleda nodded. 'That's what I understand. All they left behind were dead bodies and a note. Irv should have an image of it on our tablets by now.'

As Jenna fussed with her touchpad, waited for it to power up, Saleda continued. 'We don't have an exact headcount of the perpetrators yet. No one in the immediate area canvassed so far has any useful information, but we're still working on it since a few people at buildings nearby at the time have yet to be located.'

The image of the note left inside the bank by the perpetrators popped up on Jenna's screen, and she and Saleda huddled closer to read it simultaneously:

> The past is over and done. We must concern ourselves with the things that are to come. Do you feel it? The suggestion that begins to creep into your mind? That undefinable something that is present in one thing before you, yet lacking in another. You cannot describe it. You cannot tell just what it is. It will take a sharp instinct to detect and perceive it. Do not linger where you stand, but concern yourselves with where you will go from here, for there is not much time. We are coming, and you will not know when, until you can look past these menial words on what will become this glorified piece of paper, you will not grasp it and move on. We are coming. We *have* moved on.

'Well that's . . . *formal,*' Jenna said, not too sure what to make of the communications the killers had left. '*Any* other evidence? Weapons? Surveillance footage?'

'Weapons were all blades, from the looks of the victims, apparently, but I don't have anything more specific than that. Video surveillance at the bank was MIA – from inside the building, the parking lot, and the drive-through teller. Guess they took it with them.'

The first color of the day flashed in Jenna's mind. She noted it, catalogued it, then let it go. There would be way more, and that one couldn't possibly mean anything yet. Not until she walked the crime scene and could put it together with some of the rest of this madness.

Saleda and Jenna showed their badges to the cop manning the police-taped outline of the bank's property. He checked and double-checked their faces, then triple-checked by OKing them with the cops at the command center across the street as well as the one in charge of the scene on this side of the road.

Finally, he nodded. 'You can come on in.'

Jenna and Saleda ducked under the tape and headed toward the door, but the cop who'd checked them out walked with them, abandoning his post.

'Don't you think you'd better stay put at the divider, buddy?' Saleda jibed, her tone more chastising than inquiring.

'Actually, Lieutenant Zarecki asked me to walk you up,' the cop replied, nodding to the cop at the door, who jogged toward the crime scene tape to take over there.

An escort. How fancy. Whether it implied their importance or that the locals wanted to keep them on a tight leash was yet to be seen.

As they neared the door, the young cop stopped and turned. 'I should warn you, it's not pretty. Might want to put something over your lip to smell instead of the bodies if you carry anything.'

Jenna fished into her pocket and dabbed a dot of vanilla extract under her nose, then handed the tiny bottle to Saleda. What the hell could've happened in here that was so bad it prompted so many warnings?

While Saleda rubbed vanilla over her lip, too, the cop stared at Jenna. After a long moment, he finally opened his mouth, gaping, then half-laughed and pointed a finger at her. 'Jenna Ramey. *Doctor* Jenna Ramey, right? *You're* Doctor Jenna Ramey, aren't you?'

Jenna's neck muscles stiffened at the star-struck quality of the cop's voice. God, this had gotten old. 'Yeah. I'm her, all right.'

He shook his head, a wide smile crossing his face. 'I just can't believe I'm meeting you! I've heard so much about you!'

You and everyone else I've ever talked to.

He glanced from her, toward the crime scene, and back again. 'So, you're going to . . . you're *really* gonna . . .'

'Yes,' Jenna snapped, trying hard to keep the annoyance out of her voice. It wasn't his fault she was famous for being able to discern things about crimes based on the colors she associated with everything from letters and numbers to people and gut feelings. To him, grapheme-color synesthesia must sound like the cool super power everyone else thought it was.

'We'd better go before you ask for her autograph, because I didn't bring a pen,' Saleda said, handing the bottle back to Jenna.

'Right,' the cop said. He looked at Jenna, to the bank, and back again. 'Well, um . . . good luck with . . . it.'

'Thanks,' she said, even though the word was really meant for Saleda and her rescue.

A step away, Saleda leaned in toward her. 'Don't mention it.'

They stopped right in front of the door.

'Ready?' Saleda asked.

'As I'll ever be,' Jenna replied.

With that, Saleda swung the door open.

Despite what she'd just said, Jenna *wasn't* ready for the sight that hit her. Two bodies were splayed out on the polished marble floors next to a cheery sign advertising mortgage loan services and free online checking accounts, another was slumped against the wall surrounded by scattered, blood-smeared deposit slips. Some body *parts* were strewn around at random, turning the scene of what would at any other time be the most mundane of errands into a sickening, bloody canvas. A dead woman's body was suspended awkwardly in the air over where, presumably, her waist had caught the velvet roping on its way to the floor. A man in a pool of red, the pen chained to the counter next to him dangling above his head.

But even the horrors of the blood and gore weren't the biggest problems.

The worst part of the scene was the way the colors seemed to fly at Jenna, changing and morphing with every direction she looked. Never had she experienced this sort of wild, chaotic display of hues in her own mind at a crime scene, been unable to organize and process what they could possibly mean.

Jenna closed her eyes, shutting them all down.

'Saleda, I can't handle this. I've gotta get out of here.'

Four

Outside the bank, Saleda handed Jenna a coffee, and Jenna took a few long, deep breaths. She took a quick sip, closed her eyes.

'So, you want to tell me what happened in there?' Saleda asked, leaning against the stone wall outside the building next to Jenna.

Like I can explain this . . .

'Too many colors,' she said, hoping for understanding and not a ton of questions.

'Come again?'

'I . . . um . . .' Jenna took another sip of the piping hot coffee, searching herself for words. 'I couldn't handle the colors I started to associate with each murder I saw. There are a *lot* of different ones.'

To say the least.

Saleda let out a half-laugh. 'Thank God. I thought for a minute you were going soft on me.'

Jenna smirked. 'Hardly. I can handle the awful murder scene. It's just that the colors in my brain started making me dizzy. I'll be fine to go back in in a minute now that I'm ready for it. I think. I'm honestly not sure how to process this one. I could look at one segment of the room at a time, but I probably need to assess the crime as whole, too, if we want to get a feel for the full picture.'

Though if I knew more about the full picture, separating it would be more helpful.

A cop to their left cleared his throat, and Saleda looked toward him. 'What can I do for you?'

'I'm sorry, Special Agent Ovarez, but my commanding officer sent me out to tell you. Thought you'd want to know. We've found something else . . .'

'Another body?' Saleda asked.

The guy with the short, dark crew cut shook his head. 'No, ma'am. Well, kind of, maybe . . .'

'Out with it,' Saleda said.

'Another person,' the young officer replied. 'A live person. One who says she was here when the attack started.'

Jenna sat down across from the female employee who'd been found by the local cops closed inside the bank vault. The woman wore a navy pants suit – smart, tailored to fit her. She was seated in a metal folding chair, but even so, Jenna could tell she was short in stature. Five-foot-three, maybe, at most.

The woman tucked a strand of her copper-blonde, shoulder-length hair behind her ear. Her eyes were wide and fearful, and her pupils darted toward the door. 'Who are you? What happened to Officer Zarecki?'

'Hi, Ashlee. My name is Dr Jenna Ramey. I'm a forensic psychiatrist with the FBI. I'd like to ask you a few questions.'

'Psychiatrist?' Ashlee asked. She glanced at the door again, her hands folded tightly in her lap.

'Don't worry, Ashlee. I'm not here to analyze *you*. It's my job to try to put together the things we know about the crime and give the police officers and the FBI any information I can that might help them understand the mind of the individuals they're looking for. Let's talk about the incident,' Jenna said, careful not to call the scene upstairs a crime or refer to the murders in any way. If this woman was downstairs, it was possible she had seen none of the crime, all of it, or anything in between, and Jenna needed this information straight from her without putting any ideas in her head. 'Is that OK?'

Ashlee nodded wordlessly.

'All right. Just try to tell me what you remember. That's all I need from you,' Jenna said. She'd had to give too many interviews just like this back when she'd been the sole reason her mother had been arrested. Even as a pre-teen, her nerves had felt over the edge. And that was with only one killer stalking around, never mind the gang of them that had taken the bank by storm. Ashlee had to be terrified, and her mind was probably clouded by fear and overwhelmed at best. 'What was the first moment that you noticed something out of the everyday bank workings was going on?'

The woman sat there for a moment, quiet. She closed her eyes as though trying to see the scene in her mind. She winced. Folded her lips.

'I heard someone scream. A woman. It sounded like she was near the door,' she said softly.

'OK, good. Where were you when you heard the scream?'

'In the drive-through teller room. Behind the teller line inside the bank,' Ashlee said, her words fast and clipped, a touch of panic in her tone.

'OK. And what happened after you heard the scream?' Jenna asked, hoping for her own selfish purposes that the bank entrance had been within Ashlee's sightlines from where she was in the drive-through room and that Ashlee had looked toward it.

'I turned in the direction of the scream as I backed up closer to the wall. The yells and rushing movement out of the corner of my eye scared me. I didn't even know what exactly was happening yet, but it was just a gut instinct,' Ashlee replied, her eyes still closed. 'I couldn't see a lot from where I was pressed up by the wall, but I could make out lots of black figures moving, sprays of red. It took my brain a second to process that I was seeing people being killed.'

Damn.

'How many black figures did you see?'

Ashlee shrugged, eyes squeezed tighter. 'I have no idea. It was such a blur. But a lot. More than you'd expect. They seemed to be pouring in the door.'

'Right,' Jenna said, nodding. 'What happened after you realized what the figures were doing?'

'I dropped down to my knees by the wall, but I knew sooner or later they'd notice me. I'd seen them, after all. I kept thinking the only way I'd be OK was if I could get out before they noticed me. I crawled out of the room and went under the teller counter for cover, then I crawled to the left, toward the exit that leads downstairs to here,' Ashlee said. 'I stopped at the edge of the desk to try to peek out, see if I could make it without being seen.'

'OK,' Jenna said, waiting patiently for the next piece of the story. Obviously, Ashlee had made it downstairs alive. This was one suspense story where they knew at least the end of the chapter. The main character in this particular portion had made it.

'One of the figures grabbed my wrist,' she said.

Jenna forced herself not to react.

How the heck had she gotten away?

Jenna nodded. 'What next?'

'The person spoke. A man,' Ashlee replied.

Now she was wringing her hands in her lap, though her eyes remained shut. She shook her head profusely like she was trying to tell her own memory to forget, to not relive the nightmare.

'I begged him not to kill me. I held my other arm over my face, like I could protect myself. He could've just stabbed my stomach. Stupid.'

'Why did you think he would stab you?' Jenna asked.

'He had a weapon. Some kind of knife.'

'What did it look like?'

Ashlee squeezed her eyes tighter, and a tear trickled down her cheek. 'Long. I don't know. I can't remember. He had something like a knife. All of them did. Only they were different, too.'

'That's OK,' Jenna said. Eyewitnesses always made poor witnesses, unfortunately. 'When he spoke, what did he say?'

'He told me to take him to the safe. I kept begging him not to kill me. I figured I'd open the safe, let him clean it out. All I could think about was my family. They train us what to do during a robbery – how to call for help with silent alarms, stuff like that. But in the moment, I didn't think of any of that. I could only think about doing what he said so I could go home.'

'Understandable,' Jenna replied, calm and smooth. She needed to give the witness confidence, help her trust her own instincts. If she didn't, Ashlee could clam up. 'Anyone with half a brain would be sensitive to that. What happened next?'

'I stood up. We walked to the stairs . . . went down. Got to the safe. I turned the combination into the lock and opened the door. God. I could hear his breathing behind me.'

'Did he say anything else up to this point?'

She shook her head. 'No. Just waited. I was so scared he'd stab me in the back. God, it was so fucking terrifying.'

Now Ashlee shook. She rocked herself a little, unclasped her hands and dried them on her pants.

'When you opened the door, what happened?' Jenna asked.

'He told me to close myself in the safe so I didn't get killed. He said I was lucky. That I'd been chosen to "start the dialogue". Those were the words he used: "Start the dialogue". He told me

it was important to speak carefully when I talked to "investigators". Said the police would come. That I should pass along their
message.'

The redwood color Jenna associated with attention-seeking flashed
in. They had kept a witness alive on *purpose* to transmit a message to
the cops. The bold, chili pepper red of organization replaced the
redwood. Then, narcissistic purple. Sometimes killers secretly *wanted*
to be caught on some level. But the pathology of a *group* of killers?
Not so simple . . .

A message to pass. An organized group of killers, yet mass
murder without robbery motives, so the mafia moving money
seemed out.

A message. Organized. Mass.

The deep, dark red of sangria blanketed her mind. A color she
associated with violence rooted in causing fear. Terror.

'What message did he ask you to pass on?' Jenna asked, swallowing
hard. One of the killers had kept someone alive deliberately to tell
her – to tell the *police* – something. And left a note that they would
strike again. It could only mean one thing . . .

'He said to tell you that you should "treat all trivial things in life
very seriously—"'

'Wait,' Jenna cut in. 'Which of those were his words?'

'What he said exactly was, "Tell the cops they should treat all
trivial things in life very seriously. Tell them it is important to be
earnest."'

The words caused a wash of lapis lazuli to crash over Jenna,
the deep blue permeating her thoughts. Intelligence. Classical
intelligence.

'Thank you, Ashlee,' she said, standing. 'I may have some more
questions for you in a bit, but that's all I need right now.'

Jenna left the downstairs conference room of the bank and closed
the door behind her. Her eyes found Saleda's. 'I want to do another
walkthrough. Also, I think you'll want to get Homeland Security on
the line.'

Jenna passed Saleda and headed down the hallway toward the
stairs. She had to see the crime scene again. She could get so much
more from it now that she knew what they were dealing with.
Sort of.

In fact, she'd be able to look at each killing individually and learn even more about the group makeup, now that she knew what she was looking for.

She heard Saleda's heels clacking on the floor behind her. Her ranking officer fell into step with her. 'Homeland Security? What the fuck for?'

'Because this isn't a bank robbery gone wrong or a weird mafia-related hit,' Jenna said. 'We're dealing with a terrorist group.'

Five

Ah, visitors' day.

Isaac Keaton took a deep breath of the not-so-fresh air of the visiting area, where he was led to a little cubicle with flimsy walls. A few other supermax inmates were already here, sitting behind the fingerprint-covered Plexiglas while they talked over corded telephones to their wives, kids, parents, and legal aides. These men who had committed the worst of the worst violent crimes, who were so tough they were otherwise kept in single-occupancy control units twenty-three hours a day, would reach up to the window and mirror the palms of their five-year-old daughters, sometimes fight tears when their mother showed up for the very rare visit. The more Isaac came to this room ever since he'd started striving for good behavior points from the guards when he first set this plan into motion, the more he noticed that the air outside his cell might not be fresh, but it was full. Full of sweaty nerves, salty tears. The stench of body odor and farts and bad breath clashed distinctly with the need in the air, the hope, and the remorse.

Isaac shuffled, his ankles still shackled, around the seat of the cubicle and lowered himself into the chair. He adopted his own look of relief and happiness mixed with regret. The little twit would expect it. Need it, even, if she was to keep on track.

He found her eyes across from him and stared into them, suppressing laughter at the vacant expression staring back at him. 'Hi, buttercup. Good to see your face.'

The blonde-haired, green-eyed beauty let out a relieved laugh, flashing a smile so white he'd known the first time he'd seen it those teeth weren't a natural shade. A tear dripped down her porcelain cheek, streaking it black with her running mascara.

'Yours, too,' she breathed, and some of the tension in her shoulders relaxed.

He smiled, closed-lipped. A little bit more show, just to calm her nerves. She needed the reassuring. Always did after something like last time, when he'd been angry with her for diverting from the plan.

When his temper bested his control, he had to use a precise recipe to steer everything back on course, get Lynzee in the place he wanted her to be.

Thankfully, the recipe always worked. He'd solidified their relationship long before Lynzee was fired from the prison med ward for fraternizing with an inmate. He'd been careful, subtle. By the time anyone on staff reported his affair with the pretty young nurse, he'd not only managed to make her believe that she brought the best out in him, but that she needed him desperately. That they were soul mates and she alone understood him. That he was the only person who understood *her*. That no matter what happened, she wanted to be with him.

'Have you been sleeping better?' he asked, letting the fingers of the hand not holding the phone stretch toward her as though he wished his hands weren't cuffed so he could touch the Plexiglas, have his hand closer to hers.

She lifted a palm to the glass, pressed it to where, if he could reach, his hand might've been. 'Trying.'

He nodded. 'That's good. I want you to get some rest soon so those dark circles will go away. You're just as pretty with them, but they let me know that you're struggling.'

'Stupid evidence,' she laughed, moving her hand from the Plexiglas and wiping her eyes. 'Isaac—'

'Lynz, don't,' he cut in. He shook his head, still smiling. 'You're here now, and that's what matters. *We're* here.'

If I can taste the vomit when I say the words, you'd think you'd at least have a gag reflex when I say them.

But she didn't. She drank them up like a little plant in the desert.

'I've just been so worried you'd still be upset with me after I messed up—'

'Shh,' he admonished gently. 'I told you. It's OK.'

The last thing I need is for you to lose your focus and say something you shouldn't.

'Tell me about work,' Isaac said, the caring boyfriend. He didn't exactly *want* to hear her ramble on about her new job and why it wasn't the same as when she was here because he wasn't there. But, the change of topic steered her away from talk not fit to be discussed undisguised around guards, being recorded.

Isaac counted to one hundred and eighty in his head, careful to tune in just enough so that later whatever she told him wouldn't come back to bite him in the ass. The best plans were ruined, the most brilliant of criminals thwarted because they didn't pay enough attention to the people weaker than them. Even more brilliant minds than his had been spoiled because they'd failed to keep their generals under control. A target with the attention he or she craved was a happy target – a pawn willing to be manipulated.

Jenna Ramey's face burst forth in his mind, and for a moment, he shut out Lynzee's words. Her mother had been the smartest there was, maybe, and yet, Claudia didn't properly attend to Jenna. Let her have too many of her own thoughts. Didn't color enough of her perception. Claudia had been bested by Jenna, a costly mistake of his stepmother's he was determined to learn from.

Sure. *His* master plan had been stopped by Jenna, too, and Claudia had ended up trumping the system through a ruse he had tried and failed at himself, but his mistake had been different. He hadn't known Jenna before they met during his interrogation following a shooting last year. His mistake had been to underestimate her.

But the past was the past, and his tango with Jenna Ramey was far from over. She'd gotten the better of him and thrown him in prison, sentenced to life without parole, but he wasn't about to accept this as a defeat. Oh, no. It was just the first battle in a much larger war.

'So, did Shelby admit she was the one who took your Dr Pepper out of the fridge, or is she still trying to deny she was in the break room?' Isaac asked, latching on to Lynzee Gold's train of thought, fooling her into thinking her workplace squabbles – her *life* – was important to him. He had to, in order to change the subject and still have her think he cared. He'd let her talk for a full three minutes about herself, but it was for naught if the transition wasn't smooth. They had twenty minutes to visit, and that time could be plenty for his purposes if he shifted gears easily. It could also tick away fast if she became indignant.

'Of course not,' she replied, rolling her eyes. 'Nobody saw her go in there but me. If she 'fessed up now, it'd be worse than it would've been to begin with after she told everyone she didn't do it.'

'Ugh,' he replied. The response was more his annoyance with her banal bullshit than with the coworker and the case of the missing soda. 'Well, you just wait. Karma's a bitch . . . oh, speaking of . . . did you talk to your sister about her birthday?'

He held his breath, waiting for Lynzee's reaction as he said the words that would make sense to her. Their code to either confirm whether or not she'd taken the next step he'd asked her to or, in this case, to signal that he was about to give her more information.

She shook her head. 'Not yet. I called her, but she hasn't called back yet.'

'Ah, I gotcha,' he replied, nodding. Smug satisfaction washed over him following her reply, which let him know she was ready for his directions. He hadn't seen that little thing in her eyes that flashed when she was perturbed or disappointed. 'Well, you'll have to sign the card from me, too. I know I have to miss it, but damn, I wish I could be there. Meet your folks, too.'

Her face registered sadness, the frown clear as her eyes let go of his and turned downward.

'Lynz. Don't ever worry that this circumstance will last and that we will never meet. Understand, love. We'll have so long together, meeting everyone you've known won't even seem hard by the time we're going through our bucket lists together, checking things off. We'll be able to forget the last few years of not being together. It'll just be one more time in our lives. OK?' he said slowly. Carefully.

She nodded, but he wasn't sure she was grasping what he was saying a hundred percent. Couldn't trust that his words had gotten through to her. She was a ditz, after all.

Isaac repeated his words to her again, this time adding, 'Do not get discouraged, Lynz. We *will* be together.' For emphasis. For the show.

Lynzee sat quietly for a full ten seconds before nodding again.

'I know. Deep down, I know. It's just . . . hard,' she said, a tear trailing her nose. She wiped it with the back of her hand. Sniffled.

Isaac fought the smirk. He'd taught her so well.

'Good girl,' he said, this time really meaning the praise if not the affection. She did the job so beautifully that he almost hated that, at some point, he'd have to break her at best, kill her at worst. Though maybe killing her was more humane. She *had* performed a valuable service for him, being the vital liaison he needed and all. Was a valuable *asset*. Putting her out of the misery she'd suffer when he left and didn't marry her and have a thousand babies might be a nice reward for the loyalty.

'Time!' a guard in the doorway called.

'Gotta go, buttercup. Give your sis a hug from me. Maybe tell her the present was my idea,' he said, blowing her an air kiss.

She smiled. 'I haven't even said what I got her.'

He snickered, enjoying the way she kept up, played along. The guards would never suspect their conversations were code, because the code was so well masked. Even if they somehow zeroed in on that the talks they had were contrived, they'd never be able to decipher them.

'Still,' Isaac said. 'I want credit. I don't know what you bought, but I *do* know you have *impeccable* taste. Bye, buttercup.'

He hung up the phone, but he didn't take his eyes off her as he backed out of the cubicle. Better to give her these last few seconds of his attention, let his behaviors stand in her memory in case at any point she doubted him.

Sheep never see a wolf among them if the wolf looks like a sheep, too.

He turned away, shuffled toward the door of the visiting room to go back to his cell, thankful his acting gig was over.

When he reentered his cell, he smiled as the door slammed shut, its lock clicking into place. It was only a matter of time now before he made his move against Jenna Ramey. Showed her that it was *him* she should be afraid of. It was *him* who would come back for her.

He sat on his bed, looked up at the TV in the top corner that was tuned to the lovely televangelist channel the guards used as a torment device. He grinned, shook his head.

'And on the third day, they rolled the stone away only to see that the one they'd put there was no longer inside,' he said. 'Oh, Jenna. *Doctor* Ramey. I'm coming for you.'

Six

Back upstairs at the bank, Jenna stood in the lobby, taking in the scene again. This time, she was ready for it, knew to be careful not to look too hard at the different bodies, speculating on how they were killed. Later, it would be worth it, but for now that would only provoke too many colors to make any sense. For the moment, much more was to be gained by assessing the crime scene's bigger canvas as though it were one giant masterpiece orchestrated by one person. The person that was the leader of this terrorist group, the person who would have been the commander of the force. He or she would have had the final say on what went on here even if the plan had been a collaborative one.

With that in mind, the colors didn't seem to fly at her out of control. Instead, the gory scene was much more dilute. A horrible reality, yes, but a cohesive, dim reality rather than the bold, intense colors that had seemed to zoom around the room as if in a pinball machine when she'd first come in.

Out of the corner of her eye, she saw Porter and Teva approaching from the doorway, but only her eyes roamed the room as she otherwise kept completely still. As her teammates joined her and Saleda, she muttered the only thought she could definitively put into words at that second to help get them on to the same page: 'Every attacker has a different MO, so the violence level and profile of each individual will be different. The message is the same.'

How, I'm not entirely sure.

'Do you want to talk about the literature reference now or later?' Porter asked.

Good. Saleda had filled them in, by phone, she guessed. She shrugged, though she did know it played a role in at least part of a theory her mind was simmering on the backburner somewhere. 'Now's as a good a time as any. Oscar Wilde, *The Importance of Being Earnest*,' she said, recalling the lapis lazuli that had washed over her at Ashlee's words. 'This scene is chaotic, but the people involved aren't. Not entirely, anyway. The person at the helm whose vision we're seeing is smart. Well-educated, if the literary reference is to be believed. Made sure we were seeing everything the way he wanted us to. Wanted to be heard but not caught, I think. Left someone alive to tell the tale, ensured the video was taken away . . .' *Even though the leader obviously wanted to communicate with investigators . . .*

'That's contradictory,' Teva said. 'If they wanted us to get a message they set up explicitly, why leave a living witness but pull the video?'

'Maybe the crime scene is orchestrated one way, but the video would show us it took place somehow other than the scene implies,' Porter said.

Jenna nodded. 'Or the video would show too much or too little. Show us identifying information . . .' Really, right now, there were too many possibilities for why the group had removed the video but left a live witness.

'No matter which scenario is the right one, they had reasons for doing it how they did, I don't doubt,' a voice said.

Jenna glanced to her right to see Dodd, who had joined them. Where he'd come from, there was no telling.

'Well, terrorist groups run the gamut as far as their intentions, their motives, and the way they operate,' Saleda said.

Jenna caught herself shaking her head reactively. Stopped. Realized she was looking at a severed arm on the floor. Again, the sangria of brutality to induce fear flashed in.

'Blades are an interesting weapon of choice for a terrorist group,' she said. 'Cause a different kind of devastation entirely from the usual terror tactics like explosives or more biological weapons like poisoned gas or disease.'

'This was a decision made *for* the group, whether by one individual or a few who led them. So, no, this wasn't an instinct decision. It was just like every other choice the leadership made; for us to see for one reason or another,' Jenna said.

A deep purple flashed in, and Jenna struggled to grasp it. Too blue to be narcissism, even if it felt right. Not purple *enough* to go into the more pink fuchsia of misleading. But somehow, that was close, too. Indigo was *very* nearly the color, but still not quite the shade of deliberate intent.

Then, the color took hold of her, all of the concepts playing with each other to help her near the association, since it *was* one with a meaning for her, if only subconsciously. Russian violet. Theatrics, actors making deliberate choices to portray something to an audience they want to convey. In a way, mislead . . .

It's a performance. Acts of terror are performances designed to play to an audience.

'Practical reasons?' Dodd suggested. 'Knives are attained more easily, so younger assailants had access, maybe.'

'These people weren't all killed with hunting knives or kitchen knives,' Saleda said, glancing reflexively toward one of the dismembered bodies. 'Many are using big, unusual weapons. Machetes, big game knives.'

'Not all, though,' Teva said, 'Wounds vary in type and degree of damage from victim to victim. Only consistency is blades, it seems.'

And if the masterminds chose blades, then what was the reason? Came back to what their performance was intended to achieve. The message of the show.

Tell the cops they should treat all trivial things in life very seriously, Ashlee had quoted the killer's message.

'Tell them it's important to be earnest,' Jenna said under her breath. 'Quoted from Oscar Wilde's play. If the group left us a note to let us know they'd strike again, why leave someone behind to give us this message, too. Has to be part of the performance. I'm just not sure what it means yet.'

'So, *The Importance of Being Earnest,*' Saleda said. 'Any other thoughts based on what we're seeing here?'

'God, I don't even know,' Teva said. 'It's been a long time since it was required reading in high school.'

'Hmph,' Jenna said. 'Ages for me, too.'

'Seeing as how I could have fathered you all . . . heck, grandfathered half of you . . . I don't think I need to tell you how long it's been since I was in school,' Dodd said.

'OK, back to the scene for now, but be thinking about the literature references and who you might know who could help us other than your high school English teachers, since obviously they didn't do much for any of you,' Saleda said.

The color of store-bought vanilla ice cream flashed in. Jenna shook it away for the moment, knowing it was related more to Saleda's quip than the crime scene even if she hadn't let it linger long enough to define it.

'The literature, the note promising another attack. That rules out revenge attack, like in Oklahoma City. There, McVeigh's crime was his statement. No warnings. The messages here are a more common terror MO: fear. They want something,' Jenna said.

'And usually when they want something, the fear they want to cause is tied to it. Hence the target is tied to it. Extreme pro-lifer bombs abortion clinic. Wants to stop abortion,' Dodd said. 'Even if you're at the clinic for condoms or a cancer screening, you're going down with the docs performing the abortions.'

'Along with any fetuses still in-utero inside the building at the time.' Teva frowned. 'Killed like the people they wanted to punish for harming them. Doesn't make sense, though, because it's not like this is a pro-choice bank, operates inside a rainbow building, or has fur rugs and only hunters for employees.'

'You're right, Rookie. But you're thinking only about the want something part. Stop thinking about *who* they want dead, and think about the other half of the equation. Who do they want to fear them? Not the dead . . .' Dodd said.

'People who are alive to see the results,' Teva replied, nodding.

Sure. And after an abortion clinic bombing, that meant something. Scare the types of people who made abortions available at those clinics. But this wasn't a medical clinic or even some giant corporation raking it in on Wall Street.

But to the killers, it symbolizes something.

Jenna took another long look from one side of the room to the other, the crime scene in her vision like something she only wished were part of an action movie set.

Her gaze settled on the body of a young, white male splayed face first on the shiny wood floor. She wandered toward him, squatted beside his still frame. He was exactly where he'd fallen, according to the M.E. The first responders had left the initial scene completely intact for the FBI.

Jenna's gaze drifted from the back of his closely-cropped hair the same color as the darkest roast coffee she had in her cabinet at home to his neck, torso. He'd fallen face first into a decent-sized puddle of his own blood, and yet, the puddle he was in was closer to his stomach. The stab wound to the side of his neck – his carotid artery – wouldn't have produced that much blood and definitely didn't make sense with where the pool was in relation to where he'd fallen.

She crouched so her head was as close to level with the floor as she could get it, squinted at what she could see of the man's shoulders, chest. Soaked red down his front. She sat back, glanced at the wound to the side of his neck that most likely had finished him despite the plethora of contenders for the honor. A bit of spatter from that stab on his right shoulder, but just residue. What she'd expect.

Bending again, Jenna squinted to see his blood-soaked front. No way a jab to the carotid had soaked the collar and all visible portions of the guy's white button down. She turned her head toward where the victim's nose had cracked against the polished wood, leaned even closer. Sure enough, a deep slice stretched from under his chin across to at least his Adam's apple. Still forcing herself to tune out her colleagues' conjecture behind her, Jenna hopped to her feet and circled to the victim's other side, though she had a feeling she'd see that his foe had carried that knife swipe cleanly across his trachea, left to right.

Throat slit and *his carotid. Guy had a really, really bad day.*

Jenna blinked, sat back on her feet. The sounds in her ears buzzed as a shade of ochre flashed in. The same shade she'd seen when her dad had confronted her at age twenty about how she resisted any and all dating. She'd sat on the couch, afraid to tell him the reason she'd never wanted to go to prom or to the movies with a boy in high school, never brought a guy home to meet the family in college was because she was terrified of making the wrong choice. Of picking a mate who ended up being a psychopath. She didn't want to tell her dad that life with Claudia had caused her not to ever want relationships of her own because she was scared she'd make the same mistake he had.

The two scenarios that caused the ochre couldn't have been more different, but the jab to the victim's carotid that killed him and her father's relationship with a psychopath diminishing her urge to date had one thing in common that she associated the color with: Cause and effect.

She cocked her head, staring at the neck of the victim from this side. The carotid jab made no sense.

The killer had not gotten bored and decided to end it quickly. The victim would have suffocated from the cut trachea shortly anyway. It wasn't because he'd met a particularly vicious killer who wanted to stab him three times instead of two.

It would seem a different killer with a different style had come by and ended it a lot quicker. Different blades, styles. Lots of bloodshed . . . different people from all walks of life . . .

Jenna jumped up, surged back toward the team. 'Using blades had to be deliberate. But they clearly all had different blades, some of which had to be hard to obtain, so it wasn't a convenience choice. Maybe the leadership chose blades because people hear about bombings and shootings on the news every single day now,' Jenna said.

Porter tilted his head, considering. 'Blades are definitely unusual in a mass killing.'

'And, in a way, scarier to imagine. You're right. Explosions. Gunfire. They're on TV every day,' Teva added.

'On cable,' Saleda said, reaching to her back pocket to grab her phone. She glanced at its face. 'Got to take this.'

She stepped away, and Jenna glanced back toward the white-collared victim. 'And usually, they're visible, important targets. The World Trade Center collapsing is imagery burned into America's collective psyche, but the mental picture of people dismembered while still alive in a bank is statement-making scary, too. The goal is to get people to listen. We need to know what they want us to hear. We need to know their cause. We profile every single individual, every single victim, we try to profile their leadership, like always. But I think what might tell us most about the statement they're making is that damned Oscar Wilde quote.'

'Yes, but we already went through this, Doc. We'll all old, amnesiacs, or stoners,' Dodd said.

'Well, we need someone who isn't. Linguistics expert at Quantico?' Porter said.

'Not going to work. We need linguistics, but we also need *literature*,' Jenna replied.

Teva chuckled. 'I left all my college professors in my other pants pockets today.'

Jenna closed her eyes, hung her head as her teammates threw out names of contacts, suggestions that might work. She rubbed her temple slowly. *Not this.*

They had plenty of ideas, but none were as good as hers. And she wasn't going to be able to ignore it even if she *would* rather hack off her own foot with her car key than call her. *Riddles, word games. Mind games.* Between Isaac Keaton and Claudia, surely she'd met her lifetime quota for this particular brand of bullshit.

'I know someone,' she said, soft but sure. 'It'll take me a day or so to track her down, even with Irv to help, but I'll get him on it. She's who we need. I'm sure.'

The rest of her teammates stared at her, faces blank. Geez.

She raised her eyebrows, nodded to them as if to prod *any* of them into saying something. Anything.

'Right. So, Jenna's on the lit angle then, so we should . . .'

Porter had tried valiantly, but his trailing voice said it all. They didn't know how to move forward with this efficiently because it *wasn't* as easy as profiling the killer and moving from there. They'd try to go about usual routine, examining bodies, attempting to profile killers. That was, if they had any chance of matching up bodies to killers when, so far, all they had was the goriest room she'd ever seen and the knowledge that their terrorists all had knives, the desire to scare people, and memory retention from high school English.

Goriness to make a statement. A statement to people who lived.

Again, attention-seeking redwood flashed in.

The other thing they knew: the killers must have an allergy to media, because any terror group hell-bent on achieving statement-making scary like this bank job *had* to want the public to hear about what they'd done. This hit was designed to have psychological ramifications on people who *didn't* die inside these walls that morning. You can't scare people if no one knows about it.

'I don't get it,' Jenna muttered.

'The blood, the literature, the note, the live witness, the body parts, or something else?' Porter asked.

'Well, all those, too, but the media. Terrorists exploit the media. Manipulate it. Lure it to their little 'projects' like setting the dogs out for fresh game. But not a peep from the press,' Jenna said.

'That just changed,' Saleda said, returning from where she'd been talking in hushed tones on her cell phone. 'That was the press liaison's office at Quantico. They just patched a call from a CNC investigative journalist all the way through to Kate Balthazar herself.'

'Must be big,' Porter remarked, eyes wide in genuine surprise.

The curiosity mixed with shock in his voice was universal amongst the group. For a call to be sent from the gatekeepers through to the press liaison's office itself meant it had teeth, but to make it to the director . . .

Saleda's jaw set in a firm line. 'Big. Bad. Maybe unprecedented on our soil?' She started walking toward the door, and her voice had been so grave, the rest followed without question, though she didn't keep them in suspense.

'They weren't *not* alerting the media. Turns out they were just giving them the exclusive.'

Seven

Inside the bulletproof trailer set up outside the bank as FBI on-site headquarters, Jenna rested her elbows on the Formica countertop built into the side wall of the trailer as she stared up in horror at the footage playing on the forty-inch flat screen mounted on the rear wall.

The black and white figures darted in and out of the frame, trying to survive . . . or kill. The knowledge that the chaos she was watching had been the last few minutes of life for the people now lying inside the bank a few feet away made it the most frightening spectacle Jenna had ever viewed on a television monitor.

Spectacle.

Russian violet returned. The color of theatrics had confused her when she'd seen it earlier, but now it made sense. The perps hadn't left a witness, a message, and taken the tapes without involving the media; they'd just given the media an engraved invitation. With the mystery of the missing media solved, the live witness and the written message troubled Jenna even more. She was sure she was right in thinking the attackers wanted the general public to fear them, for the brutal attack to root itself so deeply into every mind that when their agenda came out, its success would, to some degree, already be won. Giving the tape to the media played to that strategy.

But if you want the media to show the public how it all went down frame by frame, why the other two messages?

Jenna's gaze followed the black figure with the machete-style blade. First inside the bank doors, he rushed toward the glassed-in privacy room. He entered, and with a swipe, chopped the stocky woman cowering inside almost cleanly in half. Jenna winced.

The Machete UNSUB exited the privacy room, dodging people now. From the moment he'd entered, he'd been the aggressor any time he crossed paths with someone, but suddenly, he was falling back. Letting the others do the dirty work. *Why?*

Jenna squinted. Machete UNSUB moved in a definite direction, not lost or dazed. No. He had a clear intention. She just had no clue in hell what it was.

Back at the bank door where the group had entered, he joined another black figure carrying a long sword. The two ventured right, out of view of the cameras.

Jenna jumped up and gestured at where they had exited. 'Where are they going? The two who were just here?'

'Which?' Porter asked.

'Shit,' Teva said. 'So many damned moving pieces. I've been following the same one since it started . . . the guy who looks like he stepped out of the 1800's. So I don't know who you're talking about.'

'Well, you should,' Saleda said. 'Because I've been watching Machete Kills since he went in first, and the sword guy just left off camera with him.'

Saleda's instinct seemed to have been the same as Jenna's: watch the first person in. He was bound to be the group's leader.

The tech running the footage paused it, backed it up. Pressed play again.

Jenna looked away at the exact moment she knew the lady in the privacy room was about to be cleaved in two. No need to see that moment twice.

She returned her gaze the following second though, ignoring the horrible machete scene in favor of locating the figure with the sword prior to his meeting up with Machete. Amidst the flying knives and falling bodies, she spotted the Long-Sword UNSUB on the right hand side of the video behind the teller counter alongside another attacker. The two black-clad assailants each took on one of the two tellers, the one Jenna was watching wielding his sword toward the counter and downward. The video's angle didn't show the death that resulted, but Jenna knew the victim to be the slender black female teller found lying face-first on the carpet underneath the employees' side of the countertop. Jenna had noted during the crime scene walkthrough that it appeared she had tried to crawl toward the exit when she was first knocked under the counter during the skirmish, because her initial fall landed her only a foot or so away from where her pretty blonde co-worker had taken her last breaths. But she didn't make it far. She was stabbed multiple times in her torso and thighs.

A golden color flashed in, though Jenna couldn't readily identify it.

She let it go, since it didn't match the other, more important thought in her head.

'He passes right by where Ashlee had to have been crawling under the counter toward the staircase,' she said. 'Back it up one more time.'

The tech obliged and, again, the team watched the screen as the Long-Sword UNSUB lashed at the teller the angle didn't show, then stood and exited from behind the counter. He joined up with Machete on the left side of their screen, not far from where the attackers had entered the bank, and they moved out of the frame's visibility.

'The staircase is on that side,' Dodd noted. 'Someone *did* have to escort Ms Haynie down, give her the message, and lock her in the safe, after all.'

'One person, though. Not two. She said one guy,' Teva replied.

'Doesn't mean they didn't head off together at first then split up. One had a separate task while the other scared the daylights out of our favorite living witness,' Porter said.

Jenna cringed at Porter's words. They all tended to kid at times in ways that would make anyone not in their line of work assume they needed etiquette lessons and a Bible, but for some reason, calling the one person who'd survived the carnage 'favorite' highlighted for Jenna why surviving might end up being worse for Ashlee Haynie. She'd never escape the images in her head, the screams burned in her memory.

Another color tried to break forth, but Jenna forced it back. She needed to think not get bogged down.

Then again, this sickening second by second, blow-by-blow chronicle of the deaths of twenty-one people would soon be etched in the memories of millions. CNR might've had the good judgment to keep it off the air and inform the FBI, but unfortunately, Jenna had no doubts that the terrorists had passed the footage on to other journalists, too. The FBI could yank feeds, keep it at bay as long as possible, but in the age of the hungry Internet and even hungrier media, all it would take before anyone with a broadband connection could see it would be one foreign server.

'They swiped the security footage to give to the media but left it intact,' she whispered.

'What?' Saleda asked, turning to face her.

Jenna shook her head, trying to make sense of it all. 'We thought they stole the security footage because there was something on it that would show us more to these attacks . . . something that might differ from the picture they were leaving the note and the witness to paint. But here's the footage. Obviously, it cuts off the moment they yanked the tapes, so we can't know what happened after everyone was dead and they left the building, but otherwise, it's seemingly in full and untampered with. So their sole reasoning in taking it was to deliver it to media directly, but why?'

'Or maybe they want us to *think* that's their sole reasoning,' Dodd countered.

'Maybe, but humor me for a second. Why leave a witness if you're leaving access to a full-length video?' Jenna asked.

From the side, Porter grunted a curious-sounding, 'Hmph.'

Jenna whirled to face him. 'What? What did you just notice?'

He smiled close-lipped, though it wasn't happy. Just interested.

'Vocals,' he replied.

Slate gray burst forth in Jenna's mind, the same color that had tried to peek through moments ago after Porter's comment about Ashlee Haynie being their favorite living witness. Of course. The color she associated with the sense of hearing. It wasn't just images that would be burned into Ashlee's memory. It would also be the screams, the chokes, the sputtering.

And any words they said other than what they told her to pass along to us.

'I need to talk to Ashlee Haynie again,' Jenna said. 'I need to find out what else she heard.'

Eight

'No, no, no, no, no!' Ashlee's voice got louder with every word as she shook her head, eyes squeezed shut tighter and tighter. 'I don't want to!'

'Ashlee, I wouldn't ask if it wasn't extremely important. I wouldn't make you relive that nightmare unless I thought it could help me catch the people who did this,' Jenna said softly.

'I feel like I'm going to throw up,' Ashlee said weakly.

'Agent Dodd, will you get Ms Haynie a glass of water, please?' Jenna said. 'Take a few deep breaths in through your nose and out through your mouth, Ashlee.'

Jenna watched the bank worker round her lips into an O, slowly blowing out a breath. The woman's flushed, red complexion evened, and hand trembling, she accepted the paper cup of water from Dodd. She took a slow sip.

'That's it,' Jenna said, nodding. As bad as she needed information, eyewitnesses were sketchy at recalling moments under duress. Uncooperative, hyperventilating eyewitnesses made for even worse testimonies. If the terrorists had simply wanted to pass the phrase *important to be earnest* on to the cops, they could've just written it on the same note that warned authorities they would strike again. But they hadn't.

Instead, they'd left them a living witness instructed to give the message.

Which was why Jenna now knew that whatever else Ashlee had heard come from any of their mouths was vital. They'd have known the video wouldn't have audio. They'd have also known that leaving a witness alive meant leaving a standing, testifying account of any vocalizations they made inside the building – be they statements made directly *to* the witness or not. Rookie cops might discover this nugget and think it a goldmine, but Jenna knew better.

Quite an oversight for a precise attack executed without so much as a hiccup, bank alarm, or errant cell phone call made by one of the twenty-two people inside the bank as it was being overtaken. Nope. It wasn't an oversight. Leaving Ashlee Haynie alive was deliberate.

And so was anything they allowed her to hear.

'OK,' Jenna said, her voice light and soothing. 'Now, I want you to think about the moments inside the bank after you heard the woman scream. It's going to be hard, but remember, you're physically OK. As you're imagining those minutes that your mind is fighting so hard to forget, in the back of your mind, I want you to let yourself know that it's safe to remember those things. Not comfortable. Not *OK* by any definition of the word, because no one should have to remember what I'm asking you to. But you are safe. The events are physically in the past.'

Ashlee nodded, eyes wide. She wrung her hands in her lap. 'I'll try.'

'That's all I can ask for,' Jenna said. 'OK. I want you to close your eyes and go to the moment inside the bank when you heard the woman near the door scream. Can you hear her?'

Ashlee winced. 'Yes,' she whispered.

The ache in the woman's voice stung Jenna to her core. Before she'd come back to the BAU last year, she'd spent years helping patients cope after unfathomable traumatic events, coaching them on how to control reliving their nightmares at a speed that wouldn't overwhelm them. These days, it was commonplace to consider talking through experiences healing, but in truth, for some people, calling to mind memories of the incident that had catapulted them into therapy in the first place actually exacerbated all kinds of symptoms. And, in that setting, she had a chance to develop a rapport with the patient, establish herself as an ally.

Here, Jenna knew good and well her intentions weren't first and foremost to preserve Ashlee Haynie's mental health. Her job as an investigator was to extract the damned memories inside the woman's head at whatever cost and use them to protect future lives. Never mind the life right in front of her that still needed saving.

Ashlee might've survived the attack inside the bank, but really, she wasn't so different from Jenna. The screams. The blood. They'd formed a single, defining moment of her existence. One she couldn't return from, couldn't erase.

Bloody handprints . . . the door, so close.

Ashlee Haynie might be alive, but a part of her had died inside that bank just like the others. Jenna knew it all too well.

After all, Jenna was a survivor, too.

'OK. Where are you when you hear her scream?'

A sharp intake of breath as if Ashlee was being pierced with a needle. 'Right inside the door of the drive-through teller room. I turn and see the people coming in, and I back up to the wall. I crouch down. Before I chicken out, I crawl as fast as I can out the door and across the carpet until I'm under the teller counter.'

'And what's the next thing you hear?'

Ashlee bit her lip, her face contorting in a pained expression. 'Grunts. More screams.'

'All right,' Jenna said fast, cutting off the stream of consciousness. If Ashlee got lost in the terror of the moment, she would miss any pertinent information that she might have locked in her memory. 'Try to think about the very first *singular* noise you can separate from the rest. The next thing to hit your ears that doesn't just muddle together with the other sounds in the building—'

'I can't!'

'You *can*. You're physically safe in this room, and a dozen or more FBI agents are surrounding the outside of the building now in addition to the handful surrounding you in this very room. You're safe here,' Jenna said. The bank employee might never again feel safe, and it was wrong to tell her that her trauma was over. It might be months or years. Might be never. But Jenna had learned over the years that, just after a trauma, reminding victims of their immediate physical safety – something that didn't insinuate their plight was easy or their distress was being downplayed, but rather, addressed a valid immediate concern rightly held – was one of the few things that eased panic.

Ashlee's eyes flew open, widened. 'How do you know that?' she squealed.

A shade of blue flashed in, and Jenna begged her mind to recognize it. She inwardly flipped through the shades of blue in her lexicon, mental images attached to some of them that might spur clarity. Her thoughts landed on a freeze-frame of Ayana catalogued in her mind, one where her daughter was coloring a picture of a princess in a coloring book. With a blue crayon.

Wild Yonder Blue was its name, according to Crayola. The color she associated with the normal, everyday mundane long before she'd even conceived Ayana.

Everyday life.

Of course Ashlee would question her safety even if, under normal circumstances, dozens of Feds would make a person feel untouchable. It was the reason the terrorists had chosen this normal, everyday bank in a normal, everyday place to attack. It was easy for people to convince themselves that they wouldn't be subject to a terrorist attack, in a small, off-the-radar town or unlikely place. Much harder to pretend you didn't go to the bank as part of your weekly or even monthly errands.

'Because these criminals don't want to get caught,' Jenna said truthfully.

'How could you know *that?*' Ashlee asked, blinking and staring at Jenna. 'I've seen movies where guys who leave a note . . . where the note means they secretly *want* to be found! What about *them?*'

'It's my job to read people. Criminals. It's the reason I'm called for cases like this. To give my opinion on their mindsets. It helps us form a picture of who we think they are based on what they did. It also helps law enforcement find them by predicting what they might do next. Based on this crime scene . . .' Jenna stopped. Took a deep breath. *Honesty. Honesty is still best.* 'Ashlee, I wish I could tell you my reasoning for thinking this, because I have very solid reasons to think it. But right now, with the case still under investigation and you our only reliable witness—'

'Your *only* witness,' Ashlee cut in.

'—it's important that we keep your statements uninfluenced, and that includes by us as the investigators. That said, I believe the perpetrators have tried to get as far away from the crime scene as possible because they don't want to be caught, and I believe it for reasons other than just assumptions. OK?'

Ashlee nodded, bit her lip. She seemed wary, but in a second, she closed her eyes again. The signal to resume.

'All right. Here we go,' Jenna said.

She took Ashlee back to hearing the woman scream near the door and walked her through to the point they'd left off before when Ashlee had just crawled out of the room behind the teller line to hide under the teller desk. 'Are your eyes open or closed?' Jenna asked softly. If Ashlee could focus first on a little detail about herself unrelated to the horror gripping her, maybe it would remind her she had made it through OK. Help her home in on the finer details around her.

'Closed,' Ashlee said quickly.

Jenna nodded even though Ashlee's eyes were closed now, too.

'Good. After you made it under the teller counter, was the next sound you heard close to you or far away?'

'Close,' Ashlee whispered.

'How close?'

Ashlee clenched her eyes tightly. 'Very close. Someone goes near the stairs.'

'How can you tell that's where they are?'

'Their footsteps. Running.'

The guy on the video who made a break for the stairs leading down to the vaults. Of course they hadn't actually *seen* his death play out; he was out of the video frame and into the stretch of hall that led to the stairs by the time one of the attackers caught up to him. But it definitely had played out, because they'd seen the body of the same middle-aged guy who they had seen running away on the video dead at the top of the staircase during the crime scene walkthrough.

'OK. The next sound after the running steps?'

'A yell,' Ashlee said, her body tensing. 'Then a few more slow steps. A thud.'

Sounded like she'd heard the moment the runner hit the ground, succumbing to the wounds the attacker who'd caught up to him had inflicted.

Goddamn, I wish I could help you instead of force you to remember this right now, Ashlee.

Jenna looked at her hands in her lap, closed her eyes. 'Then?'

'A voice!' Ashlee said, almost a gasp, as though she was surprising even herself.

Questions of male or female, young or old flew through Jenna's mind, but she reigned them in. 'Where did it come from? How close is it to you?'

'I'm not sure,' Ashlee said. 'Farther away than the steps. Across the room, maybe.'

'Closer to the door where you heard the scream, or in the other direction?'

'I . . . I think in the middle of them somewhere,' Ashlee said.

Jenna nodded, ignoring the colors popping in and out of her mind, fighting for dominance. *Later.*

'Good. And what did the voice say? Words?'

Ashlee nodded soundlessly.

'What did the voice say?'

'Rich . . . eh . . . loo. Like one word. Rich-eh-loo,' Ashlee said, eyes still shut tight and cocking her head as though trying to think.

Two colors surged in together, both strong and urgent. Damn this crime scene and its competing profiles.

Jenna latched on to one of them – the same deep lapis lazuli that she'd seen with 'important to be earnest.' Classical intelligence. Literature reference.

She grappled to identify the second color before it slipped away. It had been in the yellow family. Or maybe the browns? *What was the exact shade?*

But like sand through her fingers, it was gone too quickly for her to hold on to it once it had started to leak. *Fucking better not have been important.*

'OK. And after the voice, was the next sound closer than it was or farther away?'

Ashlee jumped, startled. 'Closer,' she said, panic mounting in her voice. 'A lot closer!'

'What do you hear?'

'Slams. People climbing on top of the counters. Screams! Oh, God! Nicole!'

Jenna knew she had to be thinking about the stocky blonde teller in her thirties who had died just feet from where Ashlee had been hiding.

'Deep breaths, Ashlee,' Jenna encouraged. 'What other than screams?'

'Um . . . um . . . um . . .' Ashlee stuttered, shaking her head, eyes clenched, clearly trying to sift through the horror in her head to identify something useful. 'Gurgling,' she whispered.

'OK. Keep going,' Jenna said. Ashlee did *not* need to get caught up on that noise.

'Other screams, clattering under the counter where I was,' Ashlee said. 'A bang, the counter jarring beside me.'

The other teller trying to get away from the guy with the long sword.

'What next?' Jenna prodded.

Ashlee's eyes flew open. 'I don't know anymore! The next thing I remember is my wrist being grabbed.'

Jenna forced back the colors trying to come in. She had to keep Ashlee right where she was, keep her talking. 'And then what next?'

'He told me to take him to the safe,' Ashlee said.

Consistent with her previous statement. Not that Jenna expected anything different, but when they caught the bastards responsible, Ashlee's unchanging testimony would be huge in court.

'I want you to think hard about that move from under the counter down to the safe,' Jenna said. 'Go through every movement it took to get there. Take every footstep or crawl.'

Ashlee nodded.

'As you go there, tell me what other things you notice,' Jenna said.

Eyes tightly closed, Ashlee breathed faster, heavier. 'It's such a blur. I tried hard not to look at the ground, keep my eyes toward the stairs, up. Something on the floor near there.'

A body.

'We walked down . . .' her voice trailed. 'Wait. I heard something else. Someone tell someone else something.'

'OK,' Jenna said. 'Good. What was it?'

'Someone said, "Scout, keep it together. DNA."'

Jenna blinked rapidly, surprised. Lapis lazuli flashed in. 'Are you sure that's what they said?'

Ashlee nodded hard. 'Positive.'

Jenna stayed in the moment, pushing for details like how far away the voice had been, whether it was male or female, and if anyone had reacted to the statement. Jenna walked Ashlee through the exercise all the way to the vault and being locked in, just in case her witness had anything else to reveal, but all she could think about was talking to Irv.

Finally, they reached the point when Ashlee had been found inside the safe by police, and Jenna could wrap this up. She had what she needed from Ashlee's memories; now, she needed the interview to end so she could do what had to be done with it.

'Ashlee, that must've been so difficult, and I appreciate you being brave to go through it again. You rest now. An officer will drive you to the hospital to be checked out just to be safe. If you need something to help with anxiety, be sure to ask for it. I'll be in touch in the next few days, OK?' Jenna said.

Ashlee nodded at her, looking like she was about to cry. 'I can't believe this really happened,' she muttered.

Jenna reached across, closed her hand over Ashlee's. 'It never should've.'

With that, she stood and left the room.

As soon as she closed the door, Jenna whipped out her phone. She clicked to open her texts, thinking of Irv, but smiled to see texts from Vern and Charley that said only, 'Bobblehead' and 'Clementine,' respectively. Then Yancy's text of his safe word 'Smorgasboard,' along with an 'I love you.' She exhaled. Smiled. Ayana was home safe.

She snapped back a quick text to Yancy: I love you, too, hot stuff.

Just as Jenna was about to text Irv and ask where they stood in their hunt for someone Jenna really wished they didn't have to find, she noticed Saleda descending the stairs, approaching.

'What do you think now?' her team leader asked.

Jenna sighed. *That we have one hell of a problem right now.*

'I think we should go back to Quantico and watch that video until it's so burned in our memories that we can call it up anytime, anywhere in our heads. I think we should use it to start profiling every single individual killer within the group, because I think it's going to be one of two giant steps we'll have to take to profile and nail the actual *group.*'

'I'm assuming you're going to explain why, but say I trust you for the moment. What's the other giant step?'

'Irv needs to find my literature and linguistics contact. Put the profiles of the individuals together and find her and I think we'll know a little more what we're dealing with.'

Assuming we can deal with Grey Hechinger herself first.

Nine

An electronic doorbell sounded as Yancy entered Yorke's Custom Prosthetics and Orthotics.

'Mr Yorke?' Yancy called.

'Right out!'

'Take your time,' Yancy called back then sat down in one of the two black chairs against the wall on his right side and pressed the button at the ankle on his prosthetic. The pin released, and he pulled his personal, built-in baton away from his stump and laid it on the empty chair next to him. The plastic, detailed limbs around the room loomed in his peripheral vision.

To each his own, but Yancy had always preferred the metal, even when he used his fiberglass cover over it so it looked less obvious under pants. He'd originally chosen this type of leg for its functionality since before the accident he'd loved to run, but now it was a pure survival technique. Oboe could try to chew the metal leg all he wanted and not make a dent, but choose hopping to the bathroom instead of re-legging one time during a gaming session with a plastic leg and the sausage would make himself the most expensive dachshund alive. Yancy'd learned not to underestimate the devious bastard, and it would suck *big time* to have to come in to Mr Yorke's shop and explain he'd need a new designer limb because a dog smaller than his stump had wreaked havoc on it in the two minutes he was in the john.

'Hello, hello, Mr Vogul!' Caspar Yorke called from the door at the back room as he bustled into the front. The guy was so short Yancy couldn't see him until he cleared the shelves housing boxes of liners and other prosthetic accouterments near the far end of the shop, but as soon as he appeared, he grinned, the dimples in his cheeks studding his shiny, round face. 'So sorry to keep you waiting,' he said as he passed Yancy, grabbed a chair from behind the counter by the door, and dragged it forward. He sat down in front of Yancy and folded his hands in his lap. 'What can I do for you today?'

Yancy smirked, suppressing a laugh. He'd been tight on time when he'd called a couple days ago, so he hadn't told the man why he was coming in. He'd bet anything Mr Yorke was expecting another 'rare' request. And why wouldn't he? Yancy *had* once had him design a leg with a compartment for a gun, after all.

'Eh, nothing nearly as interesting as what you're imagining, I'm afraid,' Yancy said. 'I think I just need an angle adjustment with these new kicks I got. Balance is a tad off.'

He picked up his leg from the chair beside him and showed Yorke how the socket wasn't hitting quite right, despite the shoes being the same brand of specialty sneakers he usually bought. 'Guess the slightly different style changed more than I thought it would. Can you fix me up?'

Yorke leaned closer, examining. 'I think so. Let me take this in back and make a quick adjustment. Then, we'll put it on and let you walk in it for me, see if we can do anything to fix you up totally today or if you'll have to suffer the horror of using the other custom I made you before you got the idea to request legs inspired by the Container Store.'

Yorke left, and Yancy leaned against the chair back and closed his eyes. Yorke never took long, so getting out a book or checking his social media probably wasn't even worth it.

But Jenna might've texted you back, tough guy. You've got time for that, don't you? You always do . . .

He reached in his pocket, pressed the side button as he sat up, and opened his eyes.

A quick movement from his right startled him. His head snapped toward it.

Holy shitstorm in Richmond.

Claudia Ramey stood in front of him, and she had a gun.

Ten

'What's the matter, Yance? You look surprised to see me.'

'What the fuck are you doing here?' he spat.

So. Loverboy thought this would fool her. *Or maybe he's trying to fool himself.* 'Want me to think you're more angry than afraid?' Claudia laughed. 'That's OK, I suppose. After all, I did catch you with . . . hmm . . . I guess, "your pants down" isn't quite the right phrase, is it?'

Yancy Vogul's jaw moved slightly underneath his skin as he clenched his teeth. God, that reddening in his cheeks was delicious.

Claudia winked at him. 'Don't worry. If I'd wanted to kill you, I already would've.'

'Gee. What a princess. I assume animals of the forest flock from all corners when you sing in the shower, too?'

'Of course. How do you think Bambi's mother died?'

Yancy squinted, then his gaze darted toward the back room, his smooth, fearless façade dissolving in an instant. 'What have you done with Yorke?'

'Aw, relax,' Claudia said, sitting down in the chair facing Yancy. 'I didn't kill him. He's not my type.'

'Then what *did* you do to him?' Yancy said evenly.

'Oh, nothing. Just gave him an itsy little injection that'll make sure he sleeps really well until we're done here then wakes up in time for you two to flip the fuck out together after I'm gone,' she said, making sure to imply that the shop owner would remember the attack. He didn't need to forget, after all. He hadn't seen a thing.

'So you're not here to kill me, not here to kill Yorke . . . why the hell *are* you here, Claudia? I'm guessing we don't happen to be at the same orthotics clinic today because serendipity brought us together?' Yancy jibed.

Claudia licked her lips. Smiled. This guy was about to have no choice but to make the biggest mistake he'd made so far, and he'd do it without his leg *and* his pride.

'You're right. I'm here because I knew you were coming. As adorable as it would be to have my own personal kickstand for when

I got tired, I don't *need* spare parts in order to run,' Claudia said evenly.

Yancy's nostrils flared.

'That said, it *is* time we had a chat, isn't it? Because we *aren't* that different, you and me, are we? Except for that whole I-can-enter-a-three-legged-race-at-a-picnic thing. Well, and the whole I'm a woman and you're a . . . well, you have a penis. I'm assuming it still works since Jenna's still around.'

At this, Yancy's breathing came harder, angrier, and he leaned forward where he sat as though at any moment, he might charge. This was too damned good. Shame Jenna couldn't see this, nor could Claudia trust she'd hear about it.

Yancy sat as still as he could, but all he could think about was jumping up, surprising her. Wrapping his hands around her throat and squeezing until that evil, leering smirk went lax.

'Whoa, down, boy. We wouldn't want you to do something silly and hurt yourself, now would we? We both know I'd still get away, and if you make me shoot you, who will be there to protect your dearest, beloved Jenna when I catch up to her?' Claudia said.

Yancy pressed his lips together, swallowed hard. 'You didn't follow me here to taunt me, Claudia. Even for you that's too much work.'

'See! We *are* similar creatures despite . . . all that stuff. Because even though you're one good accident – or bullet,' she said, aiming the gun at Yancy's kneecap for a split-second before leveling it back at his face, 'away from Jenna carrying you upstairs to bed the rest of your life, really, you're functioning at your peak, what with rescuing slutty damsels in distress and dumping bodies for them and everything.'

Finally, she'd come to it. He'd known she would. He'd been waiting for her to play her card ever since she'd left them the note telling them she'd seen. Knew.

But what the hell *could* she want? To hurt Jenna, all she needed to do was leak it. Incriminate him. Maybe, at worst, somehow come up with a way to implicate Jenna in the crime, too.

And yet she'd tracked him down, gotten him trapped far away from Jenna or any help – or his gun – instead. If she'd ambushed him so she could murder him and torture Jenna by sending his fingers to her one by one, she'd have started it. If her plan to torment Jenna forever had been to kill him then make sure his body was never found, she'd not be sitting here chatting. If there was one thing Yancy was positive of, it was that Claudia was getting whatever little thrills these jabs she was taking could give her while she happened to be there for another reason. She might've been bantering, but it was true that he wasn't her type. Nor was this sort of adventure. Part of the game was blending in, seeing how deep she could entrench a target – usually a man she was dating – before she yanked everything from under him. She couldn't get the same kicks from Yancy.

He knew what she was.

'So did you come all this way to compare notes? Ridicule my killing skills by showing me some pictures you snapped of my leg's hook tracks in the mud somewhere or something?'

'Actually, I came because of some other tracks you left,' Claudia said, her smile disappearing. 'I need a little favor from you, Mr Vogul.'

'Right. And I need to not be ambushed by a psychopath who's so hung up on her own past she can't use her newly found free time outside incarceration for something better than skulking around the loved ones of the one person who could put her back in again,' Yancy said.

Claudia snickered. 'Oh, but that's where you're wrong, Mr Vogul. I do have much better things to do. And it just so happens that you're the type of person I need to do it. And what I saw you do puts you in a position to ensure you will. As long as you're still good enough with computers to, say, hack into the mainframe of a hate group database and post the anonymous group members' real names and addresses from their own website because they pissed you off.'

The house's front door swung open to reveal the silent, shadowed contents of an empty home, and Beo released the breath he'd been holding.

Don't look around. Don't act suspicious.

He walked in and closed the door, hopefully by all appearances as though he had every right to be there. The sun had lowered on the horizon, and the inhabitants of the quiet suburb were all retreating inside for frozen lasagnas or to catch the evening news.

The inside of the house was a bit dim, but he didn't need a light. The foyer was still familiar, despite that it had been years since his last visit.

At one time in his life, this had felt like his second home. A place of safety and warmth. Friendship.

Trust.

Yep, Athos's parent had said never hesitate. Any time, any day; an open invitation that, during the darkest days of his life, gave him a place in the world.

Yep, once upon a time, he'd been welcome here.

He wasn't anymore. Probably for good reason, all things considered. He was the type of person who would do what he was doing now, after all. Friends or not, if Athos wasn't all in, better their friendship had ended the way it had. Better Athos walk away as a punk without a backbone, unable to muster the courage to make a difference in the world.

Better Athos turn his back on Sabine and break my sister's heart while I was a state away, lest whatever backbone he did have be tested across my knee.

As Beo's mind drifted to the cold wood of the park bench where he'd sat only hours ago, flipping one of the well-worn, tanning pages of his tattered old copy of Heller's *Catch-22*, when Atticus had plopped down on the bus stop bench next to him.

Beo had continued his reading, careful not to so much as chance a sideways glance at Atticus, as the red-hooded man had slipped a tiny thumb drive in the crook of Beo's thumb and pointer finger where it held the book.

'I don't like it much, either, dude,' Atticus had said, never looking at Beo. 'But I figure it's the best . . . maybe only . . . insurance we have.'

Beo had grunted some sort of half-assed agreement, shifting to slide the thumb drive into his pocket. He closed his book, stood up.

'Ishmael said you'd be able to get in. The authorities likely won't scratch the first layer of precautions we've taken, but if they ever do, this will waste enough of their time for us to go underground. Ishmael isn't the type to leave anything to chance.'

No. He most certainly is not.

Now, Beo pulled the thumb drive back out of his pocket as he slipped through an open set of French doors into the study. It was filled with expensive furniture, including glass-fronted bookcases that contained an outstanding collection, the contents of which were probably worth more than the average Mercedes Benz. Beo fixed his attention on the antique mahogany desk in the center of the room, however, and the computer on top of it.

He tapped a key on the keyboard to bring the PC out of sleep mode. After a few seconds, the monitor came to life, the room's only light source casting a pale glow across Beo's pale skin. Drawing in a fortifying breath, he bent to insert the USB drive.

Unpleasant business, framing one of the precious few people who didn't contribute to societies many problems. But federal agents would discover the source of the message to the reporter eventually, and when they did, Black Shadow would need a scapegoat.

And sorry, Athos. But, buddy, you're just not one of us anymore.

He smiled and clicked open the file browser, opening the word document to be copied to email. He had a few other stops to make online before this was over, but none of it would take long. After that, Athos would just need to show up when he was called. And of course he would show up. They were all still friends, after all.

Always better to have an anvil in place, ready for when the hammer of justice fell.

The look on Yancy's face wrapped Claudia in the warm, pleasant blanket of power. This was turning out to be even more fun than she thought.

'How the hell did you know about tha—'

'I think it'd probably work out best for you if you just assumed from here on out that I know *everything*,' Claudia said to cut him off. He had to be racking that poor little brain of his for how she could know all about his little escapades as the Robin Hood of the hackers, a part of his life long before he even knew Jenna. 'So do you?'

'Do I what?' he said stupidly.

'Do your thoughts leak out your stump when the tin piece is off? Does it double as a drain plug or something? Do you still have the skill set to which I just referred?' she asked, rolling her eyes.

Yancy licked his bottom lip, clearly trying to compose himself. He sucked in a few deep breaths. Blew them out.

'If you mean do I know how to hack, yes. It depends on what you're specifically wondering. Whether I *do* hack, or whether I know *how* to hack,' he said slowly.

'Well, you better hope you do. Because I'm willing to offer you a bargain,' Claudia replied, salivating at the prospect of the reaction that would surely come.

'And what bargain would that be, Lucifer?'

Claudia cackled. It was just too good. Too good because he was so right.

'I need you to hack into a database for me and retrieve a file on someone,' she said slowly. Carefully.

Yancy's eyes narrowed. 'Who?'

She smirked. 'No one related to you.'

It wasn't a lie. Not directly, anyway.

'And you're saying if I get this file for you, what?'

'I won't breathe a word to anyone about your little excursion on the night of Denny Hoffsteader's death.'

'You didn't say you wouldn't write a word,' Yancy countered.

Touché, Mr Vogul.

'Let's make this more plain then. I won't set you up to take the fall in any way for what you did, try to implicate Jenna in your little crime, or in any way use your . . . *indiscretion* . . . to harm you or anyone you love,' Claudia said, again weighing her words quickly, decisively.

Yancy closed his eyes, the misery at knowing he didn't have much choice visible in the slump of his shoulders, the resignation on his face.

'Why should I believe you?' he whispered.

'Because what else are you going to do? If you tell me no, I'll have you put away, and maybe Jenna, too. Maybe I'll kill Vern, then Ayana and Charley in front of Jenna, then Jenna on video so I can bring some footage to you in prison . . .'

Claudia could practically smell the anger and fear wafting off Yancy as he visibly struggled to compose himself, knowing he literally didn't have a leg to stand on.

'And why do you want this file?'

'Oh, never you mind,' Claudia said, her stomach flip-flopping excitedly. 'It shouldn't worry you, since like I said, it isn't related to you or your sweet, little profiler. Believe it or not, I *do* have other things to do besides lying in wait for you and my former family. Like you said, Jenna would love to have me put away, and though I'd love to sit down and have a lovely mother-daughter chat with her one of these days, I have quite a few other things on my agenda to attend to that are higher priority.' *Like Patrick Obermaier.* 'I know this is hard to believe, but I *have* made quite a few enemies over the years . . .'

'You don't say?' Yancy spat.

Claudia shrugged, still aiming the gun at Yancy's forehead. 'What can you do? You con a few people, maybe kill a couple of their family members, and they just get so pissy.'

Yancy stared at her blankly for a moment, as if he was fighting a retort. After a long pause, he finally said, 'And if I do this, you won't use what you know?'

'I'll be like a priest who took your confession,' Claudia said.

Yancy frowned. 'Right. And you won't hurt Jenna or her family?'

'I'll stay far away from your precious psychiatrist and the rest of *my* family,' Claudia sneered.

It wasn't a lie. For now.

Yancy closed his eyes, bowed his head for a long moment. He looked back up, met her gaze. 'Fine,' he said. 'I'll do it. What are the details?'

Eleven

Saleda fast-forwarded the video again at the point where the tall, skinny figure had the blonde girl, who they had now identified as twenty-six-year-old Alice Coltraine, skewered in the back with what looked like some kind of long, wavy dagger. Jenna braced for what was coming. Machete UNSUB, the man they were assuming was the group's leader, jumped into the fray once again, cleanly lopping off Alice Coltraine's head as though it was nothing more than brush in his path in the jungle. Two seconds later, Saleda paused the video.

'Look. There on the side,' she said, pointing to one of the black-clad figures who appeared to be bent over, hands on his or her knees. 'See the way their neck arches, the heavy breathing pattern in their body?'

'Dry-heaving?' Porter said.

'That must be Scout,' Saleda said.

Jenna nodded. Made sense. 'If she was threatening to throw up, it'd definitely be worth someone warning her to chill out, that it'd leave DNA at the scene.'

'What makes you think she's a woman?' Saleda asked.

Before Jenna could answer, Porter leaned forward, his elbows on the conference table. 'Not incredibly tall by any stretch of the imagination. Tiny. Body type looks female to me.'

'But back it up,' Teva said and Saleda obliged.

'See? The Machete UNSUB says something to Skewer UNSUB. If someone told Scout to keep it together right after Alice Coltraine was killed, wouldn't Ashlee have heard whatever Machete UNSUB said before that? If it's a coincidence and Ashlee was on the way to the vault before the moment in the tape that shows the UNSUB dry-heaving, guessing this is Scout might make us get everything else wrong, too.'

Jenna nodded. 'Ashlee Haynie is under duress right now anyway, so we're lucky she remembered what she did. She might remember more later, or it's possible she didn't hear the comment the Machete

UNSUB made to Skewer UNSUB at all. It might've been a whisper, or at least more quiet. Looked like a reproach.'

'I'd say the leader's scolding Tall-n-Skinny Skewer Man for having playtime when he should've been taking care of business. Bet Creepy Skewer guy was glad the leader used his machete on the girl as his punishment and not on him,' Dodd agreed. 'That said, doesn't look like the alleged leader turned toward the alleged Scout to tell her not to pitch her guts on the floor, so he either hadn't noticed or was unconcerned.'

'Let's leave that for the moment, though. What else can we tell about Scout?' Saleda said.

Jenna played back the tape in her mind, trying to focus her brain on that figure. It was useless without playing it again though. Too easy to keep eyes only on the big action. Stuff like Alice Coltraine's decapitation, sadly.

'Play it again,' she asked.

Saleda rewound the gruesome gray scale film, hit play.

'I keep losing who I think is Scout,' Porter said a few seconds in.

'Me, too. So much chaos,' Teva agreed.

Dodd reached for the remote from where Saleda had lay it on the table. 'Let's play it backwards, then.'

Jenna watched as Dodd fast-forwarded to the familiar spot where the UNSUB believed to be Scout stood, hands to knees, dry-heaving off to the side of the main action. Then, he hit the rewind button, but only after pressing pause first.

The film frames backed up much more slowly, the killings even more eerie in reverse. Body parts returned to people, blood sucked back toward wounds.

The video backtracked to show Scout killing the dark-haired teenage boy who lay spread-eagle near the mortgage loan signs. The interesting part wasn't only that she'd traced deep cuts up the fleshy undersides of his forearms with her switchblade. It was that she didn't pull her knife until he was already incapacitated.

'She runs directly at the teen as she enters, but she wrestles him into the sleeper hold, takes him down gently,' Dodd said.

Blue flashed in. First a rich, sea blue – not unlike the color of the water near her hotel the time she'd vacationed at Santa Catalina Island. Then, the shade faded to a softer, more pastel hue. The color of blue bells.

Compassion. Mercy. They were both here.

'Then, she went and dry-heaved after she killed him,' Jenna muttered under her breath.

'She felt for him. She went straight for the smallest, least imposing person. Could be for lots of reasons, but based on how she handles him, I think she didn't want someone his age to die such a gruesome death,' Saleda said.

'That's what I'm thinking,' Jenna said. 'Which suggests something else about her age.'

Porter shrugged. 'She's a mother? A kid dying in that way is hard for her to imagine?'

Jenna shook her head, but Dodd was the one who spoke up.

'Maybe, but probably not. She slit his arms, used a wrist-slitting method actually effective in suicide attempts,' Dodd said.

'So maybe she's been suicidal before,' Porter said.

'Likely,' Jenna replied, taking the remote from Dodd. 'Or something like it, anyway . . .'

'It could've been less that she felt maternal and didn't want to see a kid die so much as that she identified with him,' Porter said.

'Now, we're getting there,' Jenna said, winking.

'She also used a switchblade. So maybe she's got a street background?' Porter said.

'Can't see it close enough to tell, but I'd say so. There's a chance it could be a collector's piece or the sort of blade used to cut twine on a farm, but somehow I seriously doubt it,' Dodd said.

'Street fits. Cutters are often trauma victims. I know that's speculating, but let's face it. This whole profile is a lot of guesswork based on not a whole lot of grainy video, so why not?' Porter said.

'Wonder what the significance of the name Scout is? I get the *To Kill a Mockingbird* reference, but is it just a random book character, or is there more to it?' Saleda said.

'I think we'll need to wait for Irv to find my contact before we speculate too much on that,' Jenna muttered. God, she was hoping Irv could find Grey as much as she was dreading it.

Teva pointed to the monitor again, squinting. 'So, the taller figure that goes for the kid's mother. Definitely feminine. Maybe those two know each other, since they sort of attacked together? I mean, I realize *all* the attackers know each other. But as many of them as there are, I figure it's more likely they were closer to like-minded acquaintances when they somehow met, eventually formed the group, rather than them all being blood relatives playing bank killers as a family reunion game. But maybe some of them *within* the group are closer, had a relationship outside of just the whole, you know, *terrorist thing.*'

'Doubt it,' Dodd said. 'Scout finishes her kill, then leaves the fellow attacker – damn it. We're gonna have so many UNSUB code names before this case is over I might have to keep them written on my hand to keep track, but even I have to admit calling them just attacker or UNSUB makes it hard to distinguish any of them. But yeah, Scout does her own business, then leaves the slender UNSUB alone to do her thing while she freaks out off by herself.'

'True,' Jenna confirmed. 'And Slender UNSUB gets in trouble in the video after she kills the boy's mom, too, right?'

'Oh, yeah!' Saleda said. 'I noticed that. Two of the other attackers reacted to it . . . or at least, in movement, it *seems* they're reacting. Play it again.'

All eyes turned to the video to watch as, on the screen, Slender UNSUB rushed toward the lanky victim they now knew to be forty-three-year-old Rebekah Webb, holding some sort of small blade high, Slender UNSUB's arm even with her own forehead.

Jenna grimaced as Slender UNSUB's blade gouged directly into Rebekah Webb's right eye. The orange/pink tone of cooked shrimp flashed in. Slender UNSUB's movements weren't sloppy, which was why the shrimp color had come in instead of cornflower blue. They were determined, just not very graceful. She had a cumbersomeness about her. Even as Slender UNSUB whirled around the victim and produced a second knife, which she plunged downward into the victim's neck, she still displayed an awkwardness in her movement not hidden by the swift and decisive violent blows.

The woman collapsed as the stab to the back of her neck hit the spinal cord. Slender UNSUB smoothly removed the blade, then took a swift shot to the side of the woman's neck close to where the carotid artery would be.

'That's a lot of stabbing for one jab to the carotid,' Porter said, shaking his head.

'But she didn't die from a severed carotid,' Saleda said, flipping pages inside one of the folders. She traced a page with her finger, then, she tapped her pointer finger hard on a specific spot on the paper. 'That last stick missed the carotid. We won't know until the M.E. performs the full autopsy, but based on what he observed at the scene, he suspects she actually died from the initial injury to her eye. Thinks it hit her brain, caused a bleed. He thinks she went into shock and passed out, so they thought she was dead. When he opens her up, he suspects we'll find out the actual cause of death will be the heart stopping from lack of oxygen post-brain death.'

'Weird,' Porter muttered.

'Maybe not,' Jenna said, thinking of the shrimp color and Slender UNSUB's lack of grace. 'She went for Rebekah Webb with the first weapon already held high as she charged her. If you look back at that, it seems likely she meant to stab her in the eye the whole time.'

'Yeah, what *was* that, by the way? The first blade she used for the eye stab?' Dodd cut in. 'A kitchen knife or something?'

'Video's too grainy to tell, but size-wise, maybe.'

'There's something really amateurish and maybe even klutzy about the way she moves. I think the eye stabbing thing looks like a strategy she developed going in for whatever reason. Even I have no idea why *that* was the strategy she went for, but just the way she runs at Rebekah Webb with her arm already at face height . . .' Jenna said, her voice trailing.

'Is it coincidence the victim she rushed was close to her own height? Her own size, even. If it was a pre-determined strategy, it makes sense for her to go for the victim she thinks she can take,' Teva said.

'That implies she wouldn't have been able to take just anyone,' Jenna said. 'What makes you say it that way?'

'Well, look at the second tactic she takes. Once Rebekah Webb is incapacitated from the stab, she rounds her and takes a second knife out but uses that reverse ice pick style grip everyone in every slasher flick known to man does. It's visually appealing for horror movies, but no experienced fighter on earth is going to use it because all the victim has to do is reach up and grab her forearm or wrist to stop the downward stabbing motion. 'Only reason you choose that grip on a big knife like the one she pulls out is because you need that downward stabbing action to give enough upper body strength to deliver fatal blows.'

'And let's not forget she did *miss* the carotid artery,' Porter said.

'Of the two killers we've profiled so far, the terrorists seem to have brought with them to the massacre a barely adult street kid and another woman clearly not part of this because of her fierce skills . . . I'm thinking whatever cause has these people so committed they're willing to stab innocent bank customers to death isn't the only thing that hooked them in this far. Two people we've been able to see clear vulnerabilities in, despite the fact that they killed in cold blood. Vulnerabilities that suggest personality types. Scout's choice to slit that boy's wrists and the possibility that she's a past cutter herself mean she's likely lonely. Slender UNSUB's choice to attack first with a surprise jab at full height suggests she feels physically insecure that she could land the next blow. They're both clearly loyal to their cause, have trusted *someone* that this is their mission. What does that sound like to you?'

'The Manson Family,' Porter said with a laugh.

Saleda clicked her tongue. 'You joke, but seriously, terrorist groups can be cult-like, too.'

'And their leaders can be sociopaths, pulling their puppet strings,' Dodd said.

Twelve

'So, Scout and Slender UNSUB don't show any signs of having any emotional attachment to each other that would suggest any sort of relationship outside of the group. Scout leaves her to fly solo even here when Slender gets in trouble,' Jenna muttered, cocking her head as she stared at the monitor screen. The black and white footage could only show so much, but she still wanted Irv to enhance the video as much as possible. Any little details they could glean might prove critical.

'And yet, when that banker built like a linebacker takes Slender UNSUB by surprise, two of the other attackers *do* notice and react,' Saleda said, her eyes also set on the video. She pressed the play button and pointed to the teller counter to draw the team's focus away from the skirmish between Slender and her challenger happening near the second desk on the left side and toward decisive movement on the opposite side of the room. 'Cutthroat UNSUB reacts, starts to move in toward Slender UNSUB to assist.'

Jenna squinted at the black figure leaping off the teller counter. Short. Boxy-figure. A pinkish-purple color flashed in, and she tried to hold on to it and identify it.

'Cutthroat's right on point. Definitely one of the most violent ones. I notice it every time,' Teva said.

'How could you not? Blood sprays from her victims show up even on this damned black and white video,' Porter said.

The color trying to push through slipped away. *Damn it.*

'Worth noting that Cutthroat UNSUB is one of several double-wielders in the group. Showy,' Dodd said.

And yet . . .

'Wielding two blades *is* flashy, but not everyone in this group is doing it for the flamboyance,' Jenna said.

'I'd hope not. It's not very practical unless you happen to be super trained and a more than average degree of ambidextrous,' Dodd said from where he leaned against the conference table before taking a sip of his coffee.

'Slender UNSUB had that weird little kitchen knife and used a high, charge to the face strategy before the downward stab with the second knife, which we assume is to lend her arm strength. For her it was functional,' Jenna said, grabbing the remote from Saleda and hitting pause. '*This* UNSUB, though, Cutthroat, uses two weapons for a different reason, I think. Her kills are gory, display an unnecessary level of violence even compared to the other killers.'

'Her?' Porter said. 'You sure?'

Jenna studied the black figure again, nodded. 'The shirt is bulky, but I think I can make out breasts in there somewhere.'

'And hips,' Saleda said.

'If you say so,' Porter said, shrugging.

'Either way, Cutthroat starts back to help Slender, but then *this* UNSUB comes in . . .' Saleda pressed play again, gesturing to the place on the screen where attackers continued to spill through the bank doorway.

'Rewind that one more time,' Jenna said, focusing on the entrance. *Concentrate.*

Saleda obliged and rewound to the moment just before the hulky banker rushed Slender UNSUB.

Jenna watched with intent as the UNSUB who would rescue Slender entered the door. Maybe she'd imagined it.

But, no, the second this newest UNSUB appeared on camera, head turned, the direction his body was angled . . . he was already looking to Slender UNSUB, anticipating her needing him. The light bluish gray of protectiveness flashed in.

'They could both have personal relationships with Slender, but Cutthroat happened to be facing the direction of Slender's scuffle with the banker. She reacted, but that *could* just be because she's committed to getting the job done and getting the attackers out,' Jenna said, pushing from her mind the thought of how her last statement implied that, on some level, the killers *were* all looking out for each other, trying to get everyone out cleanly. That could be because leaving any behind would leave a trail for police to find them. She could visit that idea later. 'But the UNSUB who comes to Slender UNSUB's rescue from the doorway is already intent on saving her. See how he comes in already focused on where she is in the fray?'

Jenna hit the rewind and let the video loop through the moment once more.

'He definitely already had eyes on her the second you see him on camera,' Porter said.

'And *that* stab,' Saleda said, pausing the footage just after the UNSUB from the door reached Slender, shoved the banker attacking her on to a middle desk on the right side of the bank, and jabbed a large knife into the man's chest right at his rib cage. 'If I didn't know better I'd say it was the most bizarre attack.'

Chili pepper red flashed in. Organization. The weapon choice was peculiar, but it had obviously been planned because of its efficiency. Jenna had never seen a knife like it or the havoc it wreaked on its victim. If more killers knew about it, scary didn't begin to describe the scenarios the BAU might have to deal with.

'Do we know what that *was* yet?' Porter asked, looking to Saleda.

'It was a WASP knife,' Dodd said before Saleda could answer. 'I noticed him reloading it after he stabbed the banker. Heard about them a while back from a buddy of mine who's a diver. The thing was originally designed for sharks. Can be used like any other diving knife for the typical routine stuff on a dive, but it also has a hole in the tip to deliver the goodies. Insert knife, press button on the top, release enough compressed CO_2 into a shark – or human – to freeze all its internal organs immediately . . . and, obviously in this case, enough air to cause the body to practically blow like a tire if you forgot to remove the air compressor.'

'Shit,' Porter mumbled.

'So the WASP UNSUB could be a diver?' Teva ventured.

'Or a hunter. Used on land predators like bears, too,' Dodd said with a shrug.

Jenna leaned in to look at the paused image on the screen. Specifically, the way WASP UNSUB stood, how exact his jab was. She imaged the few seconds of video in her head as she'd seen it several times before this. WASP UNSUB had moved so swiftly. Sharp. The banker had landed on the table because when WASP UNSUB went for him, he'd applied a constant, balance-throwing forward pressure.

Denim blue flashed in. *Military.*

'Is it ever used as a tactical knife?' Jenna asked.

'Looks like it,' Dodd said, now looking at his smart phone. 'Not shocking. Perfect tool for special ops, I bet.'

Jenna nodded, whipping out her own phone and dialing Irv.

'To what search that Google alone cannot handle do I owe the pleasure, Dr Ramey?' Irv answered.

'We need to start compiling a list of military or former-military who purchased a WASP knife in the past years. Possibly crosscheck that with bank clientele and workers, though I kind of doubt you're going to come up with anything there,' she said. Mainly, the military list of WASP knife buyers would come in handy once they had other leads, but this way, they'd have it ready to check when needed.

In the background, Porter's laugh sounded over the others. 'Now we just need to know what literary role an ex-military man with a crazy-deadly diver's knife would play. I don't think Boo Radley was known for shark-killing.'

'One very vague, not-usable-at-the-moment-but-maybe-usable-in-the-maybe-near-or-maybe-far-future list coming up. What else can I do for you, my liege?'

Jenna glanced at the other team members, noting the macaroni and cheese orange-yellow of prudence that flashed in. They hadn't put together a hard and fast profile of the whole group yet, but she felt confident that it wouldn't hurt anything for Irv to be on the lookout for a few things she was sure were going to come into play.

'Maybe one more minor task, oh, hack-savvy-one,' Jenna said. She really should run this by Saleda before she did it, but that would mean risking the chance of her saying no. It wouldn't be good to get caught up in looking for things that weren't pertinent, but the literature details *were* pertinent. They had to be. 'Do some looking around for any subversive groups with some kind of tie to classic literature. The group we're looking for will be well-educated and intellectuals. Because of the type of literary references it's likely they're either college students or people who have some college education. They're a hodgepodge of personality types, so they won't all be the same sex, race, or socio-economic background, another factor that lends to the college theme since it's possibly an ideal place where a group of all walks of life might meet. They may call each other by character names or use character names for Internet handles. The group or its members will also be active on blogs and websites of newspapers and other media, probably often commenting on controversial news items or writing letters to the editor. So far, the literature references we have to go on are *The Importance of Being Earnest* by Oscar Wilde, *To Kill a*

Mockingbird by Harper Lee – the character Scout in particular – and the character of Cardinal Richelieu, who is from . . .'

Shit. Where the hell was Grey Hechinger when you needed her?

'A bunch of shit,' Irv said. 'Got it. I'm on it, though no promises. That's a really vague request until there's more to go on.'

'Thanks, Irv. By the way, any more news on—'

'No word from the Wordplay Wonder yet, if that's what you were about to ask. I'm working on it, but right now it seems like she's trying as hard to stay out of touch with you as you were with her before now,' Irv replied.

Damn it, Grey. Off your meds again, are you?

Then again, if Grey *was* going to be of use to them, she'd probably *need* to be off her meds.

'OK. Keep me posted,' Jenna said, then hung up.

She looked to Saleda, ready to take whatever lashing her leader had in store for her after giving a profile they hadn't agreed to yet. She wouldn't blame Saleda. It was blatantly seditious behavior if she'd made the call behind closed doors, but in front of the whole team *with* their leader present went beyond rebellious.

Saleda stared back at her, eyes reproachful and cold.

Then, a very long second later, Saleda rolled her eyes, smirked. 'OK, moving on. What else on this video do we have that's of use in individual profiles? If Jenna's going to get a jump on the rest of us here, we'll have this end covered so we get a participation trophy when the thing is solved.'

Thirteen

Jenna blinked, unable to believe Saleda was willing to let it go so easily. What the heck kind of leader would be OK with looking the way she'd just made Saleda look? *Quick. Engage the team with something else.*

'Slender and WASP aren't the only pair visibly working together,' Porter said before Jenna's brain had a chance to think of something to shift the topic to. 'Rewind it to right near when WASP guy enters and keep it playing.'

Saleda obliged. This time, when WASP UNSUB entered, though, Porter pointed to the door. 'Keep watching here. The kill is hard to see on the footage.'

Another black figure entered the bank, headed directly toward one of the bank managers' desks on the left side. Specifically, the farthest one from the door, passing a few other attackers actively in fights with their victims, but unconcerned by potential victims save the one who would become his target.

When the figure reached the third desk, he produced a weapon swiftly from his clothing, then stepped to the side, where his next movements were blocked by another fight going on almost directly in front of the desk as Slender UNSUB and WASP UNSUB took on another victim.

'This is one of the two victims who had blunt force trauma premortem. Those blunt force wounds didn't kill him, though. One clean, deliberate severing of his carotid did, and it was the only stab wound on his body,' Porter explained. He traced his finger in the air away from where whatever Blunt Force UNSUB was doing was now blocked by the action of WASP UNSUB and the banker at the desk in front of him and back toward the bank entrance. 'But watch – the next one in the door *also* heads straight for the third desk.'

Saleda nodded, keeping her eyes on the screen as Blunt Force UNSUB walked away, and the figure who had followed Blunt Force to where Blunt Force's victim had collapsed after a severe beating stepped in, bent down behind the third desk.

'So . . . the other victim who had pre-mortem blunt force wounds. What was his cause of death?' Teva asked.

'What can I say?' Porter said. 'There must've been a two-for-one coupon for the relentless beating, severed carotid special.'

Puce flashed in. Synchronicity.

'Well, fast-forward it to the other victim that matched that MO. Maybe from another angle, we can make out what Blunt Force's blunt object is,' Dodd said.

'And what the hell his creepy Wing Man did to the victim behind that desk after Blunt Force got bored with him,' Teva said.

Saleda pressed play, and the footage started right where they'd left off. While Wing Man UNSUB was apparently finishing off the guy behind the desk, Blunt Force UNSUB rushed in the opposite direction and, in seconds, attacked a graying man in camouflage pants and a rebel flag T-shirt. This time, even though Blunt Force UNSUB's back was to the camera as he savagely beat the man until he crumpled to the ground in front of the teller counter, unable to move, it was easy to tell Blunt Force UNSUB's weapon wasn't anything you'd expect.

'Is that a whip?' Teva asked, leaning closer to the screen as if that inch would make the granulated video suddenly crystal clear.

'No lashes on the victim,' Jenna muttered, both in answer to Teva as well as to herself. *What is he using?*

'It's . . . it looks like a cane or something. Size-wise. But not the way it bends,' Teva said.

Jenna flinched. 'It's a riding crop, I think.'

Dodd looked skeptical. 'Riding crop? Causing blunt trauma? Doubt it.'

'You're telling me in a room full of investigators not one of you is a Sherlock Holmes fan?'

Every head turned toward the door – toward the new voice – but Jenna already knew who it was. She wasn't sure *how* she'd gotten inside Quantico and made it to the door to ridicule them, nor how she was now here when Irv had already said he hadn't found her. And yet, the creamy vanilla color Jenna associated with her flashed in at the first hint of her voice, and she was sure of the face she'd see when she turned toward the doorway.

Sure enough, Grey Hechinger stood framed there, her pasty-pale white skin practically glowing in the fluorescent lights, the cascade of frizzy curls so blonde they were colorless pulled in a messy ponytail at the base of her neck.

But Grey didn't give Jenna the opportunity to introduce her, because as always, normal rules of social interaction didn't occur to Grey. They wouldn't. Ever. What would occur to her would be whatever she found most interesting. It was one of many reasons she had such trouble in social settings and appearing normal in any way.

The other reason being she was schizotypal.

Grey laughed, her head lolling back with a cheery, amused expression crossing her face. 'You already know they're calling themselves by book character names, and that this guy works with a partner. Surely you must have realized when you saw the riding crop that the guy holding it has to be Sherlock Holmes, and his surgically precise companion, very obviously, would be Mr Watson.'

Fourteen

'Everyone, meet Grey Hechinger,' Jenna said, 'my literature and linguistics contact.'

Saleda turned to Jenna, her face incredulous. Jenna simply smiled. It wasn't like she was freaking excited about this, either. But what the heck was she supposed to do? Grey was already presenting herself as the right person for this job, despite the many things that should immediately disqualify her.

Irv stepped in behind Grey. 'Sorry. She showed up at the gate asking for me, and . . . well, we were kind of—'

'Hunting me like a feral animal that wouldn't be smart enough to find its hunter first?' Grey cut in, looking at no one in particular as she glanced absentmindedly around the room like she was on a tour. Her voice was soft and amused. Almost sing-songy.

Irv's chin dipped, and his shoulders curled forward. He caught Jenna's eye. Shrugged.

Jenna waved off the nervous questions written on Irv's face. They didn't have to worry about Grey getting mad. She didn't seem it, and anger wasn't one of her go-to emotions, anyway. She was just awkward and, as usual, oblivious to rules of common courtesy. Jenna watched the woman wander around the conference room she hadn't been invited into, taking long, anything-but-furtive peeks at notes, pictures, and other case materials lying out on the table. It would never have occurred to Grey that the hunted becoming the hunter statement might've drawn a response ranging from pissed as hell at best and menacing and dangerous at worst.

'So, that online banking thing is looking better than ever,' Grey said, staring down at one of the crime scene photos that, technically, she shouldn't even be in the room with. Sure, Jenna wanted to consult her, but she'd always planned to carefully control everything in reference to the case that Grey saw, handled, heard . . .

Metallic copper flashed in, the same shade that had popped in when she and Charley had taken A to the zoo the week Dad had the flu. They'd watched in awe from behind the metal bars as the two cheetahs playfully tackled each other, rolling on the grass. She'd explained to Ayana that day, as the copper flashed in, how the cheetahs were friends, but it was only safe for humans to watch them from a distance. If the cheetahs tackled a person, it would probably be more forceful and not as friendly. *Hard to control.*

'Look, chiquita,' Porter said, taking a step toward Grey and snatching the folder Grey had been looking at off the table, 'you may have been invited here, but that doesn't mean you can tour the place like—'

'Wait a second. *Was* she invited here?' Teva cut in.

Grey turned her head toward Teva, her expression flat. 'Well, no, but . . .'

'I *had* called her several times,' Irv said. 'She *did* know we were looking for her.'

Jenna shook her head and stepped toward Irv, bit her bottom lip to stifle a humorless laugh. She closed her lips but kept wearing the sarcastic smile. 'She knew *someone* was looking for her. She didn't know who, or from where . . .' Jenna turned slowly to face Grey. 'She most definitely wasn't invited to Quantico . . .'

God help me, I thought I was done with this sort of interrogation. Ayana's three, but at least she gives straight answers.

Grey's face remained unchanged, as Jenna knew it would. The woman blinked three times, stared. 'Well, I listened to the talk message on my squawk box from a private investigator . . . PI he said. Said he got my name from someone at the college. Said he had a stalking case he was working on. Client hired him because she has a guess who the Snoopy watching her is, but the police guys don't have enough evidence to put handcuffs on him. But the PI guy got hold of a letter the stalker left for the object of his desire and wants it compared to the writing on some postcards the guessed-Snoopy wrote his sister. Said the guy at the college thought I could help determine if the stalker letter and the guessed-Snoopy's postcards were written by the same hand,' Grey said. Then she shook her head, laughed. 'Man, if *my* sister handed across some postcards to someone trying to prove me a Snoopy, I'd be pissed.' She paused, cocked her head. 'But then again, I guess if my brother was a Snoopy, I'd want him locked away for it, too. Huh.'

Jenna's face seared as she saw the disapproving, uncertain looks being exchanged in the room around her. It wasn't that Grey's peculiar speech patterns and way of structuring her sentences embarrassed her. Her fellow teammates were smart enough to discern that the weird little idiosyncrasies peppering her words and even the bizarre getup Gray wore had to be manifestations of a personality disorder.

The rusty, brown-tinged color of primer red flashed in. She'd associated it with embarrassment at least since high school, a connection that might or might not have something to do with how mortified she'd been when her Dad had dropped her off at the school dance and all the kids who'd seen her exit the '55 Chevy had told her she must be confused, that the farm equipment had to be parked out past the softball field.

Nope, she felt like a fool because of what the team had to think of *her* for seeking out the woman in the room with them. For claiming that the awkward, rambling person using a shiny black coffee mug on their conference table to check that none of her breakfast was stuck in her teeth was the most qualified expert on the planet to assist them as they worked to crack the worst case of domestic terrorism since 9/11.

Finally, Porter broke the hush in the otherwise silent room. 'So, a private investigator called you for a linguistics consult. What does that have to do with us?'

Seeming like she hadn't even heard the question, Grey continued her own train of thought right where she'd left off. 'Only, my brother wasn't. A Snoopy. Wasn't a PI, either. Neither was this guy on my squawk box,' she said, looking down at where she was moving two coffee cups around the table like they were racecars.

'How do you know that, Grey?' Jenna pressed.

Go on, Grey, give them a little taste of why they shouldn't write you off just yet.

Grey looked up at Jenna, her face flat. 'Because in the message he left on my squawk box, he asked if I would compare the writing on the postcards to the letters from the UNSUB,' she said evenly. She looked down, resumed urging her cup-cars forward on the table as though racing them. 'PIs don't say UNSUB.'

Jenna caught the impressed glance Saleda shot her way, but Grey kept talking.

'No clue what an UNSUB is, honestly. Google told me that. Term federal agents use to refer to an Unidentified Subject, it said. Didn't worry about it much, though. Maybe the PI guy retired from the FBI so he could PI. I decided I'd reply to him on the squawk box in a few days.'

'What changed the plan?' Dodd asked.

'The fact that my old roommate Keely called me to tell me someone had talked on *her* squawk box about needing to find me to return some book he borrowed. She played me the message on her squawk box, and it sure sounded like Mr PI Guy.'

Saleda glared at Irv. 'Why would you not use the same story with the roommate?'

Irv's eyes got wider. 'I don't know. I guess in the time I spend doing my job cross-referencing and data hacking for you guys that it's been years since I was a member of the A-Team?'

Grey paid them no attention. 'Well, I didn't have to be the brightest light in the candelabra to calculate that a federal agent was looking for me. I could also compute that, for some reason, he didn't want to clarify himself. All I could decide was if it was so secret, I might better find out who he was and what he found necessary of me before he came to me so that if it was bad, I could figure out what to do.'

Bothering to point out that Grey could've simply returned Irv's call would've been pointless to someone with a tendency toward paranoia, so instead, Jenna asked the only real question that mattered now. 'But how did you know to come *here?* There are FBI field offices all over the place. *Surely* he didn't call from his office phone,' she said, slowly turning to stare down Irv.

'Easy,' Grey said. 'Message he left on my squawker mentioned he couldn't pay much for the letter looking since the client was a pro bono, but if I'd do the favor, he'd treat me to lunch. Went on to postulate he knew the best barbecue place on earth,' Grey said, having abandoned the cup-cars in favor of folding a napkin as though it was origami.

Saleda rubbed her temples. 'Which brought you here *because?*'

Grey blinked again. 'Monty's. He knew Monty's. In Quantico. The only people who know about Monty's are local.'

'So you knew to come to Quantico. But how did you know to ask the guys at the gate for Irv by name?' Teva asked.

'I didn't,' Grey said, reaching into her pocket and holding up her phone. 'My squawk box handed his voice to them.'

'Right,' Irv said, shifting his weight on to the foot closest to the door. 'Well, I'll just leave you all to it and get . . . um . . . back to . . . um . . .'

'Yes, Irv, go. I can figure out how to deal with my expert FBI data analyst not knowing to buy a burner phone or come up with a convincing backstory later,' Saleda said.

Irv shrugged, palms up. 'What can I say? If anybody needs me, I'll be in my computer cave, searching for government dissenters, ideological zealots, and all that general hate sort of stuff . . . and listening to some self-help tapes on reclaiming my underappreciated, in-office balls.'

Saleda turned to Jenna. 'I need a word with you.'

Saleda's heels clicked on the tile as she walked out the door behind Irv.

Jenna glanced back at Grey, who was now pushing only one mug across the table and making a vroom sound with her lips.

'Right behind you,' Jenna said.

Saleda nodded to Jenna to close the conference room door behind her. Jenna's supervisor crossed her arms and leaned against the wall. The way her high, sable-colored ponytail stretched her eyebrows up ever-so-slightly at their corners gave Saleda's already stern face a menacing kick.

'We have twenty-one dead people whose families are being told right now their loved ones aren't coming home. For the tiny amount we have to go on to profile these terrorists, we haven't even come *close* to finishing the grainy, video-related guesswork on our plates, and another attack could be imminent. If Grey is kooky but can help us put these profiles together faster, then I'll bring her every coffee mug in my kitchen cabinets at home to play with while she does it. But if her quirks are going to be just one more chaotic, moving part of this circus I'm trying to make sense of—'

The wild metallic copper flashed in again. 'Saleda, I understand your concerns. And believe me, I know this is more than unorthodox. If you'd rather I kick Grey out of here and we just work with one of the other departments' consulting forensic linguists on this, I wouldn't fault you,' Jenna said. She'd half-hoped that Saleda would meet Grey and immediately veto the idea of bringing her in as a consult.

But she's the best.

'But you think we need her . . .' Saleda prompted.

Jenna nodded. 'Grey's brain is a virtual repository of not just literary facts but of critical literary analysis by her and by others – a nearly limitless vault of author names and historical writing themes and styles. She's a great self-taught linguist, too. No other consulting linguist or literature expert could possibly know and understand as many books as she does *and* be able to approach the situation with quite the same type of critical eye.'

'And by that you mean she has a way of looking at things differently, sees things others might miss,' Saleda said, uncrossing her arms. 'The problem is, in this case, what if she is *actually* seeing things other people miss for a reason?'

Jenna shook her head emphatically. 'She won't. She's schizotypal, falls on the autism spectrum, too. But she isn't schizophrenic or delusional.'

'Can't schizotypals have schizophrenic episodes?'

'It's rare. And there are warning signs one might be coming,' Jenna replied.

Saleda looked over Jenna's shoulder at the closed door, seeming to imagine the team and Grey behind it. 'And you diagnosed her?'

Jenna nodded. 'She was a patient. Years ago.'

'Is she reliable? Can we trust her?'

Jenna smirked. 'Trust her? Probably. Is she reliable? Definitely not. More impulsive than Dodd heading into a crime scene before the rest of us have even heard about it.'

'Well, shit. What've we got to lose?' Saleda cocked her head toward the conference room. 'Get in there and tell her welcome aboard.'

Jenna shrugged and turned the knob. Saleda was right. After all, she'd dealt with worse.

Fifteen

Irv mumbled to himself angrily as he logged into the main desktop in his office. Easy for them to say, he should know to use a burner phone and all that other MacGyver bullshit.

Instead of launching right into a search for literature-obsessed websites, the image of Grey Hechinger's rat-like face in his mind made him open the intense firewall program he had set up to monitor his network activity. Weird whim, but that batshit crazy librarian version of Luna Lovegood had him on edge. Watching the scan run always made him feel nice and in control even when everything else didn't.

Never telling Jenna that. She'd diagnose me with OCD, paranoid computer tech disorder, and procrastination by agitation-itis.

Irv pushed the chair back and kicked his feet up to the desk. They wanted him to think like Jason Bourne, they could stash him some burner phones and fake IDs in a locker in Shreveport. He'd done his best to get the job done, and he *had* found Grey Hechinger.

Not a field agent, never pretended to be one.

He took a swig from the open can of Dr Pepper on his L-shaped desk, forced himself to swallow. Of course it was warm and flat. Instead of spending that fifteen minutes of his break with his nice cold soda near the drink machine down the hall while he checked on the battle dragons he raised online from eggs to leviathans, he'd had to run to the front gate and put out fires with guards, then take Grey to the team and take a tongue lashing.

Irv glanced left over the desk at the free superheroes calendar he'd gotten from Comic-Con last year. Only a couple more weeks until vacation, and not a minute too soon. Keeping this obnoxious secret from the team wasn't quite like hiding plans for a surprise birthday party from someone. Time to figure out what to do next would be great, but just the break from making sure things stayed under wraps was needed more than anything.

Too bad vacation is more like prison than Fiji, this go 'round.

The scan results filled in the salmon-colored box on his screen in real-time, and Irv's eyes followed them.

All in a day's wor—

'What the . . .' Irv said, yanking his feet down and sitting up with a jolt. He hit the pause button to freeze the log.

Hitting keys fast and scrolling up, his heart thundered. What in the name of the number 42 was this?

Not a single entry on the long list of files before him was flagged by the watchdog software he had set up to monitor all the systems in this headquarters office of the Behavioral Analysis Unit. Amidst all the other mundane traffic logs, a series of entries caught his attention. About thirty files a page, seven pages or so. Every one showing they were viewed under his login credentials.

The system would never flag the over two hundred files, because by all appearances an approved tech analyst had retrieved them.

Only he hadn't. Irv knew he hadn't because the scan claimed the dates the files had been accessed was two years from tomorrow, in the future.

Someone covering their tracks?

'Son of a bitch,' Irv muttered, his keystrokes fast, but not as fast as he wished they could be. 'Who the hell are you, and what do you want?'

He sent the onscreen results to his printer, then canceled the routine scan. A few command lines later, and a new scan began, this time specifically filtered to show only files from the fictitious future date.

'Oh, you've messed with the wrong . . . you're going to wish— You asshole, how the hell did you . . .'

Fuming, he grabbed the stack of pages from the printer and thumbed through as the new list populated. So far, nothing new. Same file names, same directory, same login info. He reached the final page as the scan completed, then stopped short. There on the screen, one lonely line of text shone in black and white – a text file that didn't have a match on his printout because it was in a directory so many cyber miles away from all the others, it would have taken his original scan hours to turn up.

'What have we here . . .' he muttered, opening the rogue file.

A thoroughly ordinary, boring error log stared back at him, the kind applications automatically created anytime they encountered a problem, so techs or developers could troubleshoot them if needed. At first glance, all the listings appeared normal. Irv narrowed his eyes. Something was weird about this. The hacker couldn't possibly have had anything to gain out of this file, and he clearly didn't need anything out of the rest of the directory. That left only one reason to access it: to leave something behind. He searched more closely, reading each line carefully.

He lingered on one of the most recent listings and its error message:

THIS IS AN INFORMATIONAL MESSAGE ONLY. NO ADDITIONAL USER ACTION IS REQUIRED DUE TO RULES 2-33.

'Error number fifteen,' he read the rest of the line aloud. 'Error type 0B03 . . . source, home call prompt core info double limb false-dot-php . . .'

A crazy realization struck him. No fucking way.

'You son of a bitch,' he said again, this time with a different feeling entirely. 'What the hell? Why?'

His rage now converted to energy, Irv resumed typing, beginning the process of tracing every single step the uninvited guest had taken. The thirst for vengeance was gone. Right now he just needed answers. Every damn one of them.

Sixteen

From the raised voices behind the door, Jenna didn't need to be inside the conference room to know Grey was already making quite a name for herself.

And the name is nuisance.

'I'll give you that Wing Man UNSUB following around the Blunt Force UNSUB is probably Mr Watson,' Porter argued.

'And you're right. You could probably tell us more about what traits and mannerisms the pair here that apparently call themselves Watson and Holmes share with the fictional characters if the images of them on the video were enhanced. But since Irv can only run the software on one UNSUB's image at a time, we have to wait for the one he's already running on Slender to finish before requesting the new one. In the meantime, just take a seat and let us do our jobs. When we reach something we need you to consult on, we'll bring it to you.'

Nice try, but Grey Hechinger wasn't just going to get comfortable and read quietly in the corner until you needed her. Now that they'd caught Grey's interest, they had it.

I'll rescue you today, Porter, but you owe me one.

'Grey, I brought a notebook for you,' Jenna said, pulling out one of the conference table chairs and setting the legal pad on the table in front of it. She pulled the black ink pen from her pocket and set it on top. 'I need you to write down any instances on here you can think of where Sherlock Holmes is in a bank, investigating a bank, or maybe even is on a case that involves something similar to a bank: any place that stores valuables for the public, high dollar things. Especially any crimes related to those sorts of places that look like heists but then didn't end up being robberies at all. After you get that list, think about those storylines and note anything in those particular stories that might be controversial. Social issues, race issues. Political or religious scandals, maybe. Would you start that for me?'

'For the record, I totally could've handled that,' Porter said as they walked a few steps away from the table to a quiet corner closer to the video screen where they could talk out of Grey's earshot.

'I'm sure you could've gagged her,' Jenna joked. 'But this way she feels like she's working on the case using the skills that caused us to bring her here in the first place. It's more likely to keep her out of your hair indefinitely. Plus, there's the added bonus of the small chance it *could* actually yield something relevant.'

Porter narrowed his eyes comically. 'Hey, I said I could handle it. I didn't say I'd handle it *well*.'

Jenna laughed, returned to the video footage from the bank. She took a sip of her dark roast, her gaze catching the third figure to enter the bank. The Long-Sword UNSUB.

Metallic gold flashed in.

Jenna nudged Porter with her elbow, pointed at Long-Sword UNSUB. 'What about this guy? He came up when we were trying to figure out what he and Machete UNSUB were doing when they went off-screen, but we haven't really scrutinized some of the more obvious things that could go toward his profile.'

Porter gave her a sidelong glance, raised his eyebrows. 'Such as?'

'Well, he's the only one killing people with a sword that looks like it could've walked out of a history museum,' Jenna said, leaning forward and squinting, trying to make out any detailing that might be carved into the blade or its hilt.

'True. And if this crew wasn't made up of a bunch of knife maniacs stabbing people with exploding diving blades and machetes, I'd say the weirdo would catch my eye,' Porter said, 'But in this case, the only thing that might stand out would be, I don't know, a nice, regular M16.'

'Or maybe a chainsaw,' Teva said as she joined them at the projector.

'Don't give 'em any ideas. Kung Pow UNSUB with the butterfly swords left enough stray body parts in there to bring up my last seventeen meals. I'd hate to see a chainsaw in that mix,' Porter said.

Jenna's eyes found the perp Porter had called Kung Pow UNSUB. On the screen, the figure swung her blades deftly, gracefully, their slices wicked and effective.

Metallic gold flashed in again. The same color as a few moments before while watching Long-Sword UNSUB fight.

'Maybe you're on to something there,' she mumbled, holding the

metallic gold in her mind as she glanced from the Long-Sword UNSUB
to Kung Pow and back again.

'I know I am!' Porter laughed. 'Less dismemberment equals fewer
second appearances made by pancakes. I didn't realize this was a
concept that *needed* further investigation . . .'

Jenna rolled her eyes, but she focused back in on the same two
UNSUBs. 'I'm not talking about your throw-up jokes, Gilbert Godfrey.
I'm talking about Kung Pow and the butterfly swords. At first glance
none of these UNSUBs stands out; they're all different and brutal.
But actually, Kung Pow stands out for a few reasons—'

'Kung Pow UNSUB is a double-wielder,' Teva filled in.

'Yep. Two blades aren't practical in a fight for most. Might even
be a hindrance for an amateur,' Jenna said. 'But for Kung Pow, they
aren't. Which made me realize why *he*'—she paused, put her pointer
finger on Long-Sword UNSUB on the screen—'stood out in *my* mind.
The same metallic gold flashed in twice while watching this video:
when I watch Long-Sword and when I watch Kung Pow.'

'The colors,' Teva said quietly, her tone half awe, half annoyed.

'Again,' Porter said with a sigh. Full-on annoyed.

'You know me. Always gotta show off,' Jenna said. *I do so enjoy
explaining how the brain phenomenon I was put on this team to use connects
things to colors in my mind only to see faces staring back at me so blank they
look like they're trying to process every concept in Stephen Hawking's* A Brief
History of Time *at once. And yet, despite getting the same reaction every
time, instead of simply accepting the leg up my color associations give us, you
still insist on conducting these little Synesthesia for Dummies seminars any
time the colors come up, followed by a tribunal to determine whether or not
the color association should be trusted as evidence in the investigation.* 'You
want to hear it or not?'

'Of course,' Teva said.

'The metallic gold I see when I watch both of them fight I associate
with skill. Skill that comes from training. Those two aren't amateurs.
They know how to fight, and not just because they knew this day
was coming. These two were recruited for this job *because* of their
skills,' Jenna said.

Saleda had joined them and nodded, whipping out her phone and
texting. 'I'll get Irv on local martial arts centers, particularly members
or students in them who might belong to hate groups or have police
records.'

'Good. And don't forget the local colleges. Check for martial arts clubs, fencing clubs, anything of that nature. Cross-reference those students with any who might be history or literature majors or have involvement with campus organizations with literary ties or book clubs,' Jenna added. 'While we work on that, though, I think Grey can put down her catalog of Sherlock bank novels. I've got a real job for her now.'

Seventeen

'So, metallic gold meaning the two of them have mad skills with a blade translates somehow into an assignment for the Loony Librarian? How?' Porter asked.

'I *think* when you say Loony Librarian, you're referring to our expert literature and linguistics consultant, but yes.'

Jenna crossed the room to the whiteboard where Saleda had drawn boxes, one for each UNSUB, and written what was known about each. Some boxes were more spare than others, often noting no more than how many kills and what number they were through the door. Others noted the type of weapon or weapons used, if they could be made out from the grainy video. Inside four boxes, names of literary characters were written with a question mark and circled: Scout, Richelieu, Holmes, and Watson.

'We think they gave themselves classic literary aliases. They're leaving behind messages using classic literary quotes. So, our next step should be figuring out the aliases of the other nine UNSUBS. Right now, the aliases are a jumping off point to telling us more about the killers. The more individual UNSUBs we can profile, the more we can piece together what they're about as a group and how we might find them,' Jenna said.

'Don't you think it's possible it's just a gimmick? You know, they needed to be able to call each other names while running their . . . *heist* . . . or whatever it was . . . so they just said, 'OK, everybody pick a celebrity name,' or 'Let's all be superheroes!' Why assume it's anything more than just the first category that came to them?' Teva said.

'That should be obvious, Rookie,' Dodd said, clapping Teva on the back as he reached the group. 'Sure, they could just be names, but the note and witness message aren't even the only things that say literature is at the very core of this case. We know the UNSUBs picked aliases rooted in it, but we also *know* – to some degree anyway – they're playacting it. We just saw a guy beat someone half to death with a weighted riding crop, for fuck's sake. Maybe just the one sick perp has a hard-on for Sir Arthur Conan Doyle's characters and used this outing as an opportunity to cosplay and promote his terroristic agenda at the same time. But look around. Crazy weapons that don't even make sense when a few AK-47s and a grenade would've done. From the look of some of that hardware, these perps must've robbed the Smithsonian or knocked over an antique store on the way to the bank.'

Teva's face turned red, and she looked down. Quiet.

Dodd was right, but damn, he could be an ass. Especially lately, he'd seemed to have it in for Teva.

Jenna shook the thought. *Focus.*

'Dodd's right. I didn't bring butter with me to grease his big head when it gets stuck going out the door later,' Jenna said, taking a long pause to shoot him a menacing glare, 'but he's right. Their actions, words, and the couple of names Ashlee Haynie managed to remember hearing all make it seem like examining the aliases to enhance their individual profiles is warranted.'

Teva stayed quiet, staring at her toes, but if there was any awkward silence in the group, Porter hadn't noticed it.

'OK, but that's just it. We only know Scout because Ashlee heard it and we could place the timing of what was said with what was happening on the camera footage to figure out which UNSUB the alias referred to. We haven't got a clue who Richelieu is unless one of those perps was wearing a red robe and a skull cap and I just missed him the first time.'

'True,' Saleda said, 'which is why part of what will be important about this is figuring out why each perpetrator was so named. The character they chose could reflect a lot of who they are – or try to be. Reveal ideologies, personalities. Strengths or background. Maybe their fictional character came from the geographic location where they have family, or a perp chose the alias Porthos because his favorite candy bar is Three Musketeers.'

'So basically what you're saying here is, if we use *virtually nothing* to figure out something *very specific*, then bam! We'll nab our Gang of Wild Mad Literati?'

'We don't have nothing,' Jenna said, chunking a paperclip at Porter. 'We have lots of little things. We use them.'

Saleda nodded. 'And once we have profiles for every member, it'll tell us a lot about the group. If another attack is coming, it's on us to put together a map to find the who, what, when, and where to stop it. As we pick the video apart, the profiles or other literary references might intersect and show us what the heck that passage from the *Importance of Being Earnest* has to do with anything. Because we can ask our word consultant here, but I have a feeling she could ramble all day about Oscar Wilde and still not illuminate anything for us about what the attackers intended us to get from that passage *unless* we first find something in these profiles or other literary shenanigans that helps us put it into context.

Porter squeezed the bill of his ball cap in both hands, pushed it down over his eyes as he tried not to talk back. Then, his hands dropped back to his lap. 'And the Loony Librarian's going to help us pull that literary context out of our—?'

'Evidence,' Saleda cut him off. 'Yes. She is, I hope. We just need to find her a jumping off point.'

Jenna's eyes had turned back to the surveillance video, once again following Long-Sword UNSUB's every move.

'Saleda, maybe that jumping off point can be the sword. Looks old. Medieval, maybe?'

Saleda took a step closer to the screen. 'Yeah, I guess. I don't know a lot about swords.'

Dodd barked a laugh. 'Make room, make room. Let the old codger have a look.'

Dodd leaned in, squinted at the sword in the video, adjusted his glasses. 'It's French, by the look of the hilt and the blade. I'd say an infantry sword. Briquet sabre, if I know as much as I think I do. Napoleonic.'

Jenna's heart galloped. Stacks upon stacks of classics used the Napoleonic War as a backdrop. She'd been right. The Long-Sword UNSUB would be great as the next UNSUB to try to profile.

The only problem now was, she had to bring Grey over and try to explain what she needed from her.

Eighteen

'So, this guy thinks he's some character from a book?' Grey muttered, not so much judging as amused. 'And people think I'm nutsy-cuckoo.'

Jenna stifled a snicker. 'Our only clue is the sword he's carrying. Dodd thinks it's Napoleonic, a briquet sabre. Infantry issue sword. Does that . . .'

Her voice trailed, unsure how to finish. *Does knowing that sword cause a book cover to flash in your head like a color might flash in mine?*

'What Dr Ramey means is, are there any classic novels set in that era or that use weapons like that?' Dodd replied.

Grey nodded, wandering around the room, gazing upward at the ceiling as if it were scattered with nighttime stars. 'Plenty. Which would you like to hear about?'

'Oh brother,' Porter mumbled, pulling his cap down over his eyes again.

Jenna shot him a glare. Maybe they were going at this the wrong way. Expecting Grey to hear about the sword and instinctively know they wanted her to lay out all the options clearly, one by one, explaining the differences between each wasn't just unfair. It was stupid. Profiling wasn't Grey's job. It was theirs.

To tap into the kinds of connections Grey could make given the literary knowledge she possessed, the team needed to set her up to be successful.

Do your job. Ask questions. Investigate.

'Grey, what's the first book set in the Napoleonic era that comes to mind?' Jenna asked.

Grey turned to face her, doe eyes wide and honest. '*War and Peace* of course. Tolstoy. Epic story. Hundreds and hundreds of pages of five families. Rich.'

'In detail?' Saleda pushed.

'No, in money.'

Porter sniggered.

'And it's obviously about war . . .' Saleda led Grey.

But Grey had taken a seat at the table and was moving her hands in the air above it as though turning book pages. 'The French invasions. Greedy man, Napoleon. Wanted every country, so he took them.'

So, to some degree, a fight about the people in power. 'Was Napoleon portrayed negatively?'

'Oh, definitely,' Grey answered, turning and smoothing out a fictional page. 'He's a little bit of a fatty, even. Gets a rubdown in his toilet room, almost comical for someone supposedly so mighty. Thankfully the story wasn't so much about his conquering desires and more about the people feeling them.'

'What?' Porter whispered incredulously.

But Jenna was too busy trying to sort through Grey's strange word choices in order to decipher them to pay attention to how jumbled they sounded.

The people feeling them? The oppressed? Angry their own were killing and dying? Starving? The terrorists might feel or even be oppressed. Lots of activists feel they are, after all. Decide to take up the cause, do something about it.

'The whole story was about what people felt like while he was trampling their land and killing people. Not just about *that* though. Also how they felt falling in doggie love all over the place—'

'Puppy,' Porter interjected, though if Grey heard him, she ignored him.

'—and wondering why they lived at all, and if they did, what it meant. Then, in the middle of war, that Pierre sees a Russian be put to death and thinks some of the weirdest things, given the situation.'

Porter snickered, and Grey paused, turning to him as if she expected him to stop and ask a question. Jenna glared him down.

'Sorry, Grey,' Jenna said. 'You were saying?'

By then, though, Grey had caught on to the joke and she gave Porter an evil stare before going on. 'Pierre, I mean. Seeing all those Russians killed. To him, that event itself made the whole war suddenly seem unbalanced. Mad. I'll give him that. But the weird part was at the same time, he seemed to suddenly formulate in his head that men were all brothers, that mankind as a whole was actually destined to support each other. All the while, he's on his way to assassinate someone.'

Existential questions. Interesting.

'Lots of mumbling and grumbling about being rich, then the conquering making them less rich even if they gave the money away themselves. Wasn't even like Napoleon walked up and stole it. Kind of ridiculous, too, the whining, considering in the end they all end up kind of well-off anyway.'

A shade of ice blue flashed in. Endurance. Endurance from acceptance. These people didn't rise up. They endured their hardship as it came to them.

'I don't think this guy would've chosen something like Tolstoy. None of it fits. All the financial carelessness ending up all right kind of sends the message that spiritual richness is worth more than money,' Jenna said.

'And that might be a plausible message, considering they didn't steal any of the bank's money,' Dodd said. 'Unfortunately they didn't give the poor souls any time to reap the lesson.'

'If that was the lesson, they *would've* stolen the money, old man. To force them to learn money can't buy happiness and all that baloney,' Porter cut in.

'Knock it off, you two,' Saleda said.

The shade of jumbled iris blue flashed in. They could force *War and Peace* to fit if they tried, but Jenna's gut said it didn't fit right. Certain elements were there if you tossed them around, jostled them to mean what you needed them to. But the result wasn't neat.

'I don't think *War and Peace* makes sense,' Jenna said, not bothering to worry about whether the others were finished considering the possibility or not. 'Any other Napoleonic fiction where riches or money are a key element of the plot?'

Grey tilted her head thoughtfully, stared at the ceiling and whistled a tuneless, single note. The little birdie's eyes drifted back to Jenna. 'I suppose *The Count of Monte Cristo* is a choice.'

'Alexander Dumas,' Teva filled in. 'I read that in high school.'

Porter groaned and rubbed his eyes. 'Yeah, me, too. And I'd planned to *leave* it in high school.'

'Well, he was that same age but not in high school,' Grey said, looking around the room at nothing in particular.

'Who?'

Her head snapped back to face Porter, who had asked the question. 'Edmond Dantès, of course. The *main character*.'

Porter winced. He leaned toward Teva and muttered something about how they must be on Candid Camera.

Jenna kicked his shin under the table and nodded at Grey. 'Dantès, right. He was the captain of a ship or something?'

Grey nodded absentmindedly. 'Mr Perfect with the straight white teeth, I'm sure. That's always how I pictured him anyway. How his buddies did, also. They hated it.'

Grey was right. It was coming back to her now. 'Yes, his friends were jealous of him, so they have him accused of treason. He's arrested on his wedding day, I think?'

'Domino,' Grey said, pointing a finger at Jenna. 'The man he lives with in jail ends up being a much better friend to Dantès—'

'Domino?' Porter whispered.

'She means bingo,' Jenna spat back under her breath as Grey continued.

'—and before he kicks the bucket, he leaves Dantès all sorts of things, the main one being the place where a treasure is hiding.'

'The island of Monte Cristo! I remember now,' Saleda said. 'Then he escapes from prison and uses the treasure to help people who helped him and punish his enemies.'

'He stuck it to 'em for everything from having dollar signs in their eyes to being double-crossing Judases,' Grey said in an airy voice.

Auburn vengeance flashed in to match the emotional story Grey was describing. And yet, this didn't match their scene at the bank.

'We've already ruled out revenge,' Saleda said. 'Besides, here we are again at that whole robbery-without-taking thing.'

A deep red color flashed in. Almost brown. No. More purple-ish.

Jenna shook it away. She didn't want to lose track of the conversation that wasn't stopping for her. She could come back to the color.

Porter looked to Grey. 'What whimsical adventure into the age where France was run by Louis and Francis and all those other guys with names that sound like my grandmother's shall we venture into next?'

Seeing the confusion on Grey's face as she turned to Porter, Jenna quickly stepped between them. 'We can't all have names suited to drinking beer and carrying luggage, Porter,' she shot at him under her breath. 'Porter's right, Grey. Monte Cristo doesn't quite fit, but one of the elements interested me. The charged political climate during the time made it easy for his friends to frame Dantès for treason. What other books in that time and place focus heavily on the political climate?'

Grey let out a long, low whistle. 'All the ones you're talking about pretty much. We need to tighten the net some.'

Before Saleda was over her shoulder to ask, Jenna whispered, 'Narrow the list.'

Saleda shook her head. 'How do you narrow a list when you've got nothing but a sword?'

The clack of a phone vibrating across the conference table delayed anyone having to answer. Good thing, too. Jenna didn't have an angle on this yet.

Saleda picked up her ringing phone and answered.

'Yeah, Irv. Got it. I'm putting you on speaker,' she said. 'Irv thinks he's found something.' She pressed the button so they could all hear their technical analyst. 'OK, Irv. We're all here.'

'Don't get too excited, because it's definitely no assassin club roster, but I *did* stumble on to a little something I think might be worth looking into,' Irv said. 'I was digging around some of the anonymous forums people sometimes use to indulge their various misbehaviors – some harmless, petty stuff, other things a little more deviant. I've been able to get beads on miscreants in the past using sites like this because bottom dwellers know they can type angry, foreboding diatribes most forums call 'threats' and not get blocked, or show around their stash of kiddie porn without blue lights showing up outside their window.'

'And why is it they know they aren't getting caught?' Dodd growled, clenching his fists at Irv's mention of child pornography.

'It's the nature of the boards. All anonymous, no names or handles. The posts self-delete, so no records,' Irv said. 'So, I did a bit of keyword searching using some of the message from our friends, and it landed me in a cesspool dedicated to political griping. I took the liberty of flagging a poster in that charming little snake pit that I think might be related to the bank butchers,' Irv said.

'Bank Butchers,' Saleda said, frowning. 'Catchy. Almost too catchy. Don't you dare say those words within ten feet of anything with a microphone, Bluetooth, or a laptop. The group's already playing BFF with the media. No need to give them a cutesy nickname to help sensationalize it.'

'Point taken, boss,' Irv replied. 'But I do think I'd better come down and show you something. Something about this poster's words. They're just so darn *earnest.*'

Nineteen

A few minutes after he hung up with the team, Irv entered the conference room.

He tossed the file folder he'd brought down on to the table. 'Since you're all wondering, no, I made sure I took three right turns around the floor before I came in so any Russian sleeper spies would either have to stop following me or admit the tail.'

'So what'd you find that warranted something so formal as printed paper and a folder?' Jenna asked.

'Eh, I was headed on an errand anyway, so I figured I'd just bring it on my way out,' Irv said, glancing away from Jenna quickly. *Change the subject before she asks.* 'Besides, the post is deleted now, so it's not like I can just send you a link. Have a screen cap saved, but I thought given the nature of the case being so wordy, having it in hand might be helpful.'

Jenna picked up the file and opened it, scanned the page.

Irv headed for the door. They might hash out the crazy exchange he'd just gifted them with all afternoon, but sooner rather than later, the contents of that folder would culminate in a call or text to him adding another billion and five cyber-sleuthing tasks to his plate. If he was going to take care of the unwanted intruder he'd caught in his own cookie jar during that impromptu scan, he'd better do it now.

'I'll leave you fine agents to the spoils. Have to pop out of the office to take my bowties to the cleaners, but if you need me, you know where to find me,' Irv said, patting the pants pocket storing his phone.

A chuckle made him turn around. It was Saleda.

'You take your bowties to the dry-cleaners? Seriously?'

Irv gave her a playful smile. Too easy. 'What? I like the way their detergent smells, OK?'

Teva squinted. 'But you don't *wear* bowties.'

He grinned. 'That *you* know of. Buh-bye, kids!'

He turned and walked out the door.

* * *

Jenna's gaze followed Irv out the door, a shamrock green she couldn't quite put her finger on dancing in her mind. Weird. He was always sarcastic, but something about that entire encounter was over the top.

'So don't keep us in suspense. What's the forum post say?' Porter said.

The shamrock shade drifted away, and Jenna's mind jolted back to the case. She glanced at the printout of the forum post again. 'At first glance it's just a conversation about that Venture Airways flight that crashed this morning. You know the types. My penis is bigger than the pilot's – I'd have landed that jet on the cliff of the Grand Canyon or some shit like that. Three guys who, from how they talk to each other, sound like they interact regularly. Anyway, at a point, one poster's rant references *The Importance of Being Earnest*. Take a look.'

She laid the letter on the table, and the rest of the team crowded around it to read:

ANONYMOUS NO. 300672441

AS LONG AS THE STATUS QUO REMAINS, THINGS LIKE THIS WILL CONTINUE TO HAPPEN OVER AND OVER AGAIN. PEOPLE WILL DIE FOR NO REASON OTHER THAN THAT THE SAME PERSON SCREENING THAT LINE AT THE AIRPORT IS THE SAME GUY WHO COMMENTS ON SOCIAL MEDIA USING PLENTY OF SUPERFLUOUS COMMAS AND SPELLS SUPERVISOR WITH A Z. NOT THAT MR SCREENER MATTERS, CONSIDERING WHATEVER TSA APPOINTEE WHO GRADUATED WITH ALL C'S FROM COLLEGE AFTER A CALL FROM HIS DAD'S GOLF BUDDY GOT HIM IN DECIDED IT WAS TOO MUCH OF AN INCON- VENIENCE TO PILOTS TO HAVE THEM SCREENED IN THE REGULAR LINES. TOO BAD HE WAS TOO BUSY SHINING HIS MOST LIKELY TO SUCCEED PLAQUE FROM MOUNTAIN TOWNVILLE UNIVERSITY COLLEGE TO THINK OF SOMETHING AS PRUDENT AS A SYSTEM THAT WOULD BOTH ENSURE FLIGHT CREWS MADE IT TO THEIR GATES IN TIME TO CIRCUMVENT THOSE PESKY DELAYS WHILE MAINTAINING A THOROUGH SCREENING PROCESS TO PROTECT THE FLIGHT SAFETY OF MILLIONS. ——M.

ANONYMOUS NO. 300672442

DUDE, ACCIDENTS HAPPEN. ——IS

ANONYMOUS NO. 300672443

IF IT WAS EVEN AN ACCIDENT. THE GOVERNMENT PROBABLY HAD
SOMEONE ON THAT PLANE THEY NEEDED TO DISAPPEAR. SO,
POOF! —L.U.F.

ANONYMOUS NO. 300672444

YOU TWO IMBECILES THINK THIS IS FUNNY, BUT SO MANY
THINGS LIKE THIS WILL CONTINUE UNLESS THE CURRENT
SYSTEM IS GUTTED, THROWN OUT, AND REBUILT SO THAT
BEFORE YOU CAN BE THE GUY WHO DOUBLE-CHECKS THAT NO
ONE HAS A BOMB BEFORE THEY BOARD A PLANE, YOU HAVE TO
HAVE GONE TO A SCHOOL THAT REQUIRES YOU TO KNOW THAT
THE PEOPLE CONGRATULATING YOU ON YOUR GRADUATION
ARE DOING IT WITHOUT A 'D' IN THE WORD. IT'S NOT ENOUGH
TO SHRUG AND SAY, 'IT IS WHAT IT IS.' IT'S NOW IMPORTANT
TO BE EARNEST. TO BE A PART OF THE SOLUTION AND NOT THE
PROBLEM. —M.

ANONYMOUS NO. 300672445

HOW EXACTLY DO YOU EXPECT US TO DO THAT? —L.U.F.

ANONYMOUS NO. 300672446

MANY TONGUES TALK, BUT FEW HEADS THINK. THINGS ARE
HAPPENING. WE HAVE THE WISDOM, BUT WELCOME IT. WE NEED
THINKERS. PRIVATE FORUM, INVITE HAS TO COME FROM THE
ADMIN, SO WATCH FOR IT. YOU TWO HATE THIS INSANITY AS MUCH
AS I DO. HELP DO SOMETHING ABOUT IT. —M.

'Unless the important to be earnest thing is some sort of weird
slang catchphrase sweeping the nation I'm not aware of . . .' Saleda
said.

'And we can't trace an account or anything?' Teva asked.

'I guess even wizards have some limitations,' Saleda said, 'There
are no accounts to trace.'

Jenna scanned the paper again, her eyes lingering on the very last
letter of the final post on the printout. An M.

A purple-ish color flashed in. Too much of a reddish tinge to be
narcissism, but the color and the feeling she got as she looked at that

M – a signature – was cooler than the red pomegranate of confidence. No, it was definitely a mixture of the two. Both the color – a full-bodied glass of Shiraz – and what her gut told her about the state of mind of the person posting as M.

Hubris.

'Interesting that in a forum that goes as far as it does to maintain anonymity of its posters that a user would identify himself with a signature,' Jenna said.

'Well, they've talked before, be it here or elsewhere. He clearly has their contact information to invite them to this other private forum,' Dodd said.

Jenna tapped the M with her fingernail. 'But this guy, he knows what he's involved with and how important it is to avoid leaving a trail. And yet, he signs it anyway. Just an initial, one that doesn't match his real name, I'm sure. He's in an anonymous, untraceable forum with self-deleting posts. He's so sure he's got his bases covered that, like any good narcissist, he's convinced he's better than everyone else. Anyone who might be looking for him. A foolish amount of confidence in the wake of such high stakes,' Jenna said.

'You're calling narcissist, then?' Dodd asked.

Jenna nodded. 'He sure thinks he could do far better than any of these people. Grandiose sense of his own talents and ideas. And the signature just seals the deal.'

Jenna's eyes landed on Grey, who was now sitting at the end of the conference table, holding the printout of the forum post in her left hand, her right hand raised high as though she was in a high school Geometry class.

'Grey?' Jenna whispered, leaning toward her. Feeling the rest of the team's eyes on her, including Saleda's, Jenna cleared her throat, looked at Saleda. 'Saleda, I think Grey might have something to add.'

'What do you have for us, Grey?' Saleda asked.

Grey looked up at Saleda over the top of the printout. 'It's just . . . I think I might be able to figure out who he is. Or what, anyway. Another one of the books used.'

'The books they took their nicknames from?' Saleda said, suddenly intent and walking back around the table toward Grey. 'How?'

Grey pointed a bony finger at the page, traced a line of text. 'Right here. It says, "Many tongues talk, but few heads think." Madam Agent Saleda Officer, that's a quote. From Victor Hugo's *Les Miserables.*'

Twenty

Pinkish-orange apricot flashed in. Congruency.

'So *Les Miserables* joins the ranks with Sherlock Holmes, *To Kill a Mockingbird*, and one of approximately nine million novels Cardinal Richelieu managed to make a cameo in,' Jenna said.

'How *did* that guy get so famous? He's got to be the most Hollywood Cardinal ever,' Porter said.

Saleda moved to the white board and picked up a dry erase marker. 'What does the newest addition to the lineup of the book club from hell tell us about the group?'

All heads turned towards Grey.

She stared back at them, the stray frizzy wisps of blonde around her face blowing under the air conditioner vent above her, her hands folded neatly on the table in front of her, attentive.

Jenna bit her lip to keep it together. For Grey, this was behaving. She was being a polite student, and she wouldn't take subtle social cues like this when, to her, the question wasn't literal enough for her to think she could add to the conversation.

Jenna's reading of *Les Miserables* in high school seemed ages ago, and even though she and Charley had seen the musical version of Hugo's masterpiece last year at the Olney, she couldn't quite draw up the intricacies of the scenes she could picture. The one detail from the story that sprang to mind was one character's name. The mustard color of correlation flashed in. Marius.

M.

'I think our Sword Boy's nickname is Marius,' Jenna said. She turned to Grey. 'Marius was part of a radical group of students planning an uprising in the book, right?'

Grey nodded. 'The author used the students at the barricades as a device to highlight the real political unrest of the time in France.'

Teva leaned in, elbows on the table. 'I remember the students building the barricade and fighting, but to be honest, I wasn't a hundred percent on what they were trying to accomplish. All I really understood was that they didn't trust the law enforcement, because of that one complete asshole cop who dogs everyone for the stupidest stuff.'

'Javert,' Grey acknowledged. 'And yes, he was just doing his job, but you're right that he and law enforcement weren't trusted by many in that time and place; they didn't serve everyone. The uprisings of the student group and France of that time in real life were to fight pecking orders controlling everything—'

'I think what Grey means is both the book and reality reflect the social inequality in France at a time when the country had a rigid class system and people were treated according to where they fell in it,' Dodd explained.

Grey gave a nod. 'Those screwball inn keepers were rich only because they took everyone's money, but they gallivant about the whole story while Officer OCD would chase a bread thief to Mars if he had to.'

'So you're saying, in the novel, the government doesn't deal with crimes based on severity. True criminals are barely punished if wealthy, but there's hell to pay for petty crime if you're on the wrong end of the social hierarchy?' Porter recapped.

'The students were fighting the corrupt system of greed and, yes, class,' Grey said.

Jenna slid the printout of the forum post back over, skimmed it again. 'This group's rebelling against something, but it sounds like, if anything, they *want* a class.'

Dodd looked over her shoulder at the paper. 'You're right. UNSUB does seem to get his panties in a twist over punctuation errors—'

'And there's that comment about people shouldn't be allowed to graduate high school unless they can spell properly,' Saleda said.

Orchid flashed in. This group didn't want a more just society. They wanted a smarter one.

'If I had to guess, I'd say this group wants the country to be run only by the intellectual elite, which tells us they all think they belong in that categorization,' Jenna said. 'What I don't understand yet is how the attack at the bank and what they're planning next furthers that agenda.'

Dodd shook his head sadly. 'This group differs in themes, for sure. The theme of *Les Mis* has to do with the importance of love and compassion. What we saw in that bank doesn't match any definition of compassion I've heard.'

A thought tickled the back of Jenna's mind. *The scene left for them in the bank. Importance of love and compassion.*

'But they do think it's "important to be earnest,"' Jenna said. Russian violet flashed in again. 'Have any of you noticed that all four pieces of literature we've identified as being associated with this group so far also have stage play versions?'

Dodd cocked his head. 'Are they? *To Kill a Mockingbird,* sure. *Les Miserables* is obviously one. Is anything in the Sherlock Holmes series?'

Grey cleared her throat. 'Of course. Sir Arthur Conan Doyle himself teamed up with a co-writer and made up a four act play that drew from three novels in the series.'

'And *The Importance of Being Earnest* is definitely one,' Saleda said. 'I had to go watch my niece in it at her summer camp last year.'

'Is there a play with Richelieu in it?' Porter asked.

Jenna shrugged, took out her smartphone to do a quick Google search.

'Definitely. It's proper title is *Or the Conspiracy,* but it's called *Richelieu* more often than not. Written in 1839 by a British writer,' Grey chimed in.

They stared back at her, mouths gaping. She really *was* a walking database of literary information.

She stared back at them, unfazed. 'The pen is mightier than the sword. That was the big standout line.'

'Uh-huh,' Saleda said in disbelief.

'Actually, my brother and I just saw *Les Mis* last summer at the Olney,' Jenna said, an iridescent white flashing in as her inklings began to crystalize and form into a theory. She glanced at Porter, who was sitting at the conference table with his iPhone. 'Hey, Porter. Pull up the Olney Theatre Centre's website and tell me what other productions they've staged in the past year besides *Les Miserables.*'

'Sure thing,' he said, tapping letters on his phone. He scrolled down the page. 'Last season's shows included *Les Mis, A Cat on a Hot Tin Roof, Damn Yankees, A Few Good Men, Rodgers and Hammerstein's Cinderella, Pippin,* and . . . oh, look! *The Importance of Being Earnest.*'

'Could be a coincidence,' Teva said.

'Could be a big fat X marks the spot,' Dodd replied.

It might *be* a coincidence, but it wasn't a bad angle to check out. The theatric Russian violet that had flashed in at the murder scene, the choice of weapons, and the magnitude of the attack for show.

'Teva, get Irv on the line and have him cross-reference all the bank victims and employees for ties to the Olney Theatre Centre. I know this is different from our usual cases and it's most likely the victims were random, but until we have the perps in custody and know exactly how this went down, I'm not ready to write off checking victim profiles for connections. The DC sniper's victims looked random, too, but turned out they were meant to look that way so he could kill his wife and not be a suspect,' Saleda said.

'Doesn't hurt to check all the angles,' Jenna said. 'Victim connections or not, if they met through the theatre, maybe that's how they picked their character or literature piece.'

'Damn,' Teva said.

'Irv's not answering.'

Huh. For Irv, that was unusual. But even though somehow she always subconsciously thought Irv hacked databases, sent them reports, and chugged Monster energy drinks in his sleep, he *was* a real human being and probably needed to go somewhere to buy those energy drinks every once in a while. He *had* said he was running an errand.

'We could just go to this theatre, poke into some of its records ourselves,' Teva suggested.

Saleda shook her head. 'The theatre is an avenue I want to explore, but I'm not going to go traipsing down there to grill a bunch of actors and directors unless we've got something more concrete to go on.'

Grey hummed from her corner chair. 'You have one. For fun. Even the *Earnest* play thinks jobs and everything else should be fun. It says pleasure should be the only reason anyone goes anywhere.' She smiled neatly, watching her fingers slowly unravel a thread on her blouse. 'But at the same time, what M wrote from *Les Miserables* about many tongues talking . . . that isn't a line in the stage show. Only the novel.'

And while Jenna duly noted the latter portion of Grey's statement, it was the first part of it that made pear green flash in.

Trivial. The color for trivial flashed at the moment Grey mentioned the word pleasure in conjunction with *The Importance of Being Earnest* quote, claiming it was the only reason anyone should go anywhere.

A theory whipped around in Jenna's mind. 'If you ask anyone what they do in their lives they consider vital – so important they can't

skip it – most would list stuff like paying bills, going to work, weddings
. . . funerals. Not anything for fun. Fun isn't prioritized.

'The bank crew left us a note and a message. They said to take
trivial things in life very seriously. This group, they're radicals, but
they believe they're intellectually elite. They could just strike
anywhere, set off another attack without warning. I thought at first
the note warning us was just to cause fear, but I think it's more. I
think they're playing a game with us.'

'You mean you think they left us a way to find them if we're smart
enough to figure it out?' Teva said in disbelief.

Jenna smirked. 'A little test. To see if we're worthy. And the theatre
that played two shows associated with our group last year, there's a
chance it's a coincidence. But there's a chance it's not.

'Going to a play would be a trivial leisure activity. Maybe they're
telling us where to find them – or putting us at the starting gate,
anyway.'

Saleda was silent a moment, seeming to consider, before she finally
spoke. 'It wouldn't be the first time a criminal played games with
investigators. Worthy theory. Let's check out the Olney.'

Twenty-one

Irv slammed the door of his bright blue Honda HR-V. The surround-
ings weren't exactly where he'd pictured ending up once he knew
who he was tracking down, but somehow, it fit all the same.

The swooshes of skateboards flying up and down the concrete of
vertical ramps hit his ears, whoops and hollers of teens showing
off for each other on the jumps at the street-skating park inside of
Veteran's Memorial Park. Irv stepped up to the chain-link fence
enclosing the rink, his feet sinking into the grass. He wasn't wearing
the required helmet and pads required to enter the self-maintained
park. Didn't matter. He wasn't there to skate, and he couldn't even
if he had been.

This moment couldn't get any weirder. Not considering the sight
that met him inside the open-flow course. Not that hackers capable
of breaking into the FBI database with Irv's own credentials shouldn't
skateboard. It seemed as good a hobby as any. This one just happened
to be a particularly odd case. It was downright bizarre, so much that
he might've thought the GPS coordinates he'd gotten off the cell
phone might have been wrong, had a certain telltale sign not stood
beside the fence wagging his tail, giving away his pal.

Irv leaned into the fence, fingers twined in the links. 'You're just
full of surprises, Yancy.'

The skater in the neon yellow helmet hopped from his board,
landing deftly despite his metal handicap. He scooped up his plain
black board and trudged toward him. 'Yeah, well, I figured the next
step to add in the bionic man routine would be go-go-Gadget wheels.'

Yancy exited the gate and stepped past Irv to a kid who had to be
around ten, sitting on the bench facing the park. Yancy dug in his
pocket and pulled out some bills, handed them off. 'Thanks, buddy.
See you next time.'

As Yancy turned back to Irv, Irv cocked his head. 'You let just any
kid in a public park watch your dog? I'd have figured some of Jenna's
super-secret protective strategies would've rubbed off on you by now.'

Yancy smiled, squatted beside the brown dachshund, and unscrewed the cap of the water bottle sitting beside the plastic dog bowl. 'Eh, the kid can't get in the park without adult supervision, so one day when I saw them turning him away I made him a deal: watch the sausage while I skate, and I'll supervise while he does. Kid drove a hard bargain. Asked for two dollars per service as an insurance fee in case Oboe bites him. I give him three hoping I'd get lucky and he'd finally kidnap the little bastard.'

Irv chuckled. The guy talked a big game where the dog was concerned, but to be such a pain in Yancy's ass, the two sure seemed inseparable.

'So, what made you take up skating? I wouldn't have figured you'd have a lot of extra time on your hands these days with watching Ayana so much, answering dispatch, and dating,' Irv said.

'Can't be all work and no play, I guess. Decided I needed a hobby that involved something other than sitting in front of my PC while Oboe sits beside me and gets fat. Plus, there's this great coffee shop down the road that thinks I'm a veteran and always gives me free stuff, and Oboe can still do his fat thing,' Yancy said. 'But I figure since you somehow knew I was here, you still spend lots of time in front of *your* PC. All work, Irv. It's not good for you.'

You don't know the half of it.

'Idle hands are the devil's playground,' Irv cut back. He folded his arms. 'Speaking of, you've been busy, Yancy. New skating hobby aside. What I want to know is which was it for? Work or play?'

Here we go.

Yancy fought for focus against the hailstorm of thoughts railing in his mind, willed himself not to break Irv's eye contact. 'Neither.'

Sweat trickled down his neck as he squinted at the tech analyst under the hot Virginia sun. He'd known this would probably happen. Expected it, even. He was good. Bit rusty, but good enough to hack into FBI data, but even then, there were only so many ways to keep from leaving traces, and his best ideas were only ever going to be delay tactics, not magic, particularly with someone as good as Irv dogging his trail.

The image of Oboe running out of CiCi's house with the note tucked under his collar last year flashed into his mind. Then, the picture of Ayana playing on the swing set outside her new preschool. He blinked, squinted to try to hold eye contact with Irv even though the smiling image of Ayana as she held the chain links of the swing tight in her fists with pink-painted fingernails seared forward, threatening his focus.

Not now, cool guy. You practiced this for *her! It shouldn't shake you, damn it!*

Yancy swallowed hard. His gut instinct *had* been to tell Jenna. He'd made that mistake before, and he loved her more than his pride. But then, he'd gotten an e-mail with the picture of Ayana, swinging just feet away from where Yancy knew some combination of he, Charley, Vern, or Victor had stood, standing guard, ridiculous text safe words ready on their fingertips to reassure Jenna that Ayana wasn't within Claudia's grasp. He'd not only had to face the reality that their security was all an illusion of Claudia's making, that the picture was proof that, at any moment, she could swoop in and devastate them, but that a second reality was in play: everything Claudia had revealed to him and imparted to him was part of the game.

The story he'd prepared was decent, for his non-sociopathic self. One involving Jenna's ex-mother-in-law and the court battle over Ayana's collection of her father's life insurance and the files Yancy had supposedly needed to help the case. But somehow, with the moment here, confronted with the impossible cover-up he was about to face – as impressive and intricate as it might be in all the right places – it didn't feel as much the masterpiece of perfect deception it had in theory.

'Come on, man,' Irv pressed. 'You know I'm not walkin' away without knowing why the hell you hacked into secure government databases. I know you enough that I know you're not crazy. The skill to hack into FBI databases itself is proof you aren't stupid.'

God, I hope not. Here goes nothing.

Yancy took a deep breath, opened his mouth, and began to lie.

Twenty-two

As Dodd eased the SUV left to merge on to I-270 off the Capital Beltway, Jenna shifted in the passenger's seat and pressed the button to unlock the keys on her smartphone for the dozenth time. 'Still nothing from Irv,' she reported, staring at the screen. Her message box was empty, the only new activity two missed calls – both from the same unknown number and placed right around the time they left Quantico.

'Even geniuses need a bathroom break now and again,' Dodd replied.

Jenna half-laughed. 'Maybe. But it'd still be nice to know if the cross-check turned up any connections between anyone at the bank scene and people involved at the Olney Theatre before we get there. Give us a better idea where to start. Besides, even with Saleda and Teva staying behind to work the victim profiles, any helpful info from those would get to us twice as fast if they had Irv to expedite the tedious stuff.'

'And the stuff they can't get their hands on without him, too, you mean,' Dodd said, eyes on the road. He nodded. 'Yep. Even the hardest workers need their bathroom breaks.'

'That's what I'm interested in seeing *most* when we get there,' Porter grumbled from the backseat. 'After an hour on the road, I need to find a bathroom before I can even consider a meet and greet.'

'You smell that bad?' Grey said, her voice breezy.

Jenna tensed. While she and Saleda had decided it best she take Grey along, lest the team have to track her down again, and while Jenna never doubted all the ways in which the choice make things easier, it'd complicate them in plenty of others. One of those becoming apparent was Grey's dislike of Porter. While Grey's offhand remarks could be just the product of a thought process akin to blowing bubbles on a summer day, her thoughts weren't always nontoxic fluff.

'What?' Porter said, annoyance in his voice. 'I just need to take a piss, Matilda, not a bubble bath.'

'She knows that,' Jenna said, cutting him off. She shook her head. Grey had learned long ago that people viewing her as loony but harmless meant she could sneak in passive-aggressive jabs at them and get away with it. Eccentric definitely didn't equal naive.

'Well, I've got news for you then, Matilda. Your book game might be on, but your comedy routine needs some work,' Porter replied.

Jenna couldn't see Grey behind her, but she could hear her heavy, quick breathing.

'This must be the place,' Dodd said, making a right-hand turn into the modest parking lot across the street from the green-accented, white building of the Olney Theatre.

He shut the engine off, and they all climbed out. Hopefully whatever hunch they were here on would manifest results fast. The idea the group could've met here made sense with enough clues to give it weight, but this would either be a big break or a big waste of time.

Grey joined Jenna and Dodd as they started toward the theatre, still huffing angrily. Behind them, Porter slammed his door and caught up to them. Grey muttered something undecipherable under her breath.

'Hey, if you can't take it, don't dish it out, brainiac,' Porter said evenly without facing her.

Grey stopped just short of the flight of cement stairs. Jenna's phone rang as Grey whirled to face Porter.

Jenna stepped between them and held a hand up to Porter, her other hand removing her cell from her pocket. 'Please, Porter. Play nice. I'm gonna take this. It might be important.'

Jenna took three long strides away from the group, trying to ignore the man peeking out of the blinds of the window above them who had to be wondering who the heck they were. They hadn't exactly made an appointment. She'd explain after she took this call. She slowed, her heart thundering as she glanced at the phone again. The same unknown number. What if someone was trying to get in touch with her because something was wrong?

As she pressed the button to answer, questions flew through her head. Which safe words had she gotten when Ayana was at school? From who? Who was on duty to pick Ayana up, bring her home?

'Dr Jenna Ramey,' she answered, swallowing hard.

'It's about damned time. I've been trying to get hold of you for over an hour. If I didn't know better, I'd think you must've been on a plane and had it off or something,' a female voice chided matter-of-factly.

The hot coral of a paradise flower in a tropical bouquet flashed in. Reminded her of the shocking pink of boldness, but it was distinct. Brazen. Bold, yes. But confident without shame.

'Um, excuse me,' Jenna said, clutching the phone tighter. 'Who *is* this, and how did you get this number?'

'McKenzie McClendon, *New York Herald*. As for the number, you have your people, I have mine.'

Strawberry red flashed in as Jenna pictured the short, sassy auburn girl-next-door image the papers had splashed all over a few years back when the up-and-comer had chased a wild lead that had turned into the scoop of the century. The more Jenna had heard about the hungry young reporter, she had associated the color with her. She was apparently a firecracker, too – took a bribe to keep quiet, then outed the person responsible for the assassinations of the leaders of the free world anyway, all on the front page.

Jenna let out a half-laugh. *Pushy, too.*

'I'm so sorry, Ms McClendon, but we have no comment for the media at this time.'

'Don't hang up, Dr Ramey. Trust me, you'll regret it,' the cheeky voice replied.

Jenna raised her eyebrows. 'Is that a reporter threatening a federal agent? That wouldn't look pretty on the front page.'

'No, that's a reporter telling a federal agent if she's smart, she'll ix-nay the theatre, turn back around, and come to the parking lot across the street to talk to *me*.'

Jenna whipped around, the hairs on her arms standing up. 'How the hell did you know where we were? And why are you—'

McKenzie cut her off. 'This *is* a high-profile investigation, and I *am* a reporter. Flew in as soon as the bank story broke. I've obviously been following your team's every move since I got into town. Looking for a scoop. Or I *was,* anyway. Point is, you're good at your job. I'm good at mine.'

But Jenna was stuck back at the words where the yellowy-tan hue of butterscotch had flashed in. It was a color that popped in when a casual comment thrown into an ordinary conversation set off Jenna's radars as alluding to something important. 'What do you mean you *were* just a reporter trying to get a scoop? You're not anymore?'

A wicked cackle. 'I don't remember saying 'just a reporter,' but yeah, I guess you could say I've been upgraded to front row seats,' McKenzie said.

Jenna squinted into the distance, first at the parking lot where the team had left the SUV, then to the next closest lot – a tiny rectangle of gravel to the left of the theatre parking lot. A gray sedan was parked facing the road. Sure enough, leaning into it with her hip and holding her phone to her ear was auburn-haired McKenzie McClendon in jeans and hot pink high heels.

McKenzie gave a little wave. 'Well, what are you waiting for? I'm sure the theatre puts on great shows, but I've got something they could never offer you on a weekday afternoon.'

Twenty-three

Jenna and Porter crossed the street, leaving Dodd behind to babysit Grey. From what she knew of McKenzie McClendon, Jenna's hands would be full *enough* dealing with this reporter. She'd have to be an expert juggler to want to add Grey, her made up words, and bird sounds into the mix.

'Why the backup? You think I'm here to kidnap you or something?' McKenzie McClendon said, giving Porter the once-over.

'Can't be too careful,' Porter replied.

The redhead nodded. 'Fair enough.'

'What do you want, McKenzie?' Jenna asked. She didn't mean to be rude, but nevertheless, if the reporter didn't have a darn good reason for inserting herself into this investigation, Jenna was inclined to bring her in for obstruction.

'The same thing you do,' McKenzie said, leaning into her open car window and reaching to the seat.

'Oh, I doubt that,' Jenna said as she exchanged a glance with Porter. Her teammate's hand went to his holster. Girl probably wasn't dangerous, but still, like Porter had said, they couldn't be too careful.

When McKenzie turned back, she had a white envelope in her hand. Her eyes, however, were on Porter's holster . . . and his hand. 'Are you guys always so hostile with informants?'

Jenna and Porter traded looks, this time not in secret. Jenna stared at McKenzie. 'Informants?'

McKenzie shrugged, crossed her arms and leaned against the car again. 'I guess that's what I am now. Maybe witness? I didn't see anything, though, so I'm not sure. But I didn't come to cause trouble. I came to give you an e-mail that was sent to me.'

Salmon flashed in. McKenzie might be telling the truth, but she was withholding something, too.

'What does the e-mail have to do with us?' Jenna asked.

'It's from your bank killers, I believe,' McKenzie replied.

Jenna narrowed her eyes. 'How do you know?'

McKenzie smiled, as if the question amused her. 'The e-mail address. It came from yourbankstory2_14_1895.'

Porter laughed. 'Was it from at-yourfairygodmother-dot-com?'

McKenzie stared him down. Without flinching, she said, 'Actually, it's from Yahoo.' She turned to Jenna. 'And you can waste time questioning if it's real if you want to, but based on the scene at that bank, I'm guessing you're already worried something else is coming. So I'll save you the time. It's real.'

Jenna stepped forward to take the envelope out of McKenzie's hand, but the reporter pulled it back.

'Not so fast,' the reporter said.

The salmon flashed in, followed by midnight blue. The color Jenna used to see when Charley held her favorite CD hostage until she agreed to let him have the TV remote, or when Dad used a 9:30 pm bedtime to negotiate Charley into the bathtub when he was little. This was what McKenzie had been withholding. The letter was a bargaining chip.

'Fine,' Jenna said, stilling. 'What do you want?'

'An exclusive,' McKenzie said.

'With the killers?'

'With you.'

Jenna froze, ice in her veins. The reporter wanted her to talk publicly. About Claudia, of course. What else? McKenzie McClendon was already famous, could have any story she wanted. This was a terror investigation, but after what she'd covered, maybe it was just another case to her. She was interested in a scoop no one else could have.

Jenna took a deep breath, willing herself not to show her emotions.

'Fine,' Jenna said. 'After this case is over.'

McKenzie nodded, stepping forward. 'After this case.'

Jenna snatched the envelope away, and McKenzie smirked before turning back to her car

'Thanks, Jenna,' McKenzie said out of her open window, her car rolling past Jenna and Porter as they walked back toward Dodd and Grey. 'And I wasn't trying to play dirty. I have just really wanted to meet you for a long time.'

'It looks like a bunch of gibberish,' Porter said, leaning over Jenna's shoulder from the backseat of the SUV. With the letter in play, suddenly the wild goose chase into the Olney Theatre and the people connected to it wasn't the best use of their time.

'Can't be,' Jenna replied, the canary yellow of relevance flashing in. She scanned the words again:

McKenzie McClendon,

I do not write to you as so many might, appealing to your ambition, drawing on society's fear, or using some boorish, amateurish tactic like blackmail to encourage, incentivize, or intimidate you into becoming a platform for my propaganda. Yes, journalism is a needed profession by those pursuing controversial goals . . . by people such as myself who have been thrust into leadership positions to spur on others with the same aims. However, I do not need or desire a parrot.

What I need is a voice, and one with a brain behind it.

While the profession of journalism has long been hailed a noble and ethical field, fewer and fewer in the station will watch and listen, learn and think before they decide. That is, *if* they decide of their own accord. We may not live in a world of burned TRANSGRESSORS, but ignorance – willful or not – complacency, and coercion are alive and well today. Each helps our very own current culture of UNSPOKEN WORDS to masquerade as liberty.

I am not so unreasonable or out of touch that I would expect you to take my honest words as such, automatically view me objectively. In fact, most would consider it appropriate and normal to react to this letter in the opposite fashion, vilify me, and disregard the correspondence entirely. So, trust me when I tell you that if your initial reaction is that very natural one I described, I will not take offense. On the surface, it would be logical of you to assume me a monster. And because of that, I would be insolent to ask you to consider that perhaps I am not fully a monster. That of the two natures of man, I can be rightly either. I can be radically both.

I do not ask you to accept my reasoning that us being in the middle of a raging war should justify allowing the beast inside me – the one inside every man – to come out. That the only Beasts to be feared are those without reason. I only ask in the coming days that you do not abandon your own ideas as some men think all men must. I've read your columns. Know your famous stories. You were able to ignore the din and the raging current to report the valid and not just the popular. The only thing I ask of you, Ms McClendon, is that you remain UNEQUAL to your peers. I ask in the dark days that are coming not for you to think me a hero, but rather, for you to unleash your boundless curiosity, look for a nice tunnel where you can stow away and write . . . formulate your own opinions about the coming events. whatever those opinions may be. Ignore those too cowardly to seek the truth alone; by watching and listening objectively, you may on some level come to understand that these atrocities are not about the people. The people are not the point. They were – and will only be – a part of the sickness. An aspect of the sickness we will hurry to step over, for we do not kill *people*. We slaughter the principle.

We killed the pipe dream, Ms McClendon. And we are going to kill it again. Too many cowards won't, McKenzie, and that is why we must.

So, what's it going to be then, eh, Ms McClendon? It's your decision, and if we find that tunnel in which to think and hide and write, know that you can be one of the few people who still respects that at all costs and all turns, we must be allowed to make our own choices. You can truly ask yourself whether you believe in making *your* own moral choices. Most people do not have the luxury and are simply told the answer. You still have the ability to make choices – and the ability to remind others over and over again that if they do not ask themselves the same question, and often, they may end up without the option.

The capitalized words in the middles of sentences jumped out at Jenna, seemed to be chosen at random: Transgressors, Unspoken

Words, Unequal. There was something she couldn't quite put her finger on about the sentence with the, 'eh,' in it, too. It didn't fit with the careful, almost overly articulate tone of the other word choices.

She pushed away the light khaki, yellowish color she associated with things seeming out of place, sticking out given the circumstances. The words did, but she already knew that. She needed the color behind it that was trying to push through.

Indigo flashed in. *Deliberate.* She kept scanning:

> . . . My only hope, Ms McClendon, is that you will be a great source of comfort and support and in time, tell the truth as only someone as inimitable, impartial, and undaunted as you can. For I *have* made my decision. Many may think I've lost my humanity in trying to protect our society's potential, but I shall not allow them to turn me into something *other* than a human being where I have power of choice no longer. I shall not lose the power to take meaningful action. At some point, the time for reversing course will be over, and in the meantime, much more irreparable, painful damage will be inflicted.
>
> So, we are coming. I will not tell you when or where, only that we are coming. I ask you to be the one who is vigilant, Ms McClendon. It is hidden, but here. Don't wonder what makes me say that. Because whether they realize it or not, we are not the enemy, but the savior. And when you see it, tell them that, they may decide for themselves.
>
> For all the freedoms our country promotes, we are living in a world where the only freedom we truly have is the freedom to choose how we will react to the ignorant rationalizations that limit our freedoms After all, in this World we live in, we find only strength in numbers. United we stand in those, and divided, we perish.
>
> I trust you will do the right thing.

'The person seems to want McKenzie McClendon to transmit their message. Implies if she only understands it, she'll come to be on their side, then pass it on to the general public as truth,' Jenna said.

Irreparable damage. We are coming.

'It also threatens more attacks, like the note at the bank,' she continued.

She glanced back down and read the passage threatening that they were coming again. There was something . . .

This time, she forced herself to stop focusing on the threat and to pay more attention to the words after it. *It is hidden, but here.*

Lapis lazuli flashed in once again. Classical intelligence.

'My God,' Jenna muttered. 'The arrogant bastards.'

'What? What are you talking about?' Dodd asked.

'I think . . .' Jenna said, pausing to assess the lapis lazuli once more to be sure. 'I think they've given a clue in this letter.'

'Huh?' Porter asked.

'How'd you come to that?' Dodd asked.

Grey's whistling was loud in Jenna's ears. 'Don't make me say it.'

'Ah, Captain Crayon again,' Dodd replied.

'They're terrorists. They don't want to get caught. It's not in the profile. Why hide a clue in a letter the cops would see?'

Jenna ignored Dodd and twisted in her seat to look at Porter. 'They didn't hide it in a letter for cops. They hid it in one for a reporter. One known for getting to the bottom of things and not necessarily working with authorities to do it. Besides, the person at the head of this is most likely a narcissist. They'd believe no one would find it anyway.'

'Or,' Dodd said without looking at them, 'they designed it so that only someone they considered *worthy* could find it. Hid it like only they would, a test for someone who might be looking.'

Jenna smirked as the orchid of elitism flashed in. *Not a bad theory at all.* 'They consider themselves the intellectually elite, gave a reporter the chance to land a huge scoop if she was one of them. Thought she might be because of her past.'

Jenna scoured the letter in her lap once more. She had a good idea what they needed to look for within it, but since that would mean handing it off, first she needed to figure out what to do with the information once they located it.

Toward the end of the letter, her eyes landed on a single passage:

After all, in this World we live in, we find only strength in numbers.
United we stand in those, and divided, we perish.

Canary yellow flashed in her mind.

Jenna wasn't sure what, but numbers had something to do with it. She just knew.

She sucked in a hard breath. This could go well, or it could be a nightmare. But she didn't have a choice. *They* didn't. If the bank terrorists had left a clue to their next attack, they needed to get to it, and fast.

Jenna twisted again to look into the backseat, this time at Grey, who was still whistling a tuneless composition of her own making and staring out the window. 'Grey?'

Grey's whistling continued, though she did turn her head.

'I need you to look at this letter. It contains – I think – literary references. I need to know what they are,' Jenna said, passing the paper back. Remembering the strange, randomly capitalized words and the deliberate indigo that had flashed in when she'd read them, she added, 'Make sure to look at everything, but especially at the words capitalized in the middles of sentences.'

Still tweeting the shrill notes like she was some sort of kooky bird, Grey held out a hand and took the paper from Jenna.

'And Grey?' Jenna said.

Grey looked up, eyes inquisitive, mouth still bleating.

'The references have something to do with numbers. If you know what those are – or have any idea what numbers any of them could possibly be associated with,' she clarified, realizing that asking Grey to tell them what she *knew* would be a mistake that might cost them hearing any of her more unsure thoughts that could lead them in a meaningful direction, 'I need you to tell me those ideas, too.'

Grey nodded and looked back down at the paper, still whistling away.

Twenty-four

After what seemed like hours — even though it could've only been minutes from the moment Grey had stopped whistling long enough to request a pen — Grey's scribbling paused. 'I think the bank man has Ayn Rand by his toilet.'

Jenna forced back a grimace. Maybe if Grey hadn't just defaced the heck out of a piece of evidence, it'd be easier. She poised a pen at a scrap of paper she'd dug out of the SUV glove box. 'Whatcha got?'

'The last lines of paragraph three,' Grey said, and without looking, Jenna could tell she was sucking on the end of her pen, '"*Each helps our very own current culture of UNSPOKENWORDS to masquerade as liberty.*" *Unspoken Words* is capitalized, drawing attention to it. The unspoken word in *Anthem* by Ayn Rand was "ego."'

'OK,' Jenna said, scribbling notes impatiently. 'Does that have anything to do with a number?'

Grey clicked her tongue. '. . . *masquerade as liberty* . . . Yes. In the book, the main character falls in love with The Golden One, which he considers her real name. But her actual name was Liberty 5-3000.'

Jenna jotted it down. 'And that's the first reference?'

'Don't bounce your deductions,' Grey said.

Porter stared at her, wide-eyed, then looked to Jenna and blinked, confused. 'What the heck does that mean?'

'She means don't jump to conclusions,' Jenna said quickly, not wanting to lose Grey's attention or train of thought. For whatever reason, Grey wasn't giving her the references in order, but either way, they needed to get them. 'What's before that, then, Grey?'

'If he was in love with the Golden One, couldn't the number be *One*? Especially if Liberty was masquerading as it—'

'Shut up!' Jenna snapped at Porter, then turned back to Grey.

Grey glared at Porter. After a long second, she spoke, still staring awkwardly at Porter. 'That makes the fifth reference — the capitalized *Unequal* in paragraph five — an arrow pointing to the main character in the same book, *Anthem*. Equality 7-2521.'

In the same way Grey's odd speech patterns had come to make sense to Jenna, the explanation for how the numbers associated with the literary references seemed to fit. Despite the fact that they were all over the place in the order she was looking at them. Hopefully Jenna could question Grey later to make sure her reasoning was sound, but then again, when was Grey's reasoning ever going to be?

'OK,' Jenna said as she wrote the last two digits of the most recent number. 'What next?'

'Go down in that same sentence grouping—'

'Paragraph,' Jenna muttered out the side of her mouth to translate for Dodd and Porter.

'You see, "*Ignore those too cowardly to speak the truth alone*"?'

'Yes,' Jenna replied, scrolling down on the picture she'd snapped of the letter on her phone.

'Another *Anthem* toilet moment,' Grey said, laughing at her own little joke.

'OK, and what's the number?'

'In the story, a certain character who runs things says no one is allowed to think himself smarter than anyone else—'

'That's a heck of a note, considering the elitist pricks doing this,' Porter snorted.

Grey shot him a look, continuing, 'And no one can claim to have the keys to the truth by themselves.'

'Keys?' This time, Porter kept his bewilderment to a desperate, barely-there whisper beside Jenna. Grey didn't even notice him, thankfully, and she kept going.

'Collective 0-0009.'

Jenna scratched the reference down. 'Next.'

'Go back two streaks up in the same word pile—'

'Two lines up, same paragraph,' Jenna translated fast.

'Why did we skip over it in the first place?' Porter mumbled angrily.

Grey's mouth twitched as though she wanted to frown deeper, but it couldn't go any farther. '*The tunnel to stow away and write* is there. That's referred to on the very first page of Anthem, so I'm guessing number one.'

'The tunnel comes up again, doesn't it?' Jenna said, highlighter yellow, the color of repetition, flashing in as she heard the word.

'Yes,' Grey replied. 'Getting there. Go down to the second word group of the eighth word group—'

'The second paragraph of the eighth paragraph?' Porter cut in, now genuinely trying to pick up on Grey's lingo.

'The second sentence of the eighth paragraph,' Jenna said, still focusing intently on Grey. *Please don't get mad and stop on us.*

Grey turned slowly back to the paper, pausing to cut her eyes at Porter once more, but he was oblivious, scrolling madly through his own copy of the photo Jenna had sent him and Dodd, trying to catch up. 'This time, it says "*if* we *find that tunnel.*" The time before that said only to *look for* a tunnel and then the word *you* parades on,' Grey explained.

Grey had such a sharp grasp on the written word. *You might've made a really good profiler if you had the same grasp on the spoken ones.*

'I take it you were able to figure something out based on that?' Jenna said.

'The *we* in regards to the tunnel. The *we find*, in particular. In *Anthem*, Equality 7-2521 uses the tunnel to be alone, but in the story, the narrative has him referring to himself as *we*. That's on page one.'

'She can remember the word "narrative" but can't remember jump to conclusions?' Porter whispered.

'This second time the letter talks about the tunnel, I think the writer used *we* instead of a singular pronoun—'

'Singular pronoun!' Porter whispered, louder this time.

'*Forget it!*' Grey abruptly snapped, her voice spiking to full volume in the closed SUV cab. In the ensuing stunned silence, she leaned forward and snatched the pen and paper out of Jenna's hands. 'I'll do it myself.'

Jenna shot Porter as much venom as she could muster in a single glare.

Grey cast her eyes back down on the letter and began scribbling as she worked. It wasn't long before the whistling resumed.

The silence continued for some time, with Grey never slowing down. Predictably, it was Dodd who finally ventured to speak. 'Are we close to finishing up, Ms Hechinger, or . . .'

Carnation pink flashed in. Both her own *and* Dodd's impatience.

'Done with the quotes from *Lord of the Flies*, *Dr Jekyll and Mr Hyde*, *Crime and Punishment*, *Diary of a Young Girl*, and *The Iceman Cometh*. Only one story left,' Grey said, looking up, her rapid blinking in

contrast to the serene look of composure on her face. Her mouth
set, she stared at Porter. 'If you're not too busy assessing my mental
capacity, Agent, I'd like to continue with the analysis of the evidence.'
Jenna almost snorted and clapped her hand over her mouth. Beside
her, Dodd's own mouth hung open as he laughed long, hard chuckles,
and Porter sat dumbfounded in the backseat.

'Skip to after the question mark and start with the word *know*.'

Grey stopped talking and began whistling as she looked away from
them and out the window as if to say, 'Go ahead. I'll wait.' So, Jenna
scanned the passage she was referring to:

> So, what's it going to be then, eh, Ms McClendon? It's your
> decision, and if we find that tunnel in which to think and hide
> and write, know that you can be one of the few people who
> still respects that at all costs and all turns, we must be allowed
> to make our own choices. You can truly ask yourself whether
> you believe in making *your* own moral choices. Most people do
> not have the luxury and are simply told the answer. You still
> have the ability to make choices—and the ability to remind
> others over and over again that if they do not ask themselves
> the same question, and often, they may end up without the
> option.

Jenna looked up to see Dodd and Porter had both finished reading,
too, but Grey was still politely giving them time. Jenna cleared her
throat. 'Finished.'

Grey stopped whistling, turned back to them. 'That whole group
of words is *about* the book. *About* the question,' she said, her eyes
lighting up.

This was the most excited Jenna had seen Grey yet, but she wasn't
following her former patient. She hated to burst that enthusiastic
bubble since Grey was staring at them like she was waiting for them
to praise her for how clever she was or nod enthusiastically, having
seen the exciting possibility she had, too. But time . . .

'How do you mean, Grey?' Jenna asked.

Grey's bright expression turned crestfallen. She folded her lips in
to her mouth. 'Well, it's one of the story's themes, isn't it? The ability
of humanity to make its own moral choices?'

Jenna nodded, pretending to follow. Damn, it had been so long since she'd read that book in college 'OK, right. And the main character . . .' Hopefully, it would prompt Grey into giving them a refresher since the two guys seemed lost, too.

'Alex, right,' Grey nodded, seeming reinvigorated that *someone* was back with her. 'Part One has him able to make a choice between good and evil.'

'Before he and his friends go out and commit crimes,' Dodd filled in.

Jenna could've high-fived him as Grey nodded excitedly.

'Yes! Part Two, it's like the passage. He can't ask himself the question. Doesn't have the *luxury*,' Grey said, emphasizing the word from the letter. 'He's convicted.'

'So the State has taken on the role of making decisions about his moral behavior for him, in a way. He doesn't have a choice of committing more crimes in jail,' Dodd said.

'Tell that to half the criminals we've put in the penitentiary,' Porter grumbled.

'But he really doesn't have the option in the book. He's conditioned,' Jenna said, finally remembering parts of the plotline.

Grey smiled. 'Yes. Which is why Part Three's question about what it's going to be ties shoelaces into the book. It's dragging a big, fat yellow highlighter across the way the moral choices have evolution monkey-ed over the pages. The conditioning has given him no options. He doesn't have an identity to be stolen. Just to be used.'

Dodd nodded. 'I think what Ms Hechinger means is that without the option to choose morality, he's like a machine. In the book, it's apparent he can now be used as a tool for people in power to get what they want. His only choice is to give it to them or commit suicide. He tries suicide.'

Grey pointed at Dodd, a reward. 'But it doesn't work. Eventually, the government undoes the conditioning—'

'Making the final chapter's question about whether or not he'll choose to be evil now that he has the chance to make his own moral choices again,' Jenna filled in, still not sure why this told Grey anything about the reference in the letter or where to find the corresponding number the writer had intended.

'Read the word group after "*know*" again. The letter says to remind others "*over and over again*," talks about the ability to "*ask themselves the same question, and often.*" It's talking about the question *itself.* The one it knows is said in the book four times. The number *this* time is four!'

Jenna didn't ask for more proof. Her gut said to trust Grey's weird process the same way she asked the team to trust her own. She jotted the number.

'OK,' Grey said. 'Last note.'

'Praise Thor,' Porter said.

'Go down one large letter grouping—'

'Paragraph,' Porter mumbled.

'—Part of the way through. Read "*I shall not allow them to turn me into something other than a human being where I have power of choice no longer.*" This one's easy after reading about the themes earlier, because it's mirroring a direct quote.'

'Which quote, Grey?'

Or, rather, what page number?

'"*They have turned you into something other than a human being. You have no power of choice any longer.*" Page 169.'

Jenna jotted the number, then looked at her clusterfuck of scrap paper with its numbers not in order of where in the letter they were given, though she'd tried hard to keep track. *Grey, I don't know if you're a genius or a complete idiot.*

'So, we have a list of fifteen numbers. They don't readily point to anything in particular, but we're assuming they must,' Porter said.

'The dashes in the names of the *Anthem* characters could be relevant,' Dodd suggested. 'What types of numbers have dashes?'

'Phone numbers, social security numbers . . .' Jenna threw out, still writing.

'Birthdays . . .' Porter added.

'Or for that matter, what numbers are fifteen digits?' Dodd said.

'You don't have fifteen digits. You have fifteen numbers,' Grey said, staring out the window.

'Shit,' Dodd said. 'So how many *digits* do we have?'

Jenna tallied them. 'Forty-four.'

Porter groaned. 'No way we're supposed to use *all* forty-four. Not unless it's the longest GPS coordinate set on earth.'

'They'd have to be exact to a decimal point I don't think even Google Maps would record,' Jenna said, thinking.

'Some of them must be more important than others,' Grey

mused absently, now tracing a cloud on the window glass with her finger.

The Russian violet Jenna kept seeing anytime she thought about the killers' messages flashed in, followed immediately by canary yellow: relevance. The quote in the bank note!

'It is important to be earnest,' Jenna mumbled, flipping the scrap of paper over and scribbling furiously.

'What's going on?' Dodd asked. 'You have something?'

'Shh,' Jenna said, working fast. 'I don't know yet.'

She wrote the phrase the bank killers had told Ashlee Haynie to relay. Next to it, she wrote the name of the play the reference was meant to invoke: *The Importance of Being Earnest.*

The phrases were similar but obviously different. 'Grey, what does the word 'earnest' mean exactly? As many definitions as you can think of,' Jenna said. She knew the definition, but for some reason, she felt like hearing Grey's words might help the thought click.

'Earnest,' Grey said in a sing-songy voice. 'Resulting from or showing intense conviction. Serious in intention, purpose, or effort. Showing sincerity of feeling. Depth of feeling. Seriously important. Demanding attention. You want the noun or just the describer?'

'No, no. Adjective is plenty,' Jenna said, staring at the two phrases.

'Whatcha thinking, Doc?' Dodd asked quietly.

Jenna didn't take her eyes from the paper. 'If every word was chosen with intense purpose. Zeal. Intense *effort*, then would we be doing them due diligence if we discarded the fact that each *letter* might also be seriously important?'

Dodd leaned over and looked at the scrap, and she felt Porter peeking over her shoulder.

'The letter *did* say "strength in numbers." Maybe the number of how many letters are in the title but not in the phrase?' Porter suggested.

'Or vice versa. The number of letters in the phrase but not the title,' Dodd said.

Jenna glanced at the scrap. 'That would leave very few numbers. Why go to the trouble of including fifteen literary references and forty-four digits between them if you only need to hide three measly digits?'

'Ass-holery? These people *did* just slaughter a bunch of innocent people. I doubt our convenience is on their mind,' Porter said.

Jenna shook her head.

Dodd sighed heavily. 'Stop thinking with the part of your brain that's annoyed by this situation and think like a profiler. They've given us everything they have because they think a certain way. Because they *are* a certain way. Get your head out of your ass and do your job, Rookie!'

Through the thick silence, a shrill giggle cut the air.

Every head turned toward Grey.

She shrugged. 'Someone had to say it.'

Jenna smirked, turning back to the matter at hand. But it was Porter who spoke first when the silence broke.

'They're elitists. Intellectually superior in their minds, though they are obviously classically educated and most likely have some reason to believe it. So, high IQs and elitism suggests a degree of narcissism. We talked before about how they hid the clues in the letter so someone could find them if they were as smart as them, even going as far as to suggest they wanted McClendon to do so. They left another piece at the crime scene, though. If *The Importance of Being Earnest* and their reference to it is the crack to whatever the code is with these, how would McClendon know it? She wasn't privy to that information.'

Jenna shook her head, confused. 'They brought her in because, in the past, she's been smart enough to get answers. Broken rules. Maybe they figured she'd *get* privy to it.'

'Nope,' Grey said from the backseat.

Jenna shifted to look at her ex-patient, still tracing abstract shapes in trails of fingertip oil on the window. 'What do you mean, Grey?'

'Maybe the reporter would've gotten the memo from the bank in her reporter-ing, but she didn't need it. They gave it to her.'

Jenna sat up straighter. 'What? Where?'

Grey now turned from the window, held up the scribbled on printout of the e-mail McKenzie had given them. She pointed at the top. 'The address. YourBankStory2_14_1895. That's when *The Importance of Being Earnest* opened in London.'

Lapis Lazuli flashed in, followed once again by that familiar, showy Russian violet. What her ex-patient was pointing out made sense. 'Grey, you're amazing,' Jenna said.

When she had marked the two phrases as they'd decided she should, she stared at her paper:

'IT IS IMPORTANT TO BE EARNEST'

~~THE~~^{LEAVEOUT3} <u>IMPORTAN~~CE~~</u>^{LEAVEOUT2} O~~F~~^{LEAVEOUT1} ~~BEING~~^{LEAVEOUT3}

EARNEST

TAKE 8 TAKE 1 TAKE 2 TAKE 7

'Take a picture of that,' Jenna instructed. 'I'm going to forget it entirely when I flip this paper over.'

Porter snapped a photo on his phone, and Jenna turned the scrap over, her list of numbers staring back at her. Porter read her own formula to her from the picture he'd taken, and Jenna marked the numbers as he went. *Leave out three. Take eight. Leave out two. Take one.*

When they finished, Jenna could barely read her own writing:

~~5T~~

5-<u>3000</u>

<u>95</u>

1<u>4</u>~~7~~

~~7~~-2<u>5</u>2<u>1</u>

~~T~~

~~0~~-~~0~~<u>00</u>9

<u>274</u>

2<u>1</u>4

3

4-8818

4

11

169

207

'So, what about everything after the two in two hundred and four-teen?' Dodd asked.

'For that matter, what the hell just happens to be eighteen digits?' Porter asked.

Jenna shook her head. She honestly wasn't sure. She just had to trust they were on to something.

'Let's hope Irv can tell us that,' she said, and she whipped out her phone and dialed.

As she stared at the numbers on the paper while she said a silent prayer for Irv would answer, Russian violet flashed in again. It had many times since the bank.

The bank was for show. The living witness, the warning note. And now this letter was too. She wasn't sure what the performance would be, but these numbers had been meticulously laid out so that *somebody* could have a ticket.

Twenty-five

'Let me get this straight. Porter's sending me this picture, and I'm just supposed to "find something." Anything. With absolutely no direction whatsoever,' Irv's voice said through Yancy's headset.

Typing flew across Yancy's screen. He'd spent the better part of the day with Irv setting up the backdoor access into the tech analyst's office rig. Even now that the link was established, he still chewed his lip, all nerves, and reminded himself for the hundred thousandth time that Irv himself was the one who would catch him at this, and he had the man on his side.

At best, when Yancy had spewed his tale of woe at the skate park, in his wildest dreams he'd hoped to avoid jail time. Irv had listened silently, face devoid of any expression that might have given a clue as to how it was going over, until Yancy had fallen silent, exhausted and defeated.

'OK,' Irv had said.

'OK as in you'll bring Oboe to visit me in jail at least once a month?'

'OK, as in, that's good enough. I'm not going to rat you out. I'm going to offer you a job. And if you accept, I have only one rule: I won't tell Jenna what you did if you won't tell Jenna you're working for me.'

'What?' Yancy's brain had turned to oatmeal. For some reason, the first thought that had come to mind, of all the countless thoughts he could have used to try to cope with the fucked up twist of a crazy thing he had just heard, was that he should warn Irv how shitty not telling important things to Jenna always turned out to be.

Irv's hands flapped at his side in a shrug. 'I didn't come here to find my reason to send you off to prison. I already had that, man. I came here looking for you to give me a reason not to use it. You've done that. For now, I choose to believe you did what you did for a good reason, and I think you're a talented guy. Too talented to be wasted on a desk job at emergency dispatch. Not when you coming along now is so convenient for me.'

The man had secrets.

Irv had a job for Yancy, for sure, and that involved teaching him a lot more about the FBI's databases than he'd had to know to hack into them. For this one, for instance, he had to know everything Irv did.

Which meant that now, to keep Irv from telling Jenna and Saleda and The Department of Homeland Security about his attempt at the Ocean's Eleven of FBI data breaches, he sat at his own home office connected to Irv's fancy shmancy FBI office computer systems via a remote setup, intent on learning everything he could. Now that he knew what Irv wanted to do, the benefits of the gig seemed two-fold: he'd walk away from the breach, and it presented him even more opportunity to dig into Claudia's little favor and find out what she was *really* doing. Ensure Jenna really didn't have anything to worry about.

Not to mention, his newfound mentor had good reasons. Better than his, actually.

A new window popped up on Yancy's – Irv's – screen, this time, a message to Yancy: JENNA AND TEAM ONLINE. SENDING EIGHTEEN RANDOM DIGITS. THEY NEED ME TO 'FIND SOMETHING.'

Irv's laugh came through the headset. 'I'll take the gig, but only because it's my job, and I'm game for a challenge. Hang tight.' Then, 'I'm off.'

The last words were for Yancy. He gulped, adjusting his headset. Just knowing Jenna had just been on the line made his ears hot. Maybe the FBI wouldn't find out about their remote setup – after all, like Irv had said, he was the one whose job it was to look for that kind of thing – but Yancy couldn't help but feel like, somehow, Jenna would sense his presence through Irv's phone to his computer screen and all the way to him sitting here with Oboe asleep where normally his metal hook foot would be if it wasn't off right now.

'Eighteen digits, huh? Not a bank account, not—'

'Hm. No, not a *bank* account,' Irv said, and windows popped up all over the screen.

Yancy struggled to keep up with what Irv was doing visually, but the one thing he wasn't privy to in that office was the inside of Irv's brain. 'Buddy, hey. Give a bro a break. At least give me a vision. I can follow along with the subtitles, but I have to know what language they're in.'

'Sorry, man,' Irv said as windows and writing continued popping up and flying across the screen. 'Bank account gave me an idea. These bastards might've last been in a bank, but I'd be willing to bet they've spent a lot *more* time in libraries.'

Yancy watched in awe as Irv pulled a few flashy moves, library data from various systems within a hundred-mile radius of the bank crime scene scrolling across his vision faster than he could keep up.

Yancy screencapped an image of one of the segments of text that seemed to be the eighteen digits Irv was looking for, left it open in the corner of his screen to reference as the system tried to throw out any and all combinations of them.

'Whoa, stop!' Yancy said, noticing the numbers on his screenshot and the numbers scrolling in another window sync up, forming a pattern.

The text in another window stopped as Irv halted typing. 'Whatcha got?'

'The numbers in the far right database. Whatever library that is, that's our location. All of the card numbers start with 3 0009. Those are the first five digits of our eighteen!'

Irv clicked on the far right window with the matching numbers, and it burst in front of the others. 'I'll be damned,' he said. 'Every card here only has fourteen digits, but let's give it a whirl.'

The keys Irv hit manifested on Yancy's screen. 'Could it be that easy? As easy as them being in order?'

Irv continued typing, windows shooting up all over the screen again. 'Hey, sometimes the simplest answer is the most likely. Besides, from what I hear about what it took to *get* these numbers to me, if they hid this bitch in a code so only the worthy could find it, the fact that we have the digits to plug them in makes us worthy.'

The search done for the first fourteen digits of the eighteen, Irv's fancy footwork had yielded a single result now glowing at Yancy from his own computer screen: a picture of a library card.

Irv's voice cracked in Yancy's ears. 'Shut up now, I'm on the phone.' Then, 'Hey, Dr Dangerous. I had to try a few things, but I've got something for you. Head back toward Bethesda. I'm sending you an address.'

Twenty-six

After about forty minutes on the highway and ten minutes too many of Grey's whistling, Jenna led the group from the SUV down the sidewalk toward the building that housed the Suellen B. Holloway Memorial Library, which just *happened* to be attached to an elementary school in Falls Church, Virginia.

'Google Maps informs me we could hit a nice, spacious public library in this area approximately . . . I don't know, every time we *turn around*, but these creeps send us to an elementary school's media center,' Porter whispered to Jenna as they walked. 'You think this is some kind of sick threat?'

Jenna's throat tightened, and for a moment, Ayana's smiling face popped to mind, the expression the exact one she'd been wearing when Jenna had ducked out of dropping her off in her classroom to book it toward the bloody bank scene left by the killers. She stopped walking, her eyes on the ground.

Bloody handprints. Charley's face, blue and pale. So limp next to the toilet. Footsteps! Go! Run!

Charley!

'Whoa, cowgirl,' Dodd's voice jogged her back to reality, his hands clasping her biceps on either side, firm.

It felt good. She hadn't even realized until his steady pressure had rooted her that she'd been swaying on the spot.

She shook the thought away, breathed in and out, two deep, cleansing breaths, shaping her lips into a thin O so she'd be forced to exhale more slowly than her rapid heartbeat told her to. After a few seconds, she nodded to no one in particular. Opened her eyes.

'I'm OK.'

Dodd squeezed her right shoulder, and they all continued for the building. If the location *was* a threat, time was of the essence.

Stop worrying. A is safe.

I think.

They passed through the glass doorway and were met by a young, attractive blonde woman with a grin so huge and eyes so wide and bright, either she'd just downed a whole case of Red Bull or she was a fembot.

'Hi, there! I'm Hattie Zimmerman. I'm the media specialist here at Eagle Stone Elementary.'

Dodd introduced them all, and Jenna shook hands with Hattie Zimmerman when it was her turn. She took in the plump, rosy cheeks, the eager-to-help demeanor that seemed to exude from every pore the same way the uncanny sheen from her skin did.

Dodd finished by presenting Grey as a special guest consultant on the case.

If it was possible, Hattie Zimmerman smiled even wider and more intensely at the mention of Grey's expertise in linguistics and literature. 'It is such an honor! My parents just never have understood why I chose the career I did. You know what they say, though. You have to do what you love.' She turned her back, waved them along. 'Come on over to the desk. Not sure what exactly y'all are gonna need from me, but I'll do my best to accommodate in any way I can.'

The group followed Hattie's curvy hourglass frame past tables and chairs set on colorful rugs, then several rows of waist-high bookshelves. Jenna fleetingly thought of whipping her phone out and shooting Charley a quick text to check on Ayana but fought it. A was fine. She'd checked in with all three parties on patrol twice since meeting McKenzie McClendon in the parking lot and gotten the all-clear responses. *Concentrate.*

The round service counter that apparently served as the hub of the media center came into view. As Hattie slipped through one of the swinging doors and had a seat at the first of two inset cubicles, Porter caught up to Jenna and propped his elbows on the counter.

'You have to do what you love?' he said. 'I wish someone had told me that. I love eating bacon.'

Jenna looked around for Grey, expecting a jab, but Grey had wandered over to one of the shelves they'd passed and was now seated on the floor with her legs crisscrossed, a colorful picture book about butterflies open on her lap. Jenna turned back to see Hattie continuing to peck away at keys on the computer.

Finally, she tapped a key hard, then turned the monitor to face them, saying, 'There! You should be all set. This is the library card account your data analyst requested, and if you scroll through, you can view all activity on the card. When it was applied for, when received, which books were checked out, in, any late fees, etc. I still don't entirely understand how it'll help, but I guess that's why we leave it to the professionals.'

Hattie slipped through the little doorway but scooted a stool inside the command center to prop the door from clicking shut. 'Anyhoo, feel free to go on in, peruse, find whatever you need. If you run into something you need my help with, holler.'

As Hattie strolled away carrying an armful of books to return to their individual homes, Jenna entered the library command center and sat behind the computer. Irv had figured out the eighteen digits were this fourteen digit library card number and the four leftover digits after you took away the fourteen for the card were the pin number on the account. They'd have to figure out the next steps, but before they could do that, Jenna pressed Saleda's speed dial on her smartphone. She needed to relay some info, and she also needed orders.

'What do you have?' Saleda asked as she picked up.

Jenna relayed all the information she could about the individual the library card was registered to. Name, birthdate, mailing address, phone numbers, e-mail address, and then some.

'Irv sent you the picture, right?' Jenna asked.

'I have an image of the whole card on my tablet, and yes, he also sent a picture of the card's owner. You think Paul Neary is involved with the terrorists?'

Jenna stood up and paced in the confines of the round media center hub. 'No, I really don't,' she said, picturing the clean-cut face of the middle-aged, balding guy with sandy-colored sideburns who they now knew had taught sixth grade Pre-Algebra here at Eagle Stone Elementary for seven years and counting. 'I have Irv checking on him in depth, but no. I'd seriously doubt any of our UNSUBS even know the guy. If they made us dig through a letter so loaded with code that you can't find it for all the code, it wouldn't be their style to bring us straight to them.'

'Go ahead and send Porter to his classroom to interview him just in case. You and Dodd can tackle whatever you need to do there. Which, speaking of, do you have any idea what that is?'

'Frankly, I was hoping you'd have some ideas,' Jenna sighed, plopping down in the computer chair. 'I'm brainstorming, but I'm at a loss so far.'

'Let's hang up so you can send jock boy out on his mission. That'll free up two brains to think easier. Teva and I will dig through the library records as soon as Irv sends the copy he's making. In the meantime, maybe get Grey to focus on the guy's library records in conjunction with the McKenzie letter. They made this thing to lead to something. The answer's got to be here somewhere.'

Jenna nodded, glancing to where Grey was lying on her stomach, the butterfly book open on the floor between where her elbows were propped, chin resting on her fists. 'Will do. Thanks, Saleda.'

'Call if you have something. We'll check in soon if we don't hear anything.'

'Ditto, that. Bye,' Jenna said.

Porter left straight away after Jenna relayed his orders, seeming thrilled to have an escape from Grey. Dodd took the tactic of following Hattie around the library as she attended to her responsibilities, asking her questions that were ultimately hooks without teeth. Jenna took a seat back at the computer and resumed her search of Paul Neary's library records. She clicked the mouse to bring up another window on Paul Neary's library account page, this time a history of holds he'd placed on books, titles he'd requested, and a few other things.

As she scrolled through the list, she could hear Dodd's voice across the room as he lobbed question after question at Hattie. Had any strangers been to or called the library recently? Did she know if any faculty regularly attended groups designed to bring together intellectuals, like MENSA? Were any outside groups allowed to use the school facilities for get-togethers: maybe Alcoholics Anonymous held a meeting there, or maybe a women's club hosted a fundraiser?

Jenna kept thinking if only she looked hard enough, far enough . . . *stared long enough* at this account's pages, something would pop out at her. The letter had sent them here. *Something* was here.

As Jenna's ideas of how to figure out the next step circled round and round in her mind with no clear path, her agitation seemed to whip itself into a frenzy until it felt like she was about to boil over. She beat her fist hard on the marble countertop, shoved back from the desk, and stood again. There *had* to be a way to figure it out.

'Damn, that hurt! Why the hell did I do that?'

Dodd had heard her outburst and was a few feet away now, heading back to check on her. 'That counter was obviously being deliberately unhelpful. Somebody had to teach it a lesson.'

Jenna turned her hand over, expecting it to be red, but it wasn't. Still, it throbbed.

They both leaned against the counter. Jenna grimaced, squeezed the pad of her right hand, trying to massage out whatever kinks she'd jammed into it. She shook her head. 'Seriously, Dodd, I don't know *when* the last time was I've knocked the fire out of my fist that hard . . . No, wait. I actually do remember. I was at the ATM a few weeks ago . . .'

But Jenna stopped talking, walked away from the counter and Dodd. Something had flashed, and she'd missed the color by milliseconds. *Come on, brain. Let me see that again . . .*

She'd been thinking about hitting her fist on the ATM machine! Right!

This time, Jenna didn't miss the frustrated pewter blue-gray that flashed in. Just like it had when she'd been agitated at the ATM. She'd beat the side of it, pissed because she could only get three of the four digits of her PIN number to register on the screen, and she needed to pick up Pull-Ups on the way home. It was a freak connection, but it gave her an idea.

'Hattie, I need your help!' she called in a voice loud enough to make any librarian Jenna had ever known die of offense on the spot.

'Of course, of course. I'll be right there,' Hattie called.

Jenna rushed back to the computer and clicked through the account information page, double-checked the dates on when the account was opened. That no changes had been made to it. They hadn't.

Hattie rushed to the media hub.

'Can anyone besides the librarian or the card account holder access records of what books have been checked out with the card, when, etc.?' Jenna asked.

The color flash had jarred the PIN number to the forefront of her mind. It was *important* that the terrorists had given them the PIN.

Hattie shook her head. 'They would need both the account number, which is the library card number, and the PIN number.'

Jenna turned to Dodd, her heart picking up. 'Then, for some reason, they want us to look through the records of books on this guy's account. And *they* have his PIN number. We can put Irv to work on making connections to Paul Neary to get some possible leads on who might have access, but right now, it's more important we know they *have* it. They tacked on those numbers to the end of the code. If they hadn't needed them, they wouldn't have been in there.

'They wanted whoever solved the code to end up logging into Paul Neary's records—'

'Hey, guys!' Porter's voice called, and a door slammed behind him.

In the next moment, he came into vision, jogging toward them, a tall, graying man in khakis and a white button-down keeping pace just behind him, his blue-striped tie flapping side to side. Jenna's heart quickened even more. Running never meant good things.

'This is Paul Neary,' Porter said, a hitchhiker thumb over his shoulder indicating the teacher and coach. 'He does have the library card with the number we used, and he has checked out books here before—'

'But not in over two years,' Paul Neary said, seeming to only half-understand the weight of his statement. He glanced around at each agent in turn and shrugged. 'Will someone please tell me what the *hell* is going on?'

Jenna and Dodd shared a glance, then Jenna's eyes travelled to where Grey was still on the floor with her butterfly book, only now on her back, feet crossed at the ankles.

Don't get too comfortable, Grey.

She lifted her eyes back to meet Paul Neary's. 'Mr Neary, some dangerous criminals are using your library account records as part of some sort of sick scavenger hunt to find them before they hurt anyone else. We got into your account but weren't sure what to take from it. But if you haven't checked out any books with your library card in two years, I think that just changed.'

Twenty-seven

Jenna, Porter, Dodd, Grey, Paul Neary, and Hattie all huddled around a printout showing all the books he'd checked out from the Suellen B. Holloway Memorial Library since his tenure at the elementary school had begun. The list wasn't long.

But after the tedious journey through the letter's riddles, the short list of books on Paul Neary's library account was refreshing, because it looked like figuring out the next move might be short work after all. It turned out that three books had been checked out since Paul had last picked out a title himself. And all three had been taken out in the past week.

Even stranger, all three had already been checked back in.

Jenna waved away the suggestions flying in her direction, the talk of surveillance footage, interviewing everyone in the building, dissecting the school's visitor logs. They'd get to all of those, but anyone who could convince a team of fourteen people to walk into a bank in broad daylight and use blades to slaughter every man, woman, and child that happened to be in there could figure out how to get three library books checked out of this place without it being traced to him. In fact, if one of those leads led them straight to the killers' leader before this code manifested something that did, Jenna would bet all the duct tape she owned it would be a trap. A killer like this didn't want to be found. A killer like this didn't want to be caught.

Red anger flashed in. And if he *did*, he was too much like Isaac Keaton for her to give him the satisfaction without finding a way to turn the trap back on to *him* first.

'Other departments are working on those things, which are all very important. But right now, Saleda's orders are to crack this code, so that's what we're going to do. They gave us everything we needed to bring us to this library and this specific library card—'

'And then some,' Porter cut in.

'—so it stands to reason that along the way, they've given us the knowledge of how to move on from here, too—' Jenna stopped abruptly and looked at Porter. 'What did you say?'

Porter bowed his head, bent the bill of his cap. 'I know, I know, I should shut up and concentra—'

'No, no! Whatever you just said, say it again,' Jenna said, turning her back and walking two short steps away from the group, closing her eyes.

'You said that the group's letter had given us everything we needed to get to this library, and I said, "And then some,"' Porter said, confusion seeping through his usually arrogant tone.

Jenna ignored him, paying attention only to holding the color in her mind that had flashed as he'd repeated his thought. Light taupe, the same color as those ugly bridesmaids' dresses her college roommate had bought off the half-priced rack from the prior season. Leftovers.

'Oh, boy, kids,' Dodd said in a tone he usually reserved for only children and those he deemed incredibly stupid, 'you're in for a special treat today! Usually visitors only get to watch the Peacock of Many Colors strut in her natural habitat. But *you* fine people, well . . . you might just be about to catch a glimpse of the Color Wonder splaying her tail!'

Jenna ignored him, turned back around.

'*The Importance of Being Earnest* crack we used yielded eighteen numbers – fourteen for the library card, the other four for the PIN. But remember how when we used the crack on the full list of literary reference numbers Grey took out of the McKenzie McClendon letter . . .'

As her voice trailed, she fished in her pocket and found the scrap where she'd written the numbers and systematically marked them. She unwrinkled it as best she could and laid it on the counter:

5̶1̶
5̶-3000
9̲5̲
1̲4̶7̶
7̶-2̲5̲21
†
0̶-0̶0̲0̲9̲

274
214
3
4-8818
4
11
169
207

'See? The crack's last direction took the 2 in 214, but then nothing else. It didn't work to repeat it; the numbers didn't work out evenly that way, either. So, we just took the fourteen numbers and figured the rest were for something later,' Jenna said, gesturing at the seventeen leftover numbers.

Porter slid the scrap across the counter so it was next to the printout of Coach Paul's limited book history. After only a moment of silence, he jabbed the printout with his finger. 'This book. It's library number or sorting number or whatever—'

'Call number,' Hattie filled in.

'It matches the first seven of the seventeen leftover numbers. 143.4881!'

Canary yellow relevance flashed in. 'What are we waiting for? We need that book!'

'Well, here it is: *Bergson and Education* by Olive A. Wheeler,' Hattie said as she returned from the row of shelves she'd disappeared down. She laid the dusty volume on the counter. 'The copy looks old, but the actual book's older. The original version was published all the way back in 1922.'

Jenna couldn't take her eyes off the old man staring back at her from the cover of the 2012 reprint edition of the book in front of her. They'd taken monikers from classic literature, left clues from various renowned books and plays, their cemented places on required reading lists proof they'd stood the test of time. Oxford blue flashed in. Obscure.

This book, however, represented a rather large diversion from the other references they'd run into on this orchestrated quest. Sure, it was a book, and in a way, it fit the elitist mold. But not for its acclaim or because of celebrated recognition of its contribution to a genre.

Rather, at a glance, it could fit into a group of books that might've been chosen by the elitists in question only because the everyday library-goer would walk right past it. Or, at best, glance at it, assume based on its cover and existence in the philosophy section that it was boring, and put it back.

No, this book didn't fit with the other works of art the terrorists had used in their puzzle so far. Brown the shade of a coconut husk flashed in. This choice was included out of necessity.

'This book somehow holds the next step,' Jenna muttered mostly to herself. 'But what?'

'We still have ten unused digits from the seventeen leftover code numbers,' Porter said. 'Maybe those could lead to a chapter number, then page, then—'

'Line number, word number? I know we're grasping at straws, but the letter at least gave us a guide to make the jump to the page numbers. You might be right,' Dodd said, 'but the reality is we've still got ten digits here and nothing to tell us how to use them in conjunction with this lovely volume on . . . what *is* it about, anyway?'

Jenna turned toward Grey without thinking as Dodd shifted his gaze toward where their amateur literature expert was now leaning with her back against the desk, holding the hardback copy of *Bergson and Education* flat on her right palm and using her left hand to turn pages.

Grey didn't acknowledge she'd been spoken to at first, but the series of blinks that came in soft, quick flicks told Jenna she was aware she had been addressed.

Grey gently licked the tip of her pointer finger and touched it to a page corner, turned it over.

'Please, it would be better if you didn't—'

Jenna touched Hattie's arm beside her, caught her gaze, and shook her head sternly.

Hattie seemed to fight the urge to argue, but finally, she simply looked down and muttered something about germs as Jenna turned back to Grey. 'Any good?'

As usual, Grey answered any question but the one asked.

'It was put between the covers in 1922, so she might not have gotten to read it. Sad,' Grey said, as if contributing to a line of conversation. Whether she was oblivious to the fact it was one she was having in her own head or just didn't care that they were in the dark was anyone's guess, though her tone was light and thoughtful. She cocked her head, looked up as if thinking. 'Well, then again, I suppose she could've still been alive. The question would be whether or not she'd have heard of it before it was too late or even been interested.'

'Grey, you're talking about the author of this book, right? What book is it you think she wouldn't have been able to read, and what does it have to do with this one?' Jenna asked, sure to keep her words slow and polite.

Grey looked up from the book and slowly turned her head to face Jenna in an owl-like motion. 'Education reform. This book is about an evolution philosophy and education reform that would teach it.'

'Are you kidding me with this?' Porter mumbled behind Jenna.

Jenna ignored him, mustering patience and focus to extract from Grey whatever it was she had put together. Her response may not have answered the question *Jenna* had asked, but the fact that her ex-patient *had* answered Dodd's question bolstered her resolve.

'OK, and what book are you wondering if the author of this education reform book ever got to read? Why would it have mattered to her?'

Grey shrugged. 'It might not have. Some people can't stand it, so I suppose she could've gone either way.'

Focus. Eye on the prize.

'So if it might not have mattered to the author, why wonder if she'd read it?' Jenna asked, choosing the phrase very carefully so that if she actually addressed it, Grey would be all but forced to reveal something about why she had drawn a connection between the two in her mind.

'Because it's the next piece of the hunt, obviously, and it was on my mind.'

Well, then. That clears that *up.*

'What is the next piece of the hunt, Grey? Please,' Jenna said, the last word slipping out in a tone of desperation. For all they knew, the bank killers were putting on their masks again, moving to strike some target she had a chance to stop.

'Your masked men. One of them is Scout, right? From *To Kill a Mockingbird*?' Grey said.

'Yes,' Jenna said slowly, begging her own wit to be quick enough to foresee any answers or word choices that might bog Grey down.

'Well, the leftover numbers were this book's Dewey Decimal number. Kinda funny book to have in an elementary school, but I guess maybe the high school kids might need it . . .' She paused. Shrugged. 'But elementary school and Scout sitting somewhere back in one of my brain containers that opened up reminded me of a joke. Most people don't even get it, but it's a good one if you don't miss it.'

So much for not getting bogged down on any tangents.

'A joke?' Porter said in disbelief.

Not now, Porter!

But this time, Grey didn't seem bothered. In fact, she nodded fast. 'Yeah. Chapter two. *"I'm just trying to tell you the new way they're teachin' the first grade, stubborn. It's the Dewey Decimal System."*'

'What?' Porter said, his voice a mix of confusion and distaste.

'That's something Jem says to Scout,' Grey said. She let out a little laugh. 'He was trying to sound smart, saying Miss Caroline was annoyed at Scout already knowing how to read and used flashcards to dumb-down her teaching material was just because the teacher was trying out a new technique.'

'How is that a joke?' Porter asked, no longer annoyed but interested, albeit confused.

'Because it was Harper Lee sneaking in a little rubber egg—'

'Easter egg,' Jenna translated.

'—for her readers.' Grey chuckled again as if she knew Harper Lee herself and thought she was just the bee's knees. 'Jem was trying to sound smart, because by blaming Miss Caroline's methods on John Dewey, a big talker about educational reform at the time, it made it look like he understood everything they'd heard the grown people discussing about the way schools were changing and might change more.'

Jenna nodded, finally seeing it. 'But the joke was on him, because John Dewey didn't invent the Dewey Decimal System.'

'And it had nothing to do with education reform,' Porter filled in.

'Nope. But because Jem thought it did, I'd say the next place to look would be in *To Kill a Mockingbird*,' Grey said, turning back to the

Bergson book and reading intently as though she'd picked up something light for vacation.

Jenna shrugged and turned to Hattie. '*To Kill a Mockingbird.*'

The blonde nodded, already moving. 'Follow me. I know right where it is.'

Twenty-eight

When it turned out that the only copy of *To Kill a Mockingbird* that wasn't checked out wasn't on the shelf where it was supposed to be, it was actually Hattie Zimmerman's idea to check the shelf that housed the book assigned to a call number matching the only remaining digits they had yet to use from the leftover code-crack numbers.

'They used the call number to lead you to the Bergson Book,' she said sheepishly as she led them through a side area strewn with squishy beanbag chairs, then through a set of doors leading into a section of the library where the kid-friendly shapes and colors gave way to taller shelves piled with thicker books.

'I wouldn't have realized it was an option. The Bergson book's call number only had seven digits. We still have ten numbers leftover, so the thought would've never crossed my mind,' Jenna said.

Hattie dragged a step stool from the end of one aisle down the second row they came to, gingerly climbed the rungs, and stretched as tall as she could make herself. 'Well, call numbers don't have a standardized length. They all start with the same sort of thing . . . the Dewey system has ten main broad categories, so the broad category would account for the first three call number digits. But after that, every category is broken down into sub-categories over and over in order to shelve the book as specifically as possible. With certain books, the numbers are pretty short. After all, when shelving Nancy Drew books, there's really no operative need to breakdown the categories beyond fiction, mystery. But you get into some of the nonfiction stuff, and those sub-categories can get *really* specific. Can make for some nice long numbers,' she said, reaching toward the spot the book with the call number matching their final leftover numbers would normally be.

Her mouth widened. 'Yep,' she said, making a valiant push to stretch just a half an inch more, 'I think this is it.'

Her pale pink-painted fingertips brushed the top of the book just downward enough to cause it to fall to its spine, the top jutting out just enough that Hattie could grab it easily. She brought it down and handed it to Jenna.

'It *definitely* isn't shelved in the right place, but somehow I'm thinking that wasn't *our* mistake,' she said as she brushed off her trousers.

As Jenna opened the front cover of the copy of *To Kill a Mockingbird* someone had deliberately placed to eventually be found, her gaze fell on the pocket glued inside the book that, before library systems were computerized, held a card that would be taken out and filed as part of the checking out process.

Jenna strode back to the aisle opening where Dodd and Porter were waiting. She stepped between them and held the book open to display the pocket.

'What's that?' Dodd asked.

But Porter was already digging in his back pocket, snapping on latex gloves. 'It's a ticket to Hawaii, Dodd. What do you think it is? It's a note!'

As Jenna followed his lead and pulled on the pair of gloves she kept in her back pocket, Porter produced tweezers from a zipped-pocket on the inside of his jacket and gently tugged the folded piece of notebook paper out. He carried it a few steps to a square table by the window with four plastic chairs. As he sat in the closest one, Dodd pulled a plastic evidence bag from his own coat and laid it on the table. Wasn't the best for preserving clean evidence, but they had to open and read this thing, and now.

With the care of a surgeon, Porter worked the paper open until it lay flat atop the plastic bag, its black, block letters staring up at them:

IF YOU'VE FOUND THIS, IT MEANS SOMETHING SPECIAL
    ABOUT *YOU*:
YOU'RE NOT JUST INTELLIGENT, BUT YOU'VE UNEARTHED
    SOME DETAILS, TOO.
AND BECAUSE YOU'RE SO OBVIOUSLY EQUAL TO THE TASK
WE'LL SAVE YOU A STEP AND SAY, 'PULL THE INSPIRATIONS
    FOR OUR MASKS.'

TO PROVE WE'RE WORTH CONSIDERING AND THAT WE
    AREN'T INTENT TO MISLEAD,

We feel it to be a sporting gesture to gift you
    tools you don't know you'll need.
The first tool is in your hand, but it shouldn't be
    alone.
You won't need a second copy, only how to track
    it when it roams.

You'll run into another problem: an embarrass-
    ment of riches
But choose the one followed by two sequels,
    though comparatively they were misses

The sequels yield to another pair of a problem:
Double trouble, if you will
But when in doubt, start as you would with any
    series
To see if it fits the bill.

There is a third pairing which we must give, lest
    you be set up to fail
Because it's been hidden and only we see, pick up a
    whale of a tale.

When the masks are pulled and you're looking
    for a pattern or trend
You wouldn't do well to waste your time on
    words just yet,
Not when numbers are still your friend.

Our final piece of advice to give involves a
    double debut.
Line up the masks, take one from each,
And you'll get a double on one of two.

'Not this shit again,' Porter groaned. He craned his neck to see back
in the room with the beanbag chairs. 'Grey! We need your help!'

Dodd shook his head. 'We don't need Grey for this. Not all of it
at least. '*Pull the inspirations for our masks.*' That's obvious right? Since
they say one tool is already in our hand – *To Kill a Mockingbird* – they

obviously want us to pull the books that feature the individual characters that inspired each killer's literary moniker.'

That Russian violet Jenna kept seeing any time the 'show' the killers put on at the bank flashed in, and she tried to ignore the tumble in her stomach at the memory of all the blood and body parts in favor of trying to count the number of killers on the grainy black and white video. 'So we need, what? Twelve books? How many of the nicknames do we know for sure?'

It turned out, not as many as they might've hoped. They already had Scout and *To Kill a Mockingbird*, and though the team hadn't pegged any of the other UNSUBs with a nickname from the book, the poem made clear there was one. All the other copies of the book were checked out, but as the note had inferred, they didn't need them.

'If they say all we need from a checked out book is the way to track it, the numbers we're looking for on the books have to be the barcodes. Every library book's barcode sticker number would be different, though, so wouldn't the code be dependent on us picking the right checked out copy?' Porter asked, turning to Hattie.

'At some libraries, maybe. But here, all copies of a single title share the same numerical code. Individual copies are differentiated by a letter sequence tacked on *after* the barcode,' Hattie replied. She blushed. Sheepishly, she said, 'The note *does* say that numbers are your friend.'

Porter nodded, scribbling the barcode on *To Kill a Mockingbird* twice on a fresh sheet of notebook paper from the stack Hattie had set out from them. 'Next on the list?'

'"Embarrassment of Riches"' being referred to as a problem we'd have has to be talking about Richelieu. They gave us the name, but they knew good and well when they did that that we'd have about as good of a chance of finding the correct John Smith we're looking for on Facebook as we would singling out which book featuring Cardinal Richelieu they had in mind,' Jenna said.

'How true,' Porter said. 'Embarrassment is an understatement. How the heck *did* that old codger manage to show up in so many stories, anyway? He had to have bribed people. Or slept with them.'

Dodd rolled his eyes, turned around and started toward the beanbag room. 'I'll get Grey.'

Porter continued copying barcodes to his list, and, adopting a haughty tone, said, 'It's a shame about that cardinal bribing people and sexing them to be famous. Tsk. Tsk. Men of the cloth aren't supposed to conduct themselves in such a manner.'

Jenna stifled her laughter when Dodd returned with Grey and asked her ex-patient which books featuring the character of Cardinal Richelieu had two sequels.

'I wouldn't place dollars on it, because there might be another set that matches up that way, too, that I'm not thinking of, but because it said the sequels were misses, I'd go with *The Three Musketeers*. The two after it brought tears,' Grey said.

Porter looked up from his list. 'Grey? Did you just make a joke?'

Grey smiled sheepishly. Her pale cheeks tinged.

Porter gave her a single nod. 'Not bad.'

So, they retrieved and copied the barcode number for Alexander Dumas's famous tome, then pulled *Les Miserables*, banking on their hunch that the UNSUB with the long briquet sword was Marius. *Moby Dick* came next, based on the reference to the whale of a tale, though that mention had added a new level of confusion to the mix.

Porter wrote *Moby Dick*'s barcode once, then cocked his head. 'It says something else, though . . . something funny . . .'

Jenna glanced over the phrase referring to the book again, and this time, light khaki flashed in as she read the word "pairing." 'A third pairing. So there's another UNSUB with an alias from the whale book.'

Porter copied the *Moby* barcode a second time underneath the first. 'WASP UNSUB, maybe? That WASP knife was made for big game hunting. I'd think picking a fight with the whale embodiment of evil probably qualifies as big game hunting. But who's the other?'

Dodd's phone rang, and everyone in the room knew it must be Saleda calling back. She and Teva were reviewing the bank video in hopes of pulling together evidence pointing heavily to – if nothing else – some strong educated guesses about other literary nicknames the killers they had yet to label might've chosen. As he stood and walked to take the call in the other library section where the reception was better, he called back, 'After we get all these nicknames, I'm telling you, if we ever have five minutes we don't have to spend running around libraries pretending we're in a Dan Brown novel, we're gonna have a *whole* lot of fun profiling these bastards now.'

'What? You mean doing our jobs?' Porter called after him. He shook his head, now copying down the barcode off of the first of the two Sherlock Holmes books Hattie had pulled at their request. There were more Sherlock Holmes installments in existence than seemed possible, but the letter had said to treat them like any other series you'd start, and to the team, if that wasn't book one and two, they'd been doing it wrong for years.

Jenna nodded as her phone vibrated with a text. This hot trail was definitely where they needed to be for now, but the more they guessed at nicknames and books, the more antsy she was to use the choices to psychoanalyze what different life experiences and personality types could bring a group like this together.

She read the words on her screen, jumped up. 'Just got a text from Irv. With the video enhancement, they were able to call in some weapons experts and identify one of the weapons the last guy was carrying.'

Eyes on the signage labeling the book sections and range of call numbers each aisle held, Jenna rushed toward the 800's section, dashed toward the section for epic poetry. As she scanned the row, grayish-blue flashed in, as did the image of the surveillance video figure jabbing the carotid of the white-collared victim that Cutthroat UNSUB had so viciously left with blood pouring from the gash in his throat. *Something about that.*

But then, her eyes landed on the book. She snatched it up, making a beeline back to the window table and slamming it down in front of Porter.

'The weapons guys identified the short knife he was carrying as a Scaramasax dagger. That's apparently the type of dagger Beowulf used to kill the last dragon in this over-hyped Odyssey rip-off.'

Porter started copying the *Beowulf* barcode number on to his list, joking in his best mechanical computer voice: 'The word of the day is Scaramasax. Your Scaramasax is looking very healthy today, Bill.' He laughed. 'Where the hell does somebody get a Scaramasax dagger?'

'Believe me,' Jenna said, sitting down to type a text to Irv, 'if there's a Scaramasax R Us on this planet, Irv is about to find it and send me the names of anyone who has so much as breathed in it.'

Dodd appeared and set his phone in the middle of the table. 'OK, Saleda, you're on speaker. Everybody's here. Tell us you've narrowed some names down for us.'

'Right,' Saleda said, the authority in her tone easing Jenna's nerves.

With every second that went by, she just knew her cell would vibrate and they'd be called to another attack scene.

'We're looking specifically at two. One is the Slender UNSUB who attacked high, knifing her first victim in the eye. The other is the shorter guy, kinda huskier build that went straight for the athletic black guy in the suit. I remember talking when we first watched the video footage not just about how him ducking and charging into the victim low, like a football player, then stabbing him in the stomach seemed highly strategized, but also how those quick upward slashes into the auxiliary armpits suggested training, maybe military. Well, the enhanced video doesn't just show he was using a SOG Seal Pup—'

'Military tactical knife,' Porter explained to Hattie, who had nosily sidled up to the table to listen in.

'—from the clearer footage, we can tell that football charge strategy was for protection as much as to throw his victims off balance. The low protective stance was him using his body as his secondary weapon, because he couldn't hold one in the other hand. He doesn't *have* another hand.'

'So, if he was military and lost a hand . . .'

Brain, think quicker!

'He'd get a nice pretty set of discharge papers to frame for the mantle,' Dodd filled in.

'Couldn't be in the army anymore . . .' Jenna muttered, trying to force the concept to become a revelation.

Grey, who up until then had been sitting quietly at the end of the table, stirring a cup of pencils, cleared her throat. 'He's like Johnny Tremain. He was an apprentice and should've been silversmith, but a big dumb bully tricked him and made his hand so hot it melted.'

Everyone stared at her for a long moment.

Finally, Jenna pushed back from the table. 'And you're saying Johnny Tremain didn't have a hand? And, because of that, he couldn't do the job he dreamed of?'

'Kind of. He *had* a hand, it was just disfigured so bad he couldn't make it do what it needed to if he was to keep smithing the silver.'

'Close enough,' Jenna said. 'Dodd, go find Johnny Tremain.'

'Still there, Saleda?' Jenna said.

'Mm-hmm,' Saleda came back.

'So you might be able to peg the Slender UNSUB?'

'We have an idea, anyway,' Saleda said. 'For starters, on the enhancement, that kitchen knife-looking blade she used to stab actually *appears* to be a letter opener.'

Jenna pictured the frames of the surveillance footage Saleda was talking about: the tall, slim female figure and her awkward physical movement, the way she charged her victims, arm raised high. That flimsy little blade, the frailish body type . . .

'I'll buy that,' Jenna said. 'Hardly narrows it down though, does it?'

'That's the thing,' Saleda said. 'It *wouldn't*, except for that while Teva and I were reviewing the footage for the umpteenth time, something clicked between what we were seeing and a random mention in the forensic team's on-site reports.'

Jenna and Porter shared an interested look. Jenna sat up straighter. 'We're listening.'

'After Slender UNSUB killed Rebekah Webb, she struggled with the banker, remember?

'How could I forget it? The banker's torso busted like a can of biscuits after WASP boy pumped him full of almost thirty liters of CO_2. We're thinking now that he must be one of the two characters the poem claims are from *Moby Dick,* by the way,' Jenna said.

'Well, before WASP UNSUB saved Slender's day, at a point in the scuffle, Slender's letter opener was still poised face-high as is the knife in her other hand, and she's just basically lashing and trying to stab anything she can. The banker gets hold of either wrist high over her head, and for a minute, they're locked like that, each angling for leverage. After a couple seconds, he whips her left arm downward across his body, practically bending her *into* the desk beside him. The momentum of the twisting motion made her drop one knife.'

Jenna nodded to herself. 'I think I remember this.'

'Well, once he has the upper hand, he bangs her arm and wrist into the desk, trying to get her to drop the weapon she still has hold of. She didn't, obviously, because big, bad WASP man showed up, but not for lack of trying. That arm *and* the knife took a handful of good hard whacks.'

'And this helps identify her literary moniker *because* . . .' Porter said.

'I'm getting there. The forensic team had bagged a chip of some sort of iridescent material near that desk, which the initial report suggested was most likely table lacquer or ceramic, but was being sent for further tests. Well, by the time we were reviewing the footage again, trying to find connections to more of the UNSUB's monikers, we knew Slender's weapon was a letter opener. So, the blows the thing took against the desk during the fight with the banker took on new meaning, and we called over to check up on forensics.'

'Please,' Jenna said, closing her eyes, '*tell me* the chipped-off-whatever had a book title engraved in it.'

'Close,' Saleda said, a hint of pride in her voice. 'The material was identified as a composite called nacre, which is made up of crystalline and organic substances that form from the inner lining of certain mollusk shells.'

'What?' Jenna said, baffled, and beside her, Porter mouthed, 'What the fu—'

'Let me make this simple for you, Doc, since I don't have any crayons to color you a picture. You know how pearls can form inside certain mollusks, right?' Saleda asked.

'Been looking for my lucky oyster for years,' Jenna said sarcastically.

'Well, the mollusk shell secretes this nacre, and the substance forms a protective layer to shield the pearl from parasites. It's scientifically called nacre, but a lot of people know it as mother of pearl.'

Jenna's heart rate didn't so much as speed up a beat, and Porter threw his hands in the air as he shrugged. But beside the window, Grey gasped and clapped her hand over her mouth.

Jenna glared at her, then glanced at Porter, who only shook his head. She stared down at the phone lying on the table as if Saleda would be able to feel her scowl. 'What are you, Teva, and Grey putting together that's lost on the rest of us?'

The phone's speaker crackled. 'Obviously Slender's letter opener was made out of *mother of pearl*,' Saleda said, drawing out the last words so slowly it reminded Jenna of the way people sometimes thought they could make a foreigner understand a language they didn't speak.

Jenna forced herself to ignore Grey, who now had her hands clasped together in front of her and was bouncing in her chair like a child about to get her birthday presents.

'You're apparently going to have to spell it out for me, Saleda, because unless there's a book called The Letter Opener that was written by Mother of Pearl—'

'The references—'

But Grey let out an excited squeak, cutting Saleda off. 'Pearl was her daughter! Hester Prynne. She's the mother of Pearl!'

'The main character from *The Scarlet Letter,* eh? They don't seem to realize no matter what names they pick and what character personas they hide behind, they still show us things we can use,' Dodd said as he returned, laying *Johnny Tremain* on the table in front of Porter.

'They've already shown us a lot more than they probably realize. For one thing, Slender – Hester, I mean – and WASP UNSUB probably don't have a clue they did anything in the bank to betray their connection, but we had them linked from the word go,' Jenna replied.

'The Wasp Man? The *Moby Dick* Wasp Man you were talking about?' Grey asked, jumping into the conversation again, her voice softer this time. Curious. 'He and Hester Prynne . . . eat dinner together?'

Jenna didn't bother explaining to the others that asking if they ate dinner was Grey's equivalent of asking if they were in a relationship, since if they were getting used to Grey at all, this one was fairly easy to follow. Jenna nodded. 'We think they have some sort of relationship, yes. We don't know its extent, whether it's romantic or platonic. There's a chance they could even be old friends, husband and wife, or siblings. Or maybe they met in the group and just developed an emotional bond for whatever reason. No matter the type or depth, we always look for those sorts of links between people. In any of those cases, knowing about the connection could prove useful.'

Grey shook her head, but she was smiling. 'You don't understand. It already has. This inks the deal that she's Hester Prynne. It's not just the *Scarlet 'Letter'* opener or mother of Pearl now.'

Here we go.

'What is it, Ms Hechinger?' Dodd asked.

'Herman Melville was inspired by Nathaniel Hawthorne! They met, I think, in 1950,' Grey said with authority.

'And you know this because your pen pal Herman Melville wrote you a gushing letter about how he just couldn't put *The Scarlet Letter* down. Did he also write his name next to that of the author of his favorite book and enclose them in a heart with the words, "4-eva"?' Porter laughed.

Grey turned to Porter, her face cold as stone. She blinked rapidly as silence hung in the air.

'I know this because Herman Melville *dedicated Moby Dick* to Nathaniel Hawthorne. I read that. *In a book*,' Grey said, standing in a huff after her last biting words and storming off toward the beanbag chairs.

'Does it get you hard, Porter, antagonizing the mentally unstable?' Jenna snapped. 'Normally, I wouldn't defend Grey, because I've been on her little trips through Wonderland, too, and while they're interesting and colorful at first, I know they can turn into bashing your head into any mirror you see on the off chance you'd locate an exit. But right now, she *is* actually helping us. We wouldn't even have found this library and this note if not for her—'

'And what good has this little jaunt through the friendly halls of public books done for us? At this point, what it's done has taken up precious *minutes* we could've been pursuing other angles of the profiles. As I see it, we're still missing two books, and even if we somehow manage to pull them out of thin air, who's to say we won't show up at another location only to find *another* code?'

'Simmer down, Undergrad,' Dodd cut in, his voice even and calm. 'You have a very valid concern there, but arguing for more minutes and hours about whether or not we've taken the right steps up to now *definitely* won't get us closer to saving lives. I think the thing to do here is to see what we can do about getting those last two books and let this play out. See if this test of honor delivers on its promise.'

'We're tapped out of ideas about those last two here,' Saleda cut in. 'Any thoughts?'

Jenna's eyes fell to Porter's paper. The orange-tinged red of a ladybug flashed in. *Sequence.* Jenna reached for the list of barcodes and slid it toward her, a thought hitting her. She looked to Dodd.

'Tell me again what the poem says about lining up the masks,' she said, deep in thought.

Dodd pulled the evidence bag containing the still-open note from his pocket. 'Line up the masks in order – the only order we know them in is the order in which they entered the bank, and take one from each—'

'One digit from the barcode of each. OK. Got that. But which number . . .'

Jenna reached for the evidence bag, and Dodd obliged. She reread the text:

OUR FINAL PIECE OF ADVICE TO GIVE INVOLVES A DOUBLE DEBUT.
LINE UP THE MASKS IN ORDER, TAKE ONE FROM EACH, AND
YOU'LL GET A DOUBLE ON ONE OF TWO.

As Jenna read the first line, Air Force blue flashed in. One. The number one. Debut. *Debut.*

They were supposed to take the first number from each of the barcodes. The debut number!

Jenna picked up Porter's pen from the table and went down the barcode list, noting the digit each began with, placing them in order from memory, leaving two blanks for the two attackers they weren't able to link a book to. When she was finished, she handed it to Dodd since her own phone was still on the table on speaker with Saleda.

'Send these to Irv. With the two books' digits missing, there should be a hundred possible combinations of thirteen-digit numbers—'

'Ten,' Grey piped up. 'All thirteen-digit ISBN numbers begin with either a 978 or 979 prefix. Your first missing number is the second digit. That means it has to be a seven. Ten possibilities.'

Jenna took in the new information in stride, already going on. 'You get that?'

'Loud and clear,' Dodd replied.

'We need a list of all ten of those possibilities in the form of books assigned those ISBN numbers.'

Twenty-nine

Jenna's phone vibrated for the first time since they'd hung up with Saleda so she could go help Irv. She opened it to read the text:

JUST FOR THE RECORD, I'D APPRECIATE IT IF ONE DAY, YOU JUST CALLED ME FOR SOMETHING LIKE A LIST OF THE CITY'S TAKEOUT RESTAURANTS OR A BREAKDOWN OF HOW MUCH YOU COULD SAVE IF YOU SWITCHED TO GEICO.

Jenna typed back:

I DON'T DO TAKEOUT. THAT WHOLE 'NO ONE IS ALLOWED TO KNOW WHERE MY HOUSE IS' THING. AND DUCT-TAPE REPAIR DOESN'T INVOLVE A PREMIUM HIKE. GOT THE BOOKS?

Within ten seconds, the phone buzzed.

IN YOUR E-MAIL NOW. CONSIDER EASING UP ON THE TAKEOUT POLICY. I HEAR SOME OF THE GOOD PLACES HAVE CARRY-OUT.

Jenna's heart fluttered as she opened the e-mail. Now or never.

She passed her phone to Grey. 'We're looking for the book on this list that could fit or be described as getting "a double on one of two,"' Jenna said.

After the longest minute of Jenna's life, Grey let out a single laugh.

'What?' Porter said, popping up in his chair.

'What is it, Ms Hechinger?'

Grey smiled. 'This is an easy one. "*It was the best of times, it was the worst of times, it was the age of wisdom, it was the age of foolishness . . .*"'

Raspberry red flashed in as Jenna recognized the words.

'All of them, opposing pairs. All on page one,' Grey finished, grinning.

Jenna already had her phone out, speed dial pressed for Irv. She'd congratulate, praise, and otherwise say things to Grey she never thought in a million years she would after she got Irv.

When he picked up, she didn't even let him speak.

'Irv, I'll ask you for takeout menus and insurance quotes and any other boring things that will make your heart happy next week, but right now, I need you to scour the groups you've flagged online as possibly subversive with even a remote connection to classic literature and spit out the one that has a direct connection to *A Tale of Two Cities.*'

Jenna held her breath, letting the silence stand between them. This was the first time she'd ever made this kind of request and implied that she intended to wait on the phone for it. But just as she'd told him to locate *the* online group out of those he'd been culling since the attack, she stayed on the line with him now for the same reason. Ruby red, the hue a touch deeper than the pomegranate of confidence she associated with absolute certainty.

She knew it was there.

After a long minute, the typing and clicking stopped. For a second, Jenna thought she could feel her heart in her throat.

'Yep. Got it. The site and the person who created it. Shall I dictate his address to you verbally, or would you like it sent to your phone, email, and personal subversive group address coordination butler?'

Jenna laughed, hard and loud. She couldn't believe it. A break.

'Send it to your mom, Irv,' she said.

He laughed, and the phone clicked.

Jenna turned to the others. 'What are you all sitting around for? We're about to go meet the page-master.'

The SUV bounced as the front tires rolled into the driveway of 1482 Sycamore Bend in Bethesda, Maryland.

'Oho!' Dodd said, a big, surprised grin widening, 'Look, Mr Lewis must be expecting us!'

Jenna nodded. She'd seen it, too. The flash of a curtain on the lower left, a man in dark rimmed, square glasses peeking out, wary.

Dodd threw the SUV into park, and the three agents opened their doors at once. Jenna glanced back briefly at Grey. 'Grey, stay put. As soon as we clear the area as safe, we'll come get you.'

She slammed the door and jogged toward the porch, catching up to the other two, who already had their guns drawn. They'd made enough calls on persons of interest to know that a peek out the curtain could mean a perp had spotted the cops and was now making a run for it or was loading his own Glock for a showdown.

Innocent light pink flashed in, and the info Irv had sent them on Flint Lewis, creator of the group and website Irv had found with a motto based on a quote from *A Tale of Two Cities* – Black Shadow. Age thirty-one, married to Ruthie Lewis for four years. One baby daughter named Nell – thirteen months – and another on the way.

'Remember,' Jenna said, bracing for the door to open. 'Pregnant wife and one child. Careful.'

Dodd banged hard on the castle-like front door and was just opening his mouth to bark his deep, 'FBI, open up!' when the massive, dark blue door flew open, Flint Lewis standing in the hallway.

'Won't you come in?'

The tall, slender man stood aside, allowing Jenna to step through the door first. She flashed her badge, launched into her spiel. 'Mr Lewis, I'm Dr Jenna Ramey, and this is Special Agent Gabriel Dodd and SA Porter Jameson.' She cocked her head toward where the helicopter that had been clipping overhead was now setting down in a large, open front yard two houses down. 'That's Special Agent in Charge Saleda Ovarez. We're from the FBI's Behavioral Analysis Uni—'

'I know who you are,' Flint said, taking off his glasses and rubbing the lenses with a white handkerchief from his pocket.

'Oh?' she said.

'Of course. Been expecting you. I even cleared my schedule,' he replied, replacing his glasses on his face. 'Come, come. Let's sit.'

He led them through the foyer and into the living room, gestured to the two-piece sectional couch covered in deep, chocolate leather forming an 'L' shape along two adjacent walls across from a fifty-inch flat screen. As Jenna passed Flint Lewis to accept the seat, her eyes fell to the hardwood floors. No scratches, dings, or stray dust bunnies to be seen. Out of the corner of her eye, she noticed the fireplace on the far wall – the only things atop its gray-stone base an iron hearth tool set and a decorative wicker basket of kindling.

This didn't seem like a growing family's living room. No bumper pads on the hearth, baby gates in doorways to other rooms. No diapers, wipes, or toys . . . anywhere.

Hot pink flashed in. Order because of a need to control. Maybe OCD tendencies. The types of people who thought children should be seen and not heard.

From Irv's information, Jenna knew Flint was a freelance computer programmer and web designer with a background in marketing and public relations. They didn't have a lot on his early life. Home-schooled, dropped out of college when he figured out he could teach his technology professors' courses better than they could. Worked a few jobs here and there for tech companies and start-ups but settled down in the suburbs and moved his career home, too.

So where's the fam?

'Would anyone like a glass of ice water? Pellegrino?'

'No, thank you,' Jenna answered.

'Right then,' Flint said, and he took a seat in the beige suede armchair. 'Like I said, I expected you. I hate to say it. I wish I didn't have to. But as soon as I saw the bank on the news, I knew Black Shadow was involved. Knew you'd want to talk to me.'

Saleda, who had let herself in behind them and sat down, leaned in toward Flint. 'Let me make sure I understand this correctly, Mr Lewis. Are you saying that when you saw that there was a massacre at a Washington, DC, bank on the news here in Bethesda, Maryland, you immediately believed the group *you* started was behind it?'

Flint crossed his legs, shook his head. 'Not exactly, no. The Black Shadow *I* created – a place where people who were angry about problems in the government that no one would do anything about could come and vent their frustrations in a supportive, open-minded environment – ceased to exist two years ago.'

The apricot of consistency flashed in. Jenna nodded. The original Black Shadow site hadn't had much if any activity in over 24 months. 'What exactly happened to it, Mr Lewis?'

'Please, call me Flint,' he said. He clasped his hands in his lap, his knuckles whitening a bit. 'As treacherous as the name sounds, the Black Shadow forum was something more of a support group for myself, in lot of ways.'

Flint hung his head, blinking back full eyes.

'What kind of support did you find in an anti-government website?' Saleda asked bluntly.

Flint looked at her, folded his lips in, an expression that said that while he was disappointed she didn't understand, that he'd gotten the question many times before. 'Let me clarify one thing, Special Agent. I am not and was never anti-government. Anarchy would cause as many tragedies as the current problematic system does, if not more.'

A distinct shade of purple flashed in. *In the age of foolishness, we are the age of wisdom.*

The take on one of the most famous phrases on page one of *A Tale of Two Cities* – and how Irv had nailed down this as the group – had been Black Shadow's motto as stated on the website, and it underlined what Jenna had suspected all along: this group of people was very intelligent – many to the point of narcissism – and they were convinced the average mind wasn't fit to cast a vote, much less hold government office and make decisions.

'So what is it exactly that you believe about the government that led you to start Black Shadow?' Jenna asked, though she knew the answer – in part, anyway.

Flint uncrossed his legs and stood, strolled toward the tall windows behind the armchair. 'Growing up, I spent more time in hospital cancer wards than on playgrounds,' he said, turning back to face them as he reached the window. Upon seeing the surprised looks, he waved his hand. 'Oh, not me. It was my little sister. She was diagnosed with leukemia. They started chemo right away, but she went downhill fast. A bone marrow transplant was her only chance. Well, I happened to be a perfect match. Unfortunately, the transplant only put her into remission for a year. She got sick again. First, she was anemic and needed blood. Next, her kidneys started to fail, so of course, I was more than willing to give her one. She was my best friend. When she went into liver failure, my parents scheduled the surgery for me to give her half of mine. But a doctor at the hospital had started to worry my parents weren't making decisions that considered *my* well-being as much as my sister's. This doctor notified the court systems, and she was appointed my temporary legal guardian in charge of making medical decisions for me. The first time the government overstepped in my life was the moment I realized that because of them, I'd lose my sister.'

'You were only a kid,' Dodd cut in.

Flint faced him, crossed his arms over his chest. 'Yep. I was. But that's part of the problem. So was she. She went through *so* many awful treatments. She wasn't even a teenager yet when she'd had enough torture that, had she been able to choose for herself, she would've opted to die. While she still had some dignity, still felt human. But people don't believe kids can possibly be as intelligent as adults, so kids can't elect to stop treatment and end the pain . . . or decide to donate organs to give their sister a chance at a *real* life. No, the *intelligent* adults knew it was best to continue putting her through hell. More medications, more surgeries, all designed just to keep her alive a little bit longer. Here these simple-minded fools couldn't fathom that "saving" her might mean something other than preserving her ability to breathe. And yet, despite that, they were too deficient to grasp such a concept. They were allowed to make her medical decisions. They were allowed to vote! The government gave them those rights.'

He took a deep breath, blew it out. 'After that, I saw more and more examples of the government's stupidity. How the stupid did the governing. I came to believe that intellect ought to be valued in government over age or religion or any other meaningless attribution of ability put above it in the current political spectrum. If a teen had an IQ high enough to make his own medical decisions, why should his will not trump that of a person who had the lowest grades of their medical school class?'

The bright red of righteous anger flashed in first, then again, that distinct shade of purple Jenna was all too familiar with: narcissism.

Intense stuff, and not without *some* merit.

But Flint's emotions added to his inflated view of his intellect led to some skewed logic. His feelings of entitlement because he was better than others screamed of at least *one* personality trait of the dark triad. Maybe even two, since he was somewhat focused on his own self-interests. But those self-interests were motivated by something deeper – his sister's suffering, which suggested he didn't lack empathy, and his story hadn't triggered any alarms – or colors – to suggest it wasn't genuine.

So far.

'I'm so sorry about your sister,' Saleda said, steering the conversation away from a rant and gently reminding Flint who was present in the room.

He hung his head. 'I'm sorry. It's just always a tough subject.'

'We understand,' Jenna said. 'Everyone copes with grief in different ways, and it's healthy to acknowledge positive *and* negative feelings.'

It was also normal for people to find different ways of expressing those feelings. Some were healthy; some, not so much. 'I'm starting to gather that the website wasn't just a public airing of grievances but more reaching out to others who had similar pain.'

Flint nodded, Jenna's words seeming to calm him, as understanding had a tendency to do in most people. 'Of course, some people who found the site were conspiracy theorists or just general nutjobs, but I tried to moderate it well. I blocked those types from the private forums quickly. The actual group, well . . . everyone had their own reasons for being there.'

'Similar to yours?'

'Some,' Flint said, pacing again. 'Lots of lost loved ones. Painful situations and life-changing scars that in some way were the result of a government run by people not qualified to run it. In many ways, we were like an odd little family. We didn't know everything about each others' lives, but I think we were as close as you can get through a computer screen, if you can believe it.'

'Tell us about when the group started to fracture,' Jenna said.

'Well, as you can imagine, a group like this has a lot of people with very strong opinions,' Flint said.

'And a lot of wackos,' Porter muttered.

Flint ignored him. 'A couple of the more bitter members didn't find the same comfort in just talking and commiserating as the rest of us did. They sounded more and more radical, wanted to take more action. At some point, I was approached about an in-person meeting that had been set up.'

'None of you had met in person?' Saleda asked.

'No,' Flint said. 'We enjoyed each others' company and support, but by nature of what our group talked about, we were also, to some degree, afraid. Didn't give our identities on the forum at all—'

'Which is how the literary handles started?' Jenna cut in, curious.

'Kind of,' Flint said slowly. 'The handful of us there from the beginning came up with the motto, so choosing a literary character for a forum identity sort of became a trend, if you will. A couple of people did it, then everyone wanted one.'

'So, everyone named themselves, then?' Jenna asked.

'Technically, yes.'

'Why technically?'

Flint paused, seemed to consider. 'Several people talked amongst themselves as they tried to decide what names fit them. The characters were' – he pursed his lips, thinking – '*personal*. Everyone really got into their characters. It wasn't a trivial thing to anyone.'

That made sense, given all they'd seen so far.

'But even if people crowd-sourced ideas, they still chose their own, correct?'

'Technically.'

A salmon color flashed in. One she recognized easily, as it had bitten her in the rear in the past if ever she didn't readily recognize it – someone holding back. 'What am I missing?'

'One of the two I mentioned that were setting up the meetings kind of became the go-to forum authority on handle characters. He was one of the people first to pick a character after I did, but he was *definitely* the first to announce his choice in a post containing a long, in-depth analysis of the literary aspects that led him to it. Others followed suit. As the forum admin at the time, I could see when members sent private messages to one another. When character names became the 'in' thing, I noticed a lot of people were messaging back and forth with Ishmael. Though I didn't read their messages, of course, I assumed they wanted his assessment of them.'

'Ishmael?' Jenna repeated.

Flint nodded. 'I don't know a lot about his situation, really, just that he was brilliant, intense, and very resentful. He was severely disabled, though he never went into specifics of his condition. We all got the feeling he was homebound. Or that maybe he was agoraphobic.'

Jenna wasn't as sure of Flint's amateur psychological analysis as he was, but she'd ask why they'd had that 'feeling' after a few other things were straightened out. Right now, the far more interesting aspect of Ishmael was that he'd had a hand in naming the members *and* was one of the inciters of the in-person meetings.

'So if he was homebound, why set his sights on in-person meetings?' Jenna asked.

Flint shrugged. 'I can't say I know, entirely. I didn't ever go. The whole idea made me as uncomfortable as the undercurrents that came with it. If I had to guess, I'd say they probably had him on video chat. I remember him mentioning doing that for things . . . and the way he sounded when he mentioned it was one of the reasons I was sure he never left his home.'

'So the other member intent on taking action in person must've led the meetings?'

'Atticus,' Flint said without missing a beat.

Brick red flashed in. The attacker in the bank video with the machete. The one who had stepped in to finish the creepy guy's slow torture of the blonde, get things back on track. She couldn't confirm it readily, but it made sense. The letter said two characters were from *To Kill a Mockingbird,* but they'd only known Scout. The color. That was Atticus.

'What do you know about what brought Atticus to the forum?' Saleda asked.

'Bits and pieces,' Flint replied. 'I know he lost his job at some point, which I think is what led to his divorce. His little girl died. Just had a long string of such awful circumstances, and he wouldn't have joined us had it been just rotten luck.'

Damn. The sequence of events was brutal, and yet, it rang true. Jenna thought of Scout, dry-heaving after killing someone. Of Hester and her clumsy, untrained form rushing at a stranger, driven to kill. To be committed enough to their cause to take such horrendous actions, every one of their stories had to be equally compelling and terrible.

The shade of blue Jenna associated with devotion flashed in. Atticus and Ishmael had to be absolutely sure the people who joined their more radical group were completely vetted. Relationships online were strong, but for what they were planning, they needed to be very, *very* sure of these people.

'Flint, you said you were invited to the meetings. But not everyone was?'

He shook his head. 'They definitely seemed to feel people out. See if they were "with" them or not, so to speak. It was subtle, though. Manipulative.'

'How so?' Dodd asked.

'They'd test the waters with people, and then anyone they didn't deem fit – maybe they weren't hardcore enough, maybe they seemed too unsure of the more extreme ideas – they would manage to force out of the group. It's ultimately what they did to me, even though by the time it happened, I was wary enough that I was ready to walk even without the "help."'

'What do you mean by 'help'? How did it all play out?' Jenna asked.

'Like I said, I was invited to the meeting, but I didn't want anything to do with it. Some of the ones more like me, like Scarlett, who had lost a brother in the Iraq war were invited. But then you had creepy guys like Mr Darcy involved—'

Hunter green flashed in at the word creepy, then the deep crimson Jenna hated so much almost immediately after – the one that only showed up when bloodthirst was involved in violence. The man skewering the pretty, young girl in the bank. Atticus jumping in with the machete to end it. That man could be Mr Darcy.

'Mr Darcy? From *Pride and Prejudice?*' Grey asked.

Flint nodded. 'Yeah. Weird one. Was into everything Black Shadow wasn't supposed to be about. Class warfare, things like that.'

Sure. Because elitism isn't class warfare at all.

Jenna forced herself not to ask more questions about Darcy. *Focus.* 'We'll need a list of any other Black Shadow members' names you remember from that time.'

'Whatever you need.'

'So, you didn't end up going to the meeting . . .' Saleda coaxed.

'No. Thought about it a lot, but I backed out at the last minute. Shortly after, I started hearing less and less from everyone on the regular website. Those who did go left our regular forum. The way they were so cold toward me, though, prior to leaving, made me think they'd been poisoned against me somehow. Wouldn't surprise me, since many of the others not selected for this little "mission" had the same thing happen. One by one, people starting leaving the forums. Forums got boring. Pretty soon, no one hung around.'

The watery, transparent brown that reminded her so much of the lager Jenna's father would drink out of a clear stein flashed in. In her lexicon, she'd come to associate it with deviation from the norm. Irv said the last private messages on the Black Shadow forums had stopped long before the first in person meeting because there wasn't a trace of anything like this.

'Wait a minute. How were the messages about the meetings delivered?'

'The details came through their website,' Flint responded.

'They have another website? What is it?' Saleda asked.

'I don't know. It's transferred every week.'

'What does that mean?' Porter asked.

Flint narrowed his eyes. 'I want it to be clear that while I *was* privy to the information, I had nothing to do with the creation of it.'

Saleda nodded. 'Understood.'

He took a long pause. 'They attach a Trojan to a plug-in that websites can download free, like one of those news tickers or visitor counters. Anyone who downloads it is now infected. On a set date every week, the virus chooses an infected website at random and installs the New Black Shadow's website on the infected site's server.'

'That can be done?' Teva said curiously.

'Oh, easily, on certain low-security hosts. That's how it's kept from being found or easily accessed even now, I'm sure. It'll reach out to new randoms every set amount of time, copy the files over, then delete the previous ghost page. Not hard for the right people,' Flint said.

The intellectually elite.

'So if that's how the *new* Black Shadow are communicating, how do members get the web address when it changes if the sites it infects are random?' Jenna asked, thinking how they might just give it out at in-person meetings, though they couldn't have done that the first time. And now it'd be getting more and more dangerous for them to meet as a group other than for the actual attacks. Groups of that size would draw attention, particularly once the FBI gave the profile of the attackers.

'I don't . . .' Flint looked away from them all. Shifted uncomfortably. 'I don't want any part in this. I know what you'll want me to do, but I have a wife and child. Another baby coming. I can't afford to antagonize anyone. Give them any chance to remember I . . . to be on their radar.'

'To remember what, Flint?' Jenna said.

The calm and collected demeanor reflected on Flint's face up to now gave way to a panicky, troubled look. He shook his head. 'I can't. I just can't.'

'We can protect you and your family, Mr Lewis. But we can't protect a lot of innocent people who might die unless you tell us how to find that website,' Saleda said, encouraging but stern.

Flint wrung his hands. 'Please. I just want to stay out of it. Just like I did then.'

Appeal to his narcissism. 'Whether you want to be or not, Flint, you're already involved. And I hate to point it out, but you're already on their radar. They might not have meant it to lead us to your doorstep, but the little scavenger hunt they set us on, teasing us we could find them if we were worthy? It was always going to lead to Black Shadow, because that's where they started. You're not to blame, but Black Shadow was your baby. So like it or not, you're part of their game. But you started it your way. You *can* finish it your way.'

Flint bit his lip, shifted again. Then, without a word, he walked toward the kitchen area separated from the living room only by the switch from carpet to tile.

He sat down at the table, opened the black laptop in front of him. Running his fingers along the keys, they watched an e-mail account pop up. He typed a username in, saying, 'This anonymous account was given to everyone invited to the meeting. You log in to get the newest URL. If they still use the same account, that is.'

But as soon as he hit enter, the e-mails came up. They were in.

'I'll get Irv on this,' Saleda said, opening her phone. 'Need to start if we're going to crack it in time to prevent another attack.'

'It'll take a long time,' Flint muttered. 'They'll be better than that.'

Saleda held her phone, but her fingers stayed at the keys as she stared at Flint. Slowly, she put her phone back into her pocket.

'Flint, if you think you can get in . . .'

He hung his head. 'I know I've been worried about my wife and kids, but . . .'

'But what?' Jenna asked.

'But what if my family just happened to be wherever the next attack occurs? I'd never forgive myself.'

He opened the latest e-mail, copied the link. Sure enough, a login page opened.

'The login might not even still work,' he muttered, just like when trying to sign into the e-mail account. 'They probably deactivated my name when I didn't show.'

But that wasn't the case, either.

The website appeared, black with white writing on the sides, the top. But something else was going on.

It took a second for Jenna to realize what she was watching, but as her brain caught up with her eyes, so did the noises of phones vibrating and ringing in the team's pockets around her. *Shit.*

She didn't even reach for the phone. She already knew what the calls were about.

The raw video from the second attack must've been uploaded to the Black Shadow site only moments ago, because this was the call informing the team about the attack. Jenna turned heel and ran for the door.

Isaac Keaton lay back on his tiny bed with his feet crossed, a worn copy of *I Know Why the Caged Bird Sings* open in front of him. So nice of this fine super-maximum security correctional facility to give their inmates free access to a library. Granted, Level I prisoners like Isaac didn't ever *see* the library, just Li'l Book Cart Pushin' Lael, who came by once a week or so.

Thank the Miami Dolphins, though. He needed the diversion today. A pipe must have burst somewhere, because the water had stopped refilling in the john several hours ago, leaving it drier than a Southern Baptist county with no liquor stores. And of course he'd had to take a shit *all day.* The book was a decent read, at least, though he'd only selected it for the title and its special kind of irony. Had to have *some* kind of entertainment to pass the day to day. He had a jump on the plan, but patience was key.

Patience, and tapping in to the hidden culture around you.

Correctional officers and inmates alike were quick to tell new intakes there are no secrets in the penitentiary. That was bullshit. There were *plenty* of secrets in the penitentiary. Secrets Isaac was studying, practicing . . . learning.

The buzzer sounding the four o'clock head count of all the prisoners jarred the air. The C.O.s yelled at the Level II and III's, feet scuffled.

Penitentiary secret number one: the C.O.s didn't start the four o'clock head count until 4:03 because the Level II and III convicts allowed to roam the common areas in the afternoons always took a pretty second or twelve to get standing by their bunks. But because Isaac was only allowed to leave his cell once a day for one hour, he was always inside it for the chaos of cons pushing and shoving to make count, the guards bitching at anyone not moving fast or not toeing the line.

That mere four minutes of knowledge had led to *Penitentiary secret number two.*

'Border brother,' said a voice coming from the empty john. 'Inked fourteen.'

'Son of a bitch,' another voice replied. 'Where?'

'Coming down the bowling alley!'

Excitement rose in Isaac's chest, the knowledge of all the clandestine activity he'd tapped into a bigger rush than sniping those old fools on a picnic at the park. *The Aryan Brotherhood uses the pipe systems to communicate.*

Isaac tossed away his book and crossed the cell to kneel down beside the metal toilet.

Shuffling feet, yells of, 'Beat your feet!' from the C.O.s came from outside Isaac's cell.

The first voice came again. 'Car?'

He couldn't help but admire their discipline. Their ingenuity. The timing had to be deliberate. The racket of the head count covered the conversation completely. If the toilet hadn't been empty, Isaac wouldn't have heard a thing.

Isaac licked his lips. Smiled. Knowing secrets one and two was going to make penitentiary secret number three – and what it could do for him – a piece of cake.

Well, maybe not cake, but still, it would be *oh, so delicious.* After all, he was about to play a game as dangerous as any he'd played before. And yet, not a bone in Isaac's body feared he was stepping wrong. Discoveries like these were tools he owned, and tools were made to be used.

That was the part the C.O.s never got. The bigger picture was like a real-life, ultimate stakes game of Legions Ascending. As a teenager, he had become a master at stacking his deck. Isaac had perfected the art of figuring out what he wanted to accomplish, then leeching everything he could from the throwaway cards before they were discarded, collecting the perfect recipe of unique cards with powers that could combine to obliterate what stood in his path.

That was the most vital penitentiary secret he had unlocked thus far, in fact. Many had tried, but most failed. Everyone thought that to break out of a maximum security prison, you needed help on the outside, allies on the inside, intricate knowledge of the prison and its routines, and a whole lot of fucking luck.

He'd learned the layout and every single thing about the prison's routines. He had someone on the outside, and a couple of people on the inside. He even knew the final secret he needed to stack his deck.

The secret was, he didn't need luck. He had something much, much better.

Thirty

The chopper set down on the hospital helipad, the airspace now cleared by the National Guard, F18s circling in the near distance. Scary shit.

Jenna stepped out the open door, the wind from the chopper blades blowing her ponytail and the hair around her face into her eyes. Saleda was shaking hands with a man in a dark suit and sunglasses as well as with a cop who had greeted her and Teva when they stepped out of their own bird. Jenna stood behind and looked around, taking it all in. Even from the hospital roof, she could see lights flashing, crowds gathering. Police cars, ambulances. Areas taped off in yellow.

Saleda motioned to the rest of the team, and Jenna and the others followed her through the door leading into the main hospital. From the briefing they'd received from Irv while in the air, they knew the main attack had taken place on the ground floor, mostly the emergency department and waiting area. Once they'd gotten Irv on the line and had Flint Lewis give him the log-in information, Irv had had the horrific task of watching the raw video so he could tell them about the slaughter inside.

The whir of the elevator down to the floor above the emergency department was the only sound Jenna could hear other than the individual slow, long breaths of the team as they prepared themselves to enter what they knew would look like a war zone. This would be the only elevator that would open in the whole hospital thanks to the key the sergeant who had met Saleda and was now leading them inside held. The rest of the hospital was on lockdown, no one in or out. Unfortunately, too much time had passed between the attack and the first responders arriving for any lockdown to be effective. According to Irv, the attackers had been disguised as hospital workers: all in scrubs, faces masked. He was working on video feeds from every surveillance camera in the hospital, but the attackers seemed to have once again pulled the videos for their own purposes. He had footage, but only the raw attack posted on Black

Shadow's member website for their homebound disabled cohort, Ishmael.

The image of the black figure with the machete-like knife jumping in front of the tall, skinny Mr Darcy as he tortured the young girl with his fillet knife in the bank flashed in Jenna's memory. Atticus ending her life quickly, speaking fast, seemingly chastising words to Darcy on the silent video tape.

The smaller, retching figure of Scout in the bank. The frail, clumsy Hester.

A shade of blue blinked in too quickly for Jenna to catch it.

They'd been chosen because their hearts had a reason. It was how they'd gotten in, and it was how Jenna would find them. They'd have left signs, just like before.

And like before, they'd also left one witness alive.

The doors opened on the first floor, and the team exited. Saleda turned to face them.

'Thirty-two victims, all DOA. One living witness. We've got a note, we've got missing video. We've also got a *lot* of blood,' Saleda said.

Jenna braced, knowing the colors would assault her again, a barrage of the different killers MO's and how the victims had met their ends.

'I want to interview the witness,' Jenna said. She wasn't trying to get out of walking the scene by any means, but like the bank, she thought she could be more prepared to enter the onslaught of hues if she had some sort of map of the attack to start with.

'When Ms East was found under that storage cabinet in the ER lab, she was practically catatonic. She hasn't spoken a word. She was taken over to building F and is resting now in our Behavioral Health facility,' the sergeant said.

Saleda nodded. 'I feel confident if any investigator can get a useful interview from Ms East, Dr Ramey can, but we'll give Ms East a little more time to rest before we pay her a visit.'

OK, then.

The sergeant held the stairwell door open for the team, and Saleda caught Jenna's eye and cocked her head ever so slightly to come over. Jenna slipped past Porter, who'd paused to grab the tiny vial of vanilla extract he kept in his back pocket and dab some on his upper lip.

Saleda stilled on the second stair, and Jenna took the cue to pass her. Easier for the person needing to talk to be behind.

Jenna took each stair slowly as she strained for the hiss of Saleda's whisper.

'Suit guy upstairs is Homeland Security. So far, we're a joint task force, but the subtle cues are there. They want us out so they can take over.'

'But on US soil, it's our jurisdiction,' Jenna breathed.

'Bigger things are at play here than rules,' Saleda said, her voice barely audible. 'Re-election coming up, and right now, the big guy's approval ratings are lower than Porter's patience threshold with Grey. He needs his media tide to shift *big time.*'

'So, what?' Jenna hissed.

'Look, we all know the BAU are far more trained to take these asshats on. But the suits don't know that. All they know is they liked how Boston looked. A big boom, chaos. Authorities swooped in, contained it, and the terrorists were down and out in less than five days. We've already got more attacks, more people dead—'

'And a totally different group mindset, set of MO's. We give what few details we have for *this* many perps, we cause a level of chaos, false tips, and mass fear that would render just about all the tactics we're using to *actually* locate them useless,' Jenna said, the dark green skin of a dill pickle flashing in. She couldn't explain why she knew it other than the color, but she was sure Homeland Security wouldn't gain an advantage. 'It'd play right into Black Shadow's hands. We'd send more members right to their cause.'

They reached the first landing above the stairs to the door into the emergency department, currently under armed guard. Saleda paused beside Jenna.

'You're preaching to the choir. I'm holding things off as best I can, but we need to find these assholes fast.'

Good thing your PTSD has never been officially diagnosed or you'd be seriously ignoring doctor's orders right now, smart guy.

Yancy's eyes stayed glued to his screen, where he watched via his remote hookup to Irv's network the raw hospital attack footage uploaded to the Black Shadow spoofed page. The virus technique that moved the URL from site to site left Irv and Yancy little hope of tracing its origin. One of Black Shadow's members would have to have done something stupid, and unfortunately, when it came to this, it would seem they were all as smart as they believed themselves to be. So now, Irv had set up the video on loop for Yancy to hunt for anything they'd missed. Meanwhile, Irv dug through the Black Shadow site, which was currently piggybacked on the blog of some teenager who had downloaded a shady plug-in.

Oboe scratched the back door and whined. Yancy glanced away from the video. 'Oboe, I promise, I'll take you out in just a few—'

He stopped, grabbed the TV remote from his tiny, ugly coffee table. He'd left the TV on the news on mute, but now, it had caught his eye. 'What the . . .'

Yancy jabbed the volume up.

'Hey, Irv!' he said into his headpiece as he stared in awe at the TV. That sure as hell *looked like* the exact footage on his – on Irv's – computer screen. 'I think they did it again. I think they gave the media—'

'Yeah, I just got the memo. I'll tune in to the E! True Hollywood story just as soon as I bust through this motherfucker of a firewall these beasts have up . . .'

Duly noted. Yancy minimized the window of the Black Shadow website attack footage on loop and opened his own browser. A quick search on the Internet brought up the same video on several news media channels.

Yancy played the footage on a couple of different sites, not sure what he was looking for exactly. Maybe they'd highlighted certain pieces they wanted the public to see more of or had strategically cut it like a propaganda campaign. But each time, it was the same footage he'd seen on the Black Shadow member site.

He pressed play on one more rendering of the video, this time on a famous gossip website. Cringing, he watched from the usual high corner angle how chaos ensued as figures seemed to run both from and at people in every direction. Several attackers rushed past the nurses' station in the center toward what Yancy knew were doors leading to the ER waiting room, slaying all in their paths. Others seemed to rush in from the same direction and fan out, seeking any life they didn't know to be on their side. The blitz of every hallway, lab area, exam room, and supply station happened so fast that singling out many incidences was difficult. The angle ensured that many assaults were blocked from the camera by other bodies, murders in progress, backs turned. One nurse flung a rolling stretcher toward an assailant in an attempt to slow their progress, only to run into another coming from the other direction. A hospital employee nearby took a corner at full speed and skidded in a puddle of another victim's blood, wiping out flat on her rear end before her attacker caught up to finish her.

Yancy closed his eyes. Took a deep breath.

How many times can you watch this, tough guy? You OK with this many nightmares?

He shook his head. Opened his eyes and focused.

You better be. You killed Denny Hoffsteader. Bad guy or not, you deserve this, tough guy. This is what you get.

'Wait!' he yelled out loud, not even meaning to.

Yancy jabbed at his space bar to pause the gossip site footage, simultaneously reaching for his mouse to rewind the Black Shadow site footage on his computer when he realized it was on Irv's screen and he couldn't control it.

'What, dude?' Irv answered.

Yancy narrowed his eyes, zoomed in on the spot where he'd paused the gossip site footage. 'Go to the Black Shadow site footage again, start in at fifty-five, but let's take it frame by frame. I think I've got something.'

Jenna's booty-ed feet trudged through the few tiny squares of tile not smeared with blood in the inner section of the emergency department. Having re-walked the carnage of both the lobby and the ED a second time, she kept coming back to this spot. Exam Room Six.

Of all the patient exam rooms, something about this middle exam room on the wall across from the restrooms kept nagging at her. *And not just the fifteen-year-old kid who'd twisted his ankle at soccer practice killed inside it.*

She turned and re-entered the room. The two bodies of father and son lay heaped together about two feet inside the doorway. Jenna winced as, once again, she laid eyes on the bloody handprint that had been left on the white privacy curtain as it had been half-ripped from where it hung.

Charley! Have to get out . . . he was so pale. She had to be strong. Keep going. Get help for Charley. Just a few more feet . . .

Jenna shook away the memory, forced herself to focus. Not now. This wasn't the time.

Never is the time.

She pushed her feelings down hard, jammed in the internal cork she'd worked so hard to master to keep her own demons bottled, and again took in the bloody handprint. The owner of the handprint had, no doubt, used the curtain to try to stand and fight, which told Jenna it belonged to the father. The son's hands were nearing the same size, but his fingers were much skinnier, and none were covered in blood.

That, somehow, was the problem. Something about what had gone down in this room felt off, but Jenna couldn't quite put her finger on what it was. The surveillance video's range wouldn't have seen what had happened in here, though she intended to watch it back to see if anything caught her eye. But right now, all she had was the collapsed bodies and the damned colors that inevitably came and what she knew about them. And those didn't make sense, even to her.

The father had died farther inside the room. He'd been felled, seemingly, by sword wounds to the gut, as had the son. The ME was sure the dad had bled out from the stomach wounds; he couldn't say yet whether those or a dagger wound to the neck had ultimately killed the kid.

And yet, something about the dad being farther inside the room bothered her. Their positions didn't make sense. The boy was practically in front of the doorway. The dad had used the curtain for leverage, but he wouldn't have been the person seated on the exam table. Even if the dad had tried to hold off the attacker so the kid could escape, how did the boy with a probably-broken ankle get off the table and around two fighting men – one brandishing a long *sword* – only to end up with a sword wound that entered from the *front* just like his father's? A light khaki yellow color flashed in Jenna's mind. Something seemed out of place. Unless Marius had the power to clone himself, things just didn't match up. And why was Marius now carrying a dagger? That was new, too.

Had Marius somehow had trouble? Maybe the kid put up a fight and another of the assassins had stepped in to save his sword-wielding ass.

'I've had about enough of this emergency room to last me a lifetime,' Saleda said, appearing in the door. 'Dr Oscar up in acute psychiatric had me paged.'

'She's ready to let me talk to Margeaux East?' Jenna asked.

Saleda frowned. 'I wouldn't count on it. OK with going up on your own? I'm hesitant to leave the main scene with our friends from Homeland just waiting to swoop in.'

'Not a problem.'

'My phone's on me if you need it. I'm going to check in and see if any of the team have anything new, then I'll probably send at least Dodd and Teva back to Quantico to piece together more on the profiles as Irv is able to round up some victim information for them. Maybe there'll be dots to connect. What do you want me to do with Grey?' Saleda asked.

Shit. For a second in the commotion, Jenna had forgotten that this case involved Grey, like the piece of gum she couldn't get off her shoe.

'*Don't* turn her loose,' Jenna said, as much as it pained her. 'Have her shadow Dodd. That'll at least keep her from scratching Porter's eyes out.'

'You've got it,' Saleda said, turning to find the other team members.

Jenna took one last look back at the father and son before she left, then walked down the hall, staring at the red-streaked floor where the attackers had stalked their prey with blades dripping with the wounds of others before them.

The image of Scout, her hands on her knees as she dry-heaved in the bank popped into Jenna's mind again.

These people weren't born to be killers.

The shade of blue that she'd missed when it had flashed in earlier reappeared. Then, right away, the light khaki made another appearance.

'Something's just not right,' Jenna mumbled to herself, and she headed for the stairs.

'You can look in on her, but I'm afraid I have to put my foot down on this,' Dr Oscar said, leading Jenna down the corridor. 'Dr Ramey, I know you're good at what you do. I in no way mean to insult you. But it wasn't long ago that she worked up here on this very floor, and while I didn't know her, I think of her as one of our own. I know she has a long road ahead, and I want to preserve what little security she's managed to tuck herself into feeling.'

Jenna bit back her argument. It was no use. Even though Black

Shadow had left another note threatening more coming attacks, and even though Jenna knew there was more to the message inside the head of the nurse resting in the room before them, the sharp-nosed, graying psychiatrist beside her wasn't a profiler.

Jenna glanced in the square glass window into the room. A petite blonde woman, still wearing the same blue scrubs she had been when she'd come in to work that day, sat in the lone, floral-fabric chair in the room's farthest left corner, her knees bent up to her chest, feet planted in front of her rear end in the chair seat. One lily-white arm wrapped her legs, holding them to her, the other elbow propping her right arm on the armrest, her hand half-holding her head up. The other hand ran through her long, silky strands of hair the color of a pad of butter.

'Has she said anything coherent at all? Maybe repeated a phrase or even just a word?' Jenna asked, not particularly hopeful.

Dr Oscar shook her head, frowned. 'She's been like this ever since they found her folded up as tiny as she could get inside that cabinet. It's door was pulled shut and taped with the medical tape she'd had in her scrub top pocket. She'd been clutching a—'

'A pair of medical scissors,' Jenna said, a faint blue color she couldn't place flashing in like it had every time the scissors were brought up. 'I heard.'

'So awful,' Dr Oscar said. 'But, no, she hasn't said anything. She's muttered a bit, but only babble. Nothing of consequence that we've been able to discern.'

'Dr Oscar! Room 8!' a yell came from down the hall.

Dr Oscar glanced at an orderly flagging her with big arms at the opposite end of the hall, then back at Jenna. 'I'll be right back. Sorry!'

She took off running.

Jenna turned back to the window, stared in. Margeaux East continued to rock, her lips moving. She was babbling something even now.

Damn it! Jenna needed that message! More lives were at stake!

And yet . . .

Jenna glanced around. No one else in the hallway. Margeaux wasn't dangerous, and this wasn't an asylum by any means. The door wouldn't be locked . . .

The train of thought was jolted by her cell phone vibrating. Quickly and silently, she slipped her hand in her pocket and sent the call to voicemail, praying with everything in her it wasn't to do with Ayana.

It couldn't be. She has Charley, Victor, and Dad all watching. They've all been sending the right safe words on schedule.

And even if it is, this is the only chance. Now or never.

Jenna turned the knob.

Thirty-one

Jenna thudded down the staircase toward the main hospital's entrance into the emergency department, heart thundering even harder than it had been when she'd snuck out of Margeaux East's room and into a cramped alcove to avoid Dr Oscar until the coast was clear for her to sneak out of the psych ward entirely. She'd finally given in to her phone's incessant vibrating, which turned out to be texts from Saleda – telling her to rush back to the ER ASAP, there was a new development – and Irv, clueing her in to what that development actually *was*.

As she'd read his texts, the yellow from exam room six flashed in again, only this time, she realized it hadn't been just the khaki yellow of something seeming out of place she'd originally taken it for. The shade had been *so* similar, she hadn't seen it for the sand yellow it was:

BS TURNED OVER FOOTAGE TO MEDIA. MEDIA FOOTAGE ALTERED. COMPARISON TO RAW FOOTAGE FROM BS SITE SHOWS THERE WEREN'T JUST 32 BODIES. THERE WERE 33. BLACK SHADOW OFFED ONE OF THEIR OWN.

At that moment, she didn't care about Dr Oscar seeing her or even how ridiculously unethical it had been to sneak into Margeaux East's room to question her, let alone decide to pull out her voice recorder to capture the witness's babbling so she could try to make out what the woman was trying to say later.

Jenna had flown out of the alcove, her feet carrying her faster and faster toward the ER. The text hadn't said *where* the extra murder had happened, but it didn't have to. She knew where it was. It all made so much more sense. Why the Dad had died first. Why the son was closer to the door and then killed with a dagger. She hadn't seen past it because of the sword wounds, but they hadn't been the same swords.

The sand yellow represented the number two. A pair.

Jenna rounded the corner of the grisly inner portion of the emergency department from the main hospital entrance toward Hallway B – and room six – but all of the trains of thought and loaded questions she had for Saleda and the team died on her lips as she realized the latest guest had arrived to the party. It didn't take long for Jenna to gather that he wasn't happy about his literal lateness, either, and that it hadn't been intended, fashionably or otherwise. A few feet away, Saleda was drawn to full height, Porter beside her, posture aggressive as they faced the group of uniforms before them.

Jenna's gaze shifted to the arm of the officer Saleda was verbally sparring with, and the number of stars took Jenna aback. The man in the suit earlier had been a lackey sent from the Department of Homeland Security, but he had an Army general with him now.

Jenna strode forward, steeling herself to enter the mix.

'Ah, Dr Ramey,' Saleda said, noticing her approaching, seeming grateful for the interruption. 'Perfect timing.' She lanced tersely back toward the general, the police sergeant, and the man in the suit, then back to Jenna, holding her eyes fiercely as if trying to transmit something much more than simply the words she spoke. 'These gentlemen and I have been discussing the developing situation. I was just saying to them that your expertise may prove instrumental in evaluating and assessing the risk profiles of certain tactical options on the table, given the profiles we've been able to piece together.' She turned back toward the men, nodding to the general. 'General Theodore Quintrell, Military Advisor to the Secretary of the Department of Homeland Security, this is Dr Jenna Ramey, Special Agent and acclaimed forensic psychiatrist.'

The sturdy, albeit top-heavy, officer stretched out a worn, calloused hand and smiled jovially, showing off the sizable gap between his two front teeth. 'Please, do call me Ted. Formalities are for state dinners and impressing the wife.'

Jenna shook his hand, returning his smile, but only to put him at ease. The light orange that had flashed in at his words didn't jibe with the big 'ole teddy bear persona he seemed to want to impress upon her. The white hair and the double chin, rosy plump cheeks, and thick gut might've sold her that he was a military man softened in his old age if she'd met him on the street. But given the encounter she'd witnessed, the color told the real story. Funny, because she always thought of it as tiger orange, but the association actually reminded her of the orange of the black-and orange-striped Monarch butterfly.

Or rather, its mimic, the Viceroy. It looked just like the Monarch – a trick to make predators afraid to eat it since Monarchs are poisonous. But Jenna's association with the color was the exact opposite of that concept. It was a deceptive charm, one that looked innocent and even pleasant on the outside but harbored something more poisonous underneath. 'How about General Ted?'

He grinned. 'That'll work fine.'

They released hands, and Saleda nodded to the other two men in turn. 'And of course you've already met Sergeant Young and Mr Underwood.'

The two men nodded, as she did. 'Nice to see you both. Please, tell me how I can be of assistance.'

'Dr Ramey, I was just telling Agent Ovarez here that the Department of Homeland Security is increasingly worried, given the scale of these attacks, their randomness, and their brutality that with the promise of further violence from this group, our course should be swift and decisive. That's why we're working with local and state police to secure a perimeter, set up mobile command centers around and within a fifty-mile radius – thirty, if we can organize quickly enough – and through state police channels, are working with officials to issue an official shelter in place order to everyone living and working within that area. We plan to commence a door to door search by 1700 hours.'

Saleda's nostrils flared. 'What I have just been discussing with the general, however, is how such an aggressive tactic may affect the dynamics of this particular terroristic organization, given their *specific* extreme beliefs regarding governmental interference. I was informing him that it's our team's opinion that such a bold move would likely further antagonize them to escalate their violence, especially when such a manhunt has little chance of success. Based on the very few pieces of evidence we would have to identify the culprits, that is.'

The general laughed heartily. 'Miss Ovarez, forgive me, but I do believe finding one guy with a machete here, another with a samurai sword there would be fairly tale-telling.'

'None of the UNSUBs has wielded a samurai sword in these attacks,' Porter mumbled, as, next to her, Jenna could feel the angry breaths rising and falling in Saleda's chest as she fought to allow Porter's interruption to suffice in lieu of correcting the general for calling her *Miss*.

The general turned to him. 'What did you say, son?'

Porter cleared his throat, straightened his posture. 'Forgive my interruption, sir. I was just clarifying that none of the Unidentified Subjects has been known to use a samurai sword as a weapon. To date, that is.'

The general stepped to Porter's side, clapped a hand on his shoulder. 'Well, then. Guess we'll have to leave them masked men with the samurai swords be, hadn't we son?' He laughed heartily.

The acid green of disgust flashed in. Regardless of this man's game or agenda, it didn't change the fact that they were standing in the middle of a hospital emergency room turned mortuary, and here he was, laughing like he'd just told the best one-liner on the golf course.

Let's cut the shit.

'General Ted, I applaud your resolve and willingness to muster the manpower needed to put out such a strong show of effort to take back control of this situation, because the public is certainly frightened right now. No doubt their fears are on your mind, and your plan is a both a bold maneuver to capture the perpetrators of these attacks as well as an urgent display to those very scared citizens that steps are being taken to ensure their safety. But if I may speak candidly, sir, while such a strategy has its merits – it was clearly effective in Boston – based on my knowledge of this case and the profiling I have done on the UNSUBs as individuals and as a group, I must strongly encourage a different tactic be considered. Please, sir, don't waste valuable resources on trying to find the UNSUBs in a brute force, door-to-door manhunt. We can't risk antagonizing these bastards. *Especially* not when we have the new lead we do,' Jenna said, looking to Saleda as if to confirm she'd mentioned the information Irv had dropped on them.

'Yes, Miss Ovarez told me about your technical analyst's theory that one of the terrorists killed another right over from where we're standing,' the general said, glancing in the direction of where the body of a fifty-something female lab technician was now covered in a white sheet in the middle of the hallway directly between Restroom A and Exam Room Six. 'But our people have analyzed the video footage, and the area in question is so chaotic and blurred, the incident can hardly be seen at all in the whir of activity, much less be used to corroborate the wild theory of one assassin killing another, then removing the body from the crime scene. Never mind the fact that there *is* a body right where this incident supposedly occurred.'

That's the footage your *people have seen.* But while Jenna knew they could fight, show the raw footage from the Black Shadow site, this guy and everything he stood for wouldn't care. He'd made up his mind. After all, he might be a general, but he had orders, too. Make his boss look good.

'But, sir,' Saleda said through clenched teeth, trying to maintain a polite expression, 'if they took that body it is because they didn't want it identified. That has to mean that the identity of the victim could link it to the other perpetrators. Put the priority on finding that missing body, general, and I assure you, you will expedite rounding up the culprits in ways manpower and riot gear never could.'

'Young lady,' General Ted said, still smiling, but not quite as good-natured and cheerful as before, 'if there's a missing dead body out there to be found, I'm positive our men will run across it in their travels. But there are twelve terrorists who have killed over fifty people in mere days, and the time for giving them a head start to escape our clutches is over. We are putting out the shelter in place order and will be finalizing a lockdown of this city until the perpetrators are caught or dead. That is what I was sent here to do, and that is what I will be doing. We appreciate your consult and your candor, but we have a job to do, and I caution anyone who may think we should do *otherwise* to remain out of our way.'

He gave a final nod, then turned to Jenna and smiled wide, slipping right back into his grandfatherly, teddy-bear persona that Jenna was sure had gotten him many places in life. He again offered her a hand.

'Lovely to have met you, Doctor, and please, now that it looks like you folks will get to take the evening off a little early tonight, do drive safely home to your family. I bet they'll be just thrilled to have some extra time with ya.'

Jenna smiled, tight-lipped. 'They will, of course. Always fun to have a movie night with the fam.'

You know nothing about my family, asshole. And unless you're too intimidated, address my supervising officer with the title and respect she deserves.

With a curt nod to Saleda and Porter, General Ted Quintrell strolled with Sergeant Young and Mr Underwood toward the ER's exit door. The team followed, trading glances and raised eyebrows.

As they reached the exit to the street, Sergeant Young held the door open for them. After they'd each passed through, the thud behind them let them know the cop was gone.

'I'll take that as kicking us out,' Porter said. 'Fucking morons.'

'It won't smoke them out. All it'll do is cause mass hysteria. Locking people in their homes, cops in riot gear banging on doors. It's exactly what Black Shadow wants. And they'll use it to incite every bit of fear of the government they can. Try to turn even *more* normal citizens to terrorism,' Saleda ranted, kicking at the curb before sitting down on it, collapsing her head in her hands.

The shade of dull blue Jenna kept missing by a hair today returned. This time, Jenna caught it, because Saleda had just said the word. Normal.

Jenna shook her head, pacing back and forth. 'You're right. It's just what they want. More sympathizers for their cause, reason to fear those in authority to help them rise up. They planned this in hopes this would be the outcome, which is exactly why they won't be found by brute search, either. They're too smart for that . . .' Jenna stilled as jungle green flashed in. Her heart rate picked up. *Planning.*

'What?' Porter asked from where he stood on the grassy median strip. 'What're you thinking?'

Jenna smiled despite the grim scenario, her breath catching. 'Because they *did* plan it. This whole thing, almost to a fault. They had this scenario in mind, planned to use it to win support from everyday citizens. They *didn't* just plan it half-ass. To win a battle like the one they're waging – to win *government change* – you have to plan on the kind of heat General Teddy Boozer in there's cooking up. That way, when it does, you can use it. Which means you also have to plan for its ramifications and risks, because your target isn't to blow up a building and make a statement. Your target is an *end goal*. A *movement*. And to inspire a movement, you have to stay in sight . . .'

'What are you getting at, Jenna? I'm sorry to be a complete ass, but if this is some of your Color Wonder "You can see it but only with my special markers kit" crap . . . Please forgive me, but I bought a six pack of Corona last night with the money you gave me for the box,' Porter said.

Jenna half-laughed, shook her head. 'I'm just saying they figured out more than just the plan to get viewers and the plan to escape.

They also figured out how to deal if something like what happened in there today went wrong. If they could take and hide the body of anyone whose identity would mean revealing their identities, too, they could keep their covers longer. Live their normal, *everyday* lives longer. Because if the movement *does* take, they'll need to be out there with it. Visible.'

'You think they planned to kill each other all along?' Saleda asked.

Jenna bit her lip. She hadn't ruled it out, but it felt wrong. 'No, not necessarily. I think it's more likely that with that many people flinging blades around in crowded places, they were smart enough to be ready for the very real possibility that one of their own could get hurt. *Especially* considering they recruited clumsy, untrained fighters like Hester,' Jenna said.

'True. She almost got in trouble at the bank and had to be saved,' Porter said. 'So you're thinking they come to every attack prepared to get rid of one of their own as part of their escape plan? Just in case?'

'Yep. I think that's exactly what they did here, and I think they'd have been ready to do it at the bank, too,' Jenna said, the ballet slipper pink she associated with patterns flashing in. 'And I think that bank plan is exactly how we're going to figure out what they had in mind for their worst case scenario today.'

Thirty-two

'Shh!' Porter hissed as Saleda grunted.

'That was my toe,' Saleda said in a low growl.

'Sorry,' Jenna said, taking a large step into the darkness of the hallway. It was creepy, but stepping all over each other wasn't going to make it any less so. 'How close do you think we are, Porter? Can you feel anything yet?'

Porter's steady, even breathing was about the *only* moving air. Damn, a flashlight would have been nice. Or, you know, the ability to use their badges and investigate a place of interest like they would if General Fluff-n-Stuff hadn't set his beady black eyes on the Black Shadow investigation.

'From what Irv's saying, we should be about ten paces from the door,' Porter relayed. Porter was their ears; Irv had hooked the team up with a Bluetooth-like earpiece, but smaller, with no glow so it wouldn't give them away in the dark. Irv had hacked into the surveillance systems at Mt. Olive Medical Center – almost forty miles away from where the bloodbath in the emergency department at Fountains of Mercy Hospital had destroyed families and incited such palpable terror in the community. This way, Irv could guide them through the dark corridors in parts of the hospital not normally visited at this hour. Even open some doors when possible.

Jenna shivered, rubbed her arms. So many goosebumps. Man, it seemed forever since they'd sat in the warm SUV in the parking lot of the little diner across the road from Fountains of Mercy, trying to regroup. She'd sipped warm coffee – *awful* but warm coffee – as they waited for Irv to tap into the surveillance videos outside the bank, its parking lots, and even those of buildings nearby. They'd scanned the footage plenty of times before, trying to peg down a lead to chase, but this time, Irv was looking for something else.

Jenna had been wearing the earpiece at the time and had just taken a bite of a stale biscuit when Irv's voice hit her ear. 'There. Got something. They all escaped in the same vehicle outside the bank, which we all know dead-ended us at the parking garage at Fifth and Link four blocks away.'

Jenna knew all too well. The UNSUBs had exited the vehicle, fanned out, and weren't seen again. They had all left through other means of transportation, none of which were caught in the angles covered by the parking garage surveillance camera, or – that they could tell – any other cameras in the area. But this time, Irv noticed something that hadn't registered in their initial looks: the presence of a black hearse parked on the same level of the garage where the getaway vehicle had waited. None of the UNSUBs batted an eye at it at the time, so there'd been no need to give it a second thought. But right about now when they were thinking Black Shadow had a body disposal plan as an insurance policy at every stop, it was exactly the link they needed.

With a click into the same garage's surveillance, Irv confirmed the hearse still occupied the same spot. Hadn't moved. A few checks confirmed it had been stolen weeks before, but that had been enough for the team to surmise that if a hearse was the out, it only made sense for that gig's emergency dump destination to be a funeral parlor.

At first, they'd all thought for sure Black Shadow would be too smart to use the ambulance they had appropriated to be their way *into* Fountains of Mercy's Emergency Department as their way *out*, as well. It was obviously trackable. But after the bank's disposal plan and the hearse involved in it came to light, they decided that maybe the ambulance had been the perfect plan all along. After all, it was useful, especially if they needed to hide a body somewhere.

The ambulance had turned up shortly after the attack at the track beside the football field of Kegney R. Magnet Middle School, following a Fighting Phantoms football game. Apparently cheering fans, a band playing fight songs, and fresh cheeseburgers could undermine even the most devoted EMTs.

They knew this game would be going on. Ambulances have to be at all games. They staked it out, knew the EMTs left and came all the way down the hill from it. It was there for the taking.

And it had worked. Black Shadow had swapped the vehicles while everybody in the vicinity was too focused on a bunch of fourteen-year-olds tossing a pigskin to notice it.

Now, as the team tiptoed through the dark, Jenna couldn't help but imagine Charley trying to explain to Ayana why Mommy couldn't come to her mother-daughter tea party at pre-school next week because she'd been arrested for trespassing in the basement of Mt. Olive Medical, feeling through the dark for a door that would take her into the morgue. She could just hear it now: '*A, Mommy really wanted to be here, but she needed to check to see if a missing body had been snuck into a giant freezer in the bottom of a hospital where they keep the dead people.*'

'Wait, wait,' Porter said, jiggling what sounded like a door handle or knob. 'Irv can you buzz me in here?'

Jenna couldn't hear the answer through Porter's earpiece, but she was sure it was sardonic, egotistical, and best of all, affirmative. A few seconds later, a clicking sound snapped in the air, echoing through the quiet hall.

'Thanks, man,' Porter said to Irv, and he turned the knob and pushed open the door.

Saleda stepped through the entrance in front of Jenna, flipping on the lights in the anteroom, no doubt the place where the autopsies and other medical exams were done before the bodies made it into the cooler that they knew to lie beyond the thick, steel door behind them that reminded Jenna a little of the bank vault Ashlee Haynie had been closed into.

'Yep, here it is,' Porter said, leaning over one of the stainless steel counters, scanning an open manila folder. 'Listed as— Oh, for fuck's sake . . .'

After the football field, Irv had done some fancy footwork tracking various traffic cameras across the city until he was able to find the ambulance that had originally been stationed at the football game before Black Shadow swapped it out, and it had showed up on the surveillance video in the ambulance entrance to the ER at Mt. Olive Medical not long after. Irv could tap into and the electronic filing system the hospital was now using to make their patient's information more accessible— 'Yep, to me,' Irv had said as he'd perused the records.

The dead assassin had been pushed into the ER on a stretcher already covered and presented as a DOA. Black Shadow had to have either been faster than they thought was possible or their network wider than the team knew, too, because the 'EMTs' that had wheeled in the body were met by a doctor – the patient's long-time heart physician, according to his chart.

'What? They name him something cute like Peter Cottontail or Harry Potter?' Jenna asked, rolling her eyes.

'Eh, not quite *that* obvious. They're smug and think they're smart, but even they wouldn't be that outlandish. No, they went subtle this time,' Porter said.

'Define subtle,' Saleda said.

'Stine, Franklin Newman III.'

Oh, hell.

'Frank N. Stine,' Saleda and Jenna said in disgusted unison.

'Yep. He currently resides in Drawer 231. The question is, who is actually in Drawer 231 and what drawer did he come from, because I'm far more interested in its newest resident.'

They all were. After the dead assassin had been rushed in by the Black Shadow members masquerading as EMT's, curtains had been drawn for privacy under the guise of keeping his hysterical wife – no doubt also a plant – from interfering with attempts to save him. Which meant when they wheeled him downstairs, as long as they were careful to swap a John Doe into the killer's designated morgue freezer drawer, then slide the dead killer into John Doe's vacant slab, anyone who happened to open up the drawer would see exactly what the folder said they would.

Jenna had her cell phone out now, Irv on speaker. Now that they were inside the steel doors enclosing the morgue, they could risk a little more noise. Especially with Irv monitoring the cameras inside Mt. Olive Medical to warn them if anyone was coming.

'The dinosaur of a system they've got running over at Mt. Olive finally coughed up the John Doe files on record in the past year. I cross-referenced those with current occupants of our favorite morgue, and I found four. Which will it be, contestants? Will you take what's behind door number 106, door number 15, door 83, or door 182?'

Porter closed the folder. 'Well, let's go see if we can land the grand prize.'

Saleda pulled open the heavy, steel door leading into a room that had to have been designed to ensure maximum ash-color skin on all persons living *and* deceased, because the lighting effect was impressive. She headed for the first of the four drawers she spotted, keen to get it over with.

Porter and Saleda seemed to have the same idea, having both located two of the other possible drawers.

'Well, the good news is that they don't smell as bad frozen,' Porter said as they all shared one last look, a silent pact to proceed.

As Porter yanked the handle, Jenna followed suit and could hear Saleda had, as well. She rolled the slab out into the room about halfway, took a deep breath as she reached for the body bag zipper.

I could've been a professional decorator. Maybe worked in graphic design. Those use colors.

But no, after a childhood filled with terror, psychopathic mind games, and the constant threat of death, the sensible thing to do was always go into homicide investigation. Definitely healthy.

She dragged the zipper down, spread the plastic apart with gloved hands. She stared down at the elderly black male inside. Eighty, maybe. Scraggly, unkempt hair, yellowed chipped teeth. Humble, unassuming fawn flashed in as she looked at a face gaunt from too few meals, the eyes red and sad as if they'd seen even fewer hugs. Homeless, if she had to guess.

'Winner!' Porter said from across the room.

Jenna closed the plastic flaps back over the John Doe but left the bag unzipped for now, too eager to see if Porter had actually found the missing body of the dead member of Black Shadow. She crossed the room toward him, as did Saleda.

'It's definitely our guy,' Porter said.

Jenna peered into the plastic, and sure enough, though she didn't know what to expect the assassin to look like, she had no doubt it was him. For one, his head was lying on the slab, but if the board hadn't been underneath it, it likely would've hung from just strings of sinew that Atticus's blow with the machete-like knife Teva and Saleda had determined to be a kukri during their earlier, more in-depth video review hadn't managed to sever.

Brick red flashed in. Damn, she wanted to watch that footage some more for herself. See if she could confirm the suspicion forming in her mind.

And analyze it, she would. But first things first. They had to get the M.E. down here to start the process of identifying who the hell this was. And that would mean letting the rest of the players in the game in on the fact that the four of them had been very, very bad little FBI agents.

Saleda shrugged. 'Better now than never, huh?'

Jenna nodded, General Ted's round face filling her mind. Somehow, she imagined his gap-toothed smile wouldn't make an appearance next time she saw him. Even if they *were* doing everyone a favor. Identifying this killer was the fastest and best chance they had to figure out who the other members of Black Shadow were.

Saleda dialed on her cell. 'Look at it this way: if they want to kill us for going behind their backs, we were nice enough to meet them at the perfect place for it.'

She held the phone to her ear, the slight frown on her lips reading more pissed than worried. If General Build-a-Bear had just let them do their job in the first place, none of their asses would be on the line now.

Saleda spoke quick words to the police dispatcher who answered, and within seconds, the call ended. She pocketed her phone. 'That's it. They're on the way.'

Jenna clasped her hands in front of her, rocked on her heels. Nothing to do now but wait. What was the worst they could do? Send her to her room? Claudia had done way worse than that.

'This should be fun. Anyone fancy a game of I Spy while we wait?' Porter asked. 'We could use actual eyes,' he coaxed, the last part in a boyish, sing-song that would've been funny if it weren't for the fact that they were in a place that for the same reason made it completely disturbing.

Jenna shook her head and instead just paced, thinking of how many times her father had done the same thing over the years anytime he was worried. He'd been through worse than General Teddy Grahams, too. Their whole family had.

Bring it, Teddy Ruxpin. You might be the US government, but I've dealt with the bigger guns. You might think handling North Korea and Iran make you more qualified to fight these monsters. And it might, except for the fact that I've fought one you haven't. Experience with Satan is a tough one to trump.

Thirty-three

'Stupid, freakin' key, just TURN!' Jenna yelled, furiously wrenching at the key jammed in the lock, twisting harder and harder until finally the last lock of the color-coded system she'd designed turned over.

Jenna shoved the door open, slammed it, and began re-keying the locks, all the while muttering under her breath. 'Supposed to keep Claudia *out*, not *me*, for God's sake. After all, if I don't get my ass inside I'll probably be carted off to jail and held without bond.'

'Whoa! Somebody finally made your workaholism an arrestable offense? I don't know if I should send the flowers to them to thank them or forward them on to the mortuary for their funeral after you throttle 'em,' Charley said.

Jenna turned to see her brother's legs and torso sticking out from inside the cabinets under the kitchen sink. His bent elbows jutted out as his hands worked at what she assumed was the garbage disposal, and occasionally a hand popped out to feel around for a screwdriver or hammer before returning to work.

'We can use the ambulance for when you inevitably cut your hand off. Where's the duct tape?'

'Yikes,' Charley said. 'We skipped straight from "I'm too tired for you to guilt trip me about not being home more" and "Stop annoying me about this" to full on "I can give it right back, buddy,"' He slid out from under the sink enough to size her up. His eyebrows rose in surprise. 'You must've had some night.'

Jenna unsnapped her holster, took out her Glock, and popped it in the small safe she kept in the kitchen, then tossed her phone on the table and collapsed into one of the kitchen chairs. 'If you call practically breaking into a hospital morgue, digging through drawers of bodies, then being chastised like a child by an army general with the voice and face of that evil purple bear in *Toy Story 3* all because we handed him the single biggest lead on this terrorist case, then, yeah. Bad day. Is A still up?'

A squeal, frantic giggle, and the sound of running feet from the hallway answered that. A moment later, Ayana clonked into the kitchen wearing Charley's red Converse, a Pull-Up, and a pair of sunglasses. She whirled to face the hallway entrance, knees bent, grinned, and let out a giggle in between catching her breath.

'The lion TOLD YOU no more pictures, Paparazzi Ayana!' boomed a goofy version of Vern's voice from the hall. 'And now you have to pay for sneaking them!'

Jenna's dad bounded into the room and snatched Ayana off the floor, turning her little girl into a blur of kicking white legs, bouncing blonde ringlets, and a flailing arm stretched out, holding the baby monitor from her bedroom. The wild giggles continued until A could barely breathe, and Vern settled her on to his hip as finally, she allowed the monitor to be taken from her hand.

'Sometimes getting home is like watching one of those foreign game shows where people are running across a bridge of giant, Styrofoam balls, and for some reason the host gets pied in the face because someone in the audience has a banana,' Jenna said.

'Mama!' Ayana said, noticing Jenna, and she ran to her and crawled messily into her lap.

'Nah, Rain Man, it's a reality show! Top rated,' Charley said.

Ayana looked to Vern. 'Cam-ra? Wan pic-cher?'

Vern narrowed his eyes. 'I told the paparazzi it was bedtime after she snuck the last lion photo . . .'

Charley leaned in, whispering. 'The monitor is a camera. Don't ask me where she learned about paparazzi. It certainly had nothing to do with me letting her watch that episode of *Jersey Shore* where Snooki debuted her baby bump. It was like five minutes, and I swear to God, I don't even think she remembers it.'

'Mm-hmm.' Jenna smacked him in the back of his head with her palm as Ayana put on her best pouty face for Vern.

'Just one more for Ma-ma? Peeeeease?'

Vern's face melted into a smile. 'Oh, all right. But just one, then it's time to go to bed. Even paparazzi photographers have to sleep sometimes, you know.'

Ayana grinned as she hopped off Jenna's lap, taking back the monitor. She held it upside down in front of her face, the video screen facing out toward Jenna.

'A smile, Ma-ma!' Ayana said. 'One . . . two . . . four . . .'

She clicked her tongue.

'Got it!' Ayana proclaimed. She turned the monitor around to look at it. Nodded. 'Good picher, Mama!'

Jenna's chest clenched. Damn, she loved that little girl. 'Thank you, baby.'

'Tell Mommy night-night, A,' Vern said, scooping up his granddaughter.

'Nigh-nigh, Mama!' she said, letting Vern lean her in for a sloppy, wet kiss on Jenna's temple.

Jenna watched Vern carry Ayana into the hallway and disappear into her room before turning back to Charley. She stood up and reached for her usual coffee cup. 'Sometimes I swear that kid's going to grow up and want to live in a nudist colony.'

'Might as well,' Charley said. 'Between how behind we are on clean laundry and going to get a midnight snack and being surprised to find Yancy in front of the fridge in his skivvies, we're pretty damned close, anyway.'

Jenna dumped the coffee grinds into the maker, stretching to try to see into the living room. 'Where is Yancy, by the way?'

They hadn't had much time together at all lately, and as strained as things had been between them since Denny and the knowledge of Claudia's threat hanging over them, right now, she had to admit to herself nothing would be better than to feel his arms around her waist, and some long, slow kisses. Maybe even a frisky romp to channel all the wired energy General Ted's talking down had left her with into something much more satisfying.

'Not here,' Charley said.

Jenna opened her mouth to protest, but Charley held up a finger. 'Agh. Don't. We're not breaking the three guards must man the fortress rule. Victor's in the bathroom putting on his uniform, getting ready to go in. Yancy called him earlier, asked to trade shifts. Didn't say what was up, but don't worry, Rain Man. He secured an acceptable substitute and performed the changing of the guard to the letter, on schedule. No need to put him in the dog house tonight.'

Jenna turned back to the coffee pot and plugged it in, feeling a mix of relief and worry. The last time Yancy stopped telling everyone where he was and what he was up to, he had ended up getting involved in a situation over his head, killed someone while trying to rescue someone he barely knew, and landed them in their current situation where, at any moment, Claudia's blackmail hammer could fall and throw all their lives into a pit of hell.

'Rain Man,' Charley said, pushing back from the table. She felt him behind her before his hands rested on her shoulders. Gave her a light squeeze. 'He loves you. He's not going to screw that up again.'

Jenna glanced over her shoulder at him, skeptical. 'Aren't brothers supposed to hate their sisters' boyfriends because no one is good enough?'

Charley released her shoulders and walked toward the living room. 'Maybe. But sisters don't usually have to grow up in environments where curtain rods are known more for their weapon potential than, ya know, holding up curtains, so let me slide this one time, OK?'

He disappeared into the living room, and in the next few seconds, the familiar twanging of guitar strings met her ears. *Weird Charley mentioning the curtain rod tonight.* It haunted Jenna so much that sometimes his ability to act like it didn't ever enter his mind infuriated her.

'Make enough to pour me a cup?' Victor's deep voice jolted Jenna back to reality.

He stood in the doorway, finishing the buckle where his uniform pants belted over sharp, blue creases. He stepped past her and reached for a mug from the cabinet, now as at home as everyone else allowed here.

'Sure thing. I'm surprised you haven't had to go in before now, what with the manhunt of the century that's being mounted out there,' Jenna said, her voice oozing bitterness.

Victor poured his coffee, grabbed the sugar, and joined Jenna at the table. 'Should've, actually. Been putting off my captain all day so I could hang around until Yancy got back. Had to cover for him a couple of times in the past few days, actually. Hope nothing's up.'

There it was. No judgment, no condescension. Not even a request to open a dialogue or insinuate they had a problem to fix. Just the knowledge between them of what had happened, what was at stake, and that they could only pull their own weight as far as helping keep Yancy's literal skeleton in the proverbial closet. Victor didn't tell Jenna everything he'd done as they worked to make sure Denny Hoffsteader's life – and death – would never hurt this family, but she knew he'd tracked down sources, shaken up certain parties. She also knew he and Yancy had taken several late night drives without a word about where or why, always coming home resigned and stoic. She'd told Victor long ago she'd trust him to do what needed to be done to protect the family now that Claudia knew Yancy's mistake, and she'd meant it. He'd asked her to not ask, so she hadn't. In so many ways, it had been like a request Hank would've made. And yet, she might've checked behind her ex-husband, curious and even unsure of the steps he might take. It wasn't that Hank wouldn't have done everything he could to protect them or that he was somehow inadequate. He was smart, capable, and in the same situation, he would've taken bold steps to secure the situation.

Bleu de France flashed in. Just a hair different from the shade she associated with submissiveness, but the color of depending on someone all the same.

Maybe that was the difference, though. Hank would've trusted his *own* plan. And while his plan would've been every bit as much to protect his daughter and Jenna, he and Jenna didn't always share ways of thinking. Hank did things Hank's way. Got things done Hank's way. While Jenna would've trusted his intentions, she would have felt unsettled that they weren't on the same page.

His brother, however, she'd never followed to see his actions, given suggestions for strategies, or questioned his methods. She'd just known from the very day he'd promised her he'd take care of it that she didn't have to. When it came to protecting Ayana – and keeping Yancy's past in the past was vital to that – for some strange, unexplainable reason, their philosophies aligned.

Headlights flashed across the kitchen window as tires rumbled up the gravel drive. A car door slammed.

'That's my cue,' Victor said, standing and putting on his hat. 'What do you think? Will any of the people I search in the door-to-door demand I stop so they can take their picture with me?'

Jenna laughed. 'You know, of all the city-wide lockdown door-to-door manhunts I've heard of, it's actually been the cops in the riot gear that seem to get the chicks, but you never know. Maybe they'll think you're too important to risk frontlines and riot gear so they'll want your autograph.'

Victor smirked. 'Hi. Lare. Ee. Us. Cops got feelings, too, you know,' he said, giving a sniffle and wiping a fake tear from his eye.

Jenna smiled. 'I'm keeping you humble. *Someone* needs to.'

He chuckled, bent to start unlocking the front door to let Yancy in and him out. 'Well, Bad Ass, on that job, you are to be *commended*.'

Jenna leaned against the door jamming, listening as the keys clicked in their various stations. 'Hey, Victor?'

He glanced up from where he was sliding the last bolt through its casing near the floor. 'Yeah?'

'I really do doubt they're going to find anything related to Black Shadow in this door-to-door. They'll have been planning for this, and even if lightning strikes and cops end up in their homes, they'll be model citizens on their best behavior, not armed to the hilt with sawed off shotguns and tossing Molotovs out the windows. But if I'm wrong . . .'

Victor smirked, squeezed her calf with his broad hand, simply because it was the part of her closest to him. 'I'll be fine, Bad Ass. Don't you give it another thought.'

Jenna nodded as he let go and stood, swinging the door open. Yancy strode up the walk, Oboe trailing behind him, lagging on the leash as he slowed to sniff at bird poop splattered on the cement.

'Come on, buddy, it's just crap. You do it, I do it, Fox News anchors are full of it . . . just crap,' Yancy said, giving the leash a yank.

Oboe fell in line and trotted toward them. Victor and Yancy met in passing, stopped for a handshake. 'Thanks for coming today, man. I appreciate it,' Yancy said.

'Anytime, dude. Gotta run. Duty calls,' Victor said.

Victor climbed in the cruiser, and Yancy reached the door. Jenna peeled her eyes from where Victor was backing out to take in her boyfriend's deep-set eyes. She wrapped her arms around his neck and pecked his cheek while Oboe took his time waddling through, then turned to close and relock the door.

'I'm glad you decided to come over tonight,' Jenna said. 'I feel like the time we get to spend together these days is more like snap-shots rather than actual minutes or hours.'

'I know what you mean,' Yancy said, squatting to unhook Oboe's leash from his collar, then turning to get a water bowl from where it sat on the sink. 'Life's always busy, but with all this stuff with the Potomac Twelve and—'

'Is that what people are calling them? The Potomac Twelve?' Jenna asked amid a mouth full of the muffin she'd snagged from the basket on the counter. She'd spent so much time thinking about them as the bank attackers and then Black Shadow she hadn't thought that of course the public would have a name for the group by now. The team decided early on not to release the name Black Shadow for fear of tipping off its members they were on to them and give them time to run – one choice General Ted for Toffee had actually agreed with – so they'd kept it under wraps.

'Yep. I feel like I've been talking nonstop ever since I got out of bed this morning,' Yancy said.

Damn. She'd been so into her own day it hadn't even occurred to her that Yancy was probably getting dispatch calls to 911 all day with people phoning in not just the attacks but probably false alarms when people got spooked, crazies thinking they'd spotted a sign their room-mate was one of the killers. She let out a breath she hadn't realized she'd been holding, and her chest loosened ever so slightly.

Yancy looked up from where he was squatted next to Oboe, who had finished lapping up his water and had now rolled over and was stretching his back legs out to their fullest length, enjoying a belly rub. 'What was that?'

Jenna quirked her head. 'What?'

'That sigh. Like we're at the movies, and I just ordered the tickets, and you realized I wasn't going to force you to sit through a third showing of *Star Trek*.'

Jenna shook her head. 'I was worried was all.'

'About?' Yancy asked, standing and taking the chair across from her. 'Oh, wait. I get it. You just realized that the reason I had to get Victor to cover my tot fortress shift was due to the fact that there are madmen with sharp weapons running all over the region stabbing people and *not* because I'd become worried about another damsel in distress like CiCi and launched a campaign to save her.'

Jenna looked at her lap, half-laughed. 'Something like that.'

'Well,' Yancy said, standing and taking Jenna's hands in his. He gently urged her to her feet. 'While I know I deserve the doubts until I earn some of the trust back, you can rest assured that those bastard terrorists have kept me *way* too busy today to locate any princesses in towers with bully boyfriends or even anything remotely close to that. This freakin' crisis has *all* of my attention. Trust.'

As he said the last part, something changed in his voice. Sounded tired. Weary. Alice blue flashed in.

Maybe they could both use a break from the horrors they'd seen and heard all day. As antsy as she was to get news that the killer's body in the morgue had been identified and as strong as the urge was to stay up all night, obsessing over the case details while she waited, now that Yancy was here and she was, too, it felt a lot easier to follow him down the hallway into her bedroom and close the door.

As he pressed his lips against hers, his hands working her shirt upward, she let the details she'd felt so keen to analyze drift away. They'd be there in the morning, and right now, she needed this far more.

His lips parted from hers long enough for him to tug her shirt over her head and toss it on the ground. She kicked off her heels and backed toward the bed corner, perched on its end as she undid her trousers.

Yancy, now bare-chested in the dim lighting of only the little reading lamp by the bed, moved toward her and, with a lick of his lips and rubbing his hands together, bent slowly at the knees, grabbing the waist of her khakis and sinking lower and lower as he pulled them to the floor with him.

As he stood back up, towering over her, she let the strap of her bra droop off of her right shoulder, then reached across and used her hand to cause the left strap to do the same before she let herself fall back on to the bed, tempting him. As he climbed on the bed, he knelt over her, straddling her torso, a sly grin on his face, and she scooted back until her full body was on the bed, stretched diagonally across it.

'If those straps won't stay up, we might as well just do away with them, don't you think?' he said, and he playfully scooped under the small of her back with one arm, using the momentum to roll her on to her stomach. She felt his weight move from over her, the bed sink behind her as he sat back, as though waiting.

Obliging, she got to her knees and, still facing away from him, inched closer to where he waited. She reached up and twisted up the locks of hair hanging down her back, not because he needed her to, but because she was playing along.

His hands rubbed her shoulders, smoothed inward to where they dipped down. The firm, rolling massage almost made Jenna forget she was holding her hair up, but she caught it a second before she let it go.

After a moment, Yancy's hands trailed down her shoulder blades, and he leaned forward, brushing her right shoulder with a soft, warm kiss. His fingers worked at her bra clasp now, his lips still lingering next to her skin.

'You know, I pretend these things are easier to undo when I can see what I'm doing,' he breathed against her skin, 'but really, I only play it up as a difficulty because I really *really* like getting to see you from the back every now and then.'

Her beige bra dropped to the bed, the cool air hitting her bare breasts. Yancy's arms reached around her torso.

Jenna looked down, took in the sight of her breasts cupped in his hands. Felt the warmth of his chest against her back.

'You know what? I think I like this angle every now and then, too.'

Thirty-four

Jenna sat in the antique paisley armchair in the corner of her bedroom, sipping a nice fresh, dark roast with two creams, and stared out the window, watching the dragonflies zoom around the porch in a weird, intricate chase of a mating dance.

She glanced toward where Yancy still lay in bed fast asleep, his arm tucked under his pillow, clutching it to him. Last night had been everything she needed, but sleep hadn't been long enough, and unfortunately, the second it left her, the cogs in her head were whirring full force. So, she'd slipped out of bed, readied herself for a steady infusion of caffeine, and settled back into the comfy chair in her room where she could at least still creepily enjoy the cute faces her boyfriend made when he was dreaming while she mulled over the case facts nagging at her like an itch she couldn't quite find to scratch.

Really, as soon as the body was identified, things would roll. Once one perp had a name, they'd have connections: neighbors, friends, haunts, Internet footprints. Strand by strand, the impossible web would collapse as, one by one, the UNSUBs were identified, found, and caught.

So why was she so stressed about *this* case as if there was something important she'd missed that could change the game? The pieces were in play, the body being examined. Waiting was never easy, but this really was the small piece that would start the unraveling of Black Shadow's whole operation. So why? Sheer curiosity?

She ran through the hall, slick with blood. She almost fell, but grabbed the banister. Keep running! Keep running for Charley!

Jenna opened her eyes, shook the memory. Curiosity. Yeah, right.

'Morning, gorgeous,' Yancy's groggy voice said through a yawn.

Jenna glanced his way and smiled as he stretched his arms wide before sitting up and leaning back against two pillows propped on the headboard. 'Let me guess. You woke up early and were too excited to go back to sleep because you knew when I woke up you could *definitely* talk me into a day-long, winner-takes-all Settlers of Catan tournament? If that's it, though, you better hope Charley and Vern are game and that they can help explain it to Ayana, because it's really designed for five to six players . . .'

She rolled her eyes and chunked the blue throw pillow beside her chair at him. 'As thrilling as that sounds, I can't stop thinking about—'

'The Potomac Twelve attacks,' he filled in.

She folded her lips, shrugged. 'You know me well.'

He shifted to hang his leg off the bed's edge and reached for his prosthetic. 'So, what's bugging you this fine sunny morning? What colors are clashing?'

You really do *know me too well.*

'Hit me with it,' Yancy said. 'I've got my leg on, so now I can think properly . . .'

Jenna snorted. 'Well, to be honest, the whole time it's been the father and son in Exam Room Six. Something was just always off about that. The dad was killed first, but he was farther inside the room than the son. Now obviously, the son could've been farther in when Marius entered—'

'Marius?'

'The particular attacker that stabbed the father,' Jenna clarified. 'Anyway, the son could've been in a different place when Marius came into the room, making the dad the closest target and then the son tried to escape, but the sword wound in the son hit him at an angle that meant he was stabbed from the front. Did Marius kill the dad and somehow make his way back around the son so he could look him in the eye while he stabbed him?'

Yancy shook his head, picturing the surveillance footage in his own mind. 'It'd be a cool aspect to try to profile if he did, but I doubt it.' He closed his eyes, trying to picture the video. It had been so grainy, and the angle hadn't been good at all going *into* the room. It hadn't showed anything of what occurred inside it.

But then it hit him. There *was* something funny there, now that he thought about it. It had been right in that area and right around that time that one attacker had killed the other outside of that room, too.

'Could the dad's wound and the son's wound have come from different swords?' he asked.

Jenna's eyebrows raised. 'Hmm. I mean, I suppose it's *possible*, though Marius was the only long sword carrier at the bank. I didn't notice any other swords in the hospital footage, but it was hard to make out much of anything in the chaos . . .'

'I know what you mean,' Yancy muttered.

'Huh?'

'I just mean I can imagine, from what little I've seen on the gossip sites that ran it.'

But Jenna hadn't latched on to his flub, because she already had her phone in hand, texting. 'Asking Irv to send over the initial M.E. report. They won't finalize and publish official findings for a while, but in active cases they'll usually let us take a peek at their first reactions if it could help find an active perp.'

She set her phone down and hopped up. 'I'll be right back. Irv'll send reports to my tablet and I left it in the kitchen last night.'

Yancy's eyes followed Jenna out of the room, admiring how her pink-striped pajama that seemed to cover her ass *just* enough that he couldn't see anything but seemed like they might give him a peek at any instant. When she turned the corner, he hung his head then stared pointedly at his crotch. 'I have to be a good listener right now. You have to let me be good boyfriend right now!'

'Did you say something?' Jenna asked, bustling back into the bedroom.

Yancy coughed. 'Did you hear back from Irv?'

Jenna nodded, sitting down next to Yancy on the bed cross-legged. She hit a few buttons on the tablet to open a file, then swiped across it a few times searching for the page Irv had pointed out to her.

She leaned closer, reading the scrawled words of the ME, then swiped again to look at the photos of the bodies. 'Well I'll be damned,' she mumbled.

It didn't surprise Yancy, though. Not after what he'd seen on the video and the theory starting to form in his head. The dad's gut wound was definitely inflicted by Marius's briquet sabre. It entered low in the gut, but the exit wound was higher, indicative of the way the blade curved upward. The son's wound, however, was different in multiple ways. Not only did the pictorial evidence show that the entrance and exit wounds were directly across from each other with no diversion to suggest a curved blade, but the son's stab wounds also reflected two points of gashed flesh on either side of the entrance point of the sword tip. The father's wound only had one, of course, since a Napoleonic briquet sabre featured only one sharp edge. The sword the boy was stabbed with had two.

And Yancy thought he had a good idea why.

'I'm starting to get a crazy theory here,' Yancy said, his mind working overtime to figure out how to give Jenna the info she needed and keep his promise to Irv that their dealings stay between them at the same time. 'So I might be grasping at straws, but hear me out.'

Jenna nodded. 'Sure.'

'You said that at some point right around Exam Six this Atticus guy *killed* Marius before hauling his body away, right?'

'Yeah.'

'Well, I know we all are wondering why they'd kill him. I mean, if they're in the middle of an assault on the ER and some nurse happens to be a jiu jitsu master knocks him out cold, sure. You grab him and run, because if you leave him, he gets identified, and inevitably, his identity will trace back to everybody in the group. But that's not what happened. He didn't get hurt or killed by one of the victims. *They* killed him. In the middle of their own planned attack. Why?'

Jenna blinked rapidly. 'I don't know. He did something wrong. He made a mistake. He didn't stab the kid, obviously. Maybe that somehow screwed up the way the rest of the attack was supposed to go down.'

Yancy stared at the tablet, at the photo of the kid, replaying the grainy footage over and over in his mind. The guy with the long sword storms into Six. Storms out. Another attacker turns the corner and they almost bump into each other. The attacker who turned the corner turns and goes into Six. And suddenly Atticus appears and kills Marius.

'I think he made a mistake. I think he broke a rule,' Yancy said. 'Let's get Irv on the footage, but I think Atticus offed Marius because Marius walked *away* from that kid. Killed the dad, turned to do the kid but couldn't, so he left.'

Jenna nodded slowly. 'It would explain why the kid was on his way out of the room and the attacker stabbed him from the front.'

'A different attacker.'

Jenna shifted, leaned back into the pillows, stunned.

'This puts a whole new spin on the group profile, huh?' Yancy said.

She nodded. 'And honestly, I don't even know what it means. Not yet, anyway.'

From the table across the room next to the antique chair, Jenna's phone skittered across the glass until it reached the wood rim, which caught it on its side. Jenna jumped up and crossed the room, snatched it up, and read the text Irv had sent to the team:

THE M.E. GOT A HIT ON A MATCHING SCAR. MISSING PERSON
RECORD. NAMES JAMES ASNER. SENDING BRIEFING ON ASNER TO
YOUR TABLETS NOW.

She hopped back on to the bed and picked up the tablet, scrolled
through the menu to find the briefings folder. Sure enough, it was
already in the file.

Jenna read the brief out loud. 'James Asner, would be thirty-three
today. Harvard law student, went missing during his third year without
a trace. Known during his undergraduate studies there for being a
standout debate champion but also for his *many first place fencing
trophies.* Now isn't that interesting?'

'Mr Sword has a sword past. That part fits.'

'But here's the problem, according to the brief, as soon as Asner
was reported missing, the trail went cold. No leads, no sightings, no
digital footprint. Not so much as a toe print. It was like he fell off
the earth.'

'Perfect candidate for a radical terrorist group,' Yancy said.

Jenna nodded, trying hard to latch on to the color that kept sneaking
in but drifting away before she could grab hold of it. She was missing
something. Something important.

Wisps of thoughts she couldn't quite grasp taunted her as she paced
the bedroom floor. *Why? Why did they kill him? They killed him for not
killing someone. But that's off! They killed him for not killing someone.*

A shade of yellow flashed in. The thought slowly flooded Jenna's
mind. 'But this wasn't the first time he didn't kill someone. That's
what's bothering me. He was the person to lead Ashlee Haynie,
the bank survivor, down to the vault and give her the message for
us.' Still, something didn't fit, but that was part of it. 'So,' she
ventured, hoping she could talk it out of the recesses of her mind,
'the kid obviously wasn't the one survivor left. Margeaux East was.
But Marius was killed, and he didn't take her to safety. So that
wasn't his job anymore. We need to look back at the footage, see
who did . . .'

Maybe if she could figure out how the hierarchy of the lone survivor
worked, who dealt with them and why, it would help the profile even
without Margeaux East being able to deliver the message they left.

Then, before she could stop herself, Jenna confessed to Yancy about
making the tape of Margeaux East's ramblings. He insisted they listen

to it, but unfortunately, they couldn't make out any real *words*, much less literary quotes.

And while Yancy had tried to relieve her disappointment with jokes about the lines she'd crossed to make the damned thing, she couldn't believe she'd done something so drastic for something so worthless.

The yellow hue flashed in again, the same as when they'd viewed the surveillance tape.

'Ugh! But even that's still off!' Jenna vented, wringing her hands. *Come on, brain!*

Yancy sat forward, lightly wrapped his hand around her wrist. 'I can't read minds here, love. What's going on in there? Maybe I can help.'

She recounted her thinking to him about needing to see on the footage who had given a message to Margeaux East – since they knew it wasn't Marius – about how she thought the process of deciding who led the survivor might tell her more about the inner workings of the group. She collapsed on the bed in a heap. 'But the tape! That's what I just keep coming back to. The tape and the scissors. They closed Ashlee Haynie in a *bank vault,* but this girl got a cabinet? She's clearly still vulnerable to the point of being ready to attack with the only weapon she had available to her, so whoever put her there obviously didn't quite get the message across to her that the plan was for her to *live*—'

'That's because it wasn't, Jen,' Yancy cut in. He stood, pacing, gesturing wildly as he talked. 'No one put her in the cabinet. When she saw they were under attack, she ran, and when there was nowhere to run, she hid. She climbed in on her own.'

Jenna stared at him. 'How do you know that?'

Yancy looked stunned a second, but then shook his head. 'Because like you said. The tape. She taped herself in there, trying to make sure they couldn't find her, and she had the scissors ready if they did. Message Irv and have him look for it on the video, but it's the way it makes sense.'

Jenna whipped out her phone and texted Irv, but as she did, she already knew Yancy was right. It was why the colors hadn't made sense. The tape, the scissors.

She stilled, the thought so strong she couldn't fathom what it meant yet.

'Then they didn't leave a survivor at the hospital,' she said slowly, dark yellow flashing in.

Every cop learned it as Homicide 101. Assailants evolve, get better at what they do. But if you can get to the core of the early ones, the first crimes, those will give you traces of where to look. They'll always somehow connect to something the killer sees every day, does every day, knows.

She grabbed her slacks from the dresser, pulled them on as she fumbled around the room, gathering her things. 'I have to go now. I don't know what it all means, but I need to talk to Ashlee Haynie. Marius took her to that bank vault. And whether she realizes it or not, I think she knows him.'

Thirty-five

Jenna pulled up outside a ritzy-looking apartment complex called The Ivory at Castle Pines. As soon as she'd shared her hunch with Saleda and the Special Agent in Charge had confirmed, via Irv, that Ashlee Haynie seemed to have gone missing in action, the team had met at Quantico for a quick briefing and strategizing session before splitting up to start an unofficial search to locate her.

Given what she'd been through, her not showing up for her shift at another branch of Weisman Bank and Trust normally wouldn't be shocking. But the fact that the bank branch manager called to check on her and learned her phone number had been disconnected, coupled with a few more checks of Irv's, confirmed what Jenna already suspected: this wasn't Ashlee needing some down time to recuperate. She hadn't checked her email for the past twenty-four hours, despite the fact that she had regularly used her work account for personal e-mail before, too. There had been no activity on any of her credit cards, either. With the revelations in play and what Jenna was starting to piece together, the team agreed finding her was vital both to the case *and* to Ashlee's safety. They copped a plan to split up. Porter and Teva would track down James Asner's former associates at Harvard and maybe shed some more light on their one known Black Shadow member in hopes of drawing out some more angles. And while Saleda and Dodd made the rounds to speak to Ashlee's friends and family members, Jenna would swing by her apartment. Considering the signs Irv's had dug up, it was likely Ashlee wasn't there. But Jenna still wanted to take a look around her place. Ashlee being gone wasn't a coincidence, but what had happened to cause the disappearance was a bit more of a mystery. Best case scenario, she was staying with friends somewhere, depressed on their couch, or had checked herself into a mental health facility if she was suicidal and was in a hospital ward, safe and sound under suicide watch.

Disturbing hunter green flashed in. Jenna's gut said the circumstances were more alarming. Maybe Ashlee had remembered something and, realizing she *did* know Marius, fled, afraid he'd come back for her.

Or maybe Black Shadow got spooked by what happened at the hospital with Marius and decided to do away with the living liability. Even if the other members weren't aware of Marius's connection to Ashlee and it most likely being the reason he had chosen to spare her and put her in the vault to deliver the message, they knew there was a living witness, and it was likely at least that the masterminds knew of the connection because Jenna's gut *also* told her it had somehow played into their choice of what bank to attack.

Jenna and Grey climbed the staircase that led to the unit on the second level. It had only taken one carefully worded phone call to the leasing office informing them they would be dropping by to look around the apartment. Funny how even if it technically hadn't been long enough to file a missing person's case, if you said the right things, you could have the landlord agree to an unofficial visit because they thought it *was official*.

The shade of raw umber brown that Jenna associated with wealth flashed in. This apartment complex was nicer than most five-star hotels Jenna had been to and reminded her more of a resort than any apartment she'd ever set foot in.

When they reached the second floor landing, a smartly dressed African American woman in a pair of perfectly tailored gray slacks and a textured navy blazer woven with whites and grays left open to show the pretty, periwinkle silk blouse greeted them. The polite smile on her puce-painted lips was warm as she made eye contact with Jenna, offered her hand. 'Hi, there. I'm Nanette Viselli, property owner of the Ivory. So lovely to meet you, though I wish it were under less urgent circumstances.'

'Yes,' Jenna said, shaking her hand. 'I'm Dr Jenna Ramey. You actually spoke to my Special Agent in Charge, Saleda Ovarez, and she sends her appreciation for your cooperation in letting us into Ms Haynie's apartment to take a look around.'

Nanette Viselli pulled a silver key from her trouser pocket and turned to the door. As she worked the lock, she shook her head, a smile breaking across her face. 'I told my husband, knowing those two, they probably up and decided on whim to take some sort of second honeymoon. Maybe go to Scotland or somewhere to see all those medieval castles and things, as interested as they are in that . . . oh, what is that they do . . .'

They lock clicked, and she turned the knob, opened the door.

'They, Mrs Viselli?' Jenna said. 'Ashlee Haynie is married?'

Nanette stepped into the apartment's marble foyer. 'Why, yes. To JP. I'm surprised you didn't already know that. Seems like the sort of thing you guys would uncover fairly quickly.'

As she continued into the depths of the apartment, calling out just in case they were wrong and someone *was* home after all, salmon flashed in. *Yes, it is the sort of thing we usually know about right away, especially while working victim profiles of a crime.*

And yet Ashlee hadn't mentioned her husband or wanting to see him, nor had their searches into her background turned up any marriage certificates or evidence of legal marriage. Fuchsia flashed in as a strange feeling crept into Jenna's gut. They were in the right place, but she was starting to think the reason for it wasn't *quite* what she'd bargained for.

A silver-framed picture set on an antique white desk in the corner of the room pulled Jenna's attention. She picked it up and looked at the smiling couple in heavy winter coats. Ashlee Haynie and her husband JP – also known as Marius – grinning at the camera through the snow.

It suddenly all made sense. The goldenrod of deliberate overlook she'd seen when Marius had passed where Ashlee had claimed to be hiding in the bank, the spot where he'd have to have been blind to have missed her. Why the yellow – the unintentional overlook – she had seen in relation to the survivor at the hospital who was terrified and ready to fight for her life was such a contrast to the circumstances of Ashlee's survival at the bank. Marius hadn't only known her. She'd been a willing player.

'What were you saying about them liking to do something together, Ms Viselli?' Jenna asked, her eyes still glued to the image featuring the man whose body she'd seen pale and blue last night in the Mt. Olive morgue.

Nanette Viselli wandered back toward Jenna, having finally called out to every corner and toward every room. She waved her hand, chuckling. 'Aw, some kind of sword-fighting or something crazy like that! They even asked permission to use our aerobics room at the clubhouse so he could teach her some kind of thing he did with it in college. Wild, huh? If that was my husband's hobby, well, he'd just have to be on his own, because the closest you're getting me to any kind of fighting is a bidding war for a property I have my eye on!'

Nanette laughed, her teeth so bright white against that puce lipstick they looked almost unnatural, not too unlike the shiny marble columns around the fireplace she stood next to. Jenna's gaze drifted sideways from the landlady, noticing the black, lacquered shelves on the adjacent wall that started at the marble floor and stretched all the way to the ceiling itself.

Grey had seen it first and was already sauntering by the shelves as if she were a customer window shopping. Jenna crossed toward them. 'I take it they also did a lot of reading.'

Nanette stayed where she was but turned to watch Jenna and Grey examine the bookcases. 'Magnificent, aren't they? And not just the shelves. They've got quite a collection. A bit picky in taste, though.'

Jenna reached for a hardback copy of *The Catcher in the Rye*, opened it, and flipped through the worn pages. 'What makes you say that?'

'Probably more me being sore than anything,' Nanette said, taking a seat in the desk chair in front of the antique corner desk. 'Just that, well, knowing they were big readers, I recommended my niece's book to them, and well . . .'

'What?' Jenna coaxed, sensing some shame in Nanette's voice.

'They seemed interested at first and asked about it, but . . .'

'It's OK, Ms Viselli. This is just between us.'

'Well, they were nice enough, but once they found out it was only available as an e-book, any interest they'd had in it before dissolved like that,' Nanette said, snapping her fingers. 'They said it was nothing against my niece or anything, and how they were sure *her* book was fantastic, but that they just didn't buy many e-books since so many of the books available on that platform are self-published by people who wrote a first draft and put it up without ever editing it or anything. They said they had tried some but had ended up buying so many poorly written works because it was hard to tell the wheat from the chaff that they stopped buying e-books all together. Said they hadn't downloaded any in over two years and, even if they wanted to, wouldn't know where to look to find their old Books-E e-readers.'

From a few feet away came the sound of Grey grunting.

Jenna glanced over, and Grey was seated on the floor, legs criss-crossed, reading the first page of a tattered paperback version of *The Jungle*. She grunted again, this time a little louder. Let out a strange, amused laugh.

'Something funny about that, Grey?' Jenna asked

Grey didn't look up. 'If they stopped reading e-books two years ago, how come there's a new Books-E Glow on that end table,' Grey said, cocking her head toward the one of the pewter stands flanking either side of the white leather couch.

Sure enough, a Books-E Glow, the newest e-reader on the market, faced her, settled in its charging dock atop the table. Jenna glanced at the identical table mirroring it on the opposite side of the couch. No Books-E Glow, but there was a matching charging dock for one, its cord snaking behind the couch to plug into an outlet.

They both had e-readers but didn't read e-books. One was here, one missing. Most likely this one was Marius's, and Ashlee had hers with her wherever she'd gone.

And she took her Books-E with her. The one she doesn't read books on.

Flint had mentioned that the locations of the meetings were never given on the forum, that they'd found other ways. They had the email account to get the URL of the website Black Shadow members used to share things like the video footage of attacks for Ishmael to see, and yet, no details about dry-runs or the coming attacks were on those. It *had* to be getting more and more dangerous to get that big group together in person, so they couldn't be meeting every time they needed to discuss the locations and dates to show up for the next blitz. Besides, with a group as ragtag as the people who made up Black Shadow, the fact that many *were* empathetic like Marius and the dry-heaving Scout was dangerous. Atticus and Ishmael were smarter than that.

Just like the ever-moving website used to share information after talking on a stationary, forum became too risky, once again, Black Shadow's leaders had found a better way.

That better way would tell her how to stop the third attack promised in the note at the hospital. The only problem was, as much as Grey knew about literature, if they didn't know what book to look for on the e-reader – if they even *needed* to look for a book on the e-reader – her weird human trick was of no use. And as many things as Jenna could elicit from her color associations, no color in any shade or variation of the rainbow was going to flash in and explain to her how a terrorist network's system of communication through e-readers worked. In the corner of her vision, a small curio cabinet caught her attention. Inside were at least a dozen pieces of *Gone With the Wind* memorabilia, from the classic poster, to character portraits, to a figurine centerpiece of a classic southern belle.

I've found you, Scarlett.

Cutthroat UNSUB finally had a name.

The memory of her conversation with Flint Lewis resurfaced and the new Black Shadow members who had inspired him to break away from the group. A bluish hue flashed in.

Mr Darcy and Scarlett . . .

She didn't have the slightest clue how the process of communicating via the e-readers might even begin to work.

She'd let Irv look at it when she got back, but she suspected she knew someone who already had the answer.

Thirty-six

Jenna was relieved when Flint Lewis answered his phone after the first ring. This whole thing had her on edge, and while part of it was nerves that if she couldn't get hold of the one person who could crack this communication system, odds got better more people would die, another part couldn't shake off the concern about the very real danger Flint and his family were in. Danger Jenna's team had *put* them in by risking them attracting the attention of Black Shadow. Getting Flint back on their radar.

'Flint, so glad to hear your voice. Listen, I know we've already asked so much of you after you'd put this behind you, tried your best to steer clear of these awful people . . . *especially* with your sweet wife carrying the next addition to your family and a toddler to care for—'

'But,' Flint interjected, his voice flat. Angry?

Jenna bit her lip and closed her eyes. 'I need your help one more time. I wouldn't ask again. I really wouldn't, Flint,' she said, cringing through every word. She knew better than anyone about trying to get away from your past. Keep your family safe. 'But lives depend on it.'

'And what about my *family* and *our* lives? They not important enough?' came Flint's reply, his tone loud and seething.

Something was different. Something had changed since they'd run out of his home toward the scene of the hospital attack. He sounded mad on the surface, but there was more to it.

'What's happened, Flint? What's going on?'

'They *know*, Doctor,' he fumed. 'They know I logged on. I don't know how they know, but I know they do. They know I logged on, they know I dug around. I'm just . . .' he paused, his trailing words losing fire. He took a rattling breath. 'I'm just worried.'

Jenna's chest clenched. She knew the feeling better than he'd ever know.

'Help me put them away, Flint. I know how to get them, and I'm close. All I need is one piece of information I don't have.'

The silence seemed to go on for minutes until finally, Flint sighed. 'And I suppose you think I do?'

Jenna took the slight opening and launched into everything: finding Marius's dead body, identifying him and Ashlee, his apartment, the e-readers. She told the landlady's story about their aversion toward e-books, then filled him in on how she'd made the leap to them being a communication system.

'I'm sure they use them to pass information to each other without being traced, but I can't tap into it unless I know their technique. I know this is probably something they put in place long after you were out of the picture, but I guess I was hoping . . .' Jenna paused. How to explain?

Flint said nothing, but Jenna could hear him breathing heavily on the other end, assuring her he hadn't hung up.

'Please, Flint,' she said finally.

When he spoke again, his voice sounded tired, frayed at the edges. 'If they're doing what I think they are, they're using the same method as on the old forum when we wanted to get all the members to a private chat room all at once to talk about something we didn't want the Internet to keep a record of,' Flint explained.

Somehow, Jenna was pretty sure those private chats probably had more nefarious reasons, but for now, she wouldn't argue.

'How did you get in touch? Pass messages?'

'I made an account on one of the online book review sites and did a review of a book. All the members of the private forum were given the title I'd reviewed, and every day, they knew to check my account there. It would pull up my reviewer stats, and in turn, they could see if I had posted any new reviews.'

'So, if you had, I take it that they clicked out to that review, where there would be a message waiting for them hidden in it,' Jenna said, catching on.

'Something like that.'

But on an e-reader, could you click out on individual reviewer handles? Would it even show reviewers stats?

Flint seemed to have spotted the problem, too. 'I know what you're thinking, but I think I know how it works. The more messages we used, the longer the list of reviews under my handle and people got sick of wading through them, trying to figure out which was newest, *if* one was new, etc. So we simplified by deciding on a single book title. Instead of checking my review handle every day, members checked that book's page for any new reviews posted that contained the phrase 'right now' in any capacity as a part of the title of the review. It was a much more sustainable system, though I have to admit the review titles got pretty creative.'

'So how do we know what book they're checking now?' Jenna asked.

'I can't be sure,' Flint said, 'But if I had to guess, I'd say they've already told you. I'd say it'd be the book that brought you to Black Shadow in the first place. *A Tale of Two Cities.*'

'Is the review in some kind of code?' Jenna asked.

'Probably,' Flint replied.

'Can you read it?'

Flint half-laughed. 'If your point about how some things change while everything stays the same holds up. Guess we might as well see. Booting up my tablet now.'

Jenna waited, forcing herself not to ask more questions or otherwise distract Flint from looking for a hidden message in the reviews of *A Tale of Two Cities.*

Almost fifty people had been brutally murdered this week. She needed Flint to give her information. She needed at least a chance of stopping anyone from seeing this brand of horror even one more time.

'I'm almost done,' Flint said, his voice jarring Jenna from her thoughts of the bank and the hospital emergency room. 'I think I know where the next attack's going to be.'

What he said next made Jenna's heart leap into her throat. She couldn't breathe. Or swallow. So many people . . . and they didn't have much time.

Phone still to her ear, she headed for the Haynies' apartment door, grabbing Grey by the wrist and practically dragging her toward the exit without explaining to her or Nanette Viselli. All she could think was to get to her car. Go!

Hang up with Flint. Rally the team!

It was the 'Oh, no . . .' from Flint that slowed her steps toward her Blazer. She clasped the phone tighter.

'Flint? What's wrong?'

He didn't answer.

'Flint! Are you OK? Say something!'

A cough. 'Uh, there's something else in here,' he said, hoarse. 'Oh, man . . .'

'Flint? You have to talk to me, buddy,' Jenna said, prickles of worry creeping up her spine.

'Jenna, there's something about me in here.'

Jenna's breath caught in her throat. *Not this.*

'Flint, what does it say? Flint, we can help you. Protect you. What does it say?'

But there was no answer.

'Flint, are you there? Flint!'

Jenna took her phone from her ear to look at the screen. On it were two words that made Jenna's blood freeze in her veins: CALL LOST.

Thirty-seven

The Blazer's back tire skidded into a shrill screech as Jenna bore down on the gas pedal, one hand on the wheel to even out the SUV as she flew down the road, the other holding her phone to her ear.

'Come on, Saleda! Pick up. Pick up!' she yelled.

'I'm sure she would, if she could hear you from here,' Grey said, still calmly working on fastening her seatbelt. 'And even if she doesn't, with the way you all are about your squawk boxes, I'm sure she'll call you back within seconds.'

Jenna forced back the retort burning in her throat. She didn't have time to play Grey's games and wasn't about to try to explain society's relationships with their phones knowing full well Grey had no desire to understand a brand of thinking she found ridiculous. In Grey's world, the only urgent matters were matters of urgency to Grey.

Jenna hit redial on her phone after hanging up on Saleda's voice-mail. 'Come on, damn you!'

'Saleda Ovarez.'

'Fuck yes! Finally!' Jenna blurted out.

'Wow. I'm sorry I inconvenienced you,' Saleda said, sounding miffed. 'I know we're friends, Jenna, but I'm still your supervi—'

'Saleda, Black Shadow is about to hit. Today!' Jenna cut in.

'Where? How do you know this?'

'Don't waste time making me answer everything. Just rally the team and get everyone to The Mall at Holder Promenade. McClean, Virginia. I can explain everything else once you're on the road, but you have to get moving, and now!'

'McClean, Virginia?' Saleda repeated. 'OK, but you guys will all get there before we do. It's at least thirty-five minutes coming from Quantico, and that's if we do it lights blazing, running every red light we meet, and the rest of the cars from here to there happen to be in the shop today. It's about a twenty-minute drive from Bell Haven, right? Porter and Teva went to DC to talk to some guy who used to know James Asner . . . ah . . . JP Haynie at Harvard. If I'd gotten hold of them, they'd have probably gotten there about the same time you will, but neither one's answered their cells or my pages.'

Jenna blinked rapidly, clutched the phone. 'You don't think something went wrong, do you?'

'No, I'm sure they're OK,' Saleda said, and Jenna could hear Saleda's heels click-clacking rapidly on the tile floor. 'But just know you can't count on them getting there before I do, though I'm leaving now. But yeah, the last call I got from Porter, James's old friend they were interviewing suggested they talk to some Chinese Martial Arts master who used to be the principal teacher of, among other things, kung fu at Harvard who might help us put some pieces together. That's a good half an hour ago, but Porter also said they'd be turning their phones off and placing them in some bowl before they would be able to sit down with the guy to talk. Something about 'internal focus and respect.' Whatever that means. Maybe they found something useful. But either way, we can't count on them at the mall until they finish up their meeting.

'So when *you* get there, send out a team of two to circle and locate a spot to set up a base. I'll have the local cops on the way to reinforce, FBI SWAT will report to you until I arrive. Scope out the situation and don't make a move until you're sure—'

'Saleda,' Jenna said, finally finding her voice from where it had been choking from how fast her heart was beating, how hot her neck burned. Was she really about to do this? It wasn't her call. It wasn't even good judgment.

'What?' Saleda asked, sounding anxious. 'Is there more I don't know?'

'Saleda, you don't have time to drive it. You need to get there now, be there to run things. Take the chopper. You have to, because I won't beat you there,' Jenna said, heart thundering, dread mounting.

'Is something wrong? Are you broken down? I can send a car—'

'No, Saleda. I'm fine, but I'm . . .' Jenna took a deep breath. *You're doing the right thing.* 'I'm not going to McClean. I'm on Highway One heading North. I'm going to Bethesda.'

'What in the hell for?' Saleda exclaimed, confused.

Jenna gripped the wheel tighter, her knuckles whitening. She'd asked herself the exact same thing frantically in her head as she approached the turn for Highway 1. A terrorist group who'd left countless bodies in their wake were about to strike again, only this time, the team could be poised to ambush them and end this epidemic of fear that had a whole region afraid to so much as walk out their front doors. And yet, she kept hearing Flint's voice over and over, those last words he'd said before the line went dead. It wasn't just the words. It was his tone. There had been a strain in his words, an edge to the way he said them that had unsettled her as he said them. Her skin had prickled, and apple blossom had flashed in the way it would when something didn't feel right.

The second the call dropped, she knew she had to high-tail it back to Flint Lewis' home. The team would have to handle McLean. Something awful had happened, she could feel it.

Jenna spoke quickly, recounting the scene inside the Haynie apartment, the conversation about the e-readers and how it had led to her call with Flint that had ended with his deciphering Black Shadow's cryptic communication about the attack details . . . and his own knowledge that he was on their radar.

'Then, he was just gone. I dialed the number back, but it went straight to voicemail. I don't know whether to think they'd just kill him outright or—'

'No,' Saleda said. 'They'd keep him alive. At first, anyway. Find out how much he'd told us. His help finding their website tipped them off more than ever to the things he knows that are valuable, more vital to their secrecy than they'd noticed or even considered before. They won't kill him until they're sure they know what other holes he poked in their operation as well as what he knows about where our investigation stands.'

'I know I should've called in, waited for instructions, but Saleda . . .' a lump rose in Jenna's throat. As much as she wanted to be the person who rose above her demons and never looked back, as she sped down the highway, her eyes burned with tears, her hands shaking. She was only a badass because when *she* was the person on the other end of that phone call, when no matter how she fought for composure, that panic snuck in, the timbre of it seeming to be the stress inside you itself, gulping for air. She remembered the very first time she'd lost all control of the careful plans she'd made to get help and had dared a phone call to a hotline, desperate to get away from Claudia – get *Charley* away from her – that very second. She'd talked fast to the operator, trying to present herself as sane, but every now and then, her voice would quaver, and then ultimately, would hit that odd, strained note. It had sounded almost high frequency, like a cat in pain or aliens trying to communicate with their kind.

Jenna sniffed, blinked away the moisture that had built in her eyes. 'Saleda, *we* put him in danger. I know Black Shadow is bigger. I know they're the priority. But, Saleda, if something's happened to him, we're responsible for it. For him, his wife. Their kids.'

She heaved to hold back a sob as she thought of Ruthie Lewis's swollen belly in the pictures she'd seen at Flint's house. Jenna had known for a long time what being a single mother felt like, but it was only recently that she'd found out the difference in being a single mother to a child with a dead father. 'Saleda, can't we do both? Aren't we supposed to be able to save everyone?'

It was such a childish thing to blurt out, but right now, she didn't care. Her neck burned as she remembered her stepbrother Isaac's goading her about it being her weakness – the need to save everyone. Fuck him. However impossible, trying was worth more to her than anything would be to him.

On the other end of the line, Jenna could hear the helicopter's blades beginning their slow whirl. Saleda wasn't going to try to talk her out of it.

'We were never supposed to, Jenna, but that can't stop us from wanting to. Try,' her Special Agent in Charge said. 'Get to the Lewis house. Look around, see what you can see. You have gloves with you? Evidence bags?'

'Always,' Jenna answered.

'Good. Take pictures, collect any hairs, fibers. Talk to neighbors, but stay low-key. Black Shadow's agenda is something bigger than just wanting to give the finger to those they despise. They want to outlast us, and if we spook them, show them we're a step ahead, they'll just go to ground until the trail goes cold for them to rear up again.'

'I know,' Jenna replied. The only way to catch these narcissists was to keep them believing that no one was even coming close.

'There's another thing you need to know. In between all the urgent demands we've been placing on Irv, I've had him trying to track down the origin of the email Black Shadow sent to the media after the bank attack. I'd assumed it was a dead end, but Irv told me this morning he managed to trace the email account activity to a community college terminal that had been remotely accessed to send the file. He wasn't able to trace back any further.'

'So it was a dead end after all?'

'Not quite. Irv found traces of web traffic that the Black Shadow member conducted during the same session he used to send the email, including a hit to a forum that wasn't on our radar before.'

That caught Jenna's attention. 'Anything good?'

'Mostly non-relevant anti-government ranting. But he dug up a thread where some of the posters were skeptical of a couple of live protests that were taking place at the time. Another poster replied, claiming he used to feel the same way but changed his mind. Apparently, he'd been involved in a passive anti-government group when he was a teenager, along with his serious girlfriend, nicknamed Milady. Milady had been struggling with leukemia since childhood. She'd gotten them both involved because she was a fierce advocate of the right to die, and her parents had prevented her from refusing treatment. When the group turned radical, Milady went along, but the poster balked, and ended up leaving the group due to his own moral misgivings. That all changed when Milady died miserably due to complications from years of chemotherapy treatments she'd been forced to take. After that, the poster rejoined the group to fight for the cause, claiming the experience had changed him and he didn't feel like the same person anymore. That now he tries to be active, to be the man Milady wanted him to be all along.'

'I'm going to venture a guess and say 'Milady' is a literary reference,' Jenna said.

'You'd be right. Lucky for him, Irv didn't need Grey for this one. Google connected Milady with Lady de Winter from *The Three Musketeers* right away. Irv checked that against a list of old Black Shadow members Flint was able to remember from before the group became radicalized. Sure enough, Lady de Winter was on there. Right next to Athos.'

'I thought none of those names panned out,' Jenna said. After their initial questioning of Flint, Jenna had been too busy with the mall attack to worry about the list of old Black Shadow members he'd provided, but Irv would have run it at the time and contacted them if it had turned up anything. Unless . . . 'You're thinking he's our Richelieu?'

'He did say he's tried to be a better man since he lost her. Maybe that includes taking on a new name.'

Light khaki came to Jenna along with a feeling that something wasn't quite right about the conclusion. But the *Three Musketeers* character connection did seem too solid to dismiss.

'I'll have to tell Grey about this on the way back,' Jenna said. 'She'll enjoy it.'

'I'm starting to think we should be more concerned about that than we are. Maybe *she's* one of the terrorists,' Saleda joked.

Jenna smiled, despite her continued concern for Flint. 'I'll be as quick as I can in Bethesda, then I'll head your way.'

'Sounds good,' Saleda replied. 'Oh, and Jenna? Whatever you do, choose very, *very* carefully who you confide in that an attack is coming even if we do know its placement and are poised to thwart it. Homeland Security has all but said the powers that be are ready to bring this city to its knees in order to bring down Black Shadow. General Teddy gets a single whiff of a planned mall massacre, and he'll get that stamp of approval on his request for martial law. We can't secure Flint *or* take down Black Shadow if we're stuck in our living rooms watching the tanks roll by.'

'Roger that,' Jenna said, side-glancing at Grey. Unfortunately the time to be choosy about who knew about the attack had passed, and Grey's filter was flimsier than her conversational skills.

Like it or not, Grey was with Jenna until this thing was over and done. Whatever the hell *that* meant.

Thirty-eight

Before Jenna was even out of the car, she knew her gut feeling had been right. Everything about this was wrong.

Flint's silver Infiniti QX50 was still in his driveway, and his wife Ruthie's little white Bentley was parked inside the open garage, too. That in itself was strange, considering that at their last visit, even when everyone was home, they'd kept their garage closed.

Jenna headed for the back door and told Grey to wait in the car, just in case. Her foot brushed against what turned out to be a stuffed white rabbit made of corduroy with long, floppy ears. Jenna cocked her head, squatted by the toy, which had a greasy black smudge on its rump and a rip in the seam of one of its arms. If this was the type of bunny that went everywhere with Nell, she would've been missed. Jenna's stomach sank. As far as keeping burglars at bay, in this case, their narcissism must've trumped their intellectual elitist tendencies, because like so many normal homeowners they'd chosen to hide a spare key under their doormat. Or maybe figured that so many people did it, no one *actually* did it anymore. Jenna was in.

Inside, there wasn't much to see, though little things here and there nagged at Jenna, continued to fuel her suspicions that Black Shadow had taken Flint and his family. Nothing appeared stolen – expensive electronics, jewelry in the upstairs bedroom, a pink laptop computer that Jenna guessed to be Ruthie's. All still there.

In the library, Flint's glasses lay on a table beside the reading chair. He might've had in contacts, but in all his pictures, he wore glasses.

The strangest part of the scene at the Lewis house was the shelves in the library themselves. The massive, pristine collection appeared in as much order as ever, but there was something bothering Jenna about it.

Jenna strolled along the shelf, pulling hardback volumes out one at a time, glancing at a page or two as if expecting they'd seen what had happened, and if she picked the right one, it would tell her how to find them. Tolkien, *Wuthering Heights*, Virginia Woolf, George Orwell's *Animal Farm*. The collection was as extensive as it was eclectic.

Jenna's skin prickled when she came across *To Kill a Mockingbird* but was more ready when she saw *The Three Musketeers*. After all, those were both fabulous books. Black Shadow's fascination with them aside, they did *belong* in any true classic literature collection.

She put down the copy of *The Prince of Tides,* and wandered across the library toward a particular shelf that had caught her eye. The books on this shelf, which was next to the reading chair, did not form the perfect rows of books impeccably spaced from end to end.

This shelf contained the same sort of hodgepodge collection of different authors and genres, only here, they weren't nearly as organized. Some books stood upright on the shelves, spine-out, next to others standing on end but spines in, so you couldn't readily tell what they were. A vague grayish blue flashed in.

Jenna made out the spine of *Gone with the Wind*. Upright next to the stack was *The Great Gatsby,* followed by *Fahrenheit 451*. Not surprising. On the other side of the chair, a powder blue hardback of the epic poem *Beowulf*, and beside it, another copy of Dumas' *The Three Musketeers. Guess there's nothing too weird about that. I have three copies of* The Picture of Dorian Gray. *I bought one in hardback, a second paperback edition, and the third one because Ayana knocked the first paperback into the bathtub.*

The last book on the quirky little shelf leaned against the extra *Three Musketeers*. It was one of Jenna's favorites she'd read in school: Charles Dickens's *Nicholas Nickelby*.

Jenna smiled as her gaze fell on a little round picture frame no bigger than a drink coaster. She squatted a bit to get a better look. After all, had to be an important snapshot, even if it happened to be showcased inside the least ornate item in the Lewis's home.

Flint, though obviously younger, still wearing the same square frame glasses, sat in a pleather chair inside a round room that had to be a planetarium. He made a funny face at the camera as he wrapped his arms goofily around the girl next to him. A few wisps of the girl's long, dark hair clung in static strands to his shirt even as she pushed away from him, her mouth contorted in a cheesy, bad-horror movie fright face.

Rose flashed in as Jenna noticed they shared that same oval face that somehow narrowed even more at the chin. That long, thin nose that extended so far down the length of the face that it somehow seemed responsible for the way their high cheekbones had started out in one place, but angled in as sharply as they did.

As Jenna scanned the odd little shelf again, she noticed a tall stack of books on the side of the chair opposite the quirky shelf. She took a step toward it, curious, a color trying so hard to push its way through. She grappled, trying to hold on to it.

'Nice space, but he needs to put it in order by letters or something. How else can he ever find anything when he looks?'

'Grey! You scared me,' Jenna said, landing reflexively on her firearm as she whipped around. The color she'd been trying to grasp wisped away. Grey stood in the doorway holding Jenna's smartphone.

'You mean alphabetical order? I'd rather arrange them by genre,' Jenna said. 'Never have a problem finding anything.'

'But even then, you could always put a stick 'em note on all the mysteries that were red or some color that goes with 'em for you, couldn't cha? That's what I'd do if I was you . . .'

Jenna glanced back at Grey, who was wandering through the room, not looking to Jenna for an answer. Grey Hechinger. One of the few people who *sort* of understood Jenna's colors without even meaning to or realizing it. Who knew?

Out of the corner of her eye, Jenna spotted something unusual across the hall. When she got to the bathroom, Grey right behind her, she leaned forward to make out the objects that had sunk to the bottom of the full, stoppered sink. Two cell phones.

'People don't just give their iPhones bi-weekly sink baths. People who want to make sure their kidnap victims can't be traced, however . . .'

'You think someone forced them into storage?' Grey asked, worry in her voice.

'Yeah,' Jenna said, translating the question from Grey-speak into normal English in her mind as she paced the bathroom for any other signs, 'I think someone took them against their will.' Jenna reached to her pocket for her phone. 'I'll get a team out here to dust for prints. You can look, but don't touch anything, Grey.'

But as Jenna was about to dial, her phone rang.

She pressed the button to answer. 'Dr Jenna Ramey.'

'Jenna, it's Saleda. I don't know what you've found out there, but we need you to get here and *now*. Eight of the attackers have been captured, including Atticus. One was killed. The last two got away.

We could use your help to see if we can get any information to lead us to the ones who escaped before something *really* bad happens . . .'

It's over? Just like that?

Jenna grabbed her keys, motioned for Grey to follow. Something about the note in Saleda's voice as her words trailed off was more than a little unsettling. She strode through the Lewis's home and out the door, taking the steps two at a time toward the drive where her car was parked.

'Do we know which ones got away? How can something worse happen if—' Jenna cut off as her phone chimed loudly in her ear, the sound it made when she received a message during a call.

Saleda didn't wait for her to go on. 'That's what we're trying to figure out. Just get here, OK?'

'On my way,' Jenna said, hanging up the call. Trying to keep her eyes on the road, she risked a quick glance at her phone to read the message, which was from Irv:

> JUST GOT A RANSOM DEMAND FOR FLINT LEWIS AND FAMILY.
> SENDING YOUR WAY.

Of course you did.

Jenna threw her phone down, gunning the engine once more.

Thirty-nine

Jenna strode the hallways of the J. Edgar Hoover Building once they got inside, Grey fast on her heels. 'Stick close, but keep quiet,' she said quickly but without condescension.

Even Grey must've felt the gravity of the situation, because she said nothing even though Jenna caught a quick nod out of the corner of her eye.

When they reached Saleda and the team, they weren't alone. General Ted and Mr Underwood were both there, and Saleda had clearly given up on all attempts at diplomacy with the two.

Jenna swallowed hard, then strode toward them.

'In case you haven't noticed, *General*, your little shelter in place tactic didn't work! We told you they'd see you coming and plan for it. You couldn't smoke them out that way then, and you won't now.'

'And *lifting* my shelter in place order had people out in the city when they shouldn't have been. A bunch of kids at that mall could've been killed!' General Ted bellowed.

'And yet none of those kids are hurt, are they, General? Because *my* team did their job and took them down. But you sure as hell can't say that for *your* team, can you? *Your* team swooped in like a bunch of clunky-footed buffoons and made all the wrong calls. You gave the go ahead on the reckless shot. Yes, you took down the UNSUB before he could blow his bomb. Turned out this was a dry run for Black Shadow, so that bomb didn't actually exist, but hey, he won't be around for the real-time performance, right? Except that your sniper's risky-ass shot *also* clipped a wire supporting one of those big dinosaur statues in the foyer for the back to school exhibit the science museum is putting on. We have an innocent bystander in the ICU in critical condition!'

Saleda paused, closed her mouth, and looked at her feet, her head turned to stare at them so all Jenna could see was dark hair covering the side of her face.

Was Jenna imagining it, or was Saleda deliberately averting her eyes from her?

'We had to be decisive, and we were!' the general barked.

Saleda stood tall again. 'You were playing right into the terrorists' hands!' Saleda practically screamed. 'That *decisive* shot doesn't look heroic on the news. It looks careless at best, willfully negligent at worst. Now everyone within earshot of a TV or radio or holding a smartphone thinks all that matters to police is getting their guy, even if it means taking chances, gambling with innocent lives. And it is exactly what Black Shadow wants them to think. There are already protestors coming out in droves in dozens of cities all over the damned country. Including groups rallying together right here in DC. And still, you think the way to tackle it is to put out more guns, and worse, uniformed soldiers. Against our own people? You do this, and there'll be riots, General. You'll go down in history. Please don't do this. We know how to handle this. Let *us* handle it,' Saleda pleaded.

'Ha! You handled it, all right. Two of your own team couldn't even handle the drive here without crashing,' Mr Underwood piped up.

Jenna's heart galloped, and her eyes swept the room. Porter. Teva. Where were they?

Jenna pushed away the weird vibes and interjected herself into the conflict. They had more important things to deal with right now. She addressed General Ted.

'Sir, I have evidence that Flint Lewis and his family's kidnapping is connected to this case. We can't step on your toes if the president orders martial law. But until that order comes down, this case is still in our jurisdiction, and we have a duty to see it through. So please, sir. Step aside. We have suspects to interview,' Jenna said.

Once the general and his lackey were gone, Jenna forwarded the ransom note she'd received on her smartphone to Saleda and Dodd's e-mails. Saleda turned on her tablet and scanned it. However, Dodd turned to Jenna. 'Why don't we have a seat at this conference table for a minute?'

Cameo pink flashed in, and that sick, worried feeling washed over Jenna. It always seemed to precede something awful, because it only showed up whenever she got the feeling of someone trying to break something to her gently. She followed Dodd, biting her lip as Teva and Porter's faces sprang vividly to mind.

Jenna followed Dodd's lead and sat beside him, turning to face him.

'Teva and Porter are both in the ER,' Dodd said. 'Porter's arm's broken, and he sustained a severe blow to the chest. No punctured lungs, but he's having some trouble breathing, so they've got him on a ventilator until his breath support gets better. He's not thrilled about the tube, but he'll be kept sedated as long as they have to keep it in, so he can't cause too much trouble for the nurses.'

Jenna managed a half-laugh at Dodd's attempt to lighten the moment but quickly nodded for him to go on.

'Teva's a little worse off. Still in critical condition, but they think she'll make it. They think all three of them will.'

Jenna's head snapped. 'All three . . .?'

This time, Dodd looked up. His eyes narrowed, jaw set. Concerned. 'I had a feeling no one had told you yet.'

'Told me what?' Jenna said, hearing her own voice notch up in panic as Yancy's canary yellow flashed in. Dodd had said nothing about Yancy, and there was absolutely no reason Yancy would've been anywhere near that mall. But suddenly, all she could think about was how Yancy hadn't answered her last text.

'That innocent bystander that got hurt when the sniper's shot clipped one of the wires holding up those statues?' Dodd said gently.

'Yancy?' Jenna said, barely a whisper. He was supposed to be at home with Ayana and Vern and Charley. Why would he have been at the mall? It didn't make sense . . .

Dodd nodded.

'But why was he even—'

'Irv was trying to get hold of you, but he said it kept going straight to voicemail—'

'Yeah, my battery was low so I put it in standby until I was back on the road and could charge it—'

'Well, he was worrying, because he couldn't get hold of Saleda or anyone *else* inside that mall. Irv figured out they were jamming satellite signals. Which meant radio contact couldn't go in or out. But before long he realized it wasn't only to delay first responders, because when Irv hacked into the mall surveillance networks, something seemed off about the surveillance feeds. And boy was it. Turned out the footage that Saleda, General Bearito Mussolini, SWAT, and every other rescue personnel was using to strategize wasn't real-time footage. They were seeing only what Black Shadow *wanted* them to see.'

Jenna nodded slowly, disgusted. 'So they'd act based on what the cooked footage told them was happening, while outside, their BFF the media would be broadcasting the *real* footage far and wide showing the cops—'

'Irresponsible, rash, dangerous actions result in monumentally horrible fuckups,' Dodd filled in.

'And show the public that if the government can't pursue a criminal inside an everyday shopping mall without an innocent citizen ending up in intensive care, a martial law order in effect would bring disaster.'

Dodd nodded. 'So, when he couldn't get you, he called Yancy, told him what was going on. Yancy was already in his car on that side of town, so he was going to rush and warn Saleda they were being set up, try to stop the first responders from acting on bad intel from the cooked footage.'

Jenna looked down, swallowed hard. Her eyes burned, a lump hard in her throat. 'Guess he got there right on time,' she said, hating the bitter edge coating her words. He was hurt. This wasn't the time to be mad at him for rushing into danger, but it's exactly why her ears burned at the thought. Didn't he know how much she needed him? How much A loved him? How much they all did?

Her head bolted back up. 'When can I see him? Can he have visitors?'

At this, Saleda turned to face them. 'Jenna, I know your first instinct is to run to the hospital to be at his side, but trust me when I say that whatever setup he risked his life to warn us about is the same setup still in play at this very moment.' She gestured to the letter she'd been reading on her tablet. 'Whoever this mastermind Ishmael is, whether he's an invalid or not, he's clearly started something here, and he's not done. Something about this whole thing isn't right, and we have to figure out how to get to him and the others who got away before anything else happens, be it to Flint and his family or anyone else. At this point, I doubt there's anything the people pulling the puppet strings behind Black Shadow aren't capable of.'

Jenna forced the fears bombarding her about Yancy away as hard as she could. Saleda was right. They'd done this to him. They had to be stopped. She looked to Dodd. 'Dodd, can you find a quiet place for Grey to sit with the letter?' She turned to her ex-patient. 'See if you can find any hidden meanings in there, particularly to do with literature, huh, Grey?'

Grey nodded and followed Dodd to a room off to the side with a small desk. He closed her in then rejoined them.

'Keep an eye on her,' Jenna said, then faced Saleda again. 'So, which ones got away?'

'Well, Ishmael would've never been there, of course. He always hangs back because of his disability. The one the sniper popped – the one who looked liked he was wearing a suicide vest and seemed to be fiddling with what could've been a detonator? We couldn't question him for, um, obvious reasons . . . but after running his prints, turns out that not only was Fai Xiong active on the original Black Shadow forum, but he also used to be an intern in the computer lab of the community college where Irv traced that e-mail McKenzie McClendon received.'

The light khaki of something not quite right flashed in, that a computer intern would send something like that from his own lab, but she ignored it when she remembered his name. 'Fai Xiong?' Jenna repeated. 'Chinese?'

'Yep. We're guessing he must've been Richelieu. Then Marius – I mean JP Haynie . . . I mean James Asner . . . or whoever the heck he was, is dead,' Saleda said. 'So, we're missing two. One is Ashlee Haynie. The other we're trying to figure out by process of elimination.'

At the mention of Richelieu, the light khaki flashed in again, but Jenna pushed it away.

'You have them isolated, questioning them separately?' Jenna asked, already knowing that would be the case.

'Until General Grumpy Griz crashed our party and tried to horn in on our jurisdiction anyway,' Dodd said.

'So far, we've pegged the obvious ones we have in custody: Scout, Slender— I mean Hester, Watson and Holmes,' Dodd said.

'Mr Darcy is the creepy thin dude with the daggers, and Atticus is clearly the line leader with the machete,' Saleda added.

'So only two males we can't confirm?'

'We're assuming the one missing the hand is Tremain, but even so, both have lawyered up and aren't talking.'

'What about the others? Ready to talk?' Jenna asked.

'Attitudes are across the board. No lawyers so far. Some defiant, some stoic. Some, like Mr Darcy, remind me a little too much of Isaac Keaton if he happened to be playing Jack the Ripper on Halloween,' Dodd said.

'That sounds like my worst nightmare,' Jenna said, actually unsure what she was imagining, but knowing she didn't want to be anywhere near it.

'Different as the reactions may be, the story's always the same about why they were at the mall today. Every single one says because their leader told them to be there. Then they say they don't know anything else, that they aren't the boss and only do what they're told. Then, as soon as you ask about any of the others, especially Atticus, they clam up,' Saleda said.

The door to the little side office creaked open and Grey poked her head out. 'Um, are you guys busy?'

'Yeah, we're in the middle of something, Grey. Keep working on the letter, OK?' Jenna said.

Grey lingered in the doorway, her eyes shooting from one person to the next, like a shelter animal trying to determine which human would be most likely to spring her from the joint if she looked up at them with sweet, innocent eyes. She stopped on Jenna. 'Right. I can do that. I just think there's . . . the letter writer might be a person who is also involved in the group, and . . .'

'The letter writer is most *definitely* involved in the group,' Saleda said. 'Spot on. Good work, Grey. See if you can find us any clues on where Ishmael might *be*.'

Grey nodded. 'I can keep looking. I was wanting to kind of verify that you knew that the letter writer is writing for the group member who is not in the group but is taken away from the group—'

'Yes,' Jenna said. 'Ishmael is writing about taking Flint. Flint used to be Black Shadow, and now they've kidnapped him and his family. We need anything in the letter that might help us find them *or* Ishmael. Keep looking, OK?'

Grey nodded, then shut the door. Through the glass, Jenna watched her sit down and begin to pour over the letter again. Maybe she'd get lucky. They could only hope. Until then, Jenna's best shot was one of the other killers. But which?

Her mind jumped to the images of Scout on the video, her dry heaving in the bank. But no, she was street smart. That was her profile. Street smarts made her less likely to rat anyone out. *Who else . . .*

The clumsy Slender UNSUB from the video came to mind, the one who needed to be rescued by the bigger male with the WASP knife. 'What about Hester? How has she acted?'

Saleda smirked. 'Devastated. Ashamed. Afraid.'

Jenna nodded. 'Perfect.'

Forty

After skimming the folder Irv had been able to put together on what they knew about Slender UNSUB, aka Hester, aka Elise Kapra, Jenna turned the knob to the room where the thirty-three-year-old woman was being held for questioning. The others said she'd cried a little, seemed one of the most upset. But still, Jenna wouldn't know best how to tackle the interview until she had a better feel for the woman. Was she upset because she got caught or had real remorse? Her fighting style made her seem weak and clumsy, and yet, she was obviously strong – and ruthless – enough to join a band of terrorists slaughtering innocent people in droves. Until Jenna talked to Hester herself, the woman's folder couldn't tell her much at all.

Jenna stepped through the door and laid eyes on Hester, her long, thin face pale and gaunt, eyes wet with recent tears. Her bony fingers trembled, folded neatly in her lap.

'I'm Dr Jenna Ramey, Special Agent with the FBI, Ms Kapra. Or do you prefer Elise? Or Hester, maybe?'

The woman's trembling hand opened, her palms face up on the table side by side, cuffed together. 'Whichever you wish,' she said softly. Then, even quieter, 'Hester is fine.'

Jenna set the folder on the table, her cup of tap water. 'Can I get you any water or coffee, Hester?'

The woman only shook her head.

Jenna opened the folder, pretending to be looking something over, but in reality, she wanted to give Hester a chance to realize this would be an informal talk, not the third degree. If she did, maybe she'd open up. Be willing to confide in her.

'I'll cut to the chase. It'll save us time and trouble. I'm sure you're aware that most of your friends at the mall were captured and detained, also, right, Hester? All but two.'

Hester gave another nod. 'Yes. I did know that.'

'The two still out there have plans to hurt more people, Hester. Even more than all of you already have.'

Hester's bottom lip trembled.

'We need to find them before that happens, Hester. Before this gets any worse for them . . . for *you.*' Jenna leaned forward, clasped her hands on the table. 'I don't know you, Hester. Maybe you want dozens or even hundreds more people to die. But I don't think you do.'

Hester sniffled, let out an audible sob. 'Why not? I'm a monster, aren't I? That's why I'm here!' Sharp pain touched the edges of Hester's voice, a person who'd crossed lines she'd thought she could handle.

Ash gray flashed in, Hester's guilty conscience calling it forward.

'Because you didn't join Black Shadow to hurt people.' Jenna had skimmed the notes about Hester's education, her employment history. The only court record that came up in conjunction with her name happened to be a lawsuit. The file didn't tell the whole story, but Jenna could fill in the gaps. 'You see, I've been reading up on you this afternoon, Hester, and I just can't see that being why you did what you did.'

Jenna took a long pause, sipped her water. She opened the folder, sifted through the pages, and read. 'After you got your Master's in education, you took a job teaching seventh grade at a private school in Boston. You lived in the suburbs with your then-husband Joel, correct?'

Hester nodded again. Sniffled.

'It looks like your life was somewhat vanilla until I get to these pages showing where you were abruptly terminated from your teaching position and the subsequent wrongful termination suit you filed. Your husband also filed for divorce right around that time.'

'Yes,' she whispered.

'Now, I know this is a painful memory, Hester, but am I correct in understanding from this paperwork that you were terminated from your post because you had an abortion?'

Tears welled in Hester's eyes, dripped down her waxy cheeks and chin. 'Yes.'

Don't prod. Wait.

When Hester spoke again, her voice was riddled with hurt. 'When Joel and I found out we were expecting, we couldn't have been happier. It was a dream come true for us. But . . .'

Hester sniffed, her body racked with a dry sob. Jenna waited quietly.

'A few weeks later at an ultrasound, the doctors discovered my sweet baby girl . . .' Hester nearly choked on the words. She took a gasping, rattling breath. 'She had so many things against her. A chromosomal defect, a few other things. But the worst . . . the absolute *worst*,' Hester said, stopped. She blew out a slow breath, regaining composure. 'Only one chamber of her heart was formed. The doctors . . . they said there was no chance of survival.'

Jenna bowed her head, Ayana's bright eyes blazing in her mind. Her gentle giggle almost echoing in her ears. 'I'm so sorry.'

Hester bit back another sob. 'Joel left that night. He said the decision was impossible. That he couldn't face it,' Hester said. She half-laughed, shook her head. 'Funny how one person's impossible can be another person's sentence, huh?'

Compassionate Catalina blue flashed in. It was all starting to make sense. Facing that terrifying, gut-wrenching nine-month march to saying goodbye to her baby only moments after birth – and alone – Hester had opted to terminate the pregnancy. The private school got wind of it and fired her on grounds that having the procedure displayed morals not in line with the school's religious principles.

'And then, despite your exemplary record, the school let you go,' Jenna said.

Now, Hester was sobbing, and she looked Jenna right in the eye. 'Did they think I enjoyed it? Did they think I didn't feel anything? I didn't make the decision for *me*! I made it for *her*!' Tears ran down Hester's face and neck, her nose running. 'If by some miracle she had survived minutes or hours or days, none of them would have been pleasant. She'd have had absolutely no quality of life to speak of! I did it for *her*!'

'And that's why I don't think you want anyone else to die, Hester. I don't think you killed anyone because you wanted anyone to die. I think you did it because you felt like it was the only way you could get anyone to listen. Am I right?'

Hester propped her elbows on the table, collapsed her head in her hands. 'I made the most intelligent, compassionate choice I could make for my little girl, and yet they threw me to the curb. But everywhere I look, schools keep teachers with IQs so low they'd barely pass high school, just so long as they don't have any skeletons in their closets. Conform to societal norms, and as long as you can pass basic tests, feel free to mold the future minds of America.'

'I get it, Hester. I really do. The people allowed to make decisions in *so* many facets of life probably aren't nearly qualified,' Jenna said, playing to Hester's ego. Her narcissistic streak wasn't the same broad, thick band woven into some of the others' psyches, but everyone in Black Shadow was an intellectual elitist. 'But let's talk about others for a minute who *are* supposed to be qualified. Say, to lead Black Shadow.'

Hester's face darkened. She said nothing.

'All anyone seems to want to tell us today is that they did what they were told. Came where they were told to come. Is that right?'

Hester nodded.

Jenna joined her nod. 'Yep. That the boss tells them what to do. And yet, the boss isn't exactly foolproof, either, apparently. Here you all are, arrested. Caught. Your crusade to jumpstart some kind of revolution might have taken a step—'

'Because law enforcement is as predictable as Ishmael always said they would be,' Hester said.

'—but it'll take the rest of the steps without you. You'll be in prison, likely for the rest of your lives. Maybe be executed for what you've done. How it goes down for each of you, though, can be different, if you cooperate.' Jenna stood up, looked around the room. 'Because even if Ishmael was right, he isn't *here*. You're here. Your *friends* are here—'

'Those people aren't my friends,' Hester whispered.

Jenna raised her eyebrows. 'Oh? None of them?'

Hester cheeks blushed a touch.

'Yeah, most of these people might be cohorts, but at least one other guy being questioned in this building isn't just some acquaintance. Who is he to you, Hester? The guy with the WASP knife? A friend? Lover?'

Hester shook her head. 'It's complicated.'

'As complicated as mass-murdering, dirty-dozen relationships can be, I'm sure. All I know is he sure seemed to have your back. Saved your ass more than once, if the surveillance videos have anything to say about it,' Jenna said.

Hester stared at the table. 'Just leave him out of it, OK?'

Protective bluish gray flashed in – the same shade that had flashed in when Jenna had watched WASP UNSUB come to protect Hester on the bank video. *Maybe if you won't talk to help yourself, you'll talk to help him.*

'Leave him out of it? He's already *in it*, Hester. Up to his eyeballs, just like you. He might have just as good a reason as yours to be hurt or angry enough to join the cause, but he's going to hang for it anyway. Probably worse than you will. Men's prisons are rougher. He's older. Not to mention juries are harder on men in death penalty cases—'

'Stop! Please!'

Pay dirt.

'I can't stop until we find those two Black Shadow members who are still on the loose. Tell me what you know about them, where they might be or what Atticus has planned. What he's done. He'd give you two and anything he knew about you up in a heartbeat, but if you cooperate and tell us what you know about your fearless leader's plans for either the two who got away *or* other attacks, I can get you a deal. I can get one for you *and* your friend. Or whatever he is.'

Hester clenched her fists in her lap, staring at them as though deep in thought. Finally, she looked up, met Jenna's gaze. 'I don't know where Ishmael is or what he has planned. I don't know where these two people you keep talking about are or what they might be doing. But I can tell you one thing that might be useful.'

'Spill it.'

'I want a deal,' Hester said.

Jenna sat back down, leaned forward, elbows on the table. 'I will note that you cooperated fully and do my very best to ensure that it helps your case. But right now, time is of the essence, and what I can or can't do for you depends not just on what your information happens to be. It also matters that it's given to me soon enough to be able to use it to stop another disaster. So I'm afraid you'll have to take a chance on me here, Hester. You have no reason to trust me, but I can promise you this is the best and only chance for you and your friend. So, if you have something to say, say it now.'

Hester's eyes bored into Jenna's. 'Like I said, I don't know anything about Ishmael or the two who got away.'

'Right,' Jenna said.

'But you're making a big mistake in thinking Atticus is calling the shots. Atticus isn't Black Shadow's leader. Not at all. He'll tell you. Ask him yourself.'

Forty-one

Jenna stood against the door leading to the interrogation cell they'd at one time thought contained the leader of Black Shadow. Now, she didn't know what to think. Or what to expect.

She pressed her back against the wooden door, clutching a file folder of information to her chest – a hastily put-together packet that told her everything they'd been able to gather about Adam Garner – aka Atticus – since he'd been apprehended. Before she'd read through the sheets of paper inside it, she'd been ready to barge through that door, mentally spar with a psychopath so cold-blooded he had led almost a dozen other people to violently slaughter innocents by the handful and would chop off any heads his minions might have the heart to spare. She'd been internally prepping her interview of him based on her previous profile, ways she could play his own ego and arrogance against him to outwit him, coax a slip.

But now that she'd read the file, her game plan had gone out the window. *God, Yancy. I wish I could talk this one through with you. Atticus isn't at all who I thought he was.*

She stood up and took a breath. *Here goes absolutely nothing.*

Jenna opened the door, and the muscular man with the close-cropped brown hair lifted his head from where it had been resting in his hands. His features were as sharp as she'd expected, but his eyes were sunken. Tired. His eyes met hers, his gaze intent. Searching for something.

The room seemed to be getting smaller as she held Atticus's gaze. What could she possibly say to this man, knowing what she did? He was a criminal – a murderer – but for whatever she might not understand about how it had seemed like the right action to take, she could no longer look at him like a puzzle to be fiddled with or a game to be played. However badly she still needed to get inside his mind, to get information to stop more people from getting hurt, this time, she couldn't get in his head, use his own thoughts against him. She knew now those thoughts were a minefield, and tripping the wrong one would mean game over.

What the fuck would Yancy do if he was here? Jenna broke Atticus's gaze, stared down at her feet. *Think.*

He'd make a leg joke. *He'd be honest.*

Jenna looked up again and into Atticus's intense, dark eyes. 'Sir, I'm so sorry about your daughter.'

Atticus blinked. His lips parted as if he might say something but then closed again. He nodded, his strong jaw set. 'Thank you.'

Jenna pulled out a chair, sat down across from him.

'They keep asking me where the others are. What I've told them to do,' he said slowly, his voice a low, scratchy growl. 'I've tried to tell them I'm not who they think I am, but no one will listen.'

Jenna clasped her hands in front of her. 'I'm listening, Adam.'

He smirked. Let out a mirthless laugh. 'Not that I blame them, really. How could I? I'm the guy who's been running around with a kukri and doing things . . . things I never in my worst nightmares imagined I was even capable of . . .'

Jenna's thoughts drifted to the file folder on the table: lobbied Congress to change employment laws after he lost his job due to budget cuts, the divorce papers that had inevitably come when his time spent fighting for fair employment outgrew his time spent with his wife. The way his inability to keep steady employment meant only visitation rights with his three-year-old daughter instead of the joint custody he'd sought. The criminal history detailing the bar fight that had sent him to anger management classes – a mistake he'd made without a drop of alcohol on his breath – and taken those visitation rights and made them only allowable under court supervision.

The death certificate and autopsy report on his child after she died from choking on a marble – a game piece of a Chinese checkerboard set a daycare worker had allowed the children to play with without proper supervision.

'A loss so deep . . .'

'I don't think many people can fathom what they're capable of until something so horrifying comes right through their door.'

Atticus shrugged. 'Maybe *we* can't,' he said, 'but other people can.'

Jenna leaned forward. 'What do you mean when you say that?'

'You got played. Told I was the leader. But it was because we all got played. *I* got played. Maybe I can't predict my own moves, but Ishmael could. Knew what I was about, all the buttons he'd need to push. Couldn't go out himself, so he made me the figure-head. I thought I was a general leading the troops into battle. We'd change the world. Change it so smarter people were making decisions. Decisions like who was hired or fired, based on sense and intelligence and not who you know in HR. Changing things so the status quo didn't mean all you needed was a high school diploma to be legally entrusted with children's lives. Of course I was ready to lead the charge!' Atticus shook his head. 'But now I can see he just needed a fall guy. I was his fall guy. I guess we all were.'

Dodd and Saleda's mentions of all the UNSUBs talking about the mall like it was some weird family get-together popped to mind. 'You think Ishmael set you up?'

'Sure seems like it. We were told it was recon. Then we get there, a hundred cops show up and nab all of us, and only two happen to be MIA? I know our group is known for its propensity to be a bit up our own asses about our IQs, but it doesn't take a genius to sort that one out.'

But Jenna was too stuck on one phrase to laugh at the joke. Avocado green flashed in at the mention of the two MIA members. The color for triple, three. Another color tried to push through, but she forced it away, afraid of losing the nagging fragment of a thought teasing at the edge of her brain, not quite showing enough of itself. 'So you're saying two people knew the message was a trap. Or were in on it and knew it was just recon being used as a ruse. That's what you're thinking?'

Atticus shook his head. 'I'm not sure where we're getting off the same page, but this message you keep talking about. You still seem to think . . . the message about meeting up. It was about recon.'

Jenna's heartbeat picked up. 'The one through the e-reader reviews. We're talking about that message system, right?'

'Sure.'

Jenna turned to face the windowless glass and spoke to Saleda, who she knew to be directly behind it. 'Saleda, we need that e-reader from the apartment. Quick.'

Once the reader was powered up, Jenna scrolled through until she found the book page for *A Tale of Two Cities*. She swiped the touchpad until she found a review written early that morning titled, 'Don't Wait Til de Winter, Read This Classic Right Now!' She put the tablet on the table and pushed it toward Atticus.

'Show me how it works,' Jenna said, standing and rounding the table so she could look at the listing over his shoulder.

Atticus nodded, zooming the screen in to make the writing larger. He frowned as he scrolled back to the top. 'de Winter. He can't help but get in just one more little inside joke even on something as serious as recon we're scouting so we can . . .' his voice trailed off as though he was too disgusted with himself to finish the thought.

'OK, so what was the exact message?' Jenna asked, hoping to keep Atticus from getting lost in his anger.

He pointed to the star rating, which was a three. 'This mean every three letters. You write the letters out, and it'll form your message. Pretty simple if you know what you're looking for.'

Atticus took the dry erase marker Saleda had brought in for him to use and quickly jotted the letters on the white board she'd laid on the table. Jenna scanned back and forth from it to the tablet, double and triple checking that Atticus wasn't making any mistakes. As the message began to materialize, though, the words were so coherent she knew it was impossible it was a mistake or even that Atticus was using the wrong method to decipher it. Though, at this point, she almost wished he *was* capable of pulling something like that out of his hat and was tricking her. With every word of the real message revealed on the white board, Jenna's chest clenched tighter, her breathing picked up pace.

This message wasn't about an attack at all. It was just like Atticus said: the message was about recon, but it had nothing to do with the mall. It vaguely explained that two Black Shadow members had assignments off-site, and the only detail passed along in the message pertained to time slots and check in angles. The location of the mall wasn't mentioned or even alluded to. The message assumed everyone reading it already knew the location. Had been told somehow at a separate time or in another format.

That was it. Not a word about Flint, his family. A threat to them.

Burnt orange of lying flashed in as Jenna's pulse quickened, her anger spiking. If there was no mention of the mall, then the message hadn't sent her to the mall. Sent her *team* to the mall.

Sent *Yancy* to the mall.

'That's it. The two off-site were Scarlett—'

'Knew it,' Jenna blurted without meaning to.

'—and Beo.'

Goldenrod crashed in, and Jenna sucked in a sharp breath. The goldenrod. So many times in this case, the damned goldenrod!

She stormed out the door and slammed it, muttering under her breath as she bustled through the room, gathering her things. 'I saw it when Marius passed Ashlee on the bank video when he should've easily seen her. I should've known it was him when I saw it again!'

Jenna imagined Grey poking her head out of the door just a while ago, wanting to discuss the ransom note. *'I was wanting to just kind of verify that you knew that the letter writer is writing for the group member who is not in the group but is taken away from the group . . .'*

Grey had realized it even before she had.

Jenna grabbed her keys, rapped on the window to alert Grey. She gestured for her ex-patient to come with her. There wasn't any time to waste.

'What the hell are you talking about?' Saleda asked, following her down the hall. 'Where are you going?'

Jenna wheeled to face her. 'The goldenrod. When Flint revealed the whole e-book review trick to me, I asked if he ever checked the old one now and then, just to see if anything was happening. He said no. It seemed strange he wouldn't, even if just because it was a normal human reaction. The goldenrod was intentional overlook.'

'OK . . . so where are you *going*?' Saleda asked again, following her and Grey into the parking lot and to Jenna's Blazer.

Jenna opened the door and climbed in. 'If there wasn't any message about the mall attack, then the person who led us to the mall had to know about it some other way. There's only one person who led us to the mall, and if he wanted cops at the mall, it was because he'd planned it all perfectly – he'd throw all the loose ends under the bus and get the world watching for the *real* attack.'

'So you're *going* where?' Saleda pushed.

Goldenrod flashed in again, this time as a part of the image frozen in her mind of the cover of the classic copy of *Beowulf* she'd seen in Flint's house set out in that strange way on that little shelf that didn't belong.

'To Flint Lewis' house,' Jenna said. 'I don't know where the real attack will be, but you better believe Beo does.'

Forty-two

As the chopper clipped through the air, the scenery of busy, trafficked streets and tall buildings below gave way to more green, rows of houses so similar in size and style they could've been sliced with the same cookie cutter. Any second, Flint's split-level would come into view.

'Grey, when we touch down, you and I need to get inside as quickly as possible. I'll take you to the book where I saw it, but I'm going to need your help figuring out what the key is,' Jenna said.

Save for the two tiny nods she gave, Grey sat as still as a statue, belted into the chopper and clutching a tablet with the ransom note displayed on its screen.

'You're sure the ransom note's a code?' Saleda asked as the helicopter banked left toward Flint's street.

Jenna nodded. 'It's a bunch of rambling. Has to be. Just had no idea what the key to the code might be until now.'

Saleda glanced toward Grey, who was staring straight in front of her, clutching the tablet and blinking rapidly for no reason. 'And you're positive the book you saw is the key to the crack? Because of a color? Jenna, you know I respect you. And you know that even though I don't always 'get' the color stuff, that it works for you and has given us lots of leads, but if what Atticus said is right, there is an attack about to happen within the hour—'

'It's not just the color, Saleda. It was the message in the e-reader review. It said two Black Shadow operatives were on off-site assignments,' Jenna said, reaching for the handle above her. She held on, her body thrown sideways as the helicopter made its descent. She yelled louder over the din. 'It said, 'Scarlett is on an off-site assignment, and Beo has it covered.' On the surface, the other Black Shadow members thought it meant Beo was providing cover for Scarlett's operation off-site, but it didn't. If Flint is Beo, he's off doing God-knows-what, pretending to be kidnapped. 'Beo has it covered,' was another one of Flint's little Easter eggs for anyone worthy enough to find it. It meant Beo – *Beowulf* the book – "covers" the details of Scarlett's assignment.'

The chopper touched down, the blades loud in Jenna's ears.

Jenna nodded to Grey. 'It's time.' She ushered Grey to the chopper door in front of her, followed behind, and hopped out the door as Grey cleared it. She ducked and ran toward Flint Lewis's brick split-level, hair blowing everywhere, grass clippings seeming to rain up from the ground under the deafening clops of the helicopter blades.

Finally, they were inside. Jenna led Grey and Dodd through the living room and toward the library while Saleda, who was the last one in, shut the door.

Jenna stepped into the library – a place that suddenly seemed much more sinister than the last time she'd been here – her eyes trained on the strange shelf by the chair.

Dodd stopped just inside the door as Jenna crossed the room, squatted next to the stack beside the chair she'd noticed last time because *Gone with the Wind* was at its base – the only book with its spine visible to the room. She lifted the book off the top and turned it over. *A Tale of Two Cities*. The origin of Black Shadow's motto.

Her theory solidifying, one by one she plucked the books off the stack, registering each in a mental tally as she re-stacked them in front of her: *Moby Dick, Pride and Prejudice, To Kill a Mockingbird, Les Miserables, The Scarlet Letter, Johnny Tremain,* a Sherlock Holmes mystery, *The Three Musketeers,* the gold copy of *Beowulf*, another Sherlock Holmes installment. Finally, she reached the bottom, lifting *Gone with the Wind.* 'You son of a bitch,' Jenna muttered. 'You left the whole club right out in the open, hiding in plain sight.'

Grey's cough reminded her others were there, and Jenna looked to Dodd, who was standing quietly, scanning titles on other shelves without touching then, then toward where her thin, pale ex-patient stood in doorway.

Grey pointed toward the stack of books. 'Do you want me to inspect that *Beowulf*?'

Jenna's eyes narrowed as she looked to the stack of books. The goldenrod of its cover had made her think back to this stack of books, want to come back to it. But . . .

She shifted her weight, turning to face the chair behind her. Chiefly, the other books she'd left there. Kneeling on her right knee, she scanned the titles she'd known would be there even before she'd turned: *The Three Musketeers, Nicholas Nickelby,* and *Beowulf.* The second copy with a powder blue cover.

That powder blue connected in Jenna's brain, matching something she'd seen multiple times with the same person, though she hadn't been able to properly fix it in her mind before. For a moment, a second color tried to battle in, but Jenna forced it away. The powder blue was the important shade here. Most recently, it had appeared when she had searched the home of Flint Lewis, and noticed the disorganization of his bookshelf.

The scene was staged. The players all in one stack there, these books here.

'The key is in this copy,' Jenna said, handing Grey the powder blue hardback.

Grey flipped it over in her hands, scanned the back. 'This is converted differently. The gold one and this one might not spell out the same. You sure?'

Jenna nodded. Grey was right; the powder blue *Beowulf* was a different translation – a whole different version of the poem. But if Jenna knew Flint, he'd done that on purpose. Even if he'd expected someone to get as far as figuring out what book – and at his own home – to use to decipher the ransom letter's hidden message, he'd leave one more little trick. One extra test that, if you weren't smart enough, would mean you didn't get the prize.

Grey nodded, sat on the floor cross-legged. She put the book in front of her and, beside it, the tablet with the note. She stared at the two for a long moment as the quiet in the room seemed to grow around them.

Saleda stepped into the room, looked to Jenna. 'Anything?'

'Shh,' Dodd hissed calmly, finger to his lips.

Jenna's gaze, however, never left Grey. Grey wasn't stumped. She might look like it to Saleda, but Jenna knew the twinkle in those otherwise glassy eyes staring down at everything and nothing. She was thinking, trying to pinpoint something flitting around in her mind's eye.

After a long moment, Grey seemed to jolt from a stupor, blinking fast and looking around. Her gaze finally landed on what she'd been looking for, apparently, because she reached for the stack of books from where Jenna had stacked the ones all related to Black Shadow.

'This blue one might pick the lock, but the gold edition had a place marker in it,' Grey said, rifling through the stack until she came up with the gold *Beowulf* paperback.

Turning the closed book up on it's end so she could see the top pages, Grey dug her fingers in between pages, opening the book and laying it splayed open to show two random pages somewhere in the middle. Grey pointed to the corner.

'I'll be damned,' Saleda muttered.

The corner of the page on the right had been dog-eared, though only Grey had managed to notice it. But once the book was open to the page, sure enough, a single passage was underlined lightly in pencil:

> *Wise sir, do not grieve. It is always better*
> *to avenge dear ones than to indulge in mourning.*
> *For every one of us, living in this world*
> *means waiting for our end. Let whoever can*
> *win glory before death. When a warrior is gone,*
> *that will be his best and only bulwark.*

'What do we do with it?' Saleda asked.

'Flint uses numbers for the codes. Like the e-reader reviews. It's find the numbers, then they tell you which letters from the text to grab,' Jenna said. 'So . . .'

'Lines 1384, 1385, 1386, 1387, 1388, and 1389,' Grey said.

'Well, I'd have probably just said 1384 through 1389, but yeah, let's try them,' Saleda said.

Grey uncrumpled a piece of paper from her back pocket and took out a pen from another. Diligently, she used her finger to count through the words, writing down a letter every time she reached a letter within the ransom note that corresponded to the next number in the sequence of *Beowulf* lines.

'You know,' Jenna whispered to Saleda, 'You gotta hand it to 'em, though. It had to take hours to write these codes. *Tedious* hours. I can hardly find time to count letters in a crossword puzzle answer, and even then I end up having to get up before I have a chance to actually try and think of the answer.'

'Good thing he likes tedious things, because hopefully this ends with him behind bars for a long time, where he can pay attention to special details like scrubbing toilets with his own toothbrush,' Dodd said.

'Got it,' Grey said, hopping up from the floor. She handed the paper to Jenna.

'Preach, my dear sir, a crusade against ignorance; establish & improve the law for educating the common people,' Jenna read out loud. 'What the heck does that mean?'

Grey smiled. 'Dunno. But there's always someone who does . . .'

She looked toward the pocket where Jenna kept her phone, smiled slyly. Jenna grinned and snatched the phone out of her pocket, dialed Irv.

'Irv's Omnipotent After Hours, where Irv knows all at *all* the hours. What can we help you with this evening?'

'I need you to search for any public landmarks that have anything to do with this quote,' Jenna said. She read the passage to him. 'It'd be somewhere big where people pay tribute to something. Maybe a museum, a hall of fame . . . I don't know, historic sites, battle-grounds . . .'

'No need to continue this brainstorm,' Irv said. 'Got it on the first hit. Must've been late for his Mensa meeting when they wrote the code for this one, because this one was easier to spot than Dodd's toupee.'

'Be glad you're not on speaker,' Jenna said. 'Hit me with it.'

Jenna listened to Irv's answer. 'Wait! Isn't that where the people are gathering to protest the law enforcement tactics used during this case?'

Irv sighed hard. 'Yep. Activists scheduled the rally in reaction to what happened at the mall. When they first set it up, they were just demanding the heads of the operation for using excessive, reckless force, but since then, what with the curfew and all, they're saying now's the time to take a stand and refuse to become a police state.'

'Christ,' Jenna breathed, already striding toward the Lewis's door, memories flooding her of the awful day a couple of years ago when another brilliant sociopath had made victims out of the hundreds of people outside of a jail, rallying for a prisoner's right to life. *They're out there fighting for the cause* you *told them to believe in.* 'Thanks, Irv. Keep us posted on anything you find on Flint or his family's location. We'll touch base when we touch down again.'

Time was running out, and they all made their way to the chopper as Irv told Jenna she was welcome.

'And Irv? One more thing . . . If it wouldn't be too much trouble, will you call the hospital and get an update on Yancy for me? I know they say he's fine, but I don't even know what his technical diagnosis is—'

'Don't worry,' Irv cut in. 'Who needs to ask when you can hack into the system and read his file? I'll have his diagnosis, prognosis, blood type, and insurance number for you by the time you've cuffed the bad guys.'

'Thanks, Irv. You're the best.'

'That's what I've heard,' Irv said, and the line went dead.

Jenna climbed into the chopper, it's blades already clipping above, and they lifted off the makeshift helipad that was Flint Lewis's front yard, leaving thin cherry blossom trees bending and blowing in their wake.

'Back to DC,' Jenna shouted to the pilot. 'We've got to get to the Jefferson Memorial. And fast.'

Forty-three

'Set her down over there!' Saleda hollered to the helicopter pilot, pointing to a wide, grassy opening on their left.

Jenna opened the text that had just come through on her phone as Saleda leaned into her.

'East Potomac Park,' her Special Agent in Charge said, 'Don't want her to see us coming. If she spooks, she might blow the thing before we have a chance to try and talk her down.'

'We've got 'em,' Jenna said, feeling the small smile break across her face, then pulling it back. *It's not over yet.*

'Flint?' Saleda asked.

Jenna nodded. '911 in Columbia Heights got a call from the Tivoli Theatre on 14th and Park Northwest. Theatre manager came in early for preparations for box office opening for the performance tonight. He was the first one there, but the doors were already unlocked. Came in to find the lights on in the main auditorium, a couple and a baby chained up together . . .'

Jenna's heart skipped as the chubby, smiling face of Flint and Ruthie's barely-a-year-old Nell – a face she'd seen only in pictures – flashed in. Jenna ached for her, swallowed a lump in her throat. That sweet, innocent toddler already shared more in common with Jenna than any child deserved. The poor little thing didn't understand any of this now, but one day, she would understand far too well.

If she makes it.

'Jenna?' Dodd prodded, her words ambling off in the middle of her sentence the way they had clearly worrying him. 'What else did Irv say?'

Jenna looked at Dodd, tried hard to still her quivering chin. 'Th-they were chained up together on the stage, attached to all sorts of explosives.' She looked down, taking a long pause to force away the wild colors of her emotions running through her head. To still her gut reactions. Muster resolve. *They need me on the case right now. They need my head in the case.* 'Irv's already gained access to the theatre's surveillance cams, and it's definitely them.'

The helicopter lowered toward the open, grassy field of the park that sat about a mile from the Jefferson Memorial.

'Right,' Saleda said. She leaned toward the pilot. 'As soon as we land, Jenna and I will head for the memorial with the backup waiting for us.' She met Dodd's gaze and nodded, saying to the pilot, 'I need you to get this guy to the Tivoli Theatre ASAP. Hostage situation in progress. About four miles north, just north of the Columbia Heights Civic Plaza.' She turned to Dodd. 'I'll have backup and hostage negotiation teams en route. Assess the situation – especially anything that pertains or connects it to Ashlee as best you can tell – and check back in. Jenna and I will head to the memorial and spread out to try and find Ashlee.'

On a whim, Jenna pulled out her phone, texted Irv to send her any family information he had on Ashlee Haynie other than her marriage to James Asner. With James dead, maybe she suddenly realized she was in too deep, wanted out. But without her husband, who could she go to that would help her get away from Black Shadow? Who could she go to that might still take her in . . . hide her, after all she'd done. She didn't have many options if any at all. If she had parents or siblings, maybe she went to them.

'What about me?' Grey asked meekly.

Saleda paused, the question seeming to have caught her off guard. In the next second though, she gave Grey a quick nod, as if she'd had the answer on her tongue the whole time, and said, 'You'll ride along with one of the FBI backup units Quantico has waiting for us on the ground here.'

Grey nodded politely, and Jenna couldn't tell if the mousy look on her face was simply taking instructions in a serious and intimidating situation, or if maybe a little disappointment at being relegated to a spot outside of the thick of the action glowed somewhere behind Grey's wide, round eyes.

The pilot brought the chopper down gently on the grass. Saleda stepped out first, then helped Grey follow.

Jenna moved to take her turn out the door but looked over her shoulder. 'Dodd? Don't listen to a thing Flint Lewis says. Or take it with a grain of salt, anyway. I don't have his game entirely figured out yet, but the theatrics, the stage . . .'

Flint's master plan was all laid out, and just like everything he'd done until now, he would have set the stage – every actor, location, prop, and audience member – orchestrated to perfection in a way that would perfectly execute his show. Every attack leading to this moment had been spectacles tailored to convey the story Flint wanted to tell to the world, and his final act would surely be designed to give his audience a climax that would be burned into their memories forever.

'Perfect for him, huh? Though a little too matchy-matchy for me. I know he's kind of obsessed with the idea of making every piece of his weird attempt to bring about an elitist revolution take a bath in culture and verify it's IQ, but I personally like even my genius criminal masterminds to throwback to the old abandoned warehouse every now and then,' Dodd joked. 'But don't worry. I'll let the hostage negotiator listen to what he says. I'm there to listen to the things he *doesn't* say.' Dodd gave Jenna a wink. 'Though I have to tell you, I'm looking forward to the moment we let him realize we know he hasn't actually been kidnapped and is just being a prima donna. It'll tell me – tell *us* – a *whole* lot more about him.'

Jenna gave Dodd a close-lipped smile. *Exactly.*

'Now go, Doc. There's a Southern belle out there who's not quite ready to give up on the Civil War, and you've got to find her so you can let her know she's about to bomb the wrong commemorative landmark! Jefferson *had* slaves! It's *Abe's* memorial she wants!'

Jenna waved a hand at him. 'Make sure to take your ear horn with you when you go talk with the hostage negotiator, old man, because if you start talking like that to some police commander you've never met before and you don't give him good reason to put you squarely in the "old enough to be senile category" right off the bat, he might think you're in with the bad guys and have you hauled off in a straight jacket.'

'Will do,' Dodd said, chuckling.

Jenna gave him a quick grin, then turned and exited the chopper.

Jenna pulled her phone back out to find Irv's reply waiting. Every muscle in her body stiffened as she read. Ashlee *had* had a brother – a twin.

Jenna wandered over and sat on an iron bench, her eyes never leaving her phone as she read. Ashlee's brother Mitch had enlisted in the army at twenty. Then, when Bush invaded Iraq, Mitch was deployed. After Fallujah, what was left of him came home in a box.

She clicked the attachments, which turned out to be pictures: one of Ashlee and her brother as kids wearing swimsuits and holding hands on a dock, a glistening lake behind them. In the second, eight or nine-year-old Ashlee and Mitch climbing one of the many trees that made up a field covered in pink blossoms. Ashlee sitting on a low branch, leaning against the trunk with her legs stretched out as she read a Ramona Quimby book. Mitch hooking his knees over a branch on the opposite side of the trunk and hanging upside down.

Jenna scrolled through the others. Teenaged Ashlee and Mitch – both wearing deep red robes and flat graduation caps of the same color. Ashlee's cap's gold tassel dangled over her right eye as Mitch squeezed her in a bear hug, his lips pressed hard against her right cheek. The two at a theme park with their heads pressed together, making goofy faces.

Jenna swiped the tablet to see the last picture, and her breath caught. A flag-draped coffin stood in a cemetery, a handful of people in black scattered around a priest talking at a portable lectern. To his left was Ashlee, seated in one of the few chairs for the family. Hints of tears were covered by the sunglasses she wore, and her head was bowed. She stared at her feet, and in her lap, she clutched a tiny sprig of flowers.

Jenna pictured the Tidal Basin in her mind. That's where she'd find Ashlee Haynie. She just knew.

Her feet seemed to know, too.

Forty-four

Ashlee Haynie didn't even seem surprised – or alarmed, for that matter – as Jenna sat down next to her on the park bench, which was set a ways back from the Tidal Basin and the tourist path along it, nestled into the dense grove of cherry blossom trees that were a favorite of tourists visiting the city. Jenna folded her hands in her lap. Out of the corner of her eye she noticed that the deep chestnut the terrorist had dyed her hair wasn't so bad, but the short, pixie style it had been cropped into didn't seem right for the Ashlee's face shape. The disguise would've worked if she only wanted to blend into a new town and be a new person. Never if someone was looking for her.

'Thought I might find you here,' Jenna said conversationally.

A bird chirped overhead, and the gentle whispers of the Tidal Basin's ripples would've made for a serene meeting place – even for an FBI Agent and the wanted terrorist she was hunting – were it not for the yells and chants of the protestors on the steps of the memorial ruining the ambience even from a distance.

Ashlee stared straight ahead. 'No mind games, Dr Ramey. No "good cop," either. We both know you're not my friend. We both know what I did. Said straight to your face. Hell, you probably felt sorry for me. Maybe worried about me a little.'

The woman's tone was different from the act she had put on during the interview at the bank, sure. She'd been playing a role. But even so, the Ashlee speaking now didn't exude hate and the hard quality that the brutality of Scarlett's kills would suggest she would. It wasn't remorse or regret, either. Definitely not fear. Ice blue flashed in. Ashlee's tone said confidence but also gave away that she was weary. *And maybe . . . could it possibly be she's a little hurt?* But more than anything, the iced blue told Jenna what her demeanor was: resigned.

Jenna crossed her legs, nodded. 'You're right. I did worry about you. Worry about anyone who's been through something like I thought you had. And no, you're right. I know we're not friends. Neither of us wants to be. But I also know you might want some help, even if you'd never ask for it.'

'If you're here to try to talk me out of this, Dr Ramey, you really shouldn't bother. I assume you already know we're holding Flint Lewis's family hostage,' Ashlee said evenly.

The dark yellow of obliviousness flashed in. *Interesting wording.*

'Yes,' Jenna said, unwilling to give more in case Ashlee might slip and give them something they didn't already have. 'But let's talk about you some more. If you needed help, I'm here. I know you're dedicated, but even the most dedicated are only human. Killing is one thing, Ashlee, but dying is another,'

'Well, you'd better hope I can do both, because the way this bomb is rigged, if it doesn't detonate on time, the one rigged to the Lewis family will,' Ashlee said.

Now, this *was news.* In more ways than one. If it wasn't so twisted, Jenna might've laughed. If Ashlee didn't know Flint Lewis *was* Beo, he was killing two birds with one stone. He sets off another massive attack that, given the current climate, would bring the government one step closer to enacting the martial law Black Shadow needed to prove to the people that the government *would* turn on its own citizens unless the right people were put into power, and at the same time, threw yet another Black Shadow member under the bus and got rid of a loose end. Dark yellow flashed in again.

So, if you're so gung-ho about dying, then why do you seem so darn disappointed?

Aw, what the hell.

'So, are you just so noble that you can't stand the thought of an innocent family being blown to bits? Frankly, Ashlee, your past doesn't exactly show you to be a consummate humanitarian, but I have to be honest, for some reason, my gut says you don't want to die.'

That made Ashlee prickle up. Her whole body turned to look at Jenna. 'And how did you come up with that? Are you trying to say I don't have the guts to do it? Finish the mission we started? That I *believe* in?'

Jenna calmly shook her head. 'Not at all. I don't doubt your courage, dedication to your movement. Personal loss is a powerful motivator to take up a cause, but it's also the most effective fuel to drive someone to make bold moves, effect change.' Jenna paused, looked into Ashlee's eyes. 'No matter the cost.'

'So why don't you think I'll blow this thing—' Ashlee stopped mid-thought, her hardened expression morphing to one of confusion.

'How did you know a personal loss is why I believe so strongly in what Black Shadow's doing?'

'Same way I knew to look for you in this cherry tree grove while all the rest of the agents searching for you are still combing the place,' Jenna said.

Ashlee twisted a silver ring on her right hand. 'You know about Mitch.'

Jenna nodded. 'Yeah. I might not know all the details, like how Beo found out about your brother, or how he knew enough about how you felt about Mitch's death to know you were a target ripe for the picking. But I do know that however he knew those things, he was able to do what he does with everyone in Black Shadow and take those already fragile, vulnerable thoughts you had while grieving your twin and twist them around in your mind. Mold them and mess with your head until you not only blamed those in power for Mitch's death but shared Beo's own convictions about what made those people in power unfit to govern and dangerous to society. At some point, like Beo, you believed the people controlling the government were dangerous to society just like they had been to Mitch, and that had the intellectually elite been the ruling class, Mitch would still be alive.'

Ashlee stood, anger flowing through her aggressive posture. 'He would be! But no! Instead, an idiot president who can't even correctly pronounce the word "nuclear" sent my brother into a war that no evidence indicated was warranted, because, of the guys who are supposed to look at these types of situations and make intelligent decisions about them, over half barely graduated those Ivy League universities their daddies got them into. So in order for these morons to get elected, what do they do? What any sub-par, stupid human being does: they pander to the subsets of people in their constituency who are too stupid to realize *they're* stupid too,' Ashlee ranted, pacing. She stopped, faced Jenna. 'Why are you so sure I don't want to die? Because to be honest, my brother's dead, my husband's dead. Considering that doing it would be my final act to help Black Shadow finish what it started. What Beo talked me into joining. What we believed in – what *Beo* believed in – then it doesn't seem too bad a way to go.'

Two colors fought to come to the front of Jenna's mind. She pushed back the one she could worry about later, pulled the other into focus – the one that fought for dominance when Ashlee said Beo's name. Deep burgundy. Infatuation. Romantic love.

Yep. The others behind bars could wait, because unless that color was misleading her, the two who were out, about, and still very much capable of causing death and destruction seemed to happen to be the two whose networking to end up in the group hadn't *just* landed them with a connection to Black Shadow. It had also resulted in another *alliance*. That burgundy was very specific. An intense, *loyal*, alliance.

Interesting. And she doesn't know that Flint Lewis is Beo. How coy.

Unfortunately for one person in that incredibly infatuated, trusting alliance, only she subscribed to it.

'He'll be proud of you, huh?' Jenna said. 'Beo?'

'Why the hell do you care?'

'Why would you want the man who ordered your husband killed to be *proud* of you?'

Ashlee blinked, cocked her head. 'What are you talking about? Ishmael. Ishmael ordered Atticus to kill anyone who stayed their hand during a raid. That's why JP was killed.'

'Oh,' Jenna said. She pouted her lips, gave Ashlee a mocking frown. 'You didn't know.'

'Know what?' Ashlee said, her voice rising in irritation.

'Ishmael, Ashlee. He's Beo. Ishmael *is* Beo,' Jenna said, stopping short of revealing the *other* role Beo stepped into from time to time. As much as they needed to find a way to keep Ashlee from blowing hundreds of people sky high at the Jefferson Memorial, they didn't need it's reprieve to occur because Ashlee Haynie learned Beo also masqueraded as Flint Lewis and had done so that day to try to get away scot-free after she was out of the picture. And maybe Flint *did* deserve an intimate date with C4 instead of the one he'd inevitably have with Butchie McPantsdown in prison, but his wife Ruthie didn't deserve it. Or little Nell. She deserved so, *so* much more. Unfortunately, though, Ashlee would be so angry and ready to send Flint to the moon that she'd likely slice through every wire keeping that bomb live by the time Jenna so much as opened her mouth to mention the latter.

Ashlee's face went blank, and she shook her head slowly from side to side. 'That fucking dick.'

I couldn't agree more.

Ashlee threw her hands up. 'So, what now? I've fucking lived for this cause for so long . . .' The word caught in her throat as she turned her back on Jenna, took a few steps away. She shook her head hard, kicked at the ground as she barely whispered. 'You mother-fucking, lying, bag of dicks.'

Jenna moved to her, touched her shoulder. 'My supervising agent is on her way with a bomb unit. We can get this thing off—'

'I already told you,' Ashlee cut in, 'It'll set off the bomb attached to the Lewis family.' She leaned her head back, eyes squeezed shut. 'Fuck!' She opened her eyes, looked at Jenna. 'I don't want to kill any more people because I listened to that paranoid egotistical spaz maggot.'

'But if we don't diffuse the bomb, you'll still do just that.' Jenna gestured her arms wide, reminding Ashlee of the hundreds of people who would be victims if the bomb blew.

'So what do you propose, then?' Ashlee snapped.

Jenna squeezed her hand, then led her back to the bench. 'I say we sit tight and you tell me some stories about you and Mitch as kids while we wait for the bomb team. The people running the government might not all have common sense or a degree in astro-physics, but the people coming to help *you* are some of the smartest the country has to offer – both by books *and* raw talent. Trust me, Ashlee. If anyone can figure a way out of this, it's the BAU.'

Forty-five

Within five minutes of radioing Saleda, Jenna saw her superior through the filter of scraggly branches covered in pale pink blooms raining so many petals into the wind it almost looked as though Saleda was jogging through snow. Jenna stood up, waved both her arms so her Special Agent in Charge would find her faster.

Still seated on the bench, Ashlee made a small noise. A squeak of sorts. She had to be scared. And she should be. Just because she'd been duped didn't mean she wasn't still a horrible criminal. Black Shadow hadn't just killed men and women who happened to be in the wrong place at the wrong time. They'd also offed every child in their path, too. Hell, even Isaac Keaton had spared the kids.

But still, no matter what this woman had done, she was still a human being, driven by grief, anger. Jenna could be kind to her at what had to be one of the most terrifying and uncertain moments in her life. Plus, Jenna needed her to cooperate a bit longer.

'Agent Ovarez is bringing the bomb team. They should be here in just a minute or two.' Jenna sat back down beside Ashlee, patted her hand as the young woman whimpered. 'I know. Even though you knew this day could come – maybe even *would* come, nothing can prepare you for how it would feel. Fear, relief, shame, disappointment, defeat . . .'

'Suspense, unease. Loss of hope,' Ashlee replied.

Focus on the now. 'The best guys in the business are coming to work on this problem, and until they solve it, I'm going to stay right here with you. I won't leave you to go through this alone.'

Ashlee practically growled. 'Unlike *Beo*. He actually told me Ishmael decided to send me to be the one for this attack. Said it was punishment for JP's mistake.' She laughed dryly. 'And the whole time, he just wanted to get rid of me. Use me, then get rid of me. Fuckin' men.'

Jenna stood up, walked a few steps from Ashlee, biting her tongue. *I don't know, gal. Sometimes it's not just the men who mess with your head and use you. You can take that one to the bank.*

A long pause on the other end. 'Dodd? You OK?'

Dodd's voice came back in barely a whisper. 'Yes, yes. I just . . . I stepped into the balcony stairwell for a minute. Wanted to tell you one thing, just in case. Might be nothing, but worth keeping on our radar.'

'What is it, Dodd?' Jenna asked, standing up straighter, alert.

'There was . . . I don't know, Doc. It's was something he said. Or the way he said it . . .'

'Cough it up, Daddy-o,' Jenna said.

She heard long, nervous exhales almost too close to the phone speaker. What Dodd *hadn't* said yet officially had Jenna's curiosity maxed out faster than any credit card she'd ever owned.

What is *that?*

'Hey, Jenna, get over here. We've got company, and I've got no doubt I'm gonna need backup,' Saleda interrupted her train of thought as she tapped her on the shoulder from behind where Jenna had stayed on the sidewalk along the cherry blossom trees to call Dodd.

Jenna turned to Saleda, then followed Saleda's gaze to where it locked on a tall person striding toward them down the walk.

'Thanks for the info, Dodd,' Jenna said. 'I'm going to have to call you back, though. There must've been more protest signs than picnic baskets in the park, because Yogi's headed our way now, and he looks pissed.'

Forty-six

'Dr Ramey, SA Ovarez,' he said, giving them each a curt nod that told Jenna he had no intention of observing niceties. 'I'd ask why I wasn't informed of the situation at hand, but to do that would be to suggest I don't already know I'm being purposefully kept out of the loop. *However*, someone with authority that supersedes even the mighty FBI BAU wishes me to be informed of all developments so I can report to the secretary. He will want an accurate picture of the threat level and how traditional law enforcement is handling it when he makes his recommendation to the president today, of course.'

The general gestured around him to the people milling about – some tourists taking photos as well as locals enjoying the sun in addition to the protestors closer to the memorial. 'And why are these people not being evacuated? That's obviously the first step in a situation like this—'

'My apologies for interrupting, sir, but the other UNSUB? The one at the theatre? Since your people have done such an excellent and thorough job of keeping you informed, surely you're aware of his involvement, but in case you aren't, he has a bomb attached to himself, his wife, and his infant child which will detonate in the event that the bomb on Ms Haynie is disarmed,' Saleda said. 'In add—'

'And what does that have to do with not evacuating hundreds of people in danger from a nearby explosion?' the general cut in angrily.

Saleda visibly swallowed hard, breathed in one, long, deep breath. 'I was getting to that, *sir*. In addition to that particular set of extenuating circumstances, the UNSUB at the theatre – who we also believe to have been the leader who orchestrated this series of attacks – has implied that he is able to monitor her onsite here, and that should she balk on their plan by, say, alerting citizens around her to the danger and, thus, lowering the potential impact the attack might have, he has access to remote-detonate the bomb on her with no warning.'

General Ted was silent for a moment, then walked past them a few feet as if thinking.

Yeah, General Brute Force. Don't have an answer for that one, do you?

The general turned back around. 'And how do we know *she* isn't the mastermind and all this isn't some scheme to ensure she stays within full range of victims until she decides to make her move and blow everyone sky high?'

Brilliant profiling work, genius.

'Our investigation has already confirmed that the other UNSUB, Flint Lewis, is the leader of this organization. If Ms Haynie were the actual leader, why would she attach a bomb to herself that was on a set timer? Suicide bombers detonate their own vests. Ms Haynie here may have taken part in the acts of Black Shadow, but she definitely did not lead it,' Jenna said.

'And she now realizes she has been misled by Mr Lewis this whole time in an effort to manipulate her into taking part in this, and while she understands this in no way exonerates her from her culpability, she has agreed to cooperate with us to either disarm both bombs or remove hers in such a way that doesn't bring harm to the other lives attached to it,' Saleda finished.

'Oh, right! Let's not bring harm to the killer *responsible* for the massacres in the name of their so-called "cause". That would be simply *dreadful!*' the general said, walking a circle around himself, throwing his arms up.

'Sir, please keep your voice down,' Saleda said, so strong it was more instruction than request. 'Lewis claims other attacks are already set to take place even without him, but if he dies, so would the only person with information to prevent them.'

Jenna glanced over at Ashlee on the bench, who was craning her neck in their direction, trying to see what was going on. The general's rant must have caught her attention.

Jenna turned her gaze back to General Ted. 'Even if Flint Lewis wasn't holding future attacks over our heads, and *even* if it was ethical for law enforcement to choose to blow up one citizen over another without due process, I'd think even you would draw the line at sacrificing a pregnant woman and an innocent thirteen-month-old baby girl. I'm pretty sure little Nell Lewis didn't ask for a bowie knife and a ski mask for her first birthday. So, let's just hang tight, supervise, and enjoy the scenery while we let the bomb techs do their jobs.'

The general looked her square in the eye, giving her a smug, condescending smile. 'Dr Ramey, our national security is at risk. As difficult as it is to make life or death decisions, I'm charged with protecting our *country*. It's why we don't negotiate with terrorists, Doctor. Because if the life of one or two – even one of an infant – can secure hundreds or thousands, I am charged to make that pragmatic call. Now, I am taking control of this matter so that we can end this horrible day with the hundreds in this park intact, including Ms Haynie.'

'And how, pray tell, do you plan to do *that*?' Jenna asked, unable to keep the bite out of her voice. She couldn't help it. Regardless of how many wars or medals of honor the general could boast, the terrorists groups he had experience with weren't like Black Shadow. These weren't radicalized religious zealots, or nationalists.

'Black Shadow isn't your everyday, issue-driven terrorist group,' Jenna said. 'Most issue-driven groups unite because of an intense passion for a single cause like environmental extremists, fanatical animal rights groups, and even militant pro-life advocates. While Black Shadow *did* join together to fight for a shared cause, the reasons they came to be *passionate* about that cause were *far* more personal. The cause they all ended up supporting was only *very* indirectly related to the individual, intimate, and painful reasons they each came to fight for it.'

'What are you driving at, Dr Ramey?'

'Despite their different circumstances, every single member in Black Shadow ultimately ended up believing that the lack of intelligence in the government and in society was to blame for whatever in their past had harmed them in ways they would never forget or forgive. But how do you think they made that jump? To be so incensed by it that they were willing to massacre innocent people to take a stand against it required two things: a grieving victim filled with pain and anger, and someone to manipulate them into believing that mass murder was somehow the answer to that pain and anger.'

General Ted threw his arms up again. 'Well, they're still killers, Dr Ramey! How does this have *anything* to do with how I handle the matter so that everyone here at the memorial today will go home safe and sound – including our female mass murderer over there?'

'It matters because, right now, Ashlee is cooperating freely, and we're working to keep everyone safe because of that,' Saleda cut in. 'But emotions are running high, and there are a lot of feelings in play surrounding this issue. You may feel you have the upper hand, but without knowing her mindset, her pathology, her background – let's just say making the right move here is critical.'

'She may feel betrayed by Flint, may have decided she wants to live after all. But that doesn't necessarily mean she'll want him dead,' Jenna added, a sinking feeling settling over her that she knew what the general's course of action would be.

The general waved off both their words. 'I wouldn't expect her to. All we have to do is *tell her* the bomb squad has found a way to defuse the bomb attached to her without causing the explosives attached to Flint and his family to detonate. We neutralize the threat, arrest our UNSUB, and we put this one to bed.'

'You mean we lie to her,' Saleda said sharply.

'You mean we kill an innocent woman, her unborn child, and her one-year-old?' Jenna spat.

'And how do you think that'll go over in the press?' Saleda said. '"General decides to play a high-stakes variation of Russian Roulette, ends in murder of toddler and her expecting mother."'

'I think it'll be more something like how hundreds at the Jefferson Memorial were heroically saved, and with his plan thwarted, the deranged mastermind of the plot went into a rage, killing his wife and daughter before taking his own life. People don't care about the truth.' General Ted laughed. 'Most of the time, the public doesn't need the truth . . . *and* it doesn't want it.'

'I doubt Ashlee would agree . . .' Jenna's voice trailed as she turned toward the bench where Ashlee had been seated. The bomb techs were several yards away leaned over a large pamphlet unfolded about twelve times until it was flat on the grass, pointing at different sections, deep in discussion.

Jenna turned all the way around, just in case she hadn't gotten far, but there was no sight of her in any direction after a full 360.

'She's gone!' Saleda shouted next to her. She turned to the bomb techs. 'The bomb? How long left on the timer?'

The two looked at each other, eyes wide with fear. Then one coughed. 'Five minutes, ma'am.'

Jenna didn't reply. She started toward the Jefferson Memorial building, where all the protestors stood outside it, championing Ashlee's cause. She yelled over her shoulder but kept moving.

'That's what I meant about how knowing her background was critical to making the right move. And you've made it all right.

Ashlee's brother died in Iraq in a war over WMDs that didn't exist.
And if any part of her wondered if the same misinformation, the
same backdoor dealing that sent her brother to his death was still
going on in the government's leaders now, well . . . she might not
have needed the truth, sir, but by God, you just gave it to her.' Without
waiting for the general's reply, she broke into a run.

Forty-seven

With only minutes to position herself to take out the maximum number of victims – and thus ensure that after this, plus hearing more attacks were promised, the president would have no choice but to sign the order for martial law – Ashlee would head to where the bulk of the protestors were camped out. The crowd was so thick in all directions, as long as Ashlee stationed herself anywhere in or around the building or the courtyard, her mission would be a success for Black Shadow. Hell, it already was.

Jenna paused for a moment to look around, think. Get her bearings. Every direction she turned, her eyes were met with policemen in full riot gear, faceless masks wielding machine guns made for the sole purpose of war. Everything Black Shadow had wanted – worked for – was in front of Ashlee now. The government was revealing itself as an enemy. Yesterday, people had watched on TV as the Department of Homeland Security shot at innocent bystanders in a mall because of bad intel they had gotten, and today, helicopters overhead were recording segments for their nightly news that would show that these people we had trusted to serve and protect us had now been turned on us to treat us as enemies.

Where are you, Ashlee?

Jenna started meandering through the crowd again, her head whipping back and forth, trying to latch on to something that would give her an idea and fast. *She'd go somewhere significant. All of the choices Black Shadow made – their nicknames, the way they passed messages . . . when presented with a place like this, so steeped in history, Ashlee would go somewhere meaningful for the moment.*

Jenna considered the quote inscribed on one of the walls that had given away this location in the first place. The one about Jefferson's belief in the educated. But the light yellow of something feeling off had flashed in, and it felt all wrong. What else had Grey told her was inscribed on the other walls?

The orchid of elitism flashed in as a memory bounded to the forefront of her memory. The southwest wall!

Jenna ran up the steps, pushed through throngs of people with signs and bullhorns, and was rewarded with the chance to squeeze, wind, and shove her way through yet another mob inside the doors. If only she could reach the southwest wall, though, Ashlee would be there. She just knew it. It wasn't because it was one of the most famous, adorned with the iconic passage from the Declaration of Independence beginning, 'We hold these truths to be self-evident . . .' Ashlee would be there because of what *wasn't* on the wall. The inscription eliminates the right of revolution passage, which allows for the right and even the *duty* of the people of a nation to overthrow a government that is against their interests and well-being. Who'd have thought all those hours of Grey's rambling would pay off?

Suddenly, Jenna stopped cold. Sure enough, there she was. Ashlee, ten feet in front of her, back to her, looking up at the very wall that had brought Jenna straight to her.

Jesus. She had to get Ashlee out of here. Get that bomb either diffused or . . . somehow make sure that if it went off, it didn't do it where it would take hundreds of people with it.

Jenna veered to the side, hoping she could come from the angle least likely to be noticed by Ashlee until she was within distance to grab her, cuff her. What she'd do with her after that wasn't even on the table yet. One thing at a damned time.

As Jenna crept toward Ashlee, the woman's stillness, her focus on the memorial wall was almost eerie. Just about six more feet . . .

Ashlee's head turned, eyes flashing. The woman took off out of the nearest doorway, bolting down the steps, shoving people out of her way.

Jenna took the stairs two at a time, giving chase but without drawing her weapon. So many cops on duty here today for the protests. God. Jenna *had* to get to her first. If those cops saw Ashlee, identified her as a threat, and took a shot, that bomb could go off.

As Ashlee dashed across the courtyard, nearing some barricades set up around some of the police car parking set up especially to deal with the protest. If Ashlee hopped those barriers, Jenna might lose her. Too many places to duck or hide. Jenna put on a burst of speed, her lungs searing as she willed her feet to move faster. She waved people out of her way, saying, 'Please, move, move! Police business!' But it did little to stir the sardines into a frenzy, and the groups of people seemed to get slower as though she were some interesting live show.

Ashlee now straddled one of the cement barricades, almost over. How much time could possibly be left on that bomb's timer? Even though Ashlee was running away, she was still *far* too close. So many would be hurt or killed. And as she ran, Jenna was all too aware she might be one of them. At this point, running toward Ashlee was as much to save others as it was her only chance to save herself. She likely didn't have time to get out of the range of the explosion, so stopping it was the only shot.

I'll never make it to her in time.

As Ashlee went to swing her remaining leg over the barrier into the makeshift parking area, instead of simply hopping down on the other side, something caught her foot on the way over. She stumbled, then, when she thought she'd recovered and tried to take one more step, she yelped, tripping and thudding to the ground.

Jenna scaled the barricade and eased down to the other side, eyes peeled for whatever had tripped Ashlee up. *Ah. Traffic cone. Get you every time.*

Jenna rushed to Ashlee, pinned her before she could roll over. *Please don't let my knee be on the damned bomb. Please.*

She yanked Ashlee's arms behind her back, slapped them in cuffs. 'Ashlee Haynie, you're under arrest. You have the right to remain silent,' Jenna said, diligently giving the woman all of her Miranda rights. Seemed silly, knowing that underneath that coat, a clock was down to only minutes or seconds before the weapon strapped to her blew them both up, but she did it because she hadn't figured out what to do next. This was habit, and reciting the rote lines helped her stay cool. *Think. There's gotta be a way.*

'I heard what he said,' Ashlee spat as Jenna gave her a push to roll her over. 'He'd kill an innocent child. Said people didn't care about the truth. Said just tell 'em what they want to hear.'

'On your feet,' Jenna said, heaving Ashlee up under her elbows. She needed a look at the timer. Maybe she had time to get a bomb squad or SWAT . . .

'But these people out here care about the truth, and they're going to be part of it! Beo might've tricked me into getting involved, preyed on my weaknesses, but even so, he was right! What I was fighting for – what happened to my brother—'

Jenna barely listened as she ripped open Ashlee's coat, unzipped the fleece underneath it. What she saw made her heart beat double time – fifty-nine seconds.

Oh, shit.

No time to think. She glanced around her at the cop cars. *Something. Somewhere. Anywhere safe . . .*

Then, she saw it. She tried a couple of the cop cars until she found one whose door wasn't entirely shut. She pried it open, then turned and scooped Ashlee up like a baby in her arms as the woman was in mid-sentence, 'The government wanted to silence JP, too— What the hell are you—'

The hard drop into the passenger's seat knocked Ashlee's arm on a box in the middle, jammed her leg into the dash and cut her off.

A cop yelled to Jenna, running toward her. 'What the hell are you doing? That's my cruiser!'

'FBI,' Jenna yelled, 'No time to explain. She's got a bomb, set to go off in seconds. Your keys!'

The cop looked dumbfounded a moment, and Jenna could tell for a split-second the cop-side of him tried to assess the situation, handle it more logically. Use protocol.

In the next instant, though, he threw her his keys, which she caught in one hand.

Yeah, I'd rather let someone else deal with this, too, buddy.

Jenna jumped into the car, turned the key in the ignition. Tires screeched as she backed out of the spot, shifted gears, and gunned the engine in what was as close to one solid maneuver as humanly possible. The cruiser picked up speed, and the glowing bomb timer cemented in Jenna's memory was all she could think of. What number it must be down to now? Twenty, maybe. Fifteen?

She tried to force it out of her thoughts and, instead, focused on what was in front of her, the end goal rushing toward her as much as she to it. *Get there. We have to get there.*

It's the only way.

Now, Ashlee was screaming, both out of fear from the speed they were gaining, rushing down an access road far too fast to swerve or miss anything that didn't see them coming first and stop for them, as well as out of indignation that her vengeance for her brother – her revenge against General Ted for being everything she'd fought against – was being ripped from her control.

'Are you crazy? What are you doing? JP died fighting for this! I should get to finish it!' she screamed.

'Me? Crazy?' Jenna said, flooring the gas pedal, a death grip on the wheel. 'Of the two of us, I'd say I might be the *slightly* more logical one.'

Logic's driving now. The only way.

'You do realize that in thirteen seconds, *you're* going to die, too, right? You could've gone, let me finish the mission,' Ashlee said, head bowed.

Poor thing. She hasn't realized it yet.

Wouldn't be long. Jenna's heart thundered as they neared it. She unclipped her safety belt, and, with a spare pair of cuffs from the cruiser's front seat, she grabbed Ashlee's wrist closest to her, clamped one bracelet on Ashlee, the other to the steel grate of the safety partition. Ashlee stared into her eyes, stunned, but Jenna broke the stare to take the sharp veer that led to the bridge.

This is the only way.

Ashlee whimpered, then cried out, her fate finally in her sights. Jenna closed her eyes and yanked the driver's side door handle, throwing her shoulder into the door as hard as she could. She tucked hard, rolled as her body pounded to the cement, Ashlee's awful wail echoing in her ears.

Jenna's body slammed the concrete rail of the bridge, and she stopped rolling. Just in time to hear the crack of the Type III construction barricade advising the closed road, the slight crush of the cruiser hood as it slapped it away like nothing. Then, a second of silence before a splash cracked the river below, the impact so hard it almost sounded as though the car had landed on something solid.

But Jenna knew better. She'd driven so fast and in the direction she had so the car would go straight in, nose down rather than land flat and sink slowly.

I'm sorry, Ashlee. For your brother. For Mitch.

A deep, pressured pop that sounded like cannon fire echoed in the afternoon air, and a few moments later, a light mist rained down on Jenna's bare arms. She closed her eyes and pictured the photograph of baby Nell she'd seen at Flint Lewis's house that day, the sweet, chubby, cheeks that reminded her so much of Ayana's.

Sirens blared, their whoops and howls getting louder, the horns of emergency vehicles chastising drivers in holding them up. She pushed herself off her side, sat up on the bridge, and took a few breaths before using her arms to press up to test her feet. She was shaky but not hurt beyond a bit of painful road rash. That she could tell, anyway.

She would stand and wait for the first responders – for Saleda. Give a statement. But she wanted them to see her up. Alert. Of course they'd want her to go to the hospital to get checked out anyway, but this way, they wouldn't argue as much when she declined. What no one but Saleda or Dodd would know was that she'd obviously be going there, anyway.

She had to see Yancy. Kiss him. And even if he couldn't hear her or understand, she needed to tell him that despite everything that had happened, they were going to be OK, because they had to be. Only no more of this moonlighting as MacGyver business on his end. If she needed to quit the BAU, buy an expensive gaming keyboard, and sit at it around the clock until she'd mastered both Land of Valor *and* the art of professional dachshund insulting to keep them in the same playing field and happy, then he'd just have to hurry up and get out of that hospital bed, because he was going to need to come to Best Buy with her and give some advice.

Her phone buzzed as fire trucks and sheriff's cars were beginning to arrive, pulling in to park sideways across the bridge to block off the scene. She fished into her pocket. Dodd's name shined on the screen.

'Heard you had some excitement out your way,' he said evenly.

She smiled, despite herself. And even though it wasn't true yet, her gut knew it was. 'Heard you didn't,' she said. 'At least, I hope. Is Grey all right? Ruthie? Nell?'

'They're all fine,' Dodd said. He confirmed that as soon as Ashlee's bomb detonated, the timer and lights on the one attached to the Lewises disengaged. 'Your word wizard went wandering after a butterfly at some point, though. The patrol she was with said he took her to the outskirts of the action and thought she was sitting tight in the car. Next thing he knew he turned around and she was gone.'

'That's a shame. I would have liked to thank her.'

'Well, good luck trying. Something tells me she'll want some alone time to practice bird calls for a while after all this interaction with the real world.'

Jenna smirked. 'Probably.'

'You OK?' Dodd asked – outright asking if she was physically hurt, but they both knew he was asking about the emotional toll, too.

'Ah,' Jenna said, glancing in the direction of the end of the bridge where divers were already jumping into the water. 'I, uh, I did what I had to do. You said the Lewises are OK. Then I guess I'm OK,' she said, pushing Ashlee Haynie's terrified face from her mind and replacing it with chubby-cheeked Nell.

'Well, they're OK as they can be, I guess,' Dodd said. 'Like you.' He paused, then added, 'Except for Flint, maybe. Second the bomb disengaged, he was in cuffs and on his way to the Pentagon. I daresay his next adventures won't be nearly as amusing for him.'

'Poor Ruthie,' Jenna said, that sickening feeling washing over her of understanding all too well how you could never quite get over finding out someone you loved wasn't even real.

'She's shaken, but she's strong,' Dodd said. 'Both her and that kiddo will turn out all right, Jenna. And this had to happen for them to. Remember that, when you think about what you had to do. And don't worry. I already passed along a little message from you to Nell. I hope you don't mind.'

'Huh?' Jenna said, waving to Saleda as she stepped out of a black SUV down the hill and came running toward the bridge.

'Just told her that, between us, having a bad parent – you know, a *really* malignant, heinous parent—'

'Dodd, I doubt Nell knows either of those words yet,' Jenna cut in.

'—can actually be an extraordinary thing. Sure, she'll hate the gawking and the whispers. But sharing blood with an evil dragon doesn't necessarily make her an evil dragon, too. I told her that if I had my guess, I'd say it makes her just the opposite.'

Claudia's face swirled in Jenna's mind, her taunting note saying that she'd ruin them with what she knew about Yancy. 'Unfortunately, I can only vanquish a dragon when I can see her coming. Have a bead on how she plans, recognize her moves, anticipate her habits. Claudia is . . . not just fighting a dragon. It's playing chess with one, only this game's objective is getting to the battlefield, it's checkmate achieved by getting there at a time through moves your opponent must never see,' Jenna said slowly.

'That *is* true. But a rested mind can see three moves farther than one that just jumped out of a car to escape a bomb about to explode in the next ten seconds. Even *if* the board is invisible. What do you say we make a deal? You get a shower and a hug from your little girl,' Dodd said, clicking his tongue obnoxiously, 'and *maybe* go get a much-needed visit in with your man, and tomorrow, I'll show you the file I've been putting together in my off hours of all the leads I have on Claudia since she left Sumpter.'

'Dodd! You—'

'Well, somebody had to,' Dodd cut her off. 'With everyone around your house using all their spare time memorizing nonsense words and playing tag-out trio—'

'Hey!'

'*Which* is a perfectly understandable precaution, vital security task, and noble undertaking,' Dodd recovered quickly, 'I thought you might could use an extra pair of eyes and hands on the case, just to sort of start up the offensive.'

'Dodd, I don't know what to say . . .'

He laughed. 'Say you're on your way to see that sarcastic, thrill-seeking son of a gun you've got yourself mixed up with! I didn't say this before because I didn't really think you'd need much prodding. Plus, I didn't want you to hijack a car to get there—'

'Dodd, what are you talking about? Spit it,' Jenna said.

He chuckled again. 'Just get your butt to the hospital, already! I'm telling you, that joker can live through anything. He's awake, and he's been askin' for you.'

Forty-eight

'Jenna? Is that you?'

'Guess again, lover boy,' Irv said, pushing the hospital door open and stepping into the room.

'Aw, honey,' Yancy said, eyeing the PlayStation Portable in Irv's had, 'You shouldn't have.'

'Aw, it was nothin'. Don't want you gettin' out of practice. There's a tournament comin' up soon,' Irv said, handing over the sleek, handheld game console to Yancy.

'My, that's quite a thoughtful gesture,' Yancy said, looking over the gift. 'Which tells me that keeping my street cred at amateur console wars with a bunch of thirteen-year-olds and that one girl who dresses like Sailor Moon isn't the reason for this token of affection. You're not thoughtful, Irv. Definitely not. Pragmatic, maybe. Discreet, OK, and *maybe* even understanding. But thoughtful? Come on. What's this softening the blow of?'

Irv sighed, pulled up the one stiff-backed chair in the room closer to Yancy's bed. The guy looked like someone had shot his puppy.

Oh, shit! 'Oboe! Is it Oboe? Is he OK? Someone's been taking care of him, right? Jesus, I really need to have some kind of setup for someone to check on him if they ever don't hear from me for a day—'

'Cool it, wiener-lover,' Irv cut in. 'Your handsome little brown sausage is just fine.'

Yancy winced. 'You know, I really never thought I'd hear someone talk to me about my handsome little brown sausage . . .'

'Think of it as a get well present,' Irv said. Then his tone turned serious. 'Speaking of, you're right. I'm not thoughtful. At all. I'm conniving, and I just wanted to get you nice and comfy before I told you—'

'You're a suspicious bastard who never did believe what I told you about why I was hacking the FBI database, looking for a file?' Yancy said. He laughed. Irv was the best the FBI had, and far better than Yancy at a lot of the professional systems and tools the Feds had access to that he didn't, so he definitely thought Irv was the best person to train him if, for some reason – as Irv thought – he'd ever be able to get a job as an analyst. Either way, though, Yancy had more at stake with that lie he'd told Irv, and he also had approximately half Irv's morals. He'd been watching close to see if Irv showed any sign he hadn't bought it, and he'd been right to.

Irv smirked. 'How'd you know?'

'Are you kidding me? You should never play poker, Irv. You've got a mean hacking game, but when it comes to cards you hold, you've either gotta work on masking your tells or get yourself some snazzy sunglasses or something,' Yancy said truthfully. 'That day at the skate park, you might as well have worn a sandwich board advertising your to do list: check up on Yancy, fact-check Yancy's story. Go through Yancy's dirty clothes to check if he bought the expensive laundry detergent without using the coupon you gave him. Toss his garbage for evidence he actually had Chinese for lunch on Friday like he claimed.'

'Damn, dude! Easy!'

'OK, OK. I'm just joking,' Yancy said. God, he was dreading this.

Irv leaned forward. 'So, then, if what you told me you were looking for in that file wasn't true, then what *is* the truth? Just level with me, man. You can trust me.'

If only this was just about me trusting you. I do trust you. Like you, even. Which is why I'd rather not give Claudia any reasons to want you dead, like that she finds out you know about our little deal.

But, while he *had* to keep Claudia and her involvement a secret for Irv's own safety, he at least owed him some of the truth. At least, what he could give him.

Yancy sucked in a breath. Man, this would never get easier.

'I killed a guy, Irv. A cop named Denny Hoffsteader.'

Irv's jaw dropped. Whatever he'd suspected, it hadn't been this. 'What?!'

Yancy nodded. 'Remember that girl involved in the Diamond Slayer case last year with the dad who had Alzheimer's? Well, it's a long story, but I was near her house one day when this Denny guy attacked her. Tried to choke her to death.'

'No way, dude,' Irv said, his voice in disbelief.

Yancy shrugged. 'I know, right? But the even crazier part of it is, the cop was involved with CiCi because he was a pimp. So not only had I killed a cop, but I'd killed a dirty cop who was a big player in a whole prostitution ring run by dirty cops.'

'Oh, man,' Irv said, the situation's implications dawning on his face. 'And they ever find out you killed one of their own . . .'

'Yeah,' Yancy said flatly, thinking of the file he'd looked for, of everything he was leaving out.

Irv shook his head over and over before, finally, he said, 'Uh-uh. Nope. It's just not gonna happen. Not just because, deep down, you're a good guy who was just trying to save a woman who was getting beat on, and not just because Jenna needs you, though God-knows she does. But because . . .' Irv looked at the floor, shook his head some more, this time seemingly at what he didn't want to say. Finally, he looked back up. 'But because *I* need you, damn it. More than you know. But you're about to. You're about to get an earful.'

Yancy listened in quiet disbelief as Irv explained to him all the reasons he'd wanted to train him instead of turn him in. Tell Jenna what he'd done when he'd hacked the database. Yancy'd known Irv had his reasons for taking him under his wing, but Yancy could've guessed for days what those reasons were and never come anywhere close to this.

Irv also told him his plan, and now, his idea. They talked over the details, both stopping every few sentences to add a, 'shit' or a 'dammit' to the conversation, just to pay homage to the weight of what they were discussing here. What they were *deciding*.

'So that's that, then? We're agreed?' Irv asked.

Yancy nodded. What else *could* he do? 'I'm in if you're in.'

Irv gave a quick nod. 'Well, I guess the last thing to decide, then, is do you tell Jenna, or do I?'

Forty-nine

'Where's . . . O . . . boe?'

Jenna smiled at Yancy's weak attempt at acting – eyes closed, sensing someone in the room. Knowing it was her.

'Very funny, Iron Man,' she said, leaning over to kiss him. She grabbed a hard plastic chair from against the wall and pulled it up beside his bed.

'What happened?' Yancy asked. 'Did you catch them?'

'Yancy, you can't keep doing this,' Jenna said, exasperated. 'As much as I wish you were, you're not part of the team. Besides, you're already skating on the thinnest ice imaginable. What were you thinking?'

'I was thinking about doing my job, because while I hate to drop this on you, he said I could,' Yancy said.

'He? Who are you talking about? What are you talking about?'

'Irv's dying, Jenna.'

It was like a punch in the gut. Whatever she'd expected him to say, it wasn't that.

'That . . . that doesn't make any sense,' Jenna said. 'Irv's fine. I passed him on the way in here. I've been in communication with him all day.'

'Not that kind of dying,' Yancy said, seeming to search for the right words. 'He has ALS. I've been working for him, learning from him and helping him from my computer at home. Jenna, he knows about Denny. He caught me trying to . . .'

Yancy took a long pause. '. . . to dig up a file in the FBI database. Victor and I have tied up almost everything with the CiCi incident, but we were still worried about a few things we had no way of making sure stayed under control,' Yancy blew out a slow breath. 'Irv's maybe the only person on earth who could make those things go away. For good. And . . . well, he promised he would. But only if, in return, I take over for him.'

Jenna caught her mouth hanging open. 'Does Saleda know about this?'

'She will soon. Irv's gone to tell her right now. He might have months, or he might have years, but we know he won't be able to do the same things he does now for much longer. He wanted to pick his replacement instead of leaving the BAU to fend for itself. I think since he caught me, he sees me as his chance to take care of two problems at once.'

Jenna forced down the questions clamoring to be voiced, forcing herself to remember Yancy was in a hospital bed. If what he was saying was true, she could discuss it at length with Saleda later anyway.

Her face must have softened slightly, because Yancy asked tentatively, 'So . . . did you get them?'

'More or less,' Jenna said. 'We caught all but three at the mall. One died on the scene. Of the other two, one's been caught, and the other was killed before we could bring her in.'

Yancy breathed a sigh of relief. 'Good. You got that woman that got away. I was worried . . .' his voice trailed groggily. He'd been so energetic, itching to talk to her when she came in; it had been easy to forget what he'd been through. That he still had some strong drugs pumping in through his IV.

'Worried what, Yance?'

'The woman with the . . . stroller . . .' he said, then stopped. Shook his head hard. 'Whoo, sorry. Gosh, I can't believe I just now remembered her. It was the thing I was most scared of right before I blacked out. I'd seen the woman get off the elevator pushing the big heavy stroller. I can't . . . I can't remember how I knew, but it was something about how she'd nodded to the others I was sure had to be Black Shadow stationed around the food court. Signaling them somehow, like something was going to happen. And somehow I realized she was the one making the Chinese guy look like he was doing something he wasn't.'

The avocado green of three flashed in, and Jenna thought of the three names that had still been in play. She suddenly realized what had been bothering her all along about the color, and Fai Xiong.

Oh, she'd signaled to them, all right. To move in for a 'rehearsal attack' that wasn't really happening at the same time she'd set it up to look like Athos was about to detonate a bomb. They followed her signals and got apprehended by the cops, and poor Athos got his head blown off, because, that way, the numbers added up. When they went looking for leftovers not at the mall, they'd only be out for Scarlett and Beo, because 'Richelieu' had died by cop at the mall.

Her instincts when she'd seen Richelieu on the video had been right. It wasn't the facts being presented that had caused the light khaki color to keep coming up, it was the gender. The real Richelieu was a woman. Fai Xiong had been set up.

But if Flint had set up the whole thing for the others in the group to be captured, why would he let this one woman get away? Set it up so she got away. A sinking suspicion started to form.

'What did this woman look like?' she asked.

'Jet black hair, all the way down her back. Piercing green eyes. Probably the most distinctive thing about her, though, were the angles of her face.'

'Huh?'

'Her face was the most long, slender oval, only . . . there was something about the way her high cheekbones drew in toward her chin on either side of her nose, which was like this slim, delicate line that existed only to trace the length of her face in order to accentuate how perfectly symmetrical her cheekbones slanted inward on either side,' Yancy said, his eyes squinted up as though trying to picture her.

'Son of a bitch,' Jenna hissed.

Yancy's eyes widened, and he shook his head. 'No, no. I didn't have a crush on her cheekbones or anything. They were just, you know, unusual. Like seeing a guy with a pair of legs that both continue down from the knee.'

'You're a dork, and that's not what I meant,' Jenna said, her head still spinning too fast to take Yancy's leg joke bait. 'It's just that . . . you just described . . .'

Rose flashed in. Familial love. Flint's sister hadn't died after all. Come to think of it, he'd never said she had, only implied it.

'Son of a bitch,' she spat again. 'You just described the picture I saw of Flint Lewis's sister. She's alive. She was in on it. Son of a bitch!'

'Daughter, if we're getting technical.'

Jenna's smart phone was in her hand before she realized what she was doing. She typed in the Black Shadow website URL.

'Um, Jenna, that's not really something you want to tweet about.'

'I'm pulling up the videos of the attacks. I've watched those things a hundred times each, and this is the last connection I was missing. I need to see them once knowing the complete picture.'

The site took an unusually long time to load, then finally filled with an empty green background, with white text in the middle:

TO BE A WOMAN CONDEMNED TO A PAINFUL AND DISGRACEFUL
PUNISHMENT IS NO IMPEDIMENT TO BEAUTY, BUT IT IS AN
OBSTACLE TO THE RECOVERY OF POWER.

'What's the matter?' Yancy asked, seeing the puzzled look on her face. He reached out and tilted the phone in his direction. Then, he actually laughed. 'She took it down. Of course she did.'

'She's Flint's sister. She would have known every detail of what he did to help us access the site. Taking it down was probably the first thing she did when she got clear of the mall.'

'Let me see that a second,' Yancy said, gently plucking the phone out of her hand, and opening a new browser tab with his thumb. 'I don't know much about beauty, but I know a thing or two about being an obstacle.'

'What are you doing?' Jenna asked.

'Wait for it,' he said, holding up a finger. 'It's more fun for me if you wait.'

He finished typing and turned the phone back so she could see it. The browser was now filled with black text on a white background.

'You want me to read that?' Jenna asked.

Yancy glanced back at the screen, disappointed. 'Yeah, I guess it is a little underwhelming if you're not into this stuff. Hold on, this will be better.' He went to work on the phone again, but this time continued explaining. 'I installed a Trojan on the backend of the Black Shadow website. Figured it couldn't hurt. Figured Black Shadow members were smart enough to use the darkweb any time they visited the site, but when someone logs into the c-panel – the thing that lets you manage the content of the website – I have more options to work with. Let me just turn this on and we'll see if— Well, look at that. She left her laptop open.' Once again, he turned the phone around so Jenna could see.

A video loaded, showing them an empty room with a bed and a wide window near what looked like an outside door. No personal effects adorned the furniture. A hotel.

And leaning next to the TV stand was a matching set of butterfly swords.

Jenna's face broke into a wide grin. 'Is that what I think it is? Irv might have been right about you.'

Yancy smirked. 'That's her webcam feed, which I can turn on any time. Mic, too. I don't know, but I think this might make catching her a lot easier for you. Want to go through her browsing history with me? She may be smart, but we only needed to fool her once.'

Jenna nodded. 'Everyone's got a blind spot.'

Isaac walked into the visitor's area. Everything had been leading up to this. You need help from inside the penitentiary.

He settled into the chair, picked up the phone, and looked across the glass at the woman dressed in a nun's habit. You also needed help outside the penitentiary, and not just from little bimbo Lynzee.

Claudia Ramey smiled, picked up the phone, and said, 'Hello, my son.'